AUTUMN: PURIFICATION

D1500802

DAVID MOODY

INFECTED BOOKS
www.infectedbooks.co.uk

AUTUMN: PURIFICATION

Published by INFECTED BOOKS
www.infectedbooks.co.uk

This edition published 2005
Copyright David Moody 2004

A catalogue record for this book is
available from the British Library

ISBN 0-9550051-2-4

5-L1-0505-1

Prologue

Bodies.

Thousands upon thousands of cold, rancid, decaying bodies once spread across almost the entire length and width of the dead land but now crammed into the space of just a few square miles. Relentless, vicious and unstoppable shells. Creatures without direction. Creatures without purpose. Savage, instinct-driven, insect-ridden carcasses. Empty, rotting, skeletal husks which had once each had individual identities and lives and reasons to exist but which were now nothing more than emotionless collections of tattered rag, grey-green greasy flesh, withered muscle and brittle bone.

In little more than a few seconds the lives of each one of these pitiful, tortured things had been ended. Forty-seven days ago, without warning or explanation, the disease had struck and killed billions. The most brutal and unforgiving infection ever to have cursed the face of the planet tore through the defenceless population with unstoppable speed and ferocity, leaving only an unfortunate few unaffected. Now, more than a month and a half later, the full effects of the deadly germ were still making themselves known.

At the furthest edge of a cold, wet and generally featureless field, the dishevelled carcass of what had once been an affluent fifty-three year old investment banker lifted its dark, clouded eyes. Surrounded on all sides by hundreds of similarly bedraggled and featureless cadavers, the remains of the once powerful, wealthy and well-respected man shuffled awkwardly forward, slipping and sliding through churned mud, and lifted its tired arms and grabbed clumsily at those bodies which stood in its way. The body didn't know what drew it to the field, it didn't know why it was there, it didn't know what it wanted, it just

1

knew that it had to be there. Survivors. Although it didn't know what they were, it could hear them and feel them. They were different. Buried underground deep beneath the creature's feet they hid in fear and attempted to salvage some kind of life for themselves in the unnatural semi-darkness of their subterranean base. But it was impossible for them to exist without giving their location away. The world had become a lifeless, empty place, and the sounds made by the people underground echoed relentlessly through the fragile silence. The heat they produced burned like a fire. In the cold, vacuous and featureless land they attracted the corpses to them like moths round an incandescent flame.

The disease - if that really was what had caused all of this to happen - had dealt around a third of its victims a blow of unimaginable cruelty. All of those affected had been killed within seconds of infection. Most corpses - the fortunate majority - remained motionless and inert and simply rotted away where they had fallen. The remainder, however, had been sentenced to an unnaturally prolonged existence of relentless suffering. The germ had spared a key area of these creatures' brains. Somehow unaffected, a spark of primordial instinct had survived the disease, leaving the bodies physically dead but still compelled to move; lifeless but incessantly animated. And as the flesh which covered these lurching, stumbling creatures had rotted and decayed, so the unaffected region of the brain had grown in strength and had continued to drive them forward. As the brain slowly recovered basic senses had gradually returned, then a degree of control. Finally something which resembled base emotion gripped the cadavers and forced the desperate figures to keep moving. They didn't know what they were or where they were. They didn't know why they existed and they didn't know what they wanted. They had no need to eat or drink or rest or sleep or respire. Sentenced to spend every minute of every day shuffling pointlessly across the empty landscape, even the slightest sound or movement was enough to attract their limited but deadly attention.

As the days had passed since their initial infection, so the behaviour of the bodies had continued to slowly change. Apathy and emptiness began to be replaced. Restricted by their steadily worsening physical condition, the hordes of the dead became violent and increasingly aggressive. They did not have decision making capabilities, only the desire to try and silence their individual pain and protect themselves. In the empty, featureless vacuum above ground they gathered *en masse* around every disturbance or distraction, no matter how slight or insignificant, hoping to find release. Only time and decay would end the torment, but the bodies had no way of knowing whether such release would ever come.

What had begun as a few random corpses stumbling upon the underground military base by chance had now grown to be a massive crowd of vast, almost incalculable proportions. The appearance and movement of the creatures inevitably attracted more and more of them from the surrounding area. Now, several days since any of the soldiers had been above ground, almost one hundred thousand bodies fought to get nearer and nearer to the impassable bunker entrance.

The dead investment banker's way forward was blocked by more bodies. It lifted its emaciated arms again and then, with unexpected force, lashed out at the figure immediately in front. Soft, putrefying flesh was ripped from bone as the decaying office-worker tore the unprotected body in front of it apart. The sudden violence rapidly spread to the nearest cadavers on all sides and then rippled out further into the enormous crowd before petering out again as quickly as it had begun. All across this massive, decomposing gathering in random, isolated pockets the same thing was happening, triggered by each body's instinctive need to ensure its self-preservation.

Apart from the continual shuffling and fighting of the bodies and the wind blowing through the swaying branches of nearby trees, the world around the buried base appeared motionless and frozen. Even birds had learnt not to fly too close to the creatures because of the reaction their darting movements and fleeting appearances invariably caused. In spite of the fact that the dead were individually weak and clumsy, what remained of the rest of the world instinctively feared them and despised them.

Deep underground in the military base, almost three hundred survivors cowered helplessly and waited for something - anything - to happen. Despite being physically stronger than the dead, and even though they had control, intelligence and power on their side, they were afraid to move. It was obvious to all of the lost and terrified souls trapped in the concrete maze below the fields and hills that the sheer number of bodies on the surface would soon be too much for them. Their options were desperately limited. They could sit and wait, but no-one knew what they'd be waiting for. They could go above ground and fight, but what would that achieve? What use was open space and fresh air to the military? The disease still hung heavy in the contaminated air. Each one of the soldiers and their officers knew that a single breath would, in all probability, be enough to kill them. And the survivors immune to the disease who also sheltered there knew that they would fare no better from such a confrontation either. Any attempt to clear the bodies from above the base might help in the short term, but the noise and movement such an act would inevitably cause would doubtless result in thousands upon thousands more cadavers being drawn nearer to the shelter.

Below the surface the survivors and the military were forced to remain apart. The base was reasonably well-equipped and technologically advanced. Designed to cope with the expected after-effects of chemical, nuclear or biological attack, the air pumped through the underground levels was pure and free from infection. The survivors, however, were not. Decontamination had been half-heartedly attempted, but the woefully ill-prepared military commanders, scientists and advisers who controlled the base had known from the start that it had been a futile exercise. The germ could be washed away from equipment and from the soldier's protective suits, but the survivors were riddled with infection. They had been breathing the contaminated air constantly for more than a month and a half. Virtually every cell in their bodies must surely have carried the deadly contagion and, whilst it had no effect on them, even the slightest exposure might be sufficient to start the deadly chain reaction which

4

would inevitably lay waste to the soldiers and contaminate the base.

Despite their sizeable arsenal of weapons and the huge psychological and intellectual advantage which they had over the dead, the soldiers and survivors alike knew that they were trapped. The men, women and children sheltering underground lived with a constant sense of uncomfortable claustrophobia and despair. The military occupied almost all of the complex (everything beyond the entrance to the decontamination chambers) with the thirty-seven survivors having to exist in the main hanger and a few adjacent storage, utility and maintenance rooms. Space, light, heat and comfort was severely limited. After fighting through the hell above ground, however, the limitations of the military facility were readily accepted and hugely appreciated. The alternatives which awaited them on the surface were unthinkable.

1
Emma Mitchell

It's almost two o'clock.

I think it's two o'clock in the morning, but I'm not completely sure. There's no way of telling whether it's day or night down here and, if I'm honest, it doesn't matter. Whatever time of day or night it is, it's always dark. There are always some people sleeping and there are always other people awake. There are always people gathered in groups and huddles talking in secret whispers about nothing. There are always people crying, moaning, fighting and arguing. There are always soldiers moving through the decontamination chambers or coming into the hanger to check, double-check and triple-check their stockpiled equipment and machinery.

I can't sleep.

I've been lying here with Michael for the best part of two hours now. I always seem to feel guilty when we've been together like this and I can't clear my head enough to switch off and sleep like he can. I wish I could. We haven't done anything wrong. We've made love together four times in the three weeks since we've been down here and each time he's slept for hours afterwards. When I ask him why he tells me that when we've been together like this he feels more human and complete than he does the rest of the time. He tells me that what we do makes him feel the way he used to feel before all of this happened.

Sex is different now. In many ways it's sad and it reminds me of everything I've lost. In other ways it helps me to realise what I've still got. I still get scared when I think about how easy it would be to lose Michael and how lucky I am that we managed to find each other and stay together. Sometimes I'm not sure if I sleep with him because I love him, or whether it's because we just happen to be there for each other. There's no room for romance and other long forgotten feelings anymore. I don't think I'll ever have another orgasm. I can't imagine being relaxed or aroused enough to feel those kind of emotions again. When we're together there's no seduction or foreplay. All I want is to feel Michael inside me. I need the intimacy. He is the only positive part of my world. Everything is cold except his touch.

When we were above ground I hated this motorhome. I was trapped in here and it was all we had. Now it's all I want. It's where I spend most of my time. This is our little private space where we can shut ourselves away from the rest of the people we're trapped down here with. We're lucky to have this privacy and I appreciate it. The rest of them have no choice but to spend all day, every day with each other. I wonder whether they resent us? Even though I know they're probably not interested, sometimes I think that they do. I've seen the way they look at us when we're together.

I'm cold. I don't know what the temperature's like deeper underground on the other side of the decontamination chambers, but out here in the hanger it's always freezing. You can usually see your breath in front of your face. The air is motionless and still although sometimes you can smell the decay and disease outside. You'd think we'd be used to the smell of death by now, but none of us are. Yesterday I overheard a couple of soldiers talking about the air on the lower levels of the bunker. They said it's getting thinner. They said there are so many bodies above ground now that the vents and exhaust shafts around the base are gradually becoming blocked by the sheer weight of corpses crammed around them. Cooper told me he expected that to happen sooner or later. He said that most of the vents are scattered over a couple of square miles. It scares me to think just how many bodies there must be above us now for them to be having such an effect. Christ, there must be hundreds of thousands of those damn things up there.

Supplies are coming in.

Two suited soldiers have just emerged from the decontamination chambers to deliver our rations. The military don't give us much, just enough to survive. I guess they've only got so much for themselves and I'm surprised we get anything. There's going to come a point when the provisions they've hoarded in their storerooms run out. Maybe it won't matter by then. Donna Yorke keeps talking about how it's going to be different in a few months time. She says that by then the bodies will have rotted away to almost nothing and we'll be able to live on the surface again because they'll no longer be a threat to us. I hope she's right. I believe her. I've no reason not to. We can't stay down here forever.

Whatever happens to us the future is far less certain for the soldiers. Every time I see any of them I can't help thinking about what's going to happen to them. The air might still be filled with infection six years from now, never mind in six months. And how will they know if it ever becomes clear again? Are any of them going to be brave or stupid enough to take off their suits, put their heads above ground and risk breathing in? You can't see much behind their protective masks but every so often you catch a flash of stifled emotion in their eyes. They're as scared as we are. They don't trust us. Sometimes I think they hate and despise us almost as much as they do the bodies. Maybe they're keeping us here because they want to use us? Perhaps they're planning on forcing us to scour the surface to stock up their stores and provide them with food and water?

I put on Michael's thick winter coat and walk over to the nearest window to get a better view of what's happening outside. The window is covered in condensation. I wipe it away but it's still difficult to see what's going on. The lights in the hanger are almost always turned down to their lowest setting. I guess they do it to conserve power. It only gets any brighter when the soldiers are about to go outside and that hasn't happened for well over a week now. The doors have only been opened once since we've been down here. Two days after we arrived outside they tried to go out to clear the mess we'd made getting in. They started to open the doors but there were too many bodies. They burned the first few hundred of them with flame-throwers but there were thousands more behind.

I can see Cooper checking over the vehicles that he and the other people from the city arrived here in. You can tell just by

8

watching him that he used to be a soldier. Even though he has nothing to do with the rest of the military now he's still regimented and he has a level of control and confidence that none of the others possess. I often see him exercising and sometimes, when the army are out of sight, he gets small groups of people together and tries to show them how to use the military equipment left lying around here. Most of the time no-one's interested. Cooper checks the battered police van and prison truck at least once every day to make sure they're still in working order. What does he think's going to happen to them? They're not being used and apart from him no-one else has been anywhere near them in days. I asked him about it yesterday. He told me that we can't afford to take any chances. He told me that we have be ready to get out of here quickly if we need to. Much as I think Cooper is overdoing it, I keep asking Michael to make sure our vehicle will be ready when the time to leave finally arrives. And none of us are under any illusions here, we all know that the time to leave is going to come eventually. It might be today, it might be tomorrow or it might not be for six months. The only certainty we have is that we can't stay down here indefinitely.

Michael is stirring in bed.

'What's the matter?' he asks, waking up and noticing that I'm not there next to him. His eyes are dark, tired and confused as he looks around for me.

'Nothing's the matter,' I answer. 'Couldn't sleep, that's all.'

He sits up and yawns and beckons me over. I'm still cold. I get back into bed and lie down and he grabs hold of me tightly like we've been apart for years.

'How you doing?' he asks quietly, his face close to mine.

'I'm okay,' I answer.

'Anything happening?'

'Not really, just a delivery of supplies, that's all. Does anything ever happen around here?'

Still holding me tightly he kisses the side of my face.

'Give it time,' he mumbles sadly. 'Give it time.'

2

'Morning, you two,' Bernard Heath said in his loud, educated voice as Michael and Emma walked into the largest of the few rooms that the survivors were permitted access to.

'Morning, Bernard,' Emma replied. 'Bloody cold, isn't it?'

'Isn't it always?' he sighed. 'Get yourselves something to eat, the soldiers left us quite a lot last night.'

Holding onto Michael's hand, Emma followed him as he weaved through the crowded room. About six metres square, it was used by the group of survivors as a dormitory, a meeting place, a kitchen and a mess hall. In fact it was used for just about everything. As bleak, grim and imposing as its grey and featureless walls were, the fact that the room was always filled with people made it just about the best place for any of them to spend their time. In spite of the uncertainty and unease which still surrounded everything, the heat and noise made by the group of frightened and frustrated people made this room a more inviting place than anywhere else. At least here they weren't always looking over their shoulders. At least here they could, for the time being at least, begin to try and relax, recuperate and heal.

A basic shift pattern had been drawn up shortly after they had first arrived at the bunker. Although there had been the expected few missed shifts, most people seemed prepared to pull their weight and contribute by cooking or cleaning or doing whatever other menial tasks needed to be done. Rather than evade work as some of them might have done before the disaster, just about all of the survivors now willingly did as much as they could. How much of this work was done to help the others was questionable. Most simply craved the responsibility because it helped reduce the monotony and boredom of every long, dark day. As each of them had already found to their cost on many, many occasions, sitting and staring at the walls of the bunker with nothing to do invariably resulted in them thinking constantly about all that they had lost.

Emma and Michael collected their food from Sheri Newton (a quiet and diminutive middle-aged woman who seemed to always be serving food) and sat down to eat. The faces of the people sitting around them were reassuringly familiar. Donna Yorke was at a table nearby talking to Clare Smith, Jack Baxter and Phil Croft. As the couple began to eat Croft looked up and around and nodded at Michael.

'Morning,' Michael said as he chewed on his first mouthful of dry and tasteless rationed food. 'How you doing today, Phil?'

'Good,' Croft replied, wheezing. He took a long drag on a cigarette and coughed.

'You should think about giving those things up,' Michael muttered sarcastically, 'won't do your health any good. They'll be the death of you!'

Croft grimaced as he coughed and then managed a fleeting smile. It was a sign of the grim hopelessness of their situation that death was just about the only thing they could find to laugh about. The group's only doctor, he had sustained serious injuries in a violent crash when they had first approached the military bunker. The dark, dank conditions underground were not ideal and did nothing to aid his recovery. The only visible signs of his injuries which remained now were a scar across his chest and a severe limp and, as far as the rest of the group were concerned, he appeared to be getting stronger and fitter with each day. A trained and experienced medical professional, however, Croft knew that his body had sustained a huge amount of damage and that he would never be fully fit again. With his discomfort and pain seeming to increase day on day, and with the military on one side and a crowd of thousands of decomposing corpses on the other, the potentially harmful effects of smoking cigarettes was the very least of his worries.

Cooper marched angrily into the room, his sudden, stormy appearance instantly silencing every conversation and causing everyone to look round. He fetched himself a drink, yanked a chair from under the table and sat down next to Jack Baxter.

'What the hell's the matter with you?' Baxter asked.

'This place is full of fucking idiots,' the ex-soldier snapped. Since returning to the base he had steadily distanced himself from his military colleagues to the point where he now had very little to do with them. Perhaps symbolically, he now only wore the lower half of his uniform, and he only kept the boots and trousers on because they were the most practical clothes he possessed. In fact, they were just about the only clothes he had.

'Now who's he talking about?' Croft interrupted. 'Who you on about now, Cooper?'

Cooper took a swig of coffee.

'Bloody jokers in charge of this place,' he answered.

'What have they done?'

'Nothing, and that's the fucking problem.'

'What do you mean?' asked Donna, concerned. She knew Cooper well enough to know that there had to be a reason behind his sudden ranting. He was usually much calmer and more controlled than this.

'The troops won't tell me a thing anymore,' he explained. 'My guess is they've been ordered not to. I just can't understand their logic. What do they think they're going to gain from keeping us in the dark? We've seen more of what's happened out there than they have. You'd think they'd want to try and keep us on side, wouldn't you?'

'Sounds typical of what I've seen of the military so far,' Baxter said quietly. 'So is that all that's bothering you?'

Cooper shook his head.

'No,' he sighed, 'it's more than that. I've just been talking to an old mate of mine, Jim Franks. Jim and I go back a long way and I know I can trust him. Anyway, he's been telling me that they think they're going to start hitting real problems soon.'

'Supplies?' Baxter wondered.

'No.'

'What kind of problems then?' asked Emma, immediately worried.

'Big fucking problems,' Cooper continued. 'Nothing they weren't expecting, but big fucking problems nonetheless.'

'Such as…?'

'You've got to remember that I was talking to Jim through the intercom on the front of the decontamination chamber and he was trying to keep his voice down in case anyone caught him speaking to me so I didn't get a lot of detail. It's the bodies. They've been taking readings around the base and the damn things still keep coming. Jim told me that the air filtration system's still working but it's really starting to struggle and the problems we've heard about with ventilation have really started to take hold. Seems that more than half the exhaust vents are blocked or almost blocked, just like we said they would be.'

'So what are they going to do about it?' Croft mumbled, asking the question that everyone was thinking.

'There's no way of clearing the vents from down here,' he explained, 'so they're going to have to go above ground eventually.'

'But what good's that going to do?' Emma protested, immediately terrified at the prospect of the bunker doors being opened again. 'Do they think they can just clear the bodies away? As soon as they move any of them hundreds more will take their place.'

'I know that and you know that,' Cooper sighed dejectedly, 'but they don't. This is why I can't understand them not talking to us. The reality is that the people making the decisions down here don't have a fucking clue how bad things are on the surface. Until you've seen it for yourself and you've been out there in the middle of it, you just can't imagine the scale of what's happened outside, can you?'

'So how are they planning to keep the vents clear?' asked Donna. 'Like Emma says, as soon as they've cleared them more bodies will be lining up to block them again.'

'I don't know. My guess is they'll try and cover them or build something over the top. You've got to remember that this place was built not to be noticed. You'd have to look hard just to find the bloody vents 'cause they're not obvious. I think they're planning to fight their way through to them and then just do whatever they need to do to block them off. They'll try and cover the top of them or leave people out there to guard them. A trench or a wall might be enough…'

'Pity the poor bastards who get sent out there to build bloody walls,' Baxter mumbled. 'Christ, it's hard enough just being up there, never mind having to build a bloody wall. I tell you, you wouldn't get me outside for anything.'

'You reckon? Keep things in perspective, Jack,' Cooper said, looking directly at the other man, 'we've got a massive advantage over this lot at the moment because we can survive out in the open. So who says they're not going to try and use us to do whatever it is that they're planning on doing? Argue all you like, but if you've got a gun held at the back of your head, you'll do whatever they bloody well want you to do.'

'You really think it's going to come to that? You think they'll try and get us to go up there?'

'Perhaps not yet, but…'

'But what?'

'But they might do eventually. Put yourself in their shoes. You'd probably try and do the same.'

The conversation stalled as each of the survivors stopped to take stock of Cooper's words. He knew how the military minds worked better than any of them. Each of them knew that he was being frank and honest with them because there was no point trying to soften the blow. Cooper was never anything other than straight and direct. He had nothing to gain from scare-mongering or frightening the others.

'How long?' Donna asked.

'How long until what?' Cooper replied, assuming that the question had been directed towards him.

'How long before they have to open the doors and go above ground?'

He shrugged his shoulders.

'Don't know. I don't expect they know either. We'll just have to sit and wait.'

'For what?'

'For their air to start running out,' Emma interrupted quickly.

Another break in the exchange. More silent contemplation.

14

'It has to happen, doesn't it?' Michael said with a tone of honest resignation and acceptance in his voice.

'What?' mumbled Croft, only half-listening.

'I said it has to happen,' he repeated. 'It's inevitable. They call it Chaos Theory, don't they? If something can go wrong, then eventually it will go wrong.'

'Keep looking on the bright side, eh?' grinned Baxter.

'He's right,' Cooper agreed.

'We've all seen it happen,' Michael continued. 'We started off in a village hall. There was about twenty of us to start with and we thought we'd be okay but we had to get away. Three of us found ourselves a house in the middle of the bloody countryside miles away from anywhere, but that wasn't safe enough either. Built a bloody fence around it but it didn't last.'

'Same with us and the university,' Donna said, leaning closer to the others. 'Looked ideal when we first got there but the safety didn't last. Things change and we can't afford to just sit still and wait and hope and…'

'And you're right, the same thing's bound to happen here eventually,' Cooper interrupted. 'Something's got to give - more vents will get blocked, supplies will run out, the disease will manage to get in or something else will happen. It'll take luck more than anything else to keep us safe down here.'

'So what do we do about it?'

'There's not a lot we can do,' he answered. 'We just need to be ready for it when it happens, and be prepared to get out of here fast if anything goes wrong.'

3

Three days was all it took. It was mid-morning.

Michael was standing in front of the motorhome talking to Cooper about the sorry state of his battered vehicle. Although it had been cleaned and overhauled to the best of their abilities with their limited resources, the machine still looked desperately dilapidated and tired. The two men's conversation was abruptly interrupted when the hanger lights were suddenly switched on, filling the cavernous space with unexpectedly bright illumination. Having been forced to live in almost complete darkness for weeks the survivors covered their eyes and, for a fraction of a second, found themselves thinking more about the brightness and discomfort than the possible reasons why the lights had been turned on.

Michael was the first to react.

'Shit,' he cursed as he squinted and looked around, shielding his eyes, 'here they come. This must be it.'

Cooper looked up and saw that the doors to the main decontamination chamber were opening. From deep inside the base a steady stream of dark, suited figures were beginning to emerge. Close on a hundred troops filed out into the hanger. They marched quickly and quietly. Although their formation and manner lacked something of the discipline and precision Cooper had come to expect from his former colleagues, they were still clearly well organised and ready to fight.

'Christ, they mean business,' he mumbled.

'What do we do?'

'Get everyone ready to get out of here.'

The two men sprinted across the huge room, cutting through the soldier's ragged formation. The sudden light and noise had already alerted the other survivors. Anxious faces appeared in numerous doorways before Michael and Cooper were even halfway across the hanger.

'What's happening?' Steve Armitage asked.

'What's it look like?' Cooper replied. 'They're about to open the fucking doors!'

'Shit,' was all that Armitage could say. Before he could react a further crowd of panicking survivors pushed passed him and spilled out into the hanger.

'Get ready to leave,' Cooper shouted. He hoped they weren't going anywhere, but he felt duty bound to prepare the group for the worst possible scenario. 'Get everyone into the vehicles.'

Without question or delay the frightened crowd began to hurriedly make its way across the cavernous chamber towards the police van, prison truck and motorhome. Bernard Heath looked around for Phil Croft. He grabbed the unsteady medic's arm and pulled him along. Whilst he could walk, his injuries still prevented him from getting anywhere with any real speed.

'Get the kids,' Michael yelled to Donna across the small, square room where the youngest members of the group tended to gather. She did as he said, ushering the few children towards the door. Emma, frightened and moving against the flow of the others, grabbed hold of his arm.

'What's going on?' she began to ask. 'What are they doing…?'

'Get into the motorhome,' he snapped anxiously. 'I'll be over there in a couple of minutes.'

'But…' she protested. Michael pushed her away, desperate to get her to safety quickly.

'Don't ask questions,' he shouted after her, 'just get yourself over there.'

'Is that everyone?' Cooper asked breathlessly as he returned to the hanger after checking the largest room was clear.

'Think so,' said Jack Baxter as he looked back across the immense cavern. He watched nervously as the rest of the survivors attempted to cram themselves into the back of the group's three vehicles.

'You two get yourselves over there and try and get that lot sorted out,' Cooper ordered. Although he had never been formally recognised by the group as their leader, the authority and command in his voice was unquestionable. Michael and Baxter turned and ran towards the others.

Cooper stood his ground and anxiously watched the soldiers. The roar of engines suddenly filled the base and an armoured personnel carrier took up position at the foot of the ramp which led up to the main entrance doors. Two smaller jeeps were driven out of the shadows and parked behind the first vehicle. He cautiously moved forward, his military mind keen to try and work out the tactics and intentions of what was about to happen.

'Cooper,' shouted Michael as the final few survivors jostled for space in the group's battered transports, 'come on!'

Cooper ignored him and instead moved closer still to the troops. He estimated there were somewhere between eighty and a hundred soldiers in the hanger and there was no doubt that this was a major operation. He knew that the officers (who, as far as he could tell, were still buried safely within the deeper confines of the base) would never risk sending such a large number of troops above ground unless they had absolutely no option but to do so.

He took a chance. He had nothing to lose.

'Hey,' he said, standing in shadow and reaching out and grabbing the arm of the nearest suited figure. The soldier nervously span around to face him. The protective mask and breathing apparatus partially obscured the trooper's face allowing Cooper to see only his eyes. 'What's happening?'

'Vents are blocked,' he answered in a muffled but clearly young and anxious voice.

'So what's the plan?'

The soldier looked from side to side, not sure whether or not he should even be speaking to Cooper. He figured that the preparation of the troops and equipment closer to the front of the hanger was a sufficient distraction for him to risk saying a few more words.

'They reckon we can get by for now with at least two of the vents clear, so we're going out there to sort 'em and to make sure they stay working.'

'Are you staying out there?' Cooper whispered. The soldier shook his head.

'You've got to be fucking joking,' he replied quickly. 'No, that's what the jeeps are for. The vents are low on the ground. Plan is to leave a jeep straddling each vent to block them off and stop those bloody things out there from clogging them up again.'

The soldiers began to move forward. The trooper next to Cooper pulled himself free from the survivor's grip and moved up to retake his position in formation next to his colleagues. Still curious, Cooper jogged across the width of the hanger towards the others. Instead of getting into one of the vehicles with them, however, he instead clambered up onto the front of another huge military transport to try and get a better view of what was about to happen. Out of breath and red faced, Baxter appeared at his side.

'What's happening now?' he asked, panting with effort and nerves as he pulled himself up level with the other man.

'They're going to try and clear a couple of vents,' Cooper replied. 'They're planning to leave those jeeps parked on top of them to try and keep the bodies away.'

'Got to get to the bloody vents first,' Baxter mumbled. 'Do they realise what it's like out there?'

'They will in a few minutes. Anyway, they don't have any choice if they want to keep breathing. If there was another way I'm sure they'd have tried it by now. No matter what we think of them, they're not stupid...'

The conversation ended quickly as the doors began to open. At first nothing seemed to happen. But then, slowly and steadily, a dull scraping noise became audible over the rumbling sound of the military machines which stood poised to drive out into the open. A few seconds later and the first chink of light appeared. A slender shaft of harsh grey-white brightness appeared between the two gradually separating halves of the door. As Cooper and Baxter watched the width of the band of light increased as the entrance was opened further.

'Christ,' muttered Baxter under his breath. Rooted to the spot with fear he desperately tried to contain his rapidly mounting panic. 'Jesus Christ.'

As soon as the gap was wide enough bodies began to spill into the hanger. Forced forward like a thick and viscous liquid by the sheer weight of rotting flesh pushing hard against them from behind, the first corpses stumbled and lurched down the ramp towards the soldiers with surprising speed, many tripping and falling at their booted feet. The soldiers responded instinctively, pushing the bodies back and firing at them until they had managed to temporarily stem the flow of dead meat. From somewhere deep within the ranks a muffled order was given and a row of four soldiers armed with flame-throwers stepped out of the darkness. They pushed their way closer to the diseased crowd and unleashed their devastating weapons on the nearest creatures, sending controlled arcs of dripping, incandescent flame shooting out of the bunker door and up into the cold morning air. Tinder dry, the bodies caught by the fire were almost immediately incinerated.

Another order was given and the personnel carrier began to creep slowly forward, climbing steadily towards daylight and then emerging out into the open, pushing and probing deeper into the burning crowd and grinding charred flesh and bone into the ground beneath its heavy and powerful wheels. To the front and on either side the flame-thrower carrying soldiers took up protective positions and advanced cautiously, matching the massive vehicle's laborious pace and continuing to destroy as many corpses as their flames would reach. Beyond the mass of burning bodies countless more continually pushed themselves closer and closer to the disturbance, ignorant to the danger and devastation and attracted by the noise, fire, smoke and sudden movements. At the bunker entrance the two jeeps finally emerged into the mayhem, each one of them surrounded by more soldiers carrying flame-throwers and other, more conventional and clearly less effective weapons.

As the military convoy eased itself away from the front of the base uncomfortably slowly, the remaining troops formed a heavy protective line of defence across the open entrance. The cool air was filled with billowing clouds of thick, black smoke and the choking, suffocating smell of burnt meat. Suddenly unable to see what was happening from where he was watching, Cooper jumped down from his high viewpoint and moved closer to the troops.

'Cooper,' hissed Baxter, 'what the hell are you doing you bloody idiot?'

Cooper ignored him and continued to edge further forward. Now standing just short of the heavily armed soldiers he could see that the personnel carrier and its entourage had managed to carve a deep, curved groove through the centre of the immense crowd of corpses. The vehicles moved painfully slowly through the bloody mayhem, still surrounded by a circle of troops who aimed their weapons into the rotting masses which writhed and squirmed and surged all around them. Hundreds were obliterated by flame and gunfire. Undeterred, more bodies continued to stagger across the mass of burning remains.

Some three hundred metres away from the entrance to the base, the driver of the personnel carrier turned to the officer next to him.

'Where's the vent?' he demanded. 'Where's the fucking vent?'

Perhaps naively the troops had not stopped to consider the disorientating visual effect of so many bodies being packed tightly together on the ground. Shaking with nerves and fired up with adrenaline, the officer traced the path they had already taken on a map. He glanced up briefly to check his bearings but could see little through the front of the vehicle. Frantic, uncoordinated movements, jumping flame and dense clouds of heavy, noxious smoke were all that he could see.

'Should be over there,' he yelled, pointing over to his right as he continued to try and find a more accurate visual reference. The driver steered the carrier as directed, shielding his eyes from a blast of sudden brightness as more bodies were drenched with fire and destroyed. He watched in petrified disbelief as the creatures burned and yet continued to move. Inexplicably ignorant to the flames which quickly consumed them, the rotting cadavers staggered relentlessly forward until their last decaying muscles, nerves and sinews had been burnt away to nothing.

'Got it,' the driver gasped as he caught sight of the exhaust vent amongst the seething sea of figures. Standing just a few inches above the ground and surrounded by mud, moss and weeds, the location of the vent was made suddenly obvious by the movement of the bodies nearby and also by the mass of once-human remains which had accumulated around it. Drawn there by the comparative warmth coming up through the vent from the depths of the base, many bodies had become entangled with the low metal structure and had been trapped and wedged in place by the weight of countless more figures pressing forward against them. Clumsy, barely coordinated feet and legs had been twisted and had buckled under the combined weight of the huge crowd, leaving the metal vent partially obscured under mounds of cold grey flesh.

'Drive straight over the top of it,' ordered the officer. The driver did as instructed, turning the heavy vehicle towards the vent and accelerating through the bodies. The soldier moving in front of the carrier continued to soak the apparently endless crowd with fire, burning away the nearest of the hordes of lumbering cadavers which scrambled towards the convoy.

Apart from the vent this area of the field was otherwise relatively flat and featureless. The driver of the personnel carrier powered over the top of the metal covering, smashing more burning bodies away to the side and scraping away a thick layer of once-human remains. Seeing that the way was now slightly clearer, the driver of the first jeep following behind gestured for the driver of the second to leave his vehicle straddling the vent as arranged. The second driver pulled forward and stopped when the metal opening was directly under the centre of the jeep's mud and blood-splattered chassis. Leaning precariously over the side of his vehicle he saw that there was just a couple of inches clearance between the top of the vent and the bottom of the jeep. Perfect.

The other two vehicles had continued to move forwards, changing course and heading towards the next nearest vent to repeat the manoeuvre. The second driver, now suddenly vulnerable without the protection of his jeep, sprinted after the others.

From behind the row of soldiers standing in the entrance to the bunker Cooper still struggled to see what was happening.

The clouds of repulsive, stagnant-smelling smoke which the gusting wind blew back inside the base stung his eyes and filled his nose and throat with a charred, nauseating taste.

'What's happening now?' Baxter asked. As the length of time the soldiers had spent outside had increased, so the older man had slowly gained in confidence. He had now crept forward to stand just behind the shoulder of his colleague.

'Looks like they've managed to get one vent cleared,' Cooper answered. 'Can't see what they're doing now though. I've lost sight of them.'

'Do you think they're going to be able to do this...?' Baxter asked before being silenced by a sudden huge flash of flame. One of the nearest soldiers had fired a flame-thrower and had destroyed a small pocket of bodies which had somehow broken through the rest of the burning masses and which were moving dangerously close to the base.

'I don't know what to think anymore,' Cooper mumbled, struggling to keep the smoke out of his eyes and still continue to look outside. 'This is just bloody relentless, isn't it?'

'What is?'

The heat from another arc of flame sent the two men scuttling further back into the base.

'The effort,' he continued, wiping sweat and ash from his face. 'For bloody hell's sake, look at the effort that this lot are having to put in. Look at the risks they're having to take. Christ, there are about a hundred men and women out there risking their lives, and it's for the simplest of reasons.'

'What do you mean?' Baxter was confused. Cooper sensed that he was struggling to make himself understood.

'What I mean,' he said, his voice tired and flat, 'is that this is what they now have to do just so they can breathe! To keep breathing, for Christ's sake! Never mind anything else, these people have to put their lives on the line just so they can continue to breathe. It's a pretty desperate state of affairs, isn't it?'

Baxter didn't have chance to answer. The soldiers protecting the entrance suddenly lowered their weapons and dropped back. For a second the two survivors feared the arrival of an unstoppable deluge of bodies but it didn't happen. Instead the personnel carrier, followed by the five minute long return of a full complement of tired, shell-shocked and battle-dirtied troops, burst back into the bunker.

The doors began to close.

Baxter stared out into the distance for as long as he was able. The return of the powerful personnel carrier and troops had disturbed the air and, momentarily, had caused much of the dirty smoke to be dispersed. For a few seconds the survivor's view was clear and uninterrupted. He could clearly see the charred and mangled remains of hundreds of bodies lying twisted and blackened on the muddy ground. Beyond them he could see thousands more cadavers approaching the base. Like a dense, grey fog those bodies which had so far escaped destruction scrambled over the remains of those which had been obliterated, desperately trying to reach the soldiers and survivors.

The entrance was sealed. Baxter and the others relaxed. They had been ready to move if they'd had to but, for a while longer, they were safe.

4

'And that's all they're going to tell you?' Croft asked. Cooper shrugged his shoulders nonchalantly.

'That's about it,' he replied. 'To be fair I don't think there's much more to tell. They've cleared two of the vents and cremated a ton of corpses. Suppose that was all they wanted to do.'

'But will they need to clear more vents? Are they going to have to go out there again?'

'Don't know.'

'So how long do they think those vents are going to stay clear? How long's it going to be before they're clogged up with bodies again?'

'Don't know,' Cooper sighed, clearly irritated by the doctor's relentless and pointless questioning. 'Look, Phil, it doesn't matter how many times you ask me, or how many different ways you ask, I don't know anything more than what I've already told you, okay? The blokes I know have been told not to talk to me anymore.'

Several hours had passed since the soldiers had returned from outside and the doors to the base had been closed. A handful of survivors now sat in the relative comfort of the motorhome with Michael and Emma. Croft, Cooper, Baxter and Donna had needed to escape from the bunker's prison-like grey walls for a while. Although blurred and obscured by condensation, those same walls could still be seen through the windows of the motorhome. Regardless, the extra layer of separation allowed the survivors to convince themselves for a while that they were, somehow, a little further detached from their nightmarish reality than usual.

'What bothers me,' Jack Baxter said quietly, cradling a beaker of water in his hands as if it was finest malt whiskey, 'is that they're still coming. After all this time it doesn't look like anything's changed out there. I looked out there today and I could see as many bodies as I saw on the day we first arrived here, probably even more. It's been three weeks now for God's sake. Why don't they just piss off and find somewhere else to hang around?'

'Because there isn't anywhere else,' Donna reminded him. 'You know this, Jack. Even if there are hundreds more survivors scattered round the country, they'll all have probably hidden themselves away like us by now. They might not be underground, but they'll be out of sight, and they'll all have bloody huge crowds hanging round them like we have.'

'Won't make any difference whether they're underground or up a bloody mountain,' Michael added. 'Doesn't matter how quiet or careful we are, they'll eventually find us and anyone else like us.'

'I know,' Baxter mumbled dejectedly.

'Did you see what kind of condition they were in today, Jack?' Donna asked. He looked up and shook his head.

'Didn't get much chance, sorry,' he grunted sarcastically. 'I would have tried to get closer but the soldiers and the flame-throwers and the thousands of burning bodies kind of put me off. Next time I'll try and...'

'What I mean,' Donna snapped, irritated by his flippancy and completely ignoring his pathetic attempt at humour, 'is were they still as mobile as they were before? When we came down here they were starting to get really aggressive and unpredictable. I just wondered if you noticed whether they'd changed or got any worse or whether their bodies have decayed enough now to stop them from...'

'I couldn't tell,' Baxter started to, his voice suddenly humourless again. 'I couldn't really see anything much from where I was standing, and I wasn't about to try and get any closer to the...'

'It's difficult to say what kind of condition they're in,' Cooper said, cutting across the other man before he'd finished

26

his sentence. 'You have to understand that we couldn't see much more than just fire and smoke out there. What really concerns me though, is the fact that the guys who were left posted at the entrance were kept busy pretty much all the time that the doors were open.'

'What's your point?' wondered Michael.

'My point is that even though there was a bloody huge engine driving through the middle of them, some of them were still trying to get inside here. We've been saying all along that these things just react to distractions. Well that might still be true, but to my mind a personnel carrier surrounded by blokes with flame-throwers should be a damn sight more distracting than a line of soldiers standing in an open door. The bodies that came towards the base must have chosen to try and get in here.'

'You're joking, aren't you?' Baxter baulked.

'No,' Cooper replied. 'Their flesh and bone might be getting weaker, but we've suspected for weeks that they're also getting smarter, haven't we?'

'You serious?' said Croft.

'Do you really think that's what's happening to them?' asked Donna.

Cooper shrugged his shoulders.

'Don't know,' he replied. 'I'm just guessing here. It might have just been coincidence or a fluke that they found themselves close to the entrance. The bodies could have been heading towards the men out in the field and then been distracted by those that were left behind to protect the base.'

'You've got a point though,' Baxter agreed, now completely serious, 'You would have expected all of them to head for the personnel carrier and the soldiers in the field. But how could those things be getting smarter when they're rotting away?'

Several members of the group of survivors instinctively looked towards Phil Croft for an answer to their obviously unanswerable question. The fact that everyone seemed to still assume that he knew more than they did because he was medically trained never ceased to infuriate and frustrate him.

'How the hell am I supposed to know?' he snapped. 'Bloody hell, I'm getting sick of this. I keep telling you, I know as much

27

as you do.' Annoyed and tired, Croft swung himself around in his seat and pushed open the motorhome door with his feet. 'Mind if I smoke?' he asked.

'Carry on,' Michael said quietly.

'How many you down to now, Phil?' Baxter wondered.

'One and a half boxes,' he replied as he lit the remains of an already half-smoked cigarette and inhaled slowly. 'I tell you, I'm going to go out of my bloody mind if I can't get more cigarettes.'

'How long do you reckon that lot will last you?' asked Emma.

'I've been limiting myself to smoking half of one each day, so I've probably got a couple of weeks left.'

'What then?'

'Not much choice really, is there?' the doctor grumbled. 'I can give up or I can go out and get some more!'

'Where you going to go?' laughed Baxter.

'Not sure yet,' Croft smirked. 'Even if I could get out of here, I haven't got a bloody clue where we are!'

'You should try looking closer to home. Bet they've got fags and drink and everything in their stores here.'

Cooper shook his head.

'You'd be surprised, Jack. This whole operation was thrown together in minutes. They've got less kit and supplies stashed away than you'd think.'

Across from Cooper Michael sat on the edge of the uncomfortable sofa which doubled up as the bed that he and Emma shared. Emma shuffled nearer to him. She was cold and wanted to be held. He wrapped his arms around her as she rested her weight against him. The other survivors looked away, each of them feeling suddenly awkward and almost embarrassed. Emma and Michael's relative intimacy made them feel uncomfortable and unsure. Having each individually suffered so much pain and loss, the others found the idea of closeness and tenderness difficult and alien - an uneasy reminder of a world they had given up as gone forever. Having lost his long-term partner many months before the disaster, Baxter had long found dealing with this kind of emotion particularly hard.

'I always wanted a van like this,' he said suddenly, looking around and making a conscious effort to break the silence and start another conversation. 'Me and Denise were planning on getting ourselves something like this when I retired. We were thinking about selling up and living on the road for a while.'

'I wouldn't recommend it,' Michael grinned, 'it's not all it's cracked up to be. We were living on the road for a couple of weeks before we found this place, weren't we, Em? Didn't enjoy it!'

Baxter smiled.

'I've been thinking about it though,' he rambled, looking out through the motorhome window and imagining he could see something other than grey concrete walls, 'just think what it'll be like when the bodies have gone. Just picture it, we'll have the whole bloody country to ourselves. We'll be able to go where we like, when we like.'

'So where would you go?' Croft asked him.

'I think,' he began, stretching in his seat and staring up thoughtfully at the low metal ceiling above his head, 'I'll try and travel right round the coast. I'm going to wait until summer, then I'll start on the south coast and work my way west. I won't plan a route, I'll just keep going and one day I'll end up back where I started.'

'But you could have your pick of the biggest houses or whatever you wanted,' Emma said. 'You could sit on your backside and relax. You'd still want to travel and live rough?'

'I'm getting used to living rough now,' he smiled, 'it'd be strange to be comfortable again. I like the idea of moving from town to town or village to village, taking whatever I need from wherever I can find it.'

'Think you'll ever do it?' Donna asked.

Baxter looked deep down into his beaker of water and thought for a moment.

'Don't know. I hope so.'

'Think it's going to be as easy as you imagine?'

He shrugged his shoulders.

'I never said it would be easy. Anyway, there's no way of knowing, is there?'

'I can't start dreaming like you can, Jack,' Donna admitted, 'not yet, anyway. I don't know about the rest of you, but when I think about the future, I still automatically try and picture things like they used to be before this happened, just empty of people and quiet. But it's not going to be like that, is it?'

'What are you saying?'

'I can't be anything but realistic. I know we can get by for a while, but I'm anticipating every day from now on being a struggle. The more time passes since everything was normal, the less there's going to be for us to take out there. The last bits of food will rot. Buildings will start to crumble. Everything we used to know will gradually disappear.'

'Fucking hell,' Baxter groaned sarcastically, 'here's looking on the bright side, eh?'

'Like I said, I'm just being realistic, that's all,' Donna mumbled, her voice tired and resigned.

'Anyway,' Croft interjected, 'we've got to get out of here before you can start sightseeing, Jack.'

'I know,' he sighed. 'Frustrating, isn't it. We're the one's who can survive out there, and it's the bloody army who'll decide whether we can go outside or not.'

'Think they'll try and keep us down here, Cooper?' Croft asked.

'We need to stay here for a while,' Emma said.

'Unless us being here puts them at risk, I don't think they'll be in a hurry to get rid of us,' Cooper answered.

'Why?'

'I still think we might be useful to them. I'm starting to think they might have plans.'

5

'What's the matter?'

Emma had woken up alone in bed. After a moment's panic she had found Michael at the other end of the motorhome, sitting in the driver's seat behind the wheel and staring out through the windscreen into the grey, shadowy gloom of the vast hanger. The clock on the dashboard said it was almost four in the morning.

When he heard her he looked up momentarily and then looked down again.

'Nothing's the matter,' he replied. 'I was just thinking, that's all.'

'What about?'

'You know, the usual.'

'What's the usual?'

He shrugged his shoulders.

'What do you think?'

Emma sat down on the edge of the passenger seat next to him, still unsure as to what he was alluding to. A series of thoughts flashed through her mind. Was he thinking about the other survivors and the conversation they'd had earlier? Was he thinking about the soldiers or what had happened when they'd ventured outside yesterday? Or was he thinking about something else entirely? Whatever it was, it was clearly something which was weighing heavy on his mind. He scowled with concentration. His voice was abrupt and cold.

'Is it me?' she found herself wondering. 'Have I upset you or have I done something that's...?'

He shook his head and then sighed and rubbed his tired eyes.

'Why do you always assume it's got anything to do with you?' he asked. 'What could you have done to upset me? When we've got all this shit happening around us, why should it be anything you've done that's keeping me awake?'

'I don't know. Maybe if you'd talk to me and tell me what's wrong I could help. I just want to…'

Michael turned around to face Emma and reached out for her. She was shivering with cold. He gently pulled her across the front seats of the motorhome and held her close.

'It's nothing you've done,' he whispered. 'Believe me, you're just about the only thing I'm not worrying about at the moment.'

'Sorry,' she mumbled. 'It's just that when I woke up and found you weren't there I started to think that… You know what it's like, I couldn't help thinking that…'

'I know,' he interrupted.

Emma pushed her face closer towards Michael's and curled up on his lap.

'So what exactly were you thinking about?' she asked.

He nodded in the direction of the heavy entrance doors which separated the fortunate few inside the base from the immense and relentless gathering of rotting flesh outside.

'The bodies,' he answered quietly.

'What about them?'

He thought for a second.

'You remember how many were outside when we first arrived here?'

'Thousands, why?'

'Jack said he thought there were just as many of them out there today, maybe even more.'

'I know, I heard him. What's your point?'

'My point is that even though we've been buried down here for weeks, they're still managing to find us out.'

'We knew this was going to happen…'

'I know.'

'So?'

'So if they've been able to find us when we've been keeping quiet and out of sight, what the hell is going to happen now? What's going to happen now that those bloody idiots have started going out there with their guns and their flame-throwers and God knows what else?'

32

Emma squirmed uncomfortably as the implications of what he was saying became clear.

'So what do you think's going to happen?' she asked. She already thought she knew the answer, but she wanted to hear it from Michael.

'I think that every last corpse that's anywhere near here is going to end up outside those doors, trying to get inside. And then more will come, then more. And more of them means that the military's precious base is going to be put under increasing pressure to keep functioning. Sooner or later they'll have to go above ground again and then, when they do, it'll just make matters worse. Then even more of the fucking things will end up here.'

'Do you think that's really going to happen...?' she started to say.

'This is inevitable,' Michael said quietly, his voice low and unemotional. 'We've said it before, it might happen tomorrow, the day after tomorrow or the day after that. It might happen in the next hour or on the other hand it might not happen for weeks. The one thing I'm sure of is that it will happen eventually.'

6

'You on your own, Cooper?'

Cooper shuffled closer to the intercom on the heavy door which separated the main decontamination chamber and the rest of the buried base from the hanger. Well away from most of the rest of the group of survivors, he had been sitting talking to Bernard Heath when they'd become aware of sounds of movement coming from inside the decontamination area. Through a six inch square observation panel he had recognised Jim Franks, just about the last of his ex-colleagues who still dared to risk speaking to him.

'No, I've got Bernard Heath with me,' Cooper replied, his voice deliberately low. 'It's okay. Bernard's all right.'

A pause.

'Okay, mate,' the subdued and disembodied voice said. Franks and Cooper had known each other for several years and held each other in mutual respect. The rest of Cooper's former colleagues had, for a number of reasons, either been ordered or had chosen to no longer communicate with him. Many now felt uneasy around him and distrusted him because he was "out there with them" instead of being "in here with us." Others thought that being a bona-fide "survivor" somehow made him a different person to the Cooper they had known and served alongside previously. Those troops who still remained committed and loyal to the military simply feared incurring the wrath of their superiors if they dared speak to him. Others had become completely isolated and withdrawn and just didn't speak to anyone any longer.

'How you lot doing in there?' Cooper asked, huddling closer to the intercom.

'Not good,' Franks replied.

'What's happening?'

Another brief silence.

'The men are scared 'cause no-one knows what's happening or why it's happening. And we know we're on our own here now, so the jokers who are running this place are starting to think they're in charge of what's left of the fucking country and they can do what they please. We're all pretty shook up after what happened outside and it's getting pretty fucking intense down here.'

'Did you go outside?'

'Not this time,' Franks replied, 'but it'll be my turn sooner or later. You boys know better than I do what we're facing here...'

'It's not good,' whispered Heath.

'Seems to me it's fucking awful, never mind "not good",' Franks hissed. 'Jesus Christ, we've got people walking round down here talking about fields full of bodies and...'

Cooper interrupted, keen to get an answer to his original question.

'So what's happening?'

'Christ, Cooper, you know what it's like when you're getting ready for a fight. You've got some blokes who can't wait for it all to kick off so they can get going, then you've got others who spend most of their time crying into their pillows like fucking babies. All that most of us want to do is just get out of this hole, but we keep being told that what's out there is worse than what's down here and... and I don't know what the hell's going to happen but something's going to give sooner or later.'

Cooper was worried that Franks had mentioned a fight. As far as he was concerned a fight in their present position would inevitably mean risking absolutely everything for absolutely nothing.

'I wish I could give you some good news,' Cooper sighed, 'but I'd be lying to you because there's been no good news since this whole bloody thing started. Believe me though, mate, you're in the best place you could be. Make sure you stay down there as long as you can. I've told you before, every move you make up here brings hundreds of bodies swarming round you like flies. You might be stuck down there, but at least you're alive and you're not having to watch every step that you take. And if you do end up out here, you'll be trapped in your suit until you get back underground because one breath of outside air and chances are you'll have fucking had it. My advice is to keep your head down and get through this as best you can because…'

'You've got no fucking idea,' Franks snapped, raising his voice to a dangerously high level. 'For Christ's sake, Cooper, don't be so fucking naive. You know the kind of people that are down here. There's only so much of this they're going to take. There's only so much I'm going to take…'

'You don't have a choice. Go above ground again and…'

'Try telling that to this lot.'

'I know how it seems, but you've got to…'

'Remember Carlson?' Franks' desperate voice asked.

'Keith Carlson?' Cooper answered.

'Kevin,' Franks corrected. 'Remember him?'

'The chef, right?'

'That's right.'

'What about him?'

'They found him a couple of hours ago in his bunk. Stupid bloody idiot had slit his wrists.'

'Christ,' Bernard Heath sighed under his breath.

'He's not the first and he won't be the last,' Cooper answered quickly with a cold matter-of-factness.

'I know that,' Franks continued, 'the problem isn't what he's done, it's how to get rid of him. They can't decide what to do with the body. People are so fucking paranoid down here that they're talking about trying to burn it or cut it up into little fucking pieces for God's sake. I've just seen blokes fighting over the corpse.'

'Fighting, why?' Cooper asked.

'Because they want to make sure it's dead,' he replied. 'Jeavons and Coleman are standing over the fucking body watching it, ready to hack it to pieces if it starts to move.'

'It's not going to move,' Heath interrupted, his voice unintentionally condescending. 'That would probably only going to happen if the body had been exposed to the outside air before he killed himself. I don't think…'

36

'I know that and you know that,' Franks snapped angrily, 'but you try convincing a couple of hundred soldiers who are scared out of their fucking minds and who feel like they've been backed into a corner. These people are trained to fight, not to do nothing. They're talking about dumping the body outside when we go above ground again.'

'Makes sense,' Cooper said, 'but that could be weeks.'

'I don't think so.'

'Something planned?'

'It's starting to look that way.'

'What?'

'Not sure, no-one's saying much. There are a few rumours doing the rounds, that's all.'

'Such as...?'

The conversation faltered momentarily. Through the observation panel Cooper watched as Franks looked over his shoulder and checked he was safe to continue talking.

'I started to hear a few rumblings yesterday, and I've heard more today from people that I trust so it looks like there's some truth in what they're saying. Main problem is that we still can't get enough air down here and it's probably going to get worse. They cleared a couple of exhaust vents last time but they need to do more. There's no way of unblocking them from this side 'cause they'll risk infecting the whole fucking base, so at best it looks like we'll be coming up again soon to go out and get a few more of them cleared.'

'If that's at best,' Heath asked quietly, his voice filled with uncertainty, 'then what's your worst case scenario?'

Cooper glanced across at the other man, sharing his concern.

Another pause and then Franks spoke again.

'Some of the boys who went out last time,' he explained, 'told the bosses that they managed to get rid of hundreds of those things up there.'

'They did,' agreed Cooper. 'Problem is there's thousands more of them left.'

'Rumour has it,' Franks continued, 'that they're looking at trying to organise one massive push. Rumour has it we're all going above ground to torch the whole fucking lot of them.'

7

The lights came on.

Donna jumped up from her seat as the doors of the decontamination chambers began to open.

'Oh, Christ,' she mumbled anxiously, glancing across at Emma, Clare and Heath who were stood nearby and who were also staring at the slowly opening door.

Alerted by the sudden brightness in the hanger, most of the other survivors had already begun a furious and uncoordinated scramble across the vast cavern and over to their vehicles. As the first heavily-suited soldiers began to emerge from their sealed shelter the frightened crowd of men, women and children once again sprinted towards the police van, prison truck and motorhome.

A steady stream of troops again took up position on the ramp just short of the entrance doors. Standing to the side of the main column of soldiers, an officer furiously marshalled proceedings. Just as they had done the time before a number of engines were started and another armoured personnel carrier was driven out of the shadows. This time the powerful vehicle was accompanied by four jeeps and was surrounded by a phalanx of eight, flame-thrower carrying men. The men moved quickly towards the front of the short convoy, ready to escort the vehicles out into the open and burn a path for them through the crowds.

It was Saturday afternoon, three o'clock.

'What do you reckon?' Donna asked Heath. The two of them had stopped halfway across the hanger and were watching the troops intently. 'Think they're just going to try and do the same as they did before?'

'Looks that way,' he replied, his voice quiet and trembling slightly. 'I just want them to get it over with. If they're really going to do this, I just want them to do it now and stop all this stupid and pointless…'

His words were abruptly cut short as the ominous and unerringly familiar mechanical rumbling began which signalled the opening of the main doors. He nervously swallowed and licked his dry lips, unable to look away from the entrance to the bunker, too scared to keep watching but even more afraid not to. The outside world slowly began to appear. Because of the slope of the entrance ramp he became aware of the sky first - a dirty, grey-black, heavy and rain-filled sky that hung over the desolate scene and which made the day seem almost as dull and dark as night. And then it began. An unexpected split-second of silence and calm was quickly ended by a sudden torrent of bodies which began to pour into the base before being pushed back and obliterated by the soldiers with flame-throwers. From a distance Heath couldn't make out the shapes, details and actions of individual corpses - just a constantly writhing and lurching, featureless mass of movement which spilled forward before being destroyed by the flames. For a gut-wrenching and seemingly endless moment the sheer weight of advancing bodies appeared to threaten to put the front row of soldiers on the back foot, almost forcing them to move further back into the base again before they were able to dig in and push forward. Their vastly superior power and strength soon allowed them to eat into the crowd with relative ease. Brutal and one-sided, as the first battles quickly unfolded the familiar smell of burnt flesh began to fill the cavernous hanger, carried along by clouds of dirty, suffocating smoke.

'We should get ready to move,' Michael urged anxiously as he jogged across the width of the hanger. Donna reacted instantly but Heath failed to respond, transfixed by the hell he could now see outside. The personnel carrier began to drive forward, followed by the jeeps and by other heavily armoured vehicles and surrounded by a ring of troops who launched carefully controlled jets of flame into the crowd. As the troops began to move away from the base Michael ran to stand next to the other man and then took a few steps further forward.

'Cooper reckons they're really going to go for it this time,' Jack Baxter said, suddenly appearing behind the two men. 'Says they might even be trying to get rid of the whole lot of them.'

'He's right,' Heath mumbled, his voice barely audible.

'But what's the point?' Michael wondered. 'For God's sake, what good do they think it's going to do them? Get rid of them all and more and more will come. Whatever happens out there they're either going to end up back down here in this bunker or stuck outside in their suits. One way or another they'll be trapped. They might as well just cut their losses and...'

'And you can't reason with them,' Cooper said, joining the others and overhearing their conversation. He watched as the soldiers marched outside and thought for half a second about how he should have been among them. 'Try and put yourselves in their shoes,' he continued, 'we don't know much about what's happened, but we know a hell of a lot more than they do. We might not have the hardware they've got, but we're far better placed to deal with all of this than they are. All they know is they can't breathe the air outside because it will probably kill them, and that those bloody things out there are preventing them from getting the clean air they need. You can understand why they're seeing the bodies as the enemy. The only option they think they've got left now is to blow the fucking things to kingdom come and be rid of them.'

'But don't they understand...?' Baxter began pointlessly before Cooper interrupted.

'No they don't, not fully. They haven't seen half of what we've seen.'

'But the bodies won't stop, will they? They'll keep coming until there's nothing left of them.'

Outside the first troops had made steady progress. The area immediately surrounding the base - which already resembled a churned and bloody first world war battlefield - was swarming with movement. The bodies approached from all angles and were beaten and battered into the ground by adrenaline-fuelled soldiers who had been kept waiting underground too long. Every last man and woman laid into the approaching cadavers with anger and force, driven on by fear and pent-up frustration and emotion. Those who had not been above ground before, although shocked and disgusted by the bizarre and relentless battle unfolding around them, were surprised by the relative ease with which the corpses could be destroyed. Having been outside for only a few minutes, however, to many of the troops the vast numbers of the dead and their unstoppable nature had yet to become apparent.

Heavy artillery was quickly deployed with mortars and shells being fired into the endless crowd beyond the perimeter of the base. In the near distance constant explosions shook the ground and tore the bodies apart. Closer to the entrance the personnel carrier had almost reached another exhaust shaft. Walking alongside one of the vents, and shielded from the battle by the protective ring of fire which surrounded the convoy, the senior officer on the field, Jennens, watched events unfolding around him with a degree of cautious satisfaction. His men and women were already doing well, despite appalling conditions. The gloom of the afternoon's rapidly fading light was worsened by hissing rain that poured down on the scene relentlessly, drenching everything. The ferocious heat of the flame-throwers turned the grimy pools of water which had puddled in the churned, furrowed land into steam. Underneath his boots Jennens crunched charred and cindered flesh and bone into the mud.

The vent was secure. Jennens peered into the gloom beyond the scattered remains of the hundreds of bodies which had already been destroyed. He'd seen some appalling sights in his time, but never anything like this. The size and ferocity of the apparently endless crowd was remarkable and terrifying. He watched with disgust and a morbid fascination as still more of the dark, skeletal creatures scrambled, tripped and crawled through the mayhem towards his soldiers and towards certain destruction. In the midst of the confusion Cowell, one of his most trusted men, appeared at his side.

'We can do this,' he said, shouting to make himself heard through his facemask and over the wind and rain and sounds of constant battle. The muddied ground shook momentarily as a small mortar landed short of its target and exploded nearby, sending a gruesome shower of random body parts shooting into the squally air. 'If we're going to do this at all, then we should do it now.'

Jennens thought for a moment. Cowell was right. The opposition, although huge in numbers, was weak and offered no tangible resistance. Although wiping them out would not allow the soldiers any more freedom, this was unquestionably a perfect opportunity to take back some of what they'd lost. The defensive position they'd intended to take had already become offensive and attacking. If they could destroy enough bodies and beat the remainder back to a far enough distance and keep them there, they would be able to fortify the entrance to the bunker and properly clear and secure the exhaust vents. Although there was still no way the military personnel could yet survive outside the base, the officer immediately recognised the psychological importance of ridding themselves of the tens of thousands of cadavers which plagued and complicated their already miserable existence.

'Shall I give the order?' Cowell asked. Jennens looked around the battlefield again. In the short time he'd been stood there his troops had made even more progress through the diseased crowds. The enemy (if they could really be called that) were defenceless against the comparative might of the military. All the dead had were numbers. Jennens knew they had nothing to lose.

'Do it,' he commanded.

'Can't see,' complained Baxter, edging closer to the soldiers charged with protecting the hanger entrance. 'Can't see a bloody thing.'

'Stay back, Jack,' Michael warned.

A sudden familiar noise from behind the small group of survivors startled them momentarily. Cooper span around to see that the decontamination chamber doors were opening again.

'Shit,' he cursed as a second ragged column of nervous soldiers appeared from the depths of the base. There seemed to be almost twice as many of them this time.

'What's all this about?' asked Heath anxiously.

'My guess,' Cooper answered as he watched more than a hundred troops file past, 'is that they've decided to try and clear them away. This is the showdown we've been promised.'

As they emerged from the shadows into the light of the hanger the soldiers increased their speed, breaking into a gentle jog for a few paces before accelerating and sprinting out into the semi-darkness with weapons held high, ready for battle. The light outside was deteriorating rapidly. The survivors stared anxiously into the gloom as the guards at the front entrance parted to allow the re-enforcements through.

'This isn't good,' Baxter whined, feeling his stomach churn and twist with nerves. 'This is not at all good.'

As the fighting outside increased in ferocity and volume, the small group of survivors again herded towards their transports. Michael climbed into the motorhome and found it already crowded with frightened people, each of them clutching the few personal belongings they'd managed to grab hold of in the sudden confusion. In the front seats Donna had taken his usual position behind the wheel. Emma was sitting next to her.

'You two okay?' he asked, leaning into the front cabin.

'Just great,' Donna answered through teeth clenched together with nervous anticipation. She gripped the steering wheel tightly in readiness should they suddenly need to move. Emma looked up and flashed him a momentary smile.

'We're okay,' she said quietly. 'Are you going to...?'

'I'm going back to the others,' he said quickly. 'There are enough people in here already. Listen, Donna, if anything happens you just put your foot down on the fucking accelerator and get out of here.'

'Be careful,' Emma pleaded. 'Look, why can't you stay...?' she began to say but he had already gone.

There was clearly no more room in the motorhome - because of its more comfortable and open design many of the survivors had gravitated towards it rather than shutting themselves away in the insides of the more secure but claustrophobic prison truck. Michael found, however, that the prison truck (with Steve Armitage ready as ever behind the wheel) was also virtually full. Cooper called him over to the police van.

'There are only a couple in the back here,' he said, gesturing over his shoulder towards the back of the van. 'Just make sure that either you or I get behind the wheel if we need to make a move, okay?'

'Okay.'

Breathless and red faced, Bernard Heath appeared from around the back of the van.

'I've done a quick count of heads,' he wheezed. 'I think everyone's accounted for.'

Cooper nodded and then stood and watched and waited.

Outside the base a wide swathe of land had been cleared. The majority of the soldiers and machines had now been formed into long attacking lines, ready to sweep out across the land from the bunker entrance and destroy more of the bodies. Now that the jeeps had been positioned over all but one of the vents, the main objective of the excursion had been achieved. What was happening now was largely unplanned but still relatively well coordinated. From positions just behind the advancing troops heavy artillery fired over their heads and out into the distance, relentlessly pounding the land and cutting deep into the shadowy crowds, destroying countless scores of bodies. All around momentary bursts of brilliant yellow, orange and white light pierced the monochrome gloom and, like camera flashes, illuminated the grotesque hordes for a fraction of a second at a time. Deafening explosions shook the ground and rumbled through the early evening air. The troops moved steadily forward away from the entrance to the base. Progress continued to be relatively quick and largely unimpeded.

The attacking line of ground troops fanned out as they moved away from the bunker, pushing the crowds back. There remained a bloody and relatively constant gulf of several metres between the advancing soldiers and the dead. Ignorant to the danger that they faced, those creatures which had so far escaped the wrath of the military continued to move ever closer, dragging themselves over the putrefying remains of the thousands of corpses that had been destroyed before them.

'Aim for their heads,' a sergeant yelled as his troops unleashed another furious volley of bullets and flame into the seething mass of cadavers. Undeterred, the bodies continued to shuffle and trip forwards.

A short distance further down the military line, a soldier named Ellis stood up to his ankles in blood and rancid flesh and picked out individual corpses from the crowd up ahead. With the skill and concentration of a highly trained marksman he managed to shut off from the mayhem and confusion all around him and aimed at each body in turn, shooting them in the head and obliterating what remained of their brains. They dropped twitching to the ground and were immediately trampled by more dark figures advancing from behind. Conditions were becoming steadily worse with smoke, flame and rain all making it impossible to see clearly through the fading light of a dull and stormy dusk. To Ellis' left and to his right his colleagues continued to fight alongside him, each of them destroying as many bodies as they could. But still the crazed creatures continued to advance. For every one that Ellis destroyed, ten more seemed to take its place. And beyond there remained thousands more. Out of view still more and more and more of them crawled through the darkness.

'Fucking hell,' the soldier to the immediate right of Ellis cursed. 'I can't keep up with this. Christ, how many of these fucking things are there?'

They continued to shoot and the bodies continued to advance, spilling ever forward like some dark, thick liquid. Ellis didn't have time to think or speak, instead he concentrated on letting bullet after bullet fly into the rotting crowd. An unexpected arc of flame burnt through the air just ahead of him, illuminating the full horror of the scene for a few heart-stopping seconds. The twisted, grotesque faces of hundreds of corpses were suddenly exposed and Ellis found himself staring at them in disgust and revulsion, praying for the light to fade and the dark to return. The nearest corpses were less than ten metres ahead.

The ragged line of soldiers, still advancing steadily, reached a slight ditch where a meandering stream had once run diagonally across the battlefield but which had, over the course of the last few weeks, become clogged and filled with a compacted layer of rotting human remains. The trooper on Ellis' right, fighting to keep concentrating and not lose control of his frayed nerves, stumbled and slipped on the uneven ground, ending up on his hands and knees in the middle of the stagnant trench. A powerful wave of gut-wrenching nausea swept over him as he looked down into a mire of the mashed and mangled remains of decayed faces, limbs and other body parts, all instantly recognisable as such. As he pushed himself back up and tripped and stumbled further towards the approaching bodies, bile began to rise in his throat and he started to salivate. He knew that he was going to vomit, but he also knew that he had to stop himself from doing so at all costs - he couldn't take off his facemask. He turned back to face his advancing colleagues and another searing jet of fire lit up the stormy sky above him. Less than a second later a shell dropped short of its intended target and landed just metres away, exploding instantly and showering the troops with mud, shrapnel and putrefied flesh. Knocked to the ground again, the trooper panicked and scrambled back away from the front line. He was aware of a sudden stabbing, burning pain in his back, but his sickening fear and disorientation kept him moving. Once up on his feet again he reached over his shoulder and rubbed at the part of his neck and right shoulder which hurt the most. He could feel a small, jagged shard of metal which had ripped through his suit and pierced his skin. When he brought his hand back around he saw that it was covered in blood, and it was the sight of the blood on his glove which terrified him more than anything else. His suit had been compromised. Panicking, he lifted his weapon and turned back around. At first the adrenaline numbed the pain and kept him fighting.

Aware of a gap in the attacking line to his side, Ellis turned around. The wounded soldier next to him continued to fire into the swarming bodies until the infection caught him. As he emptied another round into the crowd the inside of his throat began to swell. In seconds the swellings blocked his windpipe and then began to split and bleed. Knowing he was dying, but not sure how or why, the soldier slowly turned on the spot, as if silently looking around for help or explanations. Frozen in position by a spontaneous nervous reaction, his finger remained on the trigger of his rifle, sending a seemingly endless torrent of bullets flying through the air. Ellis was the first to fall to the ground, shot through the neck. Another six men and women immediately around him were felled in seconds. Ellis saw one of them drop just metres from him.

The sounds of battle were muffled and silenced down on the ground. Weighed down by his breathing apparatus and other equipment, Ellis managed to roll over onto his back in the mud. He looked up into the cloudy sky above his head and waited. The heavy rain clattered down on his facemask, drowning out all other noise. He was aware of sudden, frantic movement and then utter darkness.

The last thing Ellis remembered was feeling the crowd of emaciated bodies smothering him as they crawled over him and marched on towards the base.

'Listen,' Cooper said as he stood by the transports next to Michael and Heath.

'What?' Heath stammered nervously.

'Something's happening.'

The men stood in silence and listened to the sounds which echoed around them.

'What?' Heath asked again.

'Can't you hear it?' Cooper whispered.

'Hear what?' Michael demanded, becoming increasingly uneasy.

'Shh...' he answered. 'Just listen.'

Michael did as Cooper said, and what the other man had implied gradually became clear. There had been a change to the sounds of battle drifting into the bunker from outside. Where before there had just been the constant pounding of gunfire and other explosions, now he could hear screams and shouts over the relentless clatter of fighting. Everything suddenly sounded desperately frantic and uncoordinated. The order and control previously demonstrated by the soldiers now seemed to be disappearing. As he watched he saw that some of the troops who had been left behind to guard the entrance to the base were edging forward, moving closer to the fight. Others were beginning to shuffle back.

'Why…?' Heath mumbled. 'What's happened…?'

'Shit, they've got no idea how many bodies there could be out there, have they?' Michael said anxiously. 'You tried to tell them, didn't you? Christ, there must be thousands of corpses for every soldier.'

'Yes, but they've got guns and machines and… It'll be all right, won't it, Cooper?' The uncertainty in Heath's voice was obvious and clear. He already knew the answer to his question.

Cooper ran the length of the hanger and up the entrance ramp until he was almost level with the guards. He peered out into the darkness. The still frequent flashes of brilliant light and flame and random explosions provided more than enough illumination to allow him to see what was happening outside. An experienced soldier, he'd seen enough ground battles to know when an army's tactics were working and when they were not. He could see at least two areas ahead of him where the bodies were now moving between the military and the base. The creatures had somehow managed to work their way through the lines of troops. Ignorant to the restrictions of fear, pain or just about any other emotion felt by the living, the dead hordes continued to surge forward past pockets of desperate and isolated men and women who were swallowed up by the decaying masses. It was an awful, nightmarish scene which held Cooper rooted to the spot with abject fear until he was distracted by the headlamps of the personnel carrier in the near distance as it turned and began to power back towards the bunker. The headlamps jerked up and down as the driver forced the powerful vehicle over the uneven ground at speed. Bodies occasionally crisscrossed in its path and were obliterated as it raced back to safety.

The corpses were close.

'What can you see?' Michael shouted to Cooper from the bottom of the ramp.

Cooper didn't answer at first, continuing instead to scan the mayhem he could see outside. There seemed to be a never-ending sea of movement ahead of him. The countless bodies which had been burned and destroyed by the last military excursion seemed to have gone - trampled underfoot by yet more corpses. He turned and ran back into the base.

'Get the engines running,' he eventually replied in a loud but calm and authoritative voice which masked the anxious, creeping terror he felt inside.

Back out in the field a combination of friendly misfires and the random movements of the bodies had now exploited four breaks in the soldier's defensive line. Already at an unexpected advantage because of the dire conditions and their incalculable numbers, the cadavers continued moving forward incessantly towards the light in the distance coming from inside the bunker. *En masse* they surged through the gaps in the ranks almost unopposed. Pockets of troops struggled to dispose both of the bodies they faced head-on and those moving through the undefended areas between them and their base. In less than fifteen minutes the balance of power on the battlefield had suddenly and unexpectedly shifted. With the coordination and order they had previously commanded now gone, the soldier's instinctive reactions and their individual selfish desire for self-preservation caused still more gaps in their defences to appear. Now there were shadowy shapes on all sides. The troops continued to fight and to shoot and to burn and destroy as many corpses as was physically possible until a single flare was launched into the sky near to where Cowell, the officer's aide, had been standing.

The flare was the signal to retreat.

'They're coming back,' Cooper yelled to the others as he sprinted towards them. He had spotted the incandescent flare hanging in the squally air and had immediately understood its meaning. Before he'd finished speaking the personnel carrier crashed back into the base, careering out of the darkness and skidding out of control. Michael and Heath dived in opposite directions as the heavy machine ploughed along the length of the hanger and then collided with the front of the survivor's police van, sending it spinning round and shunting it against the wall. Michael instinctively ran to help the survivors who had been waiting inside the vehicle and who had been unprepared for the sudden violent impact. He could hear them screaming and shouting as he yanked at the doors. One of them - an elderly man who's name he couldn't remember - was dead, his bloody face having been smashed against one of the windows.

'What the hell do we do now?' he yelled to Cooper as he pulled the remaining survivors back out into the light.

Cooper had already yanked the door at the back of the personnel carrier open.

'Get them in here,' he screamed.

Michael ushered the terrified survivors towards the military vehicle. As they quickly covered the short distance between the van and the personnel carrier the first foot soldiers returned to the base. They stumbled down the ramp, still firing indiscriminately into the darkness behind them. Seconds later the first bodies appeared. A sudden noise and a flash of movement distracted the survivors. Cooper looked up and saw that one of the jeeps had crashed into the side of the entrance door. The soldier who'd been behind the wheel was now limping into the base, struggling to keep moving forward whilst the nearest bodies reached out and began to pull him back.

'We've got to get out of here now,' Cooper decided. 'If they can't get that door closed then in a couple of minutes this place will be full of those fucking things.'

'Go!' Michael screamed at the drivers of the survivor's other two vehicles. The noise in the cavernous room was deafening and intense and at first neither Donna or Steve Armitage reacted. Michael gestured frantically and angrily towards the bunker doors until Armitage acknowledged him and began to pull forward, steering the clumsy prison truck around stockpiles of military equipment. Donna, who had never driven the motorhome before, did the same.

As the two vehicles moved towards the entrance many more soldiers and bodies swarmed into the base. Like small and insignificant ants against the vast and bland concrete backdrop, individually the corpses were slow and largely uncoordinated but their collective movement down the steep entrance ramp gave the ominous impression of speed and control. Gunfire continued to ring out and echo constantly. As more soldiers forced their way back inside, so the base became filled with more deadly gunfire and, occasionally, barely controlled flame.

From her position at the front of the motorhome Emma searched desperately through the confusion outside, hoping to catch sight of Michael. Next to her Donna tried to keep calm as she struggled to drive the heavy and unresponsive vehicle. She followed Armitage ahead of her in the truck, concentrating on staying close to his taillights. For a second she allowed herself to look up and into her door mirror. Back deeper in the base she could she frantic movement around the back of the personnel carrier. In the midst of the bloody confusion she could see Bernard Heath struggling to climb inside. She watched in helpless disbelief as he was brought down by gunfire, a stray round almost cutting him in half. A torrent of bullets thudded into his right leg, his crotch, his abdomen and his shoulder. By the time he hit the ground he was dead.

'Fucking hell,' she wailed with tears in her eyes. 'Bernard's gone down.'

'What?' Emma mumbled, spinning around desperately and trying to get a clear view through the back of the motorhome. She stared for a second at Heath's crumpled body on the ground before looking for Michael again. Where the hell was he? What had happened to him...?

Out of sight of Emma, Michael pulled the door at the back of the personnel carrier shut.

'Get moving!' he yelled as he stared out through a small, square window at the remains of his fallen friend. He lurched forward and then fell back into a seat as the soldier driving the transport slowly turned it around and pulled away.

'Put your fucking foot down,' Cooper hissed in his ear. The driver did as he was ordered, quickly overtaking the motorhome and the prison truck and powering towards the ramp. Countless staggering shapes - both living and dead - were smashed to the side.

'Which way?' the nervous trooper stammered through his cumbersome facemask as they neared the doors. Bright electric light was replaced by sudden blackness as they drove out into the open. Intense battles still seemed to be raging on all sides, providing some illumination but not enough to allow Cooper to make sense of everything that was happening around them. Knowing that the main track away from the bunker was blocked by the truck the survivors had crashed when they'd first arrived there weeks earlier, he needed to find another route away. The vehicle he was travelling in would be able to cope with any terrain, no matter how rough or uneven. The prison truck and motorhome following behind, however, would undoubtedly struggle to deal with uneven ground or anything more than the gentlest of gradients. Resigned to the fact that conditions would probably be as bad whichever direction they went in, he made a snap decision.

'Follow the line of the valley,' he ordered, gesturing left and choosing what he thought would be the most level route. He struggled to make himself heard over the engine, the rain and the relentless thud, thud, thud of the constant stream of bodies which launched themselves pointlessly at the metal sides of the personnel carrier. 'Just keep going straight,' he continued. 'We're bound to pick up a road or a track at some point.'

Driving through the bloody mayhem and devastation which continued to unfold all around them, the three vehicles disappeared into the darkness.

The hanger was filled with bodies. Individual soldiers still managed to offer a degree of resistance but their ammunition and their will to fight was almost completely gone. Terrified and exhausted, several disorientated troops had ripped off their cumbersome facemasks in desperation and were quickly infected and killed. Others were brought down by crossfire. Many more were ripped apart by vast, surging crowds of crazed bodies.

The senior officer left below ground ordered the decontamination chambers to be locked and sealed.

One hundred and seventeen troops remained buried underground.

Almost double that number were trapped on the surface, some still fighting, the majority dead or dying.

8

Being constantly thrown from side to side, Michael had to crawl the length of the personnel carrier to get to Cooper.

'So what the hell do we do now?' he demanded, knowing full well that his question was a pointless one.

Cooper had already dragged himself into the front of the vehicle and was now sitting alongside two suited soldiers. There were a further two troopers sitting in the back with Michael and three other survivors. Obviously soldiers who had been out fighting on the battlefield for some time, the survivors gave them as wide a berth as was possible in the close confines of the military vehicle. Their cumbersome protective suits were covered with a layer of mud, blood and dripping gore which had been picked up during the relentless fighting outside.

Cooper didn't even bother trying to reply to Michael's question.

'Do we just keep going all fucking night?' Michael cursed, holding on to the back of Cooper's seat as the armoured vehicle lurched down a sudden incline. He looked out through the blood-splattered glass in front of the driver. The view was frighteningly limited. 'The motorhome's got less than half a tank of fuel left,' he continued, 'we can't keep going indefinitely.'

When his comments were again met with silence from Cooper he slumped back angrily in the nearest seat and turned round to look out of the back of the vehicle. Behind them the pointless and costly battle continued to rage with frequent explosions and brilliant flashes of light illuminating the dead world for a fraction of a second at a time. The personnel carrier dipped awkwardly to one side as the ground over which they were driving became increasingly rough and uneven. Following close behind was the prison truck and, further back still, Michael was able to see the lights of the motorhome as it struggled to keep up. For a second he contemplated trying to stop the convoy so that he could try and get out and get to Emma and the others. But there were still too many bodies around to risk it. Far too many bodies.

Michael held his head in his hands and screwed his eyes shut. He tried to clear from his head some of the nightmarish images he had witnessed in the last hour but it was impossible. Everything had happened so fast. How had it all gone so very wrong so quickly? A couple of hours ago the bunker door had still been sealed and they'd been relatively safe and protected. Now they were exposed and vulnerable again, running once more without direction or defence. He thought about the people he'd seen killed - several soldiers, Bernard Heath and at least one other survivor. It had all been so pointless. He couldn't stop thinking about Bernard. He pictured him lying dead on the hanger floor, surrounded by scores of bodies and soldiers still trying to fight. Christ, he hoped he'd died quickly. He hoped he wasn't suffering. Imagine lying helplessly in the middle of that nightmare, unable to move and slowly bleeding to death, just waiting for it all to be over…

'We have to hit a road at some point,' Cooper finally said, snatching Michael back from his dark, depressing thoughts again and bringing him crashing back to reality. 'Then we'll stop and try and work out where we are.'

'Don't be fucking stupid,' the other man snapped, 'how can we stop? If we stop then we're going to…'

'If we're sensible we can afford to stop for a little while,' Cooper interrupted, his voice slightly louder - just enough to silence Michael's emotional outburst. 'We'll stop and regroup and decide what to do next. If we're quick enough there won't be time for any more than just a few bodies to find us.'

Michael nodded and grunted to show understanding but he wasn't really listening. He was trying to keep himself calm and under control. Again he found himself looking out of the window at the motorhome struggling to move across the rough terrain. He was thinking about Emma and what he would do if anything happened to her. At the same time he watched the constant, dark movement all around them as bodies turned and traipsed through the night after the uncoordinated convoy. He was trying to get used to the bitterly painful fact that they were exposed and on the run again.

In the prison truck Steve Armitage skilfully steered along the wide furrowed tracks that the military vehicle in front of him had left behind. At his side was Phil Croft, watching the scene like a hawk, terrified and shaking with nerves but still alert. In the back of the truck more survivors sat huddled in the darkness, not knowing where they were now or where they were going, each one of them wracked with an uncomfortably familiar sense of disorientation and hopeless fear.

Several metres behind the truck Donna groaned with effort as she struggled to keep control of the motorhome. It was an old, overused and unresponsive vehicle which gave a rough ride on level road at the best of times, never mind in these treacherous conditions. Inside the vehicle was deathly silent. A far more ordinary machine than the other two vehicles in front, its wide windows afforded those survivors crammed in the back a clear view of the dead world around them. It was a view which many of them would have preferred not to have seen. Now more than a mile from the military bunker, there were still vast crowds of bodies swarming across the land. Donna forced herself to keep looking forward and to concentrate on driving. She did the best she could but the motorhome was not built to move through thick, churned mud and over sudden, uneven dips and climbs. The steering was slow and heavy and the vehicle's rear end constantly threatened to slip and slide out of control. In the back no-one dared speak for fear of distracting their nervous driver.

Emma glanced up and noticed the dark silhouette of a house nestled amongst the trees on the brow of a low hill. At first she was reminded of Penn Farm and in her frightened state she didn't stop to think that where there was a building, there would almost certainly be a road, track or some other means of access. It was only when Donna slammed the brakes on that realisation dawned.

'What's the matter?' she asked, immediately concerned that they had stopped. Donna nodded her head in the direction of the two vehicles ahead. Emma peered into the darkness and saw that Cooper had climbed out of the personnel carrier. He was untying the frayed rope that was keeping a wide metal gate closed and in place. The headlamps of the three vehicles illuminated a steady stream of unsteady bodies which crisscrossed the scene randomly and began to collide with the transports. They watched as Cooper swung the gate open, kicked away the nearest corpse, and then ran back to his vehicle.

'Should be easier from here,' Donna said quietly, tired resignation very evident in her voice. 'I don't think we'll...'

Her words were interrupted by the sudden appearance of a withered cadaver which stumbled haphazardly out of the darkness towards them and slammed into the front of the motorhome. She jumped back with surprise and then leant forward and peered down at the pathetic shell which was pointlessly battering the front of the vehicle with clumsy, barely-coordinated hands. It was an appalling sight. In the time that the survivors had been underground the condition of the bodies had continued to deteriorate. This creature, judging by the length of its lank, shoulder-length hair and the remains of its ragged clothes, had once been female. The features of the lower part of its face were virtually indistinguishable. The hole where its mouth should have been was double normal size. Its jawbone hung down, looking as if it had been ripped away from one side of its head. The corpse's dark, empty eyes stared unblinking into the headlights of the motorhome.

'They're moving,' whispered Emma, forcing herself to look anywhere but directly at the body in front of them. Donna looked up and then gently accelerated, hoping that the movement of the motorhome might be enough to dislodge the body and push it to one side. When after a couple of seconds it hadn't moved, she simply pressed her foot down hard and crushed the obnoxious, disease-ridden thing beneath the wheels of her vehicle.

Following the prison truck and the personnel carrier, Donna carefully steered the motorhome through the gate and turned right onto a narrow tarmac track.

9

The convoy pushed on through the early evening and into the night, following the twisting road through the endless darkness, not knowing where it would eventually take them.

The nervous silence in the personnel carrier was uncomfortable and oppressive and yet was expected and understood. Its nine passengers were all struggling and suffering for a number of reasons. Each person was individually as anxious and uncertain as the next. Cooper kept his mind occupied by watching the road ahead constantly, scanning from side to side for bodies and hoping to find somewhere where they could stop for a while and catch their breath. They had nothing with them - no food, water, weapons or anything - and it was obvious that getting hold of some supplies whilst keeping safe had to be their first priority. He had known it was going to be like this if they'd needed to leave the base at speed. He'd intended stockpiling supplies in readiness for such an eventuality. The fact that the military had provided them with meagre rations and had maintained strict control over their equipment had made it impossible for him to build up any reserves. They'd hardly had enough to live on, never mind any to save.

In the back of the vehicle Michael stared at one of the soldiers leaning against the door. The soldier was sobbing.

'What's your name?' he asked. The suited figure turned its head and looked at him.

'Kelly Harcourt,' she replied. Michael was surprised although he knew he shouldn't have been. Under all the battlefield dirt and the heavy protective suit he'd assumed that the trooper was male. Although it was dark and most of her face was hidden by her cumbersome breathing apparatus, he could still see her eyes, her nose and the top part of her mouth. She looked too young to be in uniform.

'And is this the first time you'd been above ground?'

She nodded.

'They told us what we were going to see,' she said quietly, 'but I never expected it to be like this. I didn't think that...'

He shook his head.

'Believe me,' he sighed, 'whatever they told you, it's worse. You haven't seen anything yet.'

As quickly as it had begun the exchange ended. Michael regretted sounding so negative, but how else could he be? His awkward attempt to make conversation with the soldier had been instinctive and natural, but when he couldn't think of anything more positive to say he instead chose to say nothing. What could he possibly tell her that would make any difference to the hopelessness of her position? He couldn't help her or reassure her or comfort her. He couldn't make any promises about her safety or her health or security. He couldn't really tell her anything and that, he decided, was the hardest and most frustrating part of all. Now that they were outside and unprotected again, he truly understood just how important the military base could (and should) have been. He thought about the different places where he'd spent any length of time over the last six weeks - the community centre back in Northwich, Penn Farm and now the base - none of them had been able to provide the shelter and protection he'd craved and expected. Nowhere had been strong enough. Filled with a sudden gut-wrenching emptiness, Michael realised that in spite of his seemingly constant efforts, he had achieved nothing since the nightmare had begun. Okay, so he was still alive and in relatively good physical condition, but he was as vulnerable, cold, anxious, tired, disorientated, unnerved and helpless now as he'd been on the very first day.

Was this how it was always going to be?

Progress along debris-strewn roads was slow. The landscape through which they cautiously moved was relentlessly dark and bleak with just about the only movement coming from those random bodies quick enough to react to the noise and light produced by the three vehicle convoy. Almost an hour and a half after their unplanned and uncoordinated journey had begun, the survivors skirted round the furthest edge of relatively small town and then came upon a collection of large, nondescript buildings sited just off the main road. The soldier driving the personnel carrier slowed down. Some kind of industrial estate, when they looked deeper into the shadows they were able to make out a cinema, a restaurant, a call centre, office blocks and various dilapidated factories and several other shells of buildings in various stages of construction or demolition. It appeared that the area had been in the middle of a huge regeneration project when the project managers, the architects, the backers, the bankers, the construction workers and everyone else involved in the place had died. Michael looked around hopefully. There didn't seem to be too many bodies around, perhaps because of the relatively close proximity of the underground base. Thousands of corpses had been drawn to the bunker over several weeks. Because so many of them had ended up around the base, it stood to reason that the dead population of the surrounding areas might well have been substantially reduced. Although they may return in time, for the moment Michael guessed that they were still being drawn towards the mayhem at the base that the survivors had just left behind.

'Let's try here,' he suggested, leaning towards Cooper and the driver at the front of the vehicle.

The driver cautiously led the convoy deeper into the estate, following a winding road which connected a number of car parks the size of football pitches, largely empty save for the odd abandoned (and numerous crashed) vehicles. He was about to pull up alongside a dark and apparently lifeless restaurant when Cooper made a suggestion.

'Head for the cinema,' he said quietly. 'Everything happened early in the day. No-one would have been there when it started.'

His reasoning was sound. Most people seemed to have been killed sometime between eight and nine o'clock in the morning - long before the cinema would have been open for business. If there were any bodies inside, he thought, then at most there should only have been a few staff or cleaners.

'Go round the back,' Michael said, 'just keep going for a minute.' He followed the logic of Cooper's train of thought but he wasn't entirely convinced. The cinema may well have been quiet, but it was also designed to be dark and enclosed and the entrances and exits within each individual theatre would be limited. He was apprehensive. He didn't want to make the wrong decision and find himself trapped in such a confined and restrictive environment. 'Hold on,' he said, looking up and over to his left, 'what about that place?'

Michael gestured beyond the cinema towards a warehouse-sized shop. The driver kept moving forward, swerving instinctively but unnecessarily around three clumsy, lurching bodies which tripped out of the shadows. The warehouse was in the furthest corner of the estate and was bordered on its left side and along the back by a high chain-link fence. Beyond the fence were trees. As they approached Cooper noticed a cordoned-off loading bay nestled against the side of the building.

'Over there,' he said. 'Go through the gate.'

The driver did as instructed, carefully guiding the personnel carrier into the enclosed area. Still close behind, the prison truck and the motorhome both followed. The personnel carrier came to a sudden, jerking stop and, feeling sick through a combination of nerves and the long, rough journey, Michael clambered out quickly and jogged across the loading area. Seconds later Cooper was with him and, between them, they pulled shut a heavy gate and secured it, cutting them off from the rest of the estate. A lone body had managed to get through. Cooper grabbed its neck and smashed its head repeatedly against the back of the nearby prison truck until it fell twitching to the ground.

'Let's get everyone inside,' Michael suggested. 'If we get under cover quickly enough then we might not attract very many of them. We might even be able to spend the night here if we can…'

A sudden flurry of movement to his right distracted him. Instantly ready to batter and beat away another abhorrent body, he stopped when he saw that it was Emma. She threw herself at him and wrapped her arms around him, knocking him off-balance.

'Couldn't see you back there,' she whispered. 'I looked but I couldn't see you. I didn't know if you were here or whether you'd...'

'We haven't got time for this,' Donna hissed disapprovingly. 'Get out of sight for Christ's sake.'

The survivors and soldiers nervously emptied out of their respective vehicles and bustled into the dark building. Stonehouse, the highest ranking of the four soldiers who had travelled with them, led the way in through a side entrance which had been propped open for the last seven and a half weeks by the atrophied right leg of a dead member of staff. He held his rifle out in front of him, ready to fire but not sure what good it would do if he did. The group followed behind in a close but uncoordinated bunch and were almost completely silent until Jack Baxter spoke.

'We should make a bit of noise,' he whispered, 'just in case there's any of them in here. We should try and get them to come out of the shadows.'

'It's all bloody shadows in here, Jack,' Michael mumbled, looking around and trying to make sense of their dark and dismal surroundings. They seemed to be in a household store of sorts and they were presently standing in the middle of the electrical department. To their right was a wall of depressingly dark and dead television screens, to their left a similarly dead and powerless display of stereo equipment.

The soldier leading the group stopped moving.

'So what do we do now?' he asked.

'Get some bloody light in here for a start,' a voice from the darkness replied. Michael recognised it as belonging to Peter Guest, a quiet whisper of a man who generally kept himself to himself and to whom he had only spoken a handful of times.

'There's bound to be something in here we can use,' Donna said hopefully as she looked round through the gloom. She could hear movement nearby and, although she was almost completely certain that it was another one of her group she could hear, she wasn't totally sure.

Standing just to the side of Stonehouse, Phil Croft raised his cigarette lighter to his face, the dancing orange flame burning a bright hole in the darkness. Scrambling through the shop debris towards the light with suddenly increased speed, a body lurched at Stonehouse, knocking him off-balance and pushing him back into the huddled group of survivors. Instinctively the soldier picked himself back up, shoved the corpse back on its already unsteady feet, and then lifted his rifle and shot the pitiful creature through the head. It dropped heavily to the ground at his feet, its face a bloody mass of putrefied flesh and splintered bone.

'You bloody idiot,' Donna hissed. 'Christ, make some more noise why don't you? We'd better get some damn light sorted out now because every dead body in this fucking place will be on its way over to us.'

'Have you stopped to wonder why none of us bother carrying guns?' Baxter spat. 'A single shot might take one of them out, but there are thousands of the bloody things, and the noise you make getting rid of one will bring a hundred of them sniffing round you.'

Knowing that their words had just caused panic within the group of anxious survivors, Donna began to search the nearby shelves for something to illuminate the dark building. Others followed her lead. Kelly Harcourt, the soldier Michael had spoken to earlier, disappeared back outside and then returned with a handful of torches from the personnel carrier.

'Why the hell didn't you bring them in with you in the first place?' Donna snapped, snatching one of the torches from her.

'Give her a break,' Baxter sighed as he peered nervously into the darkness.

The torches were handed round and several circles of bright light were shone around the vast shop floor. They heard the clattering of a display unit being knocked over as at least one more clumsy body became aware of their presence and began to stumble over towards them.

'Let's stay here,' whispered Michael. 'It'll be easier if we stay in one place and wait for them to come to us.'

'How long do we wait?' a voice from behind him asked.

'As long as we have to,' he answered back. 'Why? You got anything better to do?'

The first body lumbered into view. Moving with surprising speed and dragging one useless foot behind, the creature was illuminated by the light from Donna's torch. Its face (as much of its face that remained intact) was blue-grey and waxy in appearance with dried, parchment-like skin clinging to its skull, making it appear hollow and frail. It wore the ragged remnants of a store attendant's uniform - a blue shirt (with a collar that now appeared several sizes too big because of the body's emaciation) and a red tie. Donna found the fact that the body was still wearing a tie bizarre. It even had a name badge pinned to its shirt pocket. The name had been obscured by mould and dribbles of blood and other bodily discharges which had dripped down from its decaying face over time. Cooper disposed of the body by swinging a fire extinguisher through the air and virtually knocking its listless head from its shoulders. It collapsed to the ground as three more bodies lumbered awkwardly into view.

Half an hour was sufficient time to enable the survivors to rid themselves of the last bodies and dispose of them in a heap outdoors. Pleased to finally be occupied for a while, many of the survivors then busied themselves around the building, collecting anything they thought might prove useful. The bodies outside had yet to materialise in the vast numbers the group had come to expect. When the hordes of corpses had failed to appear a handful of people had ventured out into the open for a few risk-filled minutes and gathered all the edible food and drink they could find from the kitchen of the restaurant next door and the concessions stand in the foyer of the cinema opposite. Mostly sweets, chocolate and tinned goods, it was better than nothing. By the time the men and women who had gone outside were safely back in the warehouse there were around twenty bodies gathered around the front of the building and half as many again clattering against the fence surrounding the loading bay, nothing like the massive numbers they were used to.

'They're not a problem when there's only a few of them,' Cooper explained, trying to educate Stonehouse. 'Problem is that one of them will inevitably attract another and so on and so on until you've got hundreds to deal with. And there are thousands upon thousands of the fuckers out there.'

Stonehouse sat opposite Cooper, slumped dejectedly in a chair in the area of the store where customers would previously have sat with staff and applied for credit. Baxter sat alongside them. Donna, Emma and Michael were also nearby, as were several other survivors. A short distance away the three other soldiers sat in silence on a pile of large cushions and garishly coloured beanbags which looked like they had originally been designed for use in children's bedrooms.

'So what happens next?' Stonehouse asked. Baxter looked at him with sadness and pity, trying to imagine how the soldier must have been feeling, trapped in his uncomfortable protective suit, knowing that to take it off would almost certainly result in a quick, painful and instant death. He imagined that he himself might have been able to handle it for a few hours, maybe even a couple of days, but the four soldiers now travelling with them would have to exist like this indefinitely. He didn't know how they'd be able to eat, drink or do anything else. Surely it would only be a matter of time before they had no option but to take off their suits. It was inevitable. Christ, whether they realised it or not (and he was pretty sure they did), they were just waiting to die.

'I don't know,' Cooper replied, answering the soldier's question. 'We need to stop here for as long as it's safe. We need to know exactly who and what we've got here. There are a lot of people here who need to...'

'Then what?' the soldier pressed, interrupting. He wasn't interested in hearing about the state of mind of any of the survivors. Cooper shrugged his shoulders.

'We move on I suppose.'

'Where to?'

'How the hell am I supposed to know?' he sighed. 'Bloody hell, I don't know.'

'Problem is,' Baxter said quietly, 'nowhere's safe anymore. Christ, you lot with your bloody guns and your tanks and everything else couldn't look after yourselves, could you? What hope do you think we've got?'

Cooper looked up at him and slowly shook his head.

'Come on, we've talked about this a hundred bloody times already, Jack,' he said before turning back to face the soldier again. 'The bodies are rotting. Although they're more controlled than they were before, the fact is they're still decaying.' He turned to face Stonehouse again. 'We reckon it's not going to be too long before they reach the point when they're not able to function.'

'And how long do you think that's going to be?'

'Just a few more months now.'

'A few more months? Fucking hell, are we supposed to sit here like this for a few months?'

'You might have to. Could you last that long?'

'I doubt it.'

'So what are you going to do about it?'

The soldier thought for a moment.

'Doesn't look like we've got any option but to try and get back to the base,' he replied, his voice tired and slow. 'Whatever happens we're dead if we stop out here. Might as well try and get back inside if we can.'

'You've got nothing to lose,' Baxter said.

'Seems to me we've lost everything already,' the soldier snapped.

10

By Clare's watch it was a quarter to three.

The warehouse was silent and cold. She lay restless on the floor on a thin mattress next to Donna. Together they'd dragged it over from the furniture department hours earlier. Despite being physically exhausted she couldn't relax enough to be able to sleep. Looking around in the low light it was obvious that she wasn't the only one struggling to get any rest. Perhaps as many as half of the others were awake too. Clare needed to get some sleep but she couldn't. She felt increasingly anxious and uncomfortable. Her guts were twisting with pain. Maybe it was just nerves? Perhaps it was the overdose of sugar she'd taken when she'd eaten earlier. Whatever the reason, the very thought of food now made her want to vomit. She'd had diarrhoea an hour or so ago. Christ it had been humiliating. She'd sat on a dried-out toilet pain in the furthest corner of the building and had cried with the discomfort and degradation of the experience. She was sure that everyone had been able to hear her. Even now after living rough for almost six weeks and going without even the most basic of human necessities, sometimes it was still too much for her. She was a teenage girl and, despite what had happened to the rest of the world, her body had continued to develop as it would normally have been expected to. She'd started her first period a week and a half ago. Donna had helped her and had reassured her as much as she could but it hadn't been easy - it was obvious that she was struggling too. Everyone was struggling.

Clare lay on her back and looked up at the ceiling, studying the many metal girders which supported the roof and wishing that the huge lights hanging high above her would work. She'd be prepared to risk attracting the attention of the bodies outside if she could just turn on the lights and see clearly for a while. She wanted a little light and certainty. The darkness and shadow unnerved her. She hated it even when she was in relatively familiar surroundings, but this place was cold and unknown. She hated the darkness more than ever tonight.

Her eyes were becoming heavy but still she couldn't sleep. Clare desperately needed to relax and start building up her energy reserves. She knew that as soon as day broke they'd most probably be up and out again and she didn't know when they'd next be able to stop. She didn't know if she'd have enough strength to be able to make it through tomorrow. She found it incredibly difficult to keep going when they didn't know where or what they were going to. She just hoped that tomorrow would be relatively easy and painless and...

She could hear something.

She lifted herself up onto her elbows and listened intently. There it was in the distance - a faint, mechanical sound. The world was so still that the unexpected noise seemed directionless and vague and she wondered at first whether she was just imagining it. Was it just a cruel trick her tired mind was playing on itself? The sound became fractionally louder, and she made the logical assumption that it must have been more soldiers from the base. Perhaps a few more of them had managed to get to their vehicles and get away from the bunker. Maybe they were looking for the survivors? Maybe they'd just come this way by chance? Whatever the source of the noise, it was still faint and it seemed for a while to wash in and out of range. It could have been a mile away or ten. Clare had no way of knowing where it was coming from and she was too afraid to risk getting up and going to the window and looking for it. She didn't want to be seen by any of the things outside.

It was getting louder.

She wasn't the only one who had heard it. She noticed that another couple of people (she couldn't see who) were now sitting up and listening. She leant across and shook Donna's shoulder.

'What?' Donna grumbled lethargically before suddenly remembering where she was and jumping up, worried that something was wrong or that something had happened. 'What's the matter?'

'Listen,' Clare whispered.

The noise was definitely moving closer now. It sounded like an engine of sorts, but not the engine of a car, truck or lorry. It continued to steadily increase in volume and, as it got louder, it began to change and to gradually become clear. A relentless mechanical chop, chop, chop could now be heard above the general din. Those survivors who were awake knew what it was they could hear, but they refused to believe it. Louder and louder now until the building felt like it was beginning to shake and the air was filled with the deafening sound. Michael got up and ran to the front of the warehouse, desperate to see what was making the noise and also concerned that it would attract many more unwanted bodies to the scene. All of his worries were forgotten instantly when, from out of nowhere, a brilliant shaft of bright white light suddenly swooped along the length of the industrial estate and then stopped. It took a few seconds for the reality of the situation to sink in. The reality was that there was a helicopter hovering over the warehouse, lighting up the place with a powerful searchlight.

'Is this one of yours?' Baxter asked Stonehouse as they both stood up. Behind them Cooper grabbed the nearest soldier's weapon and pushed his way over to the door through which they'd originally entered the building.

'Nothing to do with us,' the equally bemused Stonehouse replied as he and Baxter both followed Cooper out into the loading bay. They shielded their eyes from the burning light and whipping wind and ran for cover behind the prison truck as the pilot of the helicopter skilfully and carefully lowered the machine and set it down in the space between the soldier's and survivor's three vehicles. Cooper watched every metre of its rapid descent.

The very moment the helicopter was down the pilot cut its engine and extinguished all lights. The swirling rotor blades began to slow and the ground-shaking mechanical noise began to fade, leaving the all too familiar sound of bodies clattering against the wire mesh fence to become clear again. Baxter stood up to move but Cooper grabbed hold of his arm and pulled him back down.

'Wait,' he hissed, 'take it easy. We don't know who the hell this is.'

The doors on either side of the helicopter opened. Cooper watched with caution and a degree of unquestionable excitement as two people jumped down onto the tarmac. It was difficult to clearly see what was happening in the gloom of early morning. What appeared to be a well-built man and a smaller, more rotund woman stood together in front of the aircraft and scoured the scene for signs of life.

'Hello,' the man called out. 'Anyone there?'

His calls provoked a sudden and intense reaction from the crowd of corpses on the other side of the fence but nothing else. After a few seconds spent silently weighing up the options, Cooper slowly stood up and stepped out of the shadows. He held the soldier's rifle tightly in his hands, making sure it was visible, but kept the barrel very obviously pointed down towards the ground.

'Over here,' he answered. The two figures turned and, after a moment's hesitation, began to walk towards him. 'Where the bloody hell did you come from?' he demanded, relieved that these people looked relatively normal.

'Just outside Bigginford,' the man replied factually. 'I'm Richard Lawrence. This is Karen Chase.'

'Everything all right, Cooper?' Michael asked, suddenly appearing at his side, flanked by another two survivors and a soldier. A further crowd of people were stood in the doorway, watching intently.

'Think so,' Cooper mumbled in reply. He moved a little closer to Lawrence and Chase. 'How did you find us? We've only been here for a few hours.'

'Pretty easy in that thing,' Lawrence answered, nodding back towards the helicopter. He brushed his long and windswept grey hair out of his face so that he could clearly see Cooper. 'We saw the crowds a few miles back and we knew that something was happening round here,' he continued, referring to the battle at the bunker, 'so we've been on the lookout for anyone trying to get away. And you lot stick out like a sore thumb.'

'Why?'

'I've been flying helicopters for years now,' he explained, 'and it gets easy to spot things that are out of the ordinary, even today when pretty much everything's screwed up. You don't often get vehicles like the ones you've got parked around the back of places like this.'

He had a point, Cooper silently admitted to himself. The prison truck, motorhome and military vehicle did look conspicuously out of place tucked away in the shadows of the warehouse.

'How many people you got here?' Chase asked.

'Don't know exactly,' Cooper replied. 'Between thirty and forty I think…'

'Look, can we finish this inside?' Michael interrupted. He was, as always, acutely aware of the effect their prolonged appearance outside was having on the mass of bodies nearby. Cooper nodded and stood to one side to allow the new arrivals to walk past him and follow Michael into the dark building.

By the time they reached the main area where the survivors had grouped themselves just about everyone was up and awake and aware of what had happened. Nervous and subdued conversations were quickly silenced as the unfamiliar figures entered the warehouse. The centre of attention, Lawrence and Chase found themselves standing in the middle of the group feeling awkward and exposed, nodding acknowledgments to the few faces they were able to make out in the half light. Chase tugged Lawrence's arm and pulled him over to the edge of the impromptu gathering. They found themselves somewhere to sit and looked round into the many faces staring back at them.

'This is Richard Lawrence and Karen Chase,' Cooper announced as he arrived back in the room. 'They've come from Bigginford, so Christ knows how they've ended up here.'

'That's bloody miles away,' Jack Baxter muttered under his breath.

'They've got a bloody helicopter,' Phil Croft sighed, frustrated by the other man's stupid comment.

The air was suddenly filled with hushed expectation. There seemed to be so many questions to ask that no-one knew where to start. Donna cleared her throat and took up the mantle.

'So do you spend all your time flying around in the middle of the night looking for survivors?' she asked, the tone of her voice strangely abrasive and clearly lacking in trust.

'Not usually,' Chase responded, equally abrasively.

'How did you know where to find us then?'

'We've known for some time that there were probably people around here…'

'So why didn't you let us know you were about?' Baxter interrupted.

'Because we couldn't see you,' Lawrence answered, playing with his short greying ginger beard as he spoke. 'All we could see were a few thousand bodies. We knew something had to be attracting them, but we didn't know what.'

'So where were you?' Chase asked.

'Underground,' Baxter replied.

She nodded.

'I flew over this area a couple of days ago and it was pretty bloody obvious that something had happened. There was a hell of a lot of smoke around but I couldn't see what was going on. We came back again just now and saw the fighting. We thought that some of you might have got away so we spent the last couple of hours flying around trying to find you.'

The group fell silent as they each considered the explanation they'd just heard. It sounded feasible. They didn't have any reason not to believe what they'd been told.

'Tell us about the helicopter,' Emma asked. 'How have you ended up with a helicopter?'

'I've been flying for years,' Lawrence answered. 'It was my job. I used to fly people over towns for those "eye in the sky" traffic broadcasts on local radio. I was up there when this all kicked off…'

'So what happened?'

'We were in the middle of a broadcast and it got the reporter,' he replied. The pilot's face suddenly looked tired. The effort involved in talking about what had happened was considerable.

'Beautiful girl, she was,' he continued. 'She was dead in seconds. Then I looked down and I could see the world falling apart beneath me and I never wanted to land. By the time I finally touched down everyone was dead.'

The group's questions, although random and perhaps individually insignificant and unimportant, all needed to be asked. And the sudden speed of the unexpected arrival and the lack of time they'd had to think about what was happening meant that the questions were asked as and when they came to mind.

'So are there many of you?' Michael asked.

'Not as many as you by the look of things,' Lawrence replied. 'There are just over twenty of us, but we're split at the moment.'

'Split?'

He nodded.

'We've been based at Monkton airfield since all this started,' he explained, 'but we're getting ready to move on.'

'Where are you going?'

'You probably know what it's like from your own experiences, you make a damn sound out in the open these days and you find yourselves surrounded by those bloody things out there before you know what's happening. What with the helicopter and the plane...'

'You've got a plane too?' Baxter interrupted, amazed.

'Only a small one. Anyway, with the noise we make we've been surrounded by thousands of them since we first got to the airfield.'

'So where are you planning to go?' Michael asked. 'Surely it's going to be just as bad wherever you end up?'

'We've been all over the bloody place,' Baxter added, 'and we've not been able to find anywhere safe enough yet.'

'We spend our time running from crisis to crisis,' Emma sighed. 'Never seem to get anywhere worth...'

'We've found an island,' Chase said, cutting across her.

'An island?' she gasped, her mind immediately filling with images of sun-drenched beaches and golden sands.

'It's just off the northeast coast,' she continued to explain. 'It's cold, grey and miserable and there's not much there but it's a hell of a lot safer than anywhere on the mainland.'

'How big is it?' Michael asked quickly, his head beginning to spin with sudden questions. 'What kind of facilities have you got there? Are there many buildings or do you…?'

'It's early days yet,' Chase answered. 'We spent a lot of time looking for the right location and we finally think we've found it. It's a little place called Cormansey. It's about a mile and a half long and a mile wide. We think there were originally about five hundred people living there. There's one small village where most of them lived, but there are houses and cottages dotted all around the place. There's an airstrip on the far side of the island and…'

'What about bodies?' Michael wondered, desperately trying to contain his mounting interest and to keep his sudden excitement under control. Lawrence explained.

'We're planning on getting rid of what's left of the local population. We're hoping to fly a few people over each day,' he said, his voice suddenly a little more tired and slow again. 'We've only been there for a couple of days. There are six of us there now, I flew three over yesterday morning. That's how I came to be flying over here.'

'So what's the plan?'

'We've sent some of our strongest people over there to start clearing the land. They're going to work their way down the length of the island, getting rid of all the bodies they come across. Like Karen says, we think there were only about five hundred people there originally and from what we've seen it looks like more than half of them are still lying face down on the ground. As far as we can tell there aren't any indigenous survivors so that just leaves us with a couple of hundred corpses to get rid of.'

'Bloody hell,' mused Baxter in awe. Like everyone else around him he was slowly beginning to come to terms with the implications of what he was hearing. Imagine being somewhere where they were free to move and where there were no bodies. Imagine being somewhere where they could make as much noise as they damn well pleased without fear of the repercussions. It sounded too good to be true. Perhaps it was.

'Once we think we've got enough people over there we'll start moving into the village,' Lawrence continued. 'We're planning to clear it building by building until we've got rid of every last trace of them.'

'What about power and water?' the ever practical Croft asked, his mind racing. Lawrence shrugged his shoulders.

'Come on,' Donna sighed, as pessimistic as ever, 'how do we know whether any of this is true? And even if it is, how do you know if this island of yours is going to be safe?'

'They turned up here in a bloody helicopter, Donna,' Cooper said quietly, disproving of her attitude. 'My guess is they're telling the truth. Why should they lie? It might not all be as easy as they're making it sound though...'

'It's still early days and we've got a lot to do,' Lawrence said, 'but there's no reason why we can't make this work. And who knows, in the future we may well be able to get fuel and power supplies working again.'

The future, Michael thought to himself. Bloody hell, these two survivors who had suddenly appeared from out of nowhere were in a strong enough position that they could actually allow themselves the luxury of stopping to think about the future. Okay, so they clearly still had a lot of work ahead of them and the danger they faced was far from over, but at least they could sense an end to it. They could see the direction that the rest of their lives might possibly take. He, in comparison, didn't know which way he was going to run or what he was going to have to face in the morning.

The conversation continued with more previously silent survivors now finding their voices and more and more questions being asked of the new arrivals. As those questions were patiently answered the clear, sensible and rational details of the plan being presented became increasingly apparent. Individually Michael, Cooper and the majority of the rest of the group already understood the potential importance of sticking with these people.

In a moment of relative silence a single question was posed.

'Do you know what happened?' a voice from the darkness asked.

'What do you mean?' mumbled Chase.

'What happened to cause all of this?' the voice clarified nervously and with some uncertainty, not sure whether they should have dared ask.

Every other conversation stopped.

'Do you?' Lawrence asked rhetorically. No-one answered. The room was deathly silent. 'What about you?' he asked again, this time looking directly at Stonehouse and the other three soldiers grouped around him. 'You must have known something.'

'We weren't told anything,' Cooper replied.

'You're military too?'

'I was. Got myself stuck out in the open and found out by chance that I was immune?'

'What do you mean, found out by chance?'

'I took my mask off and I didn't die,' he answered quietly.

Lawrence looked into space and appeared to think carefully for a few long seconds.

'Look,' he continued, 'I can tell you what I've been told, but I can't tell you whether it's right or wrong.'

'How can he know anything?' Donna demanded angrily. 'There's no-one left who could possibly have told him.'

'You don't know that for sure...' Phil Croft attempted to protest.

'No way,' Donna continued, looking at Lawrence and Chase, 'you can't know... you just can't.'

Lawrence shrugged his shoulders nonchalantly.

'Like I said, I can tell you what I've seen and heard and you can choose whether you believe it or forget it. It makes no difference to me. My feeling is that what I've heard is right, but that doesn't necessarily mean it is.'

'Just stop all this bullshit and just fucking tell us!' Peter Guest snapped. His angry outburst was out of character for such a normally quiet, insular and withdrawn man.

As he waited to hear more, Michael stared deep into the helicopter pilot's tired face and began to ask himself whether he really wanted to listen to what he was about to say. What possible difference would it make? How would knowing what had happened change anything now? It might make him angrier. It might make the situation worse. It might even affect his relationship with Emma but he couldn't see how. Regardless of what might or might not happen, he knew that he had no choice but to listen to Lawrence. He couldn't not listen. The reality was that he might be about to find out why his world had been turned upside down so quickly and so cruelly, why everyone he had known had been killed in a single day, and why his life had become a dark, exhausting and relentless struggle.

Lawrence cleared his throat, sensing the survivor's mounting unease. He looked around the dark room, staring at each of them in turn.

'You really want to know what did this?' he asked.

Silence.

'I'll tell you what I've been told.'

11
Richard Lawrence

About a week after it started, I was hiding. Me and another bloke
called Carver had shut ourselves away in the ruins of a castle.
Sounds impressive, but it wasn't. It was just a gatehouse, a
couple of towers and a few sections of crumbling wall dotted
around a field of grass, but it had a moat that was still half-full of
water and we knew that would be enough to keep pretty much
everything out. We blocked the drawbridge and used the
helicopter to get in and out, landing it in what was left of the
main courtyard and living, sleeping and eating in a little wooden
gift shop.

We were still using the old helicopter I'd used for work but
we were getting low on fuel. We either needed to find
somewhere to fill it up or we had to get ourselves another
aircraft. On the tenth day we ended up flying low over a couple
of army bases and government buildings trying to see what
equipment they had that we could take. We didn't see anyone at
the first base, and there were just a handful of soldiers in suits
and breathing masks at the second. There were plenty of bodies
around though. I guessed that some of the military had known
what had happened, but it didn't look like many of them had
managed to get to shelter in time.

You'd have thought we'd have picked up a load of survivors
while we were out there because of the noise we made, but we
hardly found anyone. I don't know whether that was because we
just didn't see people or because they were too afraid to let us
know where they were when they heard us. It might have been
because they just weren't there. Whatever the reason, we'd
flown around a third base a couple of times without finding
anything so we moved on. We were following the motorway

south towards Tyneham when Carver spots a car moving in the distance. We follow it, and when the driver sees us he pulls over and stops in the middle of a service station car park. We land the helicopter a short distance away.

We get out of the helicopter and the driver of the car starts calling us over. He's a real awkward, gangly looking lad in his late teens. His name's Martin Smith and he's really nervous and anxious and emotional. We're the first people he's seen since it happened. He keeps bursting into tears. There are bodies all around us but he's not even looking at them and it's like he's got something more important to think about. Carver keeps the bodies at bay while I try and calm him down.

'She knows what happened,' he says as I walk up to him. 'She might be able to help. She might be able to do something.'

I'm thinking that the kid's lost his mind, and that's perfectly understandable given the circumstances because we've all come close to losing it since it happened, haven't we? He's pointing into his car. I look inside and lying across the back seat is a woman in a protective suit with a facemask and everything. It's not a military suit like the soldiers we'd seen were wearing, it's different. It looks cleaner, less practical and more scientific than what we'd seen of the army's. I open the car door and lean inside. The woman doesn't move. When I touch her shoulder she opens her eyes for a second and then lets them flicker shut again and I can see that she's in a bad way. Her face is thin and white and it's obvious that she hasn't eaten or had anything to drink since it all began. She smells as bad as the bodies and the back of her suit is soiled and dirty. I try to talk to her but I don't get any response. I can't even get her to open her eyes again and look at me. Carver shouts over to me because now there are more bodies around than he feels comfortable with and so, being as careful as I can, I pick her up and take her into the service station. Carver and Smith follow me inside. We take our chances and leave the helicopter, knowing that we'll fight our way back out to it if we have to.

I lay the woman down on a plastic bench in a burger bar. The place stinks of rotting food and rotting bodies. Carver has a quick look round for supplies but there's nothing worth taking. I sit down with Smith next to the woman, making sure we're out of sight of the windows.

I ask Smith who she is. He tells me her name is Sylvia Plant. I ask him how he came to be with her and he starts to calm down a little and tells me his story. He tells me that she was a friend of his parents and that she worked in the monitoring centre at Camber which is about thirty miles away from where we were sitting. He says she used to work with his dad a few years back, but that he hadn't seen her for a long time since his dad retired. I know the place he's talking about. It's one of those big, faceless buildings where lots of people used to work but no-one would ever talk about what they did. I start thinking he's going to tell me this woman is responsible for everything that's happened but he doesn't. He tells me that she found him about three or four days earlier. She'd been driving around since it started looking for survivors. He tells me that she was sick then because she hadn't eaten and that she'd been getting progressively worse ever since. I start to press him and I start getting hard with him because I want to know what's going on.

Smith says he asked the woman if she knew what had happened and she told him that she did. She told him that she'd been cleaning a lab when it happened, and that was why she was wearing the suit. Everyone else around her had been caught and killed. She'd said she'd walked around the building for hours looking for help. She hadn't found anyone, but she'd been able to piece together what had happened from things she'd seen. She'd used security passes belonging to dead colleagues to get into the parts of the building where she'd never been able to go before. She said that this was caused by something she'd first heard rumours about years ago. There had been stories doing the rounds for almost as long as she'd worked at Camber.

Remember the Star Wars project? Back in the eighties before the end of the cold war there was a lot of noise made about a plan to build a shield to protect countries from nuclear attack. I don't know if it ever got off the ground. According to this woman, when terrorists really started to hit their targets with force, the same countries started working on ways to protect themselves from the threat of attack by other non-conventional means. She said that they wanted to create an artificial germ which would latch onto chemicals or poisons in the air and neutralise them, that was the plan. She found out that development had been going on for some time. She also found out that a version of this 'super-germ' had been created and that it was thought to be stable. It was intelligent and self-replicating and, because of increased terrorist threats, it had already been released. Apparently that happened a couple of years ago now. Smith says the woman told him we've all been breathing the germ in every day since then.

Anyway, the woman told Smith that finally there was a chemical attack. That rang true - I remember hearing something on the news just before this all started. There was a gas attack on an airport terminal in Canada. Smith says that the woman saw reports of huge numbers of deaths in the surrounding areas, way out of line for the amount of poison that was supposed to have been released. Seems that the germ tried to do its job and neutralise the attack, but it mutated as it did it. It became toxic. Whatever happened, it set off a chain reaction that quickly spread. It was the mutated germ that did all of this. It changed to try and protect us and became something that killed just about everyone. Bloody ironic, isn't it?

Smith tells me that the woman pieced all this together from various bits of information she found. She saw records showing that communications had been lost with most of Canada, and then with the countries surrounding it. The information stopped coming altogether pretty soon after that.

You can call it bullshit if you like, but it's the only explanation I've heard so far. We can all probably come up with a hundred other reasons why all of this might have happened, but this is the only version I've heard that has any evidence to support it. Smith wasn't lying to me, he had no reason to, and the woman had no reason to lie to him either. And if she really was from the monitoring centre at Camber, then she would potentially have had access to all kinds of confidential information. I believe what I heard. Everything happened so quickly because the germ was already there. As the mutation spread, everyone died around us. There's no way we'll ever know why the corpses got up and started to move. It was designed to prevent death, and maybe it did its job after all. Maybe it destroyed the bodies but spared the brain. Whatever actually happened, it doesn't matter now.

We sat there with Smith and the woman for another few hours until it was dark. We pushed our way through the bodies back to the helicopter and flew back to base. The woman was dead by late the following afternoon. Smith is still with us.

'Rubbish,' Phil Croft snapped anxiously, disturbing a heavy silence which had descended upon the already quiet room. 'Utter rubbish.'

'Might be,' Lawrence yawned. 'Might not be. Doesn't really matter, does it?'

'And is that it?' Donna said angrily. 'Is that all you've got to tell us?'

'What else do you want me to say?'

'I don't know…'

'I've told you everything I know. What you do with it is up to you.'

The tired pilot stood up, stretched, and walked back towards the helicopter to fetch himself some food.

12

'Do you believe him?' Emma asked, looking straight into Michael's eyes.

'I believe he's telling us the truth about what happened with Smith,' he answered, 'but whether I believe the rest of his story or not is a different matter.'

'There's no reason for anyone to make it up.'

'True.'

'I remember hearing about something happening in Canada. I think it was probably the last thing I remember seeing on the television.'

'Me too, but that doesn't mean...'

'And I'm sure I've heard about that place at Camber too, and there had to be a good reason for the woman to be in a protective suit...'

'All true.'

'Bit of a coincidence that they managed to find Smith though, and that Smith found the woman or the woman found him'.

'Suppose so, but it's as much a coincidence that we were all sat in here together tonight, isn't it? It's only because of coincidence that Lawrence found us and even that you and I came across each other.'

Emma yawned and stretched her arms up into the cold early morning air.

'Ironic, isn't it?' she said quietly. 'If it is all true, I mean. Something originally put there to try and protect us ends up doing all the damage...'

'Sounds about right for this fucked up planet.'

'Anyway, it doesn't make any difference now, does it?'

'What?'

'Knowing what happened. Doesn't make me feel any different.'

Michael shrugged his shoulders.

'Lawrence's story makes sense,' he answered, 'but you're right, it doesn't matter now. We can't prove it or disprove it and even if we could it wouldn't help anyone. What's happened has happened, and that's all there is to it. There's nothing you, me or anyone else can do about it now.'

'True.'

'Reminds me of something my dad used to say,' Michael mused, allowing himself to reminisce for the briefest of moments. 'When things weren't going his way at work he'd get really wound up and sometimes we'd go for a pint together and try to put the world to rights. For a while Dad worked for a steel manufacturing company until they went bust. Every day he'd come home and tell us that they'd lost orders to other local firms or to companies overseas. Mum used to get worked up about the work going overseas but Dad said it didn't matter. He said it didn't matter where the work was going to, the fact remained that his firm had lost it. He used to say to her that if you got knocked down by a car, did it matter what colour it was? That's how I feel today. Like I said, what's happened has happened, and finding out why or what did it just isn't important. We are where we are.'

He stopped talking, turned away from Emma and quickly and discreetly wiped an unexpected tear from the corner of his eye before it had chance to trickle down his cheek. He hadn't thought about his mum and dad for days now, maybe even weeks. Like the rest of the people with him, Michael had subconsciously built a wall around the past to keep his memories separated from the present and out of sight. It hurt too much to even think about trying to deal with them.

Emma looked out of the front of the warehouse, shielding her eyes from the brilliant orange sunrise which was beginning to fill the building with bright, warm light. The long, tripping shadows of random stumbling corpses stretched across the cold, grey car park towards them.

'How you feeling?' she asked, sensing his sudden emotion and rubbing the side of his arm tenderly with her hand. He shrugged his shoulders.

'I'm okay,' he replied, subdued. 'You all right?'

Emma nodded.

'Actually, I feel quite good,' she said quietly.

'Good?'

'Well, better than I have been feeling. I don't want to get carried away here but…'

'But what?'

'But I can't help thinking that we might have found a way out of all of this. This time yesterday we were buried underground just sitting and waiting. Today we're…'

'This time yesterday we were relatively safe,' he interrupted. 'Today we're exposed and vulnerable and we've got nothing.'

'Christ, you can be such a negative, miserable bastard at times,' she complained, pushing herself away from him slightly. 'Be positive.'

'I am positive,' Michael argued, 'but I'm also realistic. Until I've seen this island and I've stood on the beach and shouted at the top of my voice and no bodies have come, I'm going to stay sceptical. We just need to be careful here and not rush into anything that's going to cost us.'

'So what are you saying? Should we just wave goodbye and let these people fly off into the sunset?'

'No, that's not what I'm saying at all, but you know what I think about chaos theory and all that stuff. If something can go wrong…'

'It will go wrong,' she sighed, completing his predictable sentence for him. 'But that doesn't mean we have to sit around and wait for it to happen for God's sake. It doesn't mean things can't work out right for us, does it?'

Michael stopped for a moment and considered her words. Perhaps she was right, maybe he was being too negative? Truth was he was too scared and he'd lost too much to risk being positive.

'Sorry,' he mumbled. 'You're right, I'll shut up.'

'I don't want you to shut up,' she said, moving closer again. 'I just want you to give this a chance. Have an open mind. Come on, Mike, think about what we could get out of this if things work out. If this island is everything they say it is, then before long you and I could have a house together. We could have our own bedroom with a proper bed. We could have a kitchen, a garden, a living room… We could have space…'

'We thought we'd got all of that at Penn Farm.'

'I know, but this is different. If it hadn't been for the bodies then we'd probably still be at Penn Farm, maybe even somewhere better. Bloody hell, if it hadn't been for the bodies then we could be anywhere we damn well please. And now we're talking about going somewhere where there aren't any bodies.'

'No we're not,' Michael sighed, slipping back into his negative mindset again, 'not yet. At the moment we're talking about going to an island and clearing a couple of hundred bodies from it. There's a big difference.'

Emma shook her head. For a split second she considered answering him but she didn't bother. She knew it wasn't worth it when he was in this kind of mood. She turned and walked away, tired of arguing pointlessly. Michael watched her go. He didn't want to upset her or alienate her. More than anything he wanted to protect her and shield her from everything that was happening around them. He couldn't stand to see her running away with half an idea that might eventually end up costing them everything.

For a while he sat alone and watched the bodies outside.

13

The time had come for them to make their move.

It had been almost unanimously agreed that trying to get to the airfield and join the other survivors there was the only sensible option available to the group. Logical alternatives were nonexistent. There was nowhere else to go.

In the days and weeks since they'd arrived at the underground base, the structure and composition of the group had changed little. Until yesterday when they had been forced to leave the shelter their situation had, on the whole, remained fairly constant. During their time below ground in isolation most people had been content to sit back, to blend into the background and watch everything happen around them without actively contributing. Other more confident people - Cooper, Michael, Baxter and Donna for example - had, by default, begun to take control and organise. In the cold and uncertain light of day this morning, however, there had been a sudden and subtle shift. The introduction to the equation both of the soldiers (who had until yesterday maintained an enforced and cautious distance from the group) and the two survivors who had arrived in the helicopter seemed to have somehow altered the structure and behaviour of the fragile collection of frightened people. Perhaps they had also been affected by hearing Lawrence's possible explanation of what had happened to the rest of the world although, realising its ultimate insignificance, few people had actually spent much time thinking about it. Whatever the reason, the group's situation had changed dramatically, and individuals who had previously seemed content to hide in the shadows now pushed themselves to the fore, desperate not to get overlooked and left behind.

'I'll do it,' Peter Guest said anxiously, stepping around Jack Baxter and grabbing a map from Richard Lawrence's hands. 'Show me where we are.'

Lawrence took the map back and folded it down to a more manageable size. He pointed to the general area where they were presently hiding. He had spent the last half hour writing down basic directions to Monkton airfield for the survivors to follow and had just asked for a volunteer to navigate. Showing more enthusiasm than he had done at any time during the previous month, Guest anxiously began to read through the directions and cross-referenced them to the map, plotting the route to Bigginford and the airfield beyond.

'You travel with Cooper in the personnel carrier then,' Michael suggested. 'Armitage can follow behind in the truck and I'll follow him.'

'Not in your motorhome you won't,' Steve Armitage said from across the room. He'd been outside to check over the three vehicles and had just returned, breathless and cold. He wiped his greasy hands on a dirty rag which he threw into a dark corner. 'It's knackered. Axle's broken. I'm not surprised after the journey we had last night.'

'Shit,' Michael cursed.

'What are we going to do now then?' Emma asked, feeling strangely saddened by the loss of their vehicle. Although she had often detested being inside it, she had spent a lot of time there with Michael. It was where they had been able to be alone and intimate. She had come to think of it as their own private space. A small, uncomfortable and increasingly cramped and squalid private space, granted, but it had been their own.

'We'll have to go out and find something else,' said Donna who, until then, had been sitting nearby and listening silently. 'We're going to need another vehicle. There's bound to be something round here that we can use.'

'There still aren't too many bodies around out there,' Armitage added. 'I reckon we'll be all right to go and look around providing we're sensible and we're not outside too long. Maybe a few of us should go out and work our way through the car parks?'

'Can't we try and manage with just two trucks?' Emma wondered. Michael shook his head.

'Don't think so,' he answered. 'We might have been able to fit everyone in at a push, but I think we need to try and take as much stuff from here as we can get our hands on. Seems stupid to leave it all behind now we're here, doesn't it? We don't know when we might need it.'

'He's right,' Cooper agreed. No-one argued.

'You're going to have to get yourselves two vehicles,' Stonehouse announced. Stood at the back of the small group of people, the soldier stood up. An imposing figure in his heavy protective gear, flanked by one of his men and with his rifle held at his side, his sudden movement silenced the survivors.

'Why's that?' Cooper asked, genuinely confused.

'Because we're going back to the base,' he replied. 'It's our only option.'

'Don't be fucking stupid,' snapped Croft. 'The place was overrun. You can't go back there.'

'We can and we will. We can't stay out here.'

'But we need your…'

'We need to get back underground. We're completely fucked if we stay up here.'

'Doesn't look like you've got much choice,' Michael hissed. 'You're dead whatever you do. Might as well come with us and…'

'And what? Sit and watch you lot run? Sit in these bloody suits and wait to die? Sit and…'

'At least you'd be giving us a chance,' Croft yelled, his face suddenly red with emotion. 'Do things your way and everyone loses.'

'Tough.'

'Bastard,' he spat and he lurched towards the soldier, limping and wincing as he landed heavily on his feet, aggravating his still painful injuries. Stonehouse lifted a single gloved hand and pushed the doctor to one side. Already off-balance, he fell awkwardly to the ground at the soldier's booted feet. Stonehouse lifted the butt of his rifle and held it poised inches above Croft's upturned face.

'Leave it, Phil,' Cooper said. He turned to face Stonehouse. 'Just go.'

'What the fucking hell are you doing?' Croft demanded as he crawled away from Stonehouse. 'Have you gone completely fucking mad?'

Cooper looked down at him.

'No,' he replied.

Stonehouse stood and watched, unnerved by the unexpected response he had received from his ex-colleague. He had anticipated some kind of resistance from him at least.

'Christ,' the incensed doctor continued as he picked himself up and brushed himself down, 'there are only four of them. We need that vehicle, Cooper. We'll end up driving to Bigginford in a convoy of twenty bloody cars if we're not careful.'

'No we won't,' Cooper said calmly. All eyes were on him. He began to walk towards the exit and away from the confrontation when he suddenly stopped, turned round and ran back in the opposite direction, diving through the air and smashing into Stonehouse and the soldier standing next to him. In the sudden confusion the two soldiers were knocked flying and sent tumbling to the ground. Stonehouse was on all fours. Cooper grabbed hold of his facemask underneath his chin and yanked it off his face. The second soldier, immediately aware of what was happening, began to scramble away. Cooper jumped onto his back and pulled and tugged at his suit, his mask and his breathing apparatus until it came free and he could see the soldier's exposed body underneath. Aware of the other two soldiers running away and fleeing deeper into the vast store, he stood back and readied himself should the troopers on the ground attack.

Stonehouse was the first to drag himself back up onto his feet. He ran angrily towards Cooper, grabbing his rifle off the floor as he moved. By the time he'd managed to stand completely upright the infection had caught him. Choking, and with a look of pained surprise on his frozen face, he fell back on top of the other soldier who was already suffocating. Fighting for breath, he shook and convulsed, still grasping his rifle tightly.

Eyes bulging, he stared at the faces of Cooper and the others who stared back at him as he asphyxiated and died.

'You killed them,' gasped Donna in revulsion. The survivors stood and stared in disbelief. 'You killed them you bastard.'

'They were dead already,' Cooper responded with disdain.

14

Michael, Baxter and Cooper ran together through the silent car parks scattered around the industrial estate, desperately searching for another suitable vehicle to get them to the airfield. The number of bodies around was still lower than they'd expected and it stood to reason that the bulk of the population who had died in this area had, over the days and weeks, been dragged away in the direction of the military base. All three men were acutely aware of the fact that the danger was reduced but far from gone, and that more random bodies might appear at any moment.

'Van,' Michael said as he pushed his way past another lurching corpse. 'Over there.'

He pointed to the far right corner of the large rectangular car park they had just entered. On its own next to a red-brick office building was a red mail van. On the tarmac in front of it lay the gnarled body of a postal delivery worker. The woman's motionless corpse was twisted and withered like a piece of washed-up driftwood. The strap of an empty mail bag was wrapped around her neck, its contents having long since been scattered and blown away by the wind.

Cooper ran round and yanked open the driver's door. Michael frantically grabbed the keys from the corpse's wizened hand and threw them over to him before turning back and kicking out at two bodies which had stumbled uncomfortably close. He had Stonehouse's rifle slung across his back. With nervous uncertainty he swung it round and primed it as Cooper had earlier shown him how. He'd taught him how to shoot while they'd been underground but, until now, he'd never actually needed to fire a weapon. Bullets were okay when they were faced with just a handful of corpses, but Michael and the others usually had to deal with many, many more than this. Holding his breath he brutally shoved the barrel of the rifle into the dark hole in the middle of one body's face where its nose had once been and pulled the trigger. A deafening crack rang around the car park, echoing off the walls of every building in the immediate vicinity. Michael was knocked back by the unexpected force of the weapon. He tripped and fell as a shower of crimson gore and splintered bone erupted from the back of the creature's head.

'Push it!' Cooper shouted from the front of the van. He couldn't get it started. The engine wouldn't turn over. Michael picked himself up and shot the second body in the side of the head before swinging the rifle around onto his back again and running round to the rear of the vehicle where Baxter was already pushing. He shoulder charged the van, the impact helping it to roll forward slightly. Cooper jumped out of his seat and began to push and shove against the driver's door and steering wheel.

'Christ, Cooper, have you still got the bloody handbrake on?' Baxter half-joked, red-faced and wheezing as he strained against the back of the van. 'Come on!' He threw his full weight forward again and, with his head to one side, stared anxiously at more gangling, decomposing bodies which were creeping dangerously close.

With all three of the men pushing the van finally began to achieve some momentum. It started to roll across the width of the car park with relative ease and Cooper hurled himself back inside. He slammed his foot down on the clutch and tried again to start the engine. After a few painfully long seconds of ugly mechanical groaning and straining, the machine finally spluttered into life. He accelerated away, clearing the engine and leaving Michael and Baxter to run after him through belching clouds of dirty fumes which spilled from the van's exhaust after weeks without use. He quickly turned the vehicle around and returned to collect the others, taking only the briefest of diversions to plough down two meandering cadavers which pointlessly stumbled after them.

Breathlessly, and without saying another word, the men motored back to the warehouse.

***

Inside the building Emma had managed to find the two remaining soldiers who had disappeared in fear of their lives. They were hiding together in a large storeroom.

'Just leave us alone,' one of the soldiers spat as they heard Emma approaching. His voice was high-pitched and strained, full of desperation and fear. 'That bloke's a fucking psychopath. He's always been the same. He'll fucking kill us.'

The frightened trooper cowered away in the shadows. Metres away from him Kelly Harcourt pressed herself back against a storage rack hoping she would melt into the shadows, her heart thumping in her chest.

'He's no psychopath,' Emma said as she took a few cautious steps further into the room, trying to pinpoint the exact location of the two frightened figures. 'He's a survivor, that's all.' She peered into the room, sure that she had just seen a flicker of movement. 'You'd probably have done the same if you were in his position.'

She didn't find it easy defending Cooper's virtually indefensible actions, no matter how relieved she was that he had acted so quickly. She'd also forgotten that, many weeks ago now, these two troopers had served alongside him. Perhaps there was much about his character they knew that she didn't.

'He'll do it again,' the male soldier whimpered. 'All he's got to do is open our suits and we've fucking had it. That's all that any of you have to do.'

'But no-one's going to do that to you, are they?' Emma sighed. 'Why the hell would we?'

'You'll do it if you have to,' Harcourt shouted, the sudden volume and direction of her voice giving her location away. 'You'd kill us just as quickly as you get rid of those bloody things outside.'

'Personally I couldn't, but maybe you're right, maybe some people could. The point is we shouldn't have to. The only reason that Cooper did what he did was to safeguard the group. He's just looking out for himself and for the rest of us, that's all. As long as you don't do anything to put us at risk, you'll be okay and...'

She stopped talking. Just ahead and to her right Kelly Harcourt slumped against the racking and slid down to the ground. Emma could see one of her feet sticking out into an aisle. She slowly walked towards her and crouched down at the side of the terrified soldier. Her facemask was clouded and blurred with condensation. She lifted her head and looked up at Emma.

'I don't know what to do,' Harcourt admitted, struggling to keep her composure. The anger and fear in her voice had suddenly given way to desperation and pain. 'I can't handle this.'

'It's all right,' Emma soothed, putting a gentle hand on her shoulder. 'We're all struggling to handle this, we just drag ourselves along from day to day.' She paused, not sure if Harcourt was listening or whether it was even worth continuing. 'Listen, I don't believe in bullshit so I'll be straight with you, you two have got the worst deal of all here. You're stuck between a rock and a hard place. You're trapped in those bloody suits and it must be hell, but you don't have much of a choice, do you? You can try and get back to your base, you can stay here or you can come with us. Like I said, as long as you don't put anyone at risk then…'

'Then what?' she demanded. 'Then your friend won't kill us.'

Emma sighed with frustration. She stood up and began to walk back towards the door, keen to get back to the others.

'Look, we're too busy trying to keep ourselves alive here. No-one's interested in killing you.'

Without waiting for a response she turned and walked away.

15

Strangely calm and uncharacteristically oblivious to the potential threat of the growing crowd of restless bodies on the other side of the chain-link fence, the survivors readied themselves to leave. Their brief and unexpected respite at the warehouse had given them precious time to regroup and reorganise themselves and the arrival of Lawrence and Chase in the early hours had given some direction to their frantic and previously directionless escape from the bunker. Now without the motorhome many of the group had been crammed into the back of the personnel carrier, which had proved to be slightly less cramped and more comfortable than the back of the prison truck. Cooper took the wheel of the military vehicle with Peter Guest at his side while Steve Armitage took up his now familiar seat at the controls of the second truck. Armitage had begun to fiercely guard his position. Apart from the fact that very few other people could have driven the truck, the responsibility, power and control which he attached to the role made him feel worthwhile and alive. Strange, he thought, that what had previously always felt like such an ordinary and menial task should now give him such purpose.

Fewer survivors travelled in the back of the prison truck than on earlier journeys. The spare space was taken up by the supplies and equipment which the group had stripped from the warehouse. Just a handful of people travelled in the final vehicle in the convoy - the bright red and uncomfortably conspicuous post van. Donna sat in the driver's seat with Jack Baxter on the passenger side and Clare sat between them. Behind them were the two remaining soldiers, surrounded by yet more supplies. Donna watched them in her mirror. Harcourt seemed genuinely afraid and didn't appear to be a threat. Her male colleague, however, was far more unpredictable and less trustworthy. His name (she had recently discovered) was Kilgore. A short, wiry-framed and nervous man, he was too jittery and agitated for her liking.

Fifteen minutes earlier Lawrence and Chase had left in the helicopter, taking with them two of the younger survivors. The remaining group of people had crowded round and watched in awe as the powerful machine had lifted up into the clear blue early morning sky. Having spent weeks underground and cowering away in the silent shadows, to witness the aircraft rise with such majesty, strength and sheer bloody noise and arrogance had been a humbling and strangely emotional experience. As the helicopter disappeared into the distance the sounds made by the rabid bodies smashing themselves furiously against the metal fence had suddenly seemed louder than ever. The closeness and anger of corpses reminded the survivors of the relentless danger which faced each one of them.

Before leaving Cooper and Guest had gathered the other drivers around them to talk about the proposed route in detail one last time. It was crucial that they all knew the route and the potential problems they might face along the way. Using road atlases he had found in the warehouse, Guest had highlighted the directions they needed to take and had quickly handwritten a set of rough notes to be carried in each vehicle. He was desperately keen to share with the others the information which Richard Lawrence had earlier shared with him.

'You see,' he explained, talking with unprecedented energy and interest, 'they've obviously not had to spend much time on the ground and so this was the most direct route they were able to come up with. Now I've not personally spent a lot of time in this part of the country so I'm not completely sure where we're...'

'Do me a favour,' Armitage sighed, 'just shut up and let me have my bloody map, will you?'

Undeterred, Guest continued.

'Lawrence told me that they've not seen any particularly large gatherings of bodies between here and Bigginford.'

'What's large supposed to mean?' asked Cooper. 'Twenty-five of them? Two thousand? Half a million?'

'Don't know,' he quickly admitted, keen to continue with his explanation. 'Anyway it looks like we'll be able to stick to the motorways for a good part of the journey. They're probably not going to be clear, but from what they've seen from the air they think we should be able to work our way through.'

'What about cities?' Jack Baxter anxiously wondered. 'We're going to stay away from the cities as best we can, aren't we?'

'We'd like to,' Cooper answered quickly, deliberately denying Guest the opportunity to respond, 'but we've got to try and balance out safety and risk. To get to Bigginford we're going to have to get pretty close to the centre of Rowley.'

'What does pretty close mean?' Armitage demanded.

'Like I said, it's going to be about balancing safety with risk. If we bypass Rowley then you're right, we'll probably avoid a whole load of potential trouble spots. The problem is, we'll also end up adding a hell of a lot of distance and time onto the length of the journey. Obviously we'll be in a better position to make a final decision when we're nearer to getting there, but personally my opinion is that we'll be better off following this route. I'd rather take a chance and take the quicker option than risk running out of fuel because we've driven further than we needed to. We could end up stuck out in the middle of nowhere.'

'I don't like it,' Baxter complained.

'No-one likes any of this,' Cooper sighed, 'so let's just see how the land lies when we get there, okay? Chances are no-one's been anywhere near Rowley for weeks. Most of the bodies will probably have drifted away. We've probably got as much chance finding them in the middle of a field than finding them waiting in the cities.'

'Suppose.'

Guest seized on a momentary lull in the conversation to start talking again.

'Cooper's right, Rowley might be a problem, but once we're through it should pretty much be plain sailing until we get to the airfield.'

'Plain sailing?' Armitage grunted. 'Bloody hell, nothing's been plain sailing for months now.'

'Did Lawrence tell you much about the airfield?' Baxter asked.

'He said it was a private airfield,' Cooper replied. 'He said it was pretty small with one runway and a few buildings. There's supposed to be a fence running all the way around to keep trespassers and plane-spotters out.'

'Does it keep bodies out though?' he mumbled.

'At the moment,' Cooper answered.

'What do you mean by that?'

'Chances are they've got the same kind of problems we had at the base and back in the city.'

'Such as?'

'By now I expect they've been surrounded by hundreds of bodies. Probably thousands of them.'

Sitting anxiously and waiting to leave, the sudden strength and resilience which the survivors had somehow managed to build up during the last few hours had now all but disappeared.

Their sudden flight from the military base yesterday had been a terrifying and directionless descent into the night. Since stopping at the warehouse, however, and now that they had made contact with Lawrence and Chase, their situation seemed to have steadily improved. With many bodies appearing to have been drawn towards the underground bunker over recent days and weeks leaving the surrounding area relatively clear, and with the airborne survivors unexpectedly presenting the group with a possible escape route from their nightmare, their fortunes seemed to have changed for the better. Crammed into their vehicles again, though, and faced with the prospect of lurching headlong into the unknown once more, every last person – ex-military and civilian alike – felt sick to the stomach with nerves.

Cooper, Donna and Armitage started their engines and slowly moved towards the exit. Once all three drivers had given a signal to each other confirming they were ready to leave, Michael undid the latch and let the tall gate swing silently open. No longer restrained, noxious cadavers immediately began to lurch and spill towards him, crisscrossing in front of him on unsteady feet. He sprinted the short distance to the back of the personnel carrier, pushing several of them aside, climbed into the vehicle and slammed the door shut. Cooper began to move slowly forward, leading the convoy back out into the dead world.

16

A welcome combination of good fortune and sensible planning allowed the three vehicles to reach the first section of motorway less than half an hour after leaving the desolate industrial estate. It was almost half-past ten when they joined the main road, and the earlier bright morning sun had long since been swallowed up and hidden by impenetrable dark cloud. A light mist had descended, bringing with it dull gloom and a fine, persistent rain.

Peter Guest, acting as Cooper's navigator, had again become withdrawn and quiet, reverting to his more familiar demeanour and losing the sudden confidence, energy and interest he had somehow managed to previously find. No-one was surprised. Cooper had anticipated having problems with him, as had Michael.

'Junction twenty-three,' Cooper said under his breath. Guest anxiously checked his map again, frantically trying to confirm that they were still on the right road. The fact that they hadn't changed direction since he'd last checked didn't seem to matter. The further they had moved away from the warehouse, the more nervous and unsure he had become.

'All right, Cooper?' Michael asked, pushing his way closer to the driver.

'I'm okay,' he replied, concentrating on the road ahead. Michael struggled to peer out through the front of the personnel carrier. His view was restricted and he craned his neck to clearly see the cluttered tarmac strip which stretched out in front of them. In the gloom it wasn't easy to see the direction the road took. The mist obscured much of the landscape around them and the ground ahead seemed to be carpeted with a tangled layer of dead bodies and rusting machinery. The vehicle Cooper controlled was sufficiently powerful to be able to push a path through the debris and decay, allowing the others to follow in its wake. Rowley, the second largest town for a hundred square miles, was now just over ten miles away.

'Grim, isn't it?' Michael grumbled unhelpfully from just behind Cooper's shoulder.

'This place was grim at the best of times,' he replied under his breath.

Allowing for heavy traffic and other delays, on a clear day a few months ago the journey they had just completed from the warehouse to Rowley would probably have taken the best part of two hours. Today, however, it had taken the survivors almost six hours to reach the outskirts of the town. Although they had been relatively fortunate and had not come across many serious obstacles along the way, progress through the ruined land had been painfully slow at times. Cooper was beginning to get tired – his head ached with the effort of having to concentrate so hard for so long. He desperately wanted to stop for a while to rest and close his eyes and stretch his legs but he knew that it was impossible. The personnel carrier's headlamps, although not helping much in the poor conditions, seemed to constantly illuminate random, fleeting movement on all sides. Whereas the noise and activity at the military base had seemed to act as a magnet for the thousands of bodies wandering aimlessly across the land and had kept them away from the industrial estate and the warehouse, there obviously had been few such distractions in this part of the country. Lumbering, shadowy shapes seemed to continually emerge from the mist and then disappear into the darkness again as the personnel carrier, prison truck and van motored past them. It was too dangerous to even consider stopping here.

'Which way, Peter?' Cooper asked, annoyed that he had to keep pressing the other man for directions. They were rapidly approaching a fork in the road which had, until just a few seconds earlier, been cloaked and hidden by the mist.

'Don't know,' the other man stammered. His thoughts had been elsewhere and Cooper had taken him by surprise. In sudden blustering, pointless panic his eyes darted around the map on his lap which he'd been following by torchlight. He searched desperately for the answer to Cooper's question.

'Come on, you should know this,' the ex-soldier snapped angrily at him, allowing his exhaustion and unease to show. 'For Christ's sake, you're the one with the fucking directions in front of you!'

'Think I've got it,' he said, looking up and squinting into the darkness to try and read a dull, moss-covered road sign. 'Take the 302.'

Guest's delay and indecision resulted in Cooper having to yank the personnel carrier over to the left to force the heavy vehicle to quickly change direction before they passed the junction.

'You sure about this?' he asked as he drove down a dark roadway which curved round and down to the right and then snaked back under an elevated section of the carriageway which they had just been following.

'This is right,' Guest said quietly, trying his best to appease Cooper. 'I'm sure it is. We need to follow this road for another couple of miles, cross the river and then find the road to Huntridge and we should have bypassed the city centre.'

Cooper swerved the personnel carrier around a rusting double-decker bus which had toppled over onto its side and which now straddled virtually the full width of the road. The prison truck followed close behind followed, in turn, by Donna driving the post van.

'Jesus Christ,' she cursed as she forced the van's two off-side wheels up a grass verge to squeeze past another wreck. Although much smaller than the other vehicles, she didn't have the power to smash the remains of cars, bikes, trucks and other obstacles out of the way as Cooper and Armitage did. Rather than clear a way through for her, as the other two drivers battered their way forward through the wreckage the debris they created was frequently dragged back out into the middle of the road behind them and left directly in her path.

Like Guest in the front of the first vehicle, Jack Baxter was also studying the maps.

'Not far now,' he mumbled, preferring to keep his head down rather than look up at what was happening around him, despite the fact that looking down made him feel nauseous and travel-sick. As if the long and precarious drive wasn't difficult enough, whenever he looked outside he could see the grey shifting silhouettes of bodies dragging themselves pointlessly towards the convoy. The speed of their vehicles, although not as fast as they perhaps would have liked, kept them safe enough. Jack knew that they would be okay as long as they kept moving, but the fact that they were so close to the bodies again unnerved and frightened him.

The road the survivors were now following was a ring road which would eventually skirt around the main part of the city centre. A wide and recently built expressway, its surface was covered with the scattered remains of the city and surrounding district's population. As their proximity to the lifeless heart of Rowley increased, so too did the amount of twisted metal and rotting flesh which lay around them and which threatened to block their way forward. Many, many people had fallen and died here on the city's outskirts when the rush hour crawl had been savagely cut down by disease almost eight weeks ago. No-one travelling through the decay today was surprised. It was nothing they hadn't expected to see.

Donna was used to the grey gloom outside being interrupted by the bright rear brake lights belonging to the two vehicles she followed as they twisted and turned to weave their way through the mayhem. In fact, she had spent much of the time intentionally trailing the lights rather than trying to follow the road which was frequently difficult to make out amongst the constant carnage. Her heart began to thump in her chest with nervous anticipation when, without warning, both the personnel carrier and the prison truck suddenly stopped moving. Clare, still sitting in the seat next to her, had somehow managed to fall asleep for a few precious seconds, her exhaustion and the constant movement of the van combining to finally overcome the effects of her fear and unease. She quickly lifted her head again in panic when the van lurched to an unexpected halt.

'What's the matter?' she demanded anxiously, looking frantically from side to side. 'What's happened?'

'Don't know,' Donna answered quietly. She glanced into the wing mirror as a random corpse tripped out of the darkness and collided heavily with the side of the van, the clattering impact ringing out loudly and shattering the general quiet of the dying day. The two soldiers sitting in the back jumped up as the creature began to hammer on the metal side of the vehicle. Seconds later and there were four more of them doing the same. Donna looked up again and saw that there were already several more crowding and jostling around the back of the prison truck just ahead.

'Why have we stopped?' Kilgore demanded anxiously from the darkness behind her. Much as he really didn't want to look, he wished that the light would improve so that he could see what was happening around them. He turned and peered cautiously out through the window in the back door of the van. More corpses were emerging from the heavy mist all around them.

'What the hell is he doing?' Baxter asked under his breath as they watched Michael jump out of the back of the personnel carrier and run around to the front of the vehicle. He disappeared from view and Donna instinctively pulled the van further forward so that they could get a better view of what was happening. She stopped when they were level alongside the prison truck.

'Christ,' she mumbled in disappointment and disbelief, 'what are we supposed to do now?'

A short distance ahead of them was a narrow bridge. At either end of the bridge were traffic lights which had once regulated the flow of vehicles from one side to the other but which were now as dark, lifeless and devoid of colour as the rest of the blanched world around them. The traffic lights had been necessary because the road which spanned the length of the bridge was just a single lane in width. Just over halfway along it a medium-sized truck had crashed and had somehow spun round through almost ninety degrees, leaving it wedged awkwardly between the decorative concrete walls which lined either side of the crossing. Twenty feet or so below the bridge was a wide river, its once relatively clear water now turned a stagnant dirty green-brown by the seeping pollution it carried with it away from the nearby city.

'So what do we do now?' demanded Clare. Jack looked down at the map on his lap again.

'There are two more bridges,' he answered. 'One's about three miles further north, the other four or five miles back the way we came.'

'Shit,' Donna cursed angrily.

Hidden from view of the many nearby bodies by virtue of the mist, the narrowness of the bridge and the various vehicles around it, Michael ran back to the personnel carrier after having surveyed the obstruction ahead of them. Managing by chance to somehow find a way through, a single corpse hurled itself at him from out of nowhere, seeming to explode furiously out of the shadows without warning. Caught by surprise, he took the full force of the impact head on and could do nothing more than stand still for a moment, pushed back against the side of the transport and with the inescapable smell of dead, rotting flesh suddenly filling his lungs and causing him to gag. Instinctively he lifted his arms to protect himself and recoiled in disgust as he grabbed hold of the decaying cadaver. Most of its ragged clothing having long since been ripped and torn away, his fingers sliced easily through the greasy flesh which covered its foul-smelling torso. Closing up the fingers on his right hand, and wincing as dead skin flapped and the remains of putrefied organs dripped and dribbled down his arms, he held onto the creature's suddenly exposed ribcage before pushing back against it, running forward and throwing it over the side of the bridge. Out of sight, the body fell for several long seconds before landing in the water below and being carried away by the strong current. Wiping his hands on a patch of wet grass at his feet and then drying them on the back of his trousers, Michael quickly scrambled back into the personnel carrier.

'You okay?' Emma asked. He nodded.

'Fine,' he answered as he made his way forward towards Cooper. 'It looks like it's just the truck blocking the road. It's pretty well wedged in. I don't think we'll be able to move it by hand. You'll have to try and push it off the side of the bridge.'

Cooper didn't waste time acknowledging Michael. Instead he accelerated slowly and began to trundle cautiously but steadily towards the blockage. The prison truck, now surrounded by somewhere between forty and fifty uncontrollable cadavers, scrambling and fighting constantly, also began to move. In the post van Donna, surrounded by a slightly smaller but no less animated or violent crowd, waited nervously for space before following close behind.

'See where the corner of the bonnet is sticking out?' Michael asked breathlessly, leaning into the front of the personnel carrier to speak to Cooper and pointing at the crashed truck just ahead of them. 'If you hit it there and give it a shove you should be able to push it through the wall.' Again Cooper didn't respond, choosing instead to concentrate on trying to work out the physics of the situation in the few short seconds remaining until they made contact. Michael seemed to be right, the truck was positioned in such a way that if he did manage to catch it properly, its back-end would be forced through the concrete balustrade and out over the edge.

'What's that?' Jean Taylor, a middle-aged housewife asked. She was sitting next to Michael, peering over Cooper's shoulder and out through the front of the vehicle and across the bridge.

'What?' Cooper grunted. Jean lifted her finger and pointed ahead.

'Over there,' she replied. Michael looked up and saw that there was movement on the other side of the wrecked truck. The mist was slightly thinner on the far side of the bridge. He stared into the dull greyness. He could see bodies. There were at least ten or twenty of them. No, wait, there were many more. Perfectly timed, the wind gently blew more of the fog away, revealing for an instant a densely packed crowd of vacuous figures filling the narrow carriageway across the river. As they watched the constantly shifting mass of decaying shapes, several of the creatures near to the front of the gathering began to rip and tear at the corpses surrounding them. Crazed and incensed by the arrival of the vehicles, the bodies destroyed those that stood between them and the light and noise made by the approaching survivors.

'Why are there so many of them?' Jean asked, her voice reduced to little more than a slight and nervous whisper. The answer to her question, although no-one said as much, was simple. The sound that the convoy had made had travelled through the late afternoon air and had attracted the attention of just about every wandering corpse which happened to have been in the local area. The creatures on both sides of the river had been drawn to the sound and had instinctively gravitated towards it. Those on the other bank had moved towards the disturbance with the narrow bridge being their only means of crossing. The growing crowd had been channelled by the sides of the bridge. In the same way that the wreck of the truck was preventing the survivors from moving forward, so it had also stopped the bodies from getting any closer. Oblivious to the obstruction, more and more of them had, as ever, continued to relentlessly herd towards the survivors, causing a swollen bottleneck of diseased, decaying flesh to be formed.

Cooper was aware of the bodies, but he was still concentrating on shifting the truck. Did he ram it or just push against it with slow and steady force? The machine he was driving was powerful and responsive. Rather than risk injuring his passengers by crashing into the blockage and trying to smash it out of the way, he instead elected to take the more cautious option. He increased his speed just slightly so that he had sufficient momentum and steered towards the protruding corner of the truck which Michael had pointed out. The survivors in the back of the personnel carrier lurched forward and then back in their seats as the two vehicles made contact and as metal began to grind and strain against metal.

'Come on,' Michael hissed under his breath, willing the crippled vehicle in front of them to move. It shifted back a couple of inches but then stopped when the rear driver's-side wheel became wedged up against the kerb. Cooper accelerated again and pushed harder. No movement. He pushed harder again and then, after what felt like an endless wait, the truck finally gave way to the pressure being exerted upon it. The back wheels jumped up into the air as the twisted chassis shot back a further few inches. Another push from Cooper and then the scrape and rumble of cracking, crumbling concrete could finally be heard. Peter Guest leant over to his left and watched as a sudden torrent of dust and broken masonry tumbled down into the polluted waters below.

'You've almost done it,' he wittered nervously, keeping one eye on the bodies ahead. 'Give it another push and it'll be...'

Tired of waiting and now more sure of his actions, Cooper accelerated with force, smashing into the front of the truck again and this time sending it flying back through the bridge wall. For a split-second it remained balanced precariously, pivoting and teetering on the edge agonisingly before tipping back, flipping over and crashing down on its roof into the river. The moment his path was clear Cooper accelerated again, now powering into the crowd of bodies with massive force, cutting them down in a torrent of blood, bone, disease and decay and obliterating them instantly.

Suddenly able to move with relative freedom and speed again, the convoy pushed its way across the narrow bridge with ease and continued to skirt around the remains of the dead city.

17

Passage along the roads on the other side of the river was relatively clear and trouble free. Within a couple of miles the road they had been following opened up again into a dual carriageway. Last used during what had probably been one of the busiest times of the day in terms of volume of traffic some eight weeks ago, the side of the road which led into town was clogged with the disappointingly familiar sight of hundreds upon hundreds of ruined vehicles, some frozen and still, others with the emaciated remains of their drivers and passengers still trapped inside, fighting to get out as the survivors neared. By comparison the road in the opposite direction was virtually empty. Few vehicles seemed to have been travelling away from Rowley when the infection had first struck. Cooper led the convoy across the central reservation, smashing his way through an already damaged section of metal barrier. Driving on the wrong side of the road felt annoyingly uncomfortable and strange, but it was also unquestionably easier.

A brief respite in the mist and rain increased the light levels of the late October afternoon for a short while. The road followed a long, gentle arc with woodland on one side and, in the near distance on the other, the shadows of the city of Rowley. No matter how much time had elapsed since the germ – if that really was what had done all the damage – had struck and destroyed so much, the sight of a once busy and powerful city drenched in total darkness and without a single light shining out was still unnatural and unsettling. Having been isolated and shut away for some time, it presented the survivors with a stark reminder of the incomprehensible scale and magnitude of what had happened to the defenceless world around them.

Peter Guest now seemed a little more composed again.

'In about half a mile we should reach a series of roundabouts on this road,' he explained, carefully following every inch of their progress on his map. 'Keep going straight until we hit the fifth one, then it's left. Another twenty miles or so after than and we should just about be there.'

Michael crouched on his knees on the floor in the back of the personnel carrier and washed his hands with strong disinfectant they'd taken from the warehouse, trying desperately to get rid of the smell of dead flesh which had stained him. Emma sat at his side, watching him intently and occasionally looking up and out of the window. Every few seconds the light from one of their vehicles would catch in a window of an empty building or in the windscreen of a motionless car and would reflect back for an instant, making her look twice and wonder whether there was anyone there. She knew there would be no-one, but she had to keep looking just in case.

His hands stinging, Michael finished what he was doing and sat back down next to her, collapsing heavily into his seat as the personnel carrier swerved around the first roundabout, knocking him off-balance.

'You okay?' Emma asked.

'Fine,' he replied.

'You stink.'

'Thanks.'

She didn't know which was worse – the smell of death and decay (which they were all becoming disturbingly accustomed to) or the overpowering stench of the strong chemicals Michael had doused his hands with.

The couple hadn't spoken much all day. There had been so many distractions and interruptions that it hadn't been possible for them to speak for any length of time. It had been one of those now all too familiar depressing days filled with fear and uncertainty, when many people seemed to have been so wrapped up in their own dark thoughts that they hadn't been able to (or hadn't even wanted to) share them with anyone else. Now that the end of their journey seemed to be approaching, however, the mood among the survivors in the personnel carrier appeared to have lifted slightly.

'I was thinking,' Michael began, leaning against Emma and whispering quietly to her, 'if this works out then I want to try and get over to that island as soon as I can. I think we both should.'

'Why?' she asked, her voice equally quiet and secretive.

'Because if you believe everything we've heard then it could well be the place where we end up spending the rest of our lives. I want to make sure we get everything we need out there.'

'That's a bit selfish, isn't it? What about...?'

'I'm not suggesting doing anything at the expense of any of the others,' he explained quickly, keen to make it clear that he wasn't being completely self-centred, 'I just want to be sure we get what we need. And I'm not just talking about you and me either, I'm talking about all of this lot too.'

He looked around the personnel carrier at the other people travelling with them. It was disheartening that even now after having spent so much time together, the group remained fragmented and disparate. The survivors generally seemed to fall into either one of two very distinct categories – those who talked about the future and those who wouldn't. Interesting, Michael thought, that he could name all those who had at least tried to look forward and make something of the little they had left. The others – those who sat still and silent and wallowed in self-pity and despair – remained comparatively nameless, faceless and characterless.

Michael still clung onto the slim hope that they could carve themselves something of a future from the remnants of the past. But the chances and opportunities presented to them seemed increasingly slender and difficult to spot and take. He knew he had to make the most of every chance which came his way, no matter how small, and he wasn't about to entrust what was left of his uncertain future to someone he didn't know anything about or who didn't know anything about him. He had to admit that as positive as he genuinely did feel, the prospect of meeting this new group of survivors made him feel slightly uneasy.

'All I'm saying,' he said to Emma, keen to labour his point, 'is that we need to make sure we stay in control here. This little bit of control is all we've got left.'

***

Two vehicles behind, tempers were beginning to fray.

'Will you two just shut up and stop your fucking moaning,' Donna sighed, glancing over her shoulder at the two soldiers slumped in the back of the van. 'All you've done for the last hour is complain. If you haven't got anything positive to say, don't say anything at all.'

'I've got plenty to say,' Kilgore snapped back. 'Problem is you won't listen.'

'You might as well take your bloody mask off and give us all a break,' she hissed.

'Come on, Donna, that's a bit harsh isn't it?' Baxter whispered across the front of the van, his voice quiet enough not to be heard from the back. 'Just let it go, he's not worth it. He's just a bloody idiot who's scared to death. They both are, you can see it in their faces.'

Donna watched in the mirror as Kilgore angrily sat back in his seat like a chastised child, crossed his arms and turned and stared out of the window. It wasn't worth fighting back. He'd been arguing with Donna for several miles about something pointless (he couldn't even remember what had started it now). He really didn't like her. She was blunt and opinionated. She had a big mouth, a bad attitude and such an air of superiority at times that he wanted to hit her. Fucking woman, he thought, thinks she's better than Harcourt and me because she can breathe the air without a bloody suit. Bitch.

'We should kick them both out now,' Donna said out of the corner of her mouth. 'I don't know why we're even bothering to bring them with us. We should do what Cooper did to the other two and...'

'Come on,' he sighed, 'you know as well as I do why Cooper did what he did. This is different. At the end of the day they're just people like you and me. They might even be able to breathe if they could take a chance and...'

'I'll slit their fucking suits and we'll see how they get on,' she muttered angrily to herself.

Baxter shook his head sadly. He knew – he hoped – that she didn't mean what she was saying. Maybe it was just the tension

112

and uncertainty of the long day getting to her like it was getting to him? Not wanting to prolong the conversation he returned his attention to his maps again.

The convoy rapidly approached the third of the five roundabouts they expected to come across in relatively quick succession along the road to the airfield. Tired, Donna sat up in her seat and dropped the van back a little way to allow her to get a better view of the road ahead. In the centre of the island in the middle of the carriageway was a large stone war memorial which she could see outlined against the darkening sky. At its base it had been hit by a juggernaut that had obviously lost control when its driver had died. The huge lorry was twisted round awkwardly with its cab leaning over to one side and half its wheel-base lifted off the ground.

'Take it easy round here,' Baxter warned as the two vehicles ahead of them slowed down to navigate their way through and around the crash scene.

A body hurled itself out of the darkness and into the way of the personnel carrier, distracting Cooper momentarily. In the brief and sudden confusion he over-steered and clipped the back of the crashed juggernaut, bringing it thumping back down onto all of its wheels again. Armitage, following too close behind, then collided with the military vehicle in front, shunting it forward and, at the same time, also causing the juggernaut to be shoved fractionally further forward into the base of the memorial too. Cooper glanced up and, seeing that the tall stone monument had been disturbed, increased his speed and drove quickly towards the exit that Peter Guest was furiously pointing to. Armitage followed.

'Shit,' Donna yelled as she watched the truck and personnel carrier disentangle themselves and move on. From a little way back she could see that the monument, already unsteady, had been seriously weakened by the impact and subsequent vibrations. As the prison truck powered away, the pointed top of the memorial began to sway and tilt. Its collapse appeared inevitable. Rather than take any unnecessary risks, Donna stopped the van and they watched from a distance as it fell, the tall stone needle crashing heavily to the ground and splitting into three huge pieces as it smashed into the tarmac. Even before the dust had settled it was obvious that the road they needed to take was blocked.

'Bloody brilliant,' Donna said dejectedly, shaking her head and rubbing her tired eyes.

'Doesn't matter, just go round the roundabout the other way,' Baxter suggested anxiously. 'Do anything, just keep moving.'

Donna pulled forward and began to steer anti-clockwise around the island, doing her best to concentrate on following the road and ignoring the numerous swarming bodies which had been attracted by the arrival of the vehicles and the sudden crash and confusion they had caused.

'Which exit?' she demanded.

They were now travelling around the roundabout in the opposite direction to that which they had originally intended.

'Third,' Baxter shouted. 'No, fourth.'

His nervous indecision, coupled with the intense pressure, the random movement of corpses all around her and the various obstructions which littered the road, caused Donna to choose the wrong exit. It was a split second decision and she made the wrong choice. They had expected to continue along the wide main road they'd already been following for miles. The narrowness and unexpected direction of the road they were now on made her mistake immediately obvious.

'Damn,' she cursed, slamming on the brake and stopping. She looked back in her mirror and saw that the road behind was rapidly filling with bodies. Two crashed cars made it difficult to reverse back easily. Up ahead she could see the taillights of the personnel carrier and prison truck rapidly moving away from them along the right route. 'I can't turn round here,' she said, looking around desperately for a way out.

'Keep going forward!' Baxter shouted as bodies began to slam against the sides of the van. 'Just keep moving. I know where we are on the map. I'll get us back on track in a few minutes.'

Frustrated, unnerved and angry with herself and with Baxter for making the mistake, Donna drove further down the road as quickly as she dared, dividing her attention between concentrating on the road and trying to keep staring into the darkness in the general direction in which the other two vehicles had disappeared.

'They'll find us,' Cooper said abruptly, hoping to silence Guest who was already wittering and babbling about the whereabouts of the missing van.

'But they could be anywhere...' he began to protest.

'Listen,' Cooper interrupted, his voice clearly tired but still level, calm and full of authority, 'they've taken a wrong turn, that's all. They've got maps. They're not stupid. They'll find us.'

'But what if...?'

'They'll find us,' he said again. 'And if they don't then they'll just make their way to the airfield like we agreed. They're going to expect us to keep following the route we've planned. Stopping and turning around or leaving this road now will make things harder for everyone.'

18

In the post van the situation was deteriorating rapidly. Nervous recriminations and arguments had begun. More bad decisions had been made.

'You told me to go right,' Donna yelled.

'I said left!' Baxter snapped back. 'Tell her, Clare, I said left, didn't I?'

'I'm not getting involved,' Clare said nervously from her seat which was literally in the middle of the argument. 'Anyway, it doesn't matter who said what, just get us out of here, will you?'

Whatever the instruction had or hadn't been from Baxter, the fact remained that they were now lost. In the fading light each dull and shadowy street looked virtually the same as the next and as the last. Street names and other signs were overgrown and covered with moss and weeds, making them almost impossible to read at the frantic speed at which the van was travelling. With bodies constantly marauding nearby they had no option but to keep moving quickly. It had only taken a couple of wrong turns to confuse and completely disorientate the survivors.

'Haven't we been down here before?' Clare mumbled.

'How could we have been here before?' Donna demanded angrily. 'For God's sake, we've been driving straight for the last ten minutes. We haven't turned round. How the hell could we have been here before?'

'Sorry, I just thought...'

'We took two left turns and one right, remember? Since then I haven't done anything except drive straight. Now shut up and let me concentrate.'

'Take it easy on her,' Baxter whined, 'she's only trying to help.'

'If it wasn't for you and your bloody directions we wouldn't need help.'

'Come on, let's not go there again. We both screwed up. I got it wrong and you got it wrong and now we're...'

'Now we're in a real bloody mess because...'

'I still say we should try and find somewhere to stop for a minute or two to try and work out where we've gone wrong,' Kelly Harcourt suggested, doing her best to end the pointless arguments. 'All we need to do is...'

'We can't stop,' Donna explained, cutting across her. 'For Christ's sake, don't you understand anything yet? This place is crawling with bodies. We can't risk not moving.'

'But why not?' the soldier pressed, her voice calm and level in comparison to the others. 'Seems to me we can either stop now and take a chance or just keep driving round in circles all bloody night until we run out of fuel and end up stopping anyway.'

Donna didn't respond.

'Maybe she's right,' Baxter said after a few long seconds had passed. 'We should find somewhere to park the van until we're sure of where we're going again. We don't have to get out or anything. Even if a hundred bodies manage to find us, if we keep quiet then they'll disappear off before long.'

'Bloody hell, Jack,' Donna sighed as she steered round the rubble and other scattered remains of a shop, the front of which had been decimated by an out of control ambulance. 'How I are you? All it takes is for a couple of those things to start banging and hammering on the van and we'll have bloody hundreds of them around us in no time. They don't just lose interest and turn round and disappear anymore, remember?'

Baxter didn't answer. He just sat in his seat and looked out into the darkness around them feeling frightened, frustrated and slightly humiliated. He returned his attention to the map in front of him and tried again to work out where they were. He hated travelling. He began to think he'd even be prepared to take his chances on foot with the remains of the decaying population outside just to be able to escape from the volatile confines of this damn van.

'Find a landmark,' Harcourt suggested.

'What?' Clare mumbled.

'I said we should find a landmark,' she repeated, clinging onto the side of the van as Donna swerved and weaved down another cluttered road. 'We need to try and find something recognisable so that we can orientate ourselves to the map.'

'It's pitch black,' Donna snapped. 'How the hell are we supposed to find a fucking landmark when we can't see anything?'

Hoping for inspiration, she turned left and drove down another narrow street. More residential in appearance than most that they had so far driven along, here more cars seemed to be parked than had crashed, perhaps indicating that it had not been a particularly busy throughway. On either side of the road were houses; very dark, ordinary and unremarkable Victorian terraced houses. The relative normality of the scene managed to silence the raised voices and bring a temporary respite to the relentless arguments. It had been a long time since any of the survivors or soldiers had found themselves anywhere so inoffensive, unobtrusive and reassuringly familiar. For a few seconds Baxter's fear and nervousness gave way to a stinging, stabbing pain and a desperate sadness as the ordinary sights which suddenly surrounded them forced him to again remember all that he had lost.

'What about a church?' suggested Harcourt, pointing out the silhouette of a large and imposing building nestled behind the row of houses to their right.

Resigned to the fact that they were going to have to take a chance and stop, Donna drove quickly towards the church. Two right turns in quick succession and they were there. She steered the van down a narrow service road which bent round to the left before opening out into a small rectangular car park. In front of them, and slightly to the left, was the church, on the other side a school.

'We going to stop out here or take a chance inside?' Harcourt asked from the back. She turned and peered out through the rear window. A single body was tripping awkwardly down the service road after them. Contrary to what Donna thought, the soldier was quickly beginning to understand that although insignificant on its own, the body would inevitably bring more of the damn things to the scene in no time.

'Inside,' Baxter suggested, leaning forward and looking directly at Donna for a reaction. 'In for a penny, in for a pound. Come on, this place looks pretty quiet and you've been sat behind the wheel for hours.'

'Everywhere's quiet, you idiot,' she moaned. 'Doesn't mean it's safe though, does it? We're putting our necks on the line here for no reason…'

Donna didn't want to move, but she didn't want to sit outside, exposed and vulnerable, either. Her resistance was instinctive. As she stared up at the front of the church she thought long and hard. She had to admit that it did make sense to try and make the most of this unexpected break in the journey.

'To hell with it,' Baxter whispered, 'our necks are on the line whatever we do. Let's do it.'

'Okay,' she sighed reluctantly as she watched the solitary body approaching the van. Exhausted, she pushed herself out of her seat and clambered out. The three survivors and two soldiers sprinted over to the dark school building and quickly disappeared inside, leaving the body to crash clumsily into the side of the van and then turn and stumble after them.

19

The airfield was close. Cooper knew that they were near, not just because Guest had been talking constantly and with renewed nervousness for the last ten minutes, but also because there were suddenly many more bodies around than there had been previously. The city was behind them and the road they now followed ran between wide, open fields. All around he could see dark, stumbling figures. Some were distracted briefly by the noise made by the trucks carrying the remaining survivors, but most continued to shuffle steadily forward in the same general direction as the two vehicle convoy was moving. With a lack of any other obvious distractions nearby it was logical to assume that the living and the dead were all heading towards the same destination.

'How far?' Michael asked from the back of the personnel carrier.

'Just a couple of miles now I think,' Guest replied.

'How do we get in when we get there?'

Michael's question was sensible but no-one answered. Guest and Cooper exchanged momentary glances before returning their attention to the maps and the road respectively. Michael slumped back in his seat next to Emma. He hadn't really expected any response. As foolish as it might now have seemed, getting access to the airfield hadn't been something that had been discussed at any great length with Lawrence and Chase. The two airborne survivors had been noncommittal and vague about this end of the journey, telling the others that they would know when they arrived and that they'd make sure they had a clear passage to safety. From the distance and relative comfort of the warehouse hours earlier it had seemed reasonable to believe them. Now, however, as they rapidly approached their final destination and the crowds of cadavers which would inevitably be waiting there, nerves and doubt were beginning to take hold.

'So how are we going to get inside?' Emma whispered, taking care not to talk too loudly.

'No idea,' he grunted in reply.

Michael's concern increased tenfold as they followed a bend round in the road and, for the first time, were able to see the airfield in the distance. Located in the middle of a wide plain which the road they followed now gently descended towards, it was instantly recognisable for a number of reasons. Firstly, and most obviously in the gloom of early evening, because of the light which shone out from what he presumed was an operations room or observation tower of sorts. The only artificial light the survivors had seen since leaving the warehouse earlier in the day, it burned brightly in the night like a beacon. The light initially drew Michael's eyes away from the rest of the scene. Gradually, however, he began to look around a little further. He saw that the building with the light stood just off-centre in the middle of a vast fenced enclosure, alongside a single dark concrete strip. The land around the building was clear for several hundred metres in all directions, and the entire estate was ringed by a tall fence. On the other side of the fence was the second more obvious and far more ominous indication that the survivors were close. Around all of the perimeter of the site for as far as they could see from the road, a dense, heaving crowd of bodies had gathered. Thousands upon thousands of them swarming like dark, shadowy vermin against the inky-blue backdrop of the night. From where he was sitting it was difficult to estimate with any accuracy, but it seemed to Michael that in most places the crowd ahead of them was at least a hundred bodies deep.

Toying with the idea of stopping short of the base and trying somehow to attract the other survivors from a distance, Cooper cautiously slowed the personnel carrier down.

'Something wrong?' Guest asked anxiously. Cooper shook his head.

'No,' he replied quickly, his voice quiet as he peered into the distance, looking hopefully for some movement on the airfield.

'Are they really going to see us? Do you really think they're going to…?'

Tired of Guest's relentless noise, the ex-soldier looked across at him, silencing his increasingly irritating babbling with a single glance. Although conditioned by years in the forces and too professional to let his feelings show readily, Cooper was also beginning to feel a little unsettled and the other man's nerves didn't help. He reassured himself by trying to put himself in the position of the people at the airfield. From where he was he had a clear and uninterrupted view of them so they, no doubt, should have the same of him. As bright and distinct as the light from their observation tower was so, surely, would the light from their vehicles be also. He was sure they would soon see them approaching. As their distance from the airfield steadily reduced, however, his doubts returned and he nervously prayed for something to happen. He couldn't risk going much further forward without a sign that they had been seen. Driving too close to such an enormous crowd without an escape route would be tantamount to suicide.

'There,' one of the survivors shouted from close behind him. 'Look!'

Michael sat up and leant forward to try and get a better view of what was happening. It was difficult to make out detail from a distance, but their slightly elevated position on the approach road allowed him to see definite movement on the airfield. Several small lights – torches and lamps perhaps – were moving away from the observation tower towards a dark shape at one end of the equally dark runway. Was that the helicopter they had seen earlier? As he watched it became clear that it was. After a delay of a few seconds the powerful machine climbed into the sky and then hovered some thirty or forty feet above the ground. Even from a distance and over the engine of the personnel carrier they could hear its rotor blades slicing through the cold night air.

'This is it,' said Cooper as he began to increase his speed again. The road continued its gentle descent towards the airfield. As they approached the helicopter began to gracefully move out to meet the survivors, switching on its bright searchlight as it hovered over the road, illuminating the route they needed to follow. The brilliant burning light also illuminated a sizeable section of the seething, violent crowd of decomposing bodies which surrounded the airfield, the sudden incandescence causing them to react with increased and relentless ferocity.

'How are we supposed to get through that lot?' Guest sensibly asked.

'Just drive straight through them, I suppose,' Cooper answered, 'same as we always do.'

'But there are hundreds of them.'

'There are always hundreds of them,' he sighed as he struggled to look ahead and follow the line of the dark road.

'And who's getting out to close the gate or block up the hole in the fence afterwards?' Emma asked, equally sensibly.

As they neared the airfield it became apparent that the helicopter was beginning to lower. When a gap of no more than ten feet remained between its landing skids and the heads of the corpses, it stopped moving. Hundreds of gnarled, withered and desperately grabbing hands reached up pointlessly towards the powerful machine. Weak, slight and ragged, the bodies were being thrown about and buffeted by the violent, swirling wind created by the helicopter's blades.

'What the hell are they doing now?' Michael asked, craning his neck to get a clear view. He watched in confusion as the survivors in the back of the helicopter allowed themselves to hang out over the sides of the aircraft. Anchored in position and held tightly by rudimentary safety harnesses, two figures emptied large cans of liquid over the crowd directly below. As they worked the pilot (Lawrence, presumably) gently moved the helicopter from side to side, ensuring that as many bodies as possible were drenched with the substance. When the canisters were empty they were dropped into the enraged mass of shadowy shapes below, smashing several of them into the ground and knocking many more aside. The speed of the operation suddenly began to increase as the helicopter quickly lifted higher.

'Slow down again, Cooper,' Guest suggested. For once Cooper listened to him. He cautiously reduced their speed.

One of the figures in the back of the helicopter lit something – a torch or flare or a bottle of something flammable, it was difficult to tell from such a distance – and casually let it drop into the crowd below. The bright flame seemed to be falling forever, spinning over and over until it reached the cadavers below. In an instant the substance which had soaked many of them combusted, exploding and burning through the night air and destroying scores of rotten bodies.

'Here we go,' Cooper muttered under his breath before slamming his foot back down and sending the vehicle careering at speed towards the airfield. The bodies which had been destroyed left a relatively clear area at the point where the road entered the enclosure. As the personnel carrier and the prison truck hurtled towards the fence more survivors emerged from the observation tower and sprinted towards the perimeter. A group of six men and women pulled open a solid-looking gate that had previously been hidden by the mass of corpses swarming nearby.

More bodies were approaching, stumbling over the charred remains of those that had already fallen. The helicopter swooped and dived through the air above them, distracting them and keeping them away from the two vehicles which were quickly disappearing into the compound.

The gate was closed.

20

'I don't know,' Baxter sighed, his voice little more than a whisper. 'I'm not sure. I don't see why we can't just wait here for a few hours longer and then try and get to the airfield. What difference is a couple of hours going to make for God's sake?'

Donna was already beginning to regret this unscheduled delay in their journey to the airfield. She should have gone with her instincts. She wished now that they'd taken their chances and just kept driving until they'd managed to get themselves back on course. It was clear that the others didn't share her views. Clare, Baxter and the two soldiers were content to sit and wait for a while and then make their move. She listened to the opinions of her fellow survivors and respected them. She didn't care what the soldiers thought.

'Let's forget it until morning,' Clare suggested. 'We might as well. We're pretty safe here, aren't we? It's almost dark know.'

'She's got a point,' Kelly Harcourt agreed. 'It makes sense to wait until it's light before we move. It'll be easier to see where we're going in the light.'

'I don't want to wait,' Donna argued. 'We're vulnerable if we stay out here. I think we should go now.'

'Seems to me we're vulnerable everywhere,' the female soldier said dejectedly from behind her facemask. Whilst the three survivors stood and shivered in the cold, she and Kilgore had been sweating under heavy layers of protective clothing. What she'd have given to feel the cold wind and rain on her face again...

'We've been here for over an hour now,' Baxter continued, 'and there still aren't that many bodies around out there, look.'

He gestured for Donna and the others to look through the window which he was standing next to. The group had hidden themselves away in a first floor classroom in the small school which lay nestled in the shadows of the imposing church they'd originally planned to shelter in. Donna peered down into the carpark below and saw that he was right. There were very few bodies nearby, and most of them seemed to be wandering around as aimlessly as ever, seemingly oblivious to the presence of the survivors in the school. A handful of them had crowded around the van and were pressing their diseased faces against the windscreen. She could see other dark figures around the edges of the carpark. Strange how they seemed to almost be keeping their distance.

'As long as we keep quiet and out of sight we should be okay, right?' mumbled Harcourt.

'It doesn't matter when we get to the airfield, as long as we get there,' Baxter continued, trying to convince himself as much as anyone else. 'They're not going to be in a position to pack up and leave tomorrow, are they? Lawrence said they've only just started flying people out. It's not like we'll get there and they'll all have gone already, is it?'

Clare sat on a low desk a short distance away and listened to the end of the conversation with disinterest. She leant down and picked up a book from where it had fallen on the wood-tiled floor. The name on the front of the book was Abigail Peters who, she worked out from the school year she was in, had been nine or ten when she'd died. Baxter stopped talking. He looked across at her sadly and watched her flicking through the pages of the book. Poor kid, he thought, as much as what had happened had been hard for any of them to comprehend and try and deal with, in many ways it must have been infinitely more difficult for her.

Baxter found their surroundings unnerving and sad. Everywhere he looked he could see evidence of young lives ended without justification or reason. It was hard seeing the innocence of childhood shattered so brutally as it had been by everything that had happened. Fortunately the school day seemed not to have started when it had begun. They had entered the building through the main reception area and, apart from the body of a teacher they'd noticed stumbling between upturned chairs in an assembly hall, the building looked to have been

126

virtually deserted. On the way up to their relatively secluded classroom hideout (it was one of only two rooms not on the ground floor) they had been able to see the playground at the front of the school. There they had found a disturbing, but not wholly unexpected sight which still shook them and affected each one of them deeply even after all they had already seen. Lying in the playground were between thirty and fifty dead children, all wearing their school uniform. Around them lay the bodies of their parents and teachers. From their elevated position they could see more corpses on the other side of the school entrance gate. More innocent young lives ended on their way to class.

'Where's Kilgore?' Donna asked, disturbing Baxter's dark thoughts.

'What?' he mumbled, looking round. He could see Clare and Harcourt, but the other soldier was nowhere to be seen.

'Did anyone see him leave?'

No response.

Donna, followed closely by Baxter, quickly left the classroom and ran down the long, straight staircase which led to the ground floor. The creak and slam of another classroom door at the far end of another corridor off to their right gave away Kilgore's location. Picking their way cautiously through the shadows, the two survivors made their way down towards him.

'What the hell are you doing?' Baxter hissed as they entered the room and confronted the missing soldier. He was crouching down in front of a glass tank. The remains of three decomposed goldfish were floating on the top of six inches of murky green water.

'All the animals are dead,' he replied, 'look.' He gestured towards another two tanks which were adjacent to the first. At the bottom of one was the dead and dehydrated husk of a lizard, at the bottom of the second three mounds of mouldy fur which had once been gerbils, mice or hamsters. 'Poor little buggers.'

'Kilgore,' Donna seethed, incensed by the man's selfish stupidity, 'get yourself out of sight will you. Get back upstairs with us.'

'Why? What do you mean get out of sight? There's no-one here to see me, is there? I'm just looking at...'

'We can't afford to take these kind of risks just because you fancy having a look around. You're putting us in danger by...'

'I'm not putting anyone in danger,' he protested. 'I'm not doing anything.'

'Just get back upstairs.'

Donna marched out of the room and back up to the classroom. Kilgore followed, not agreeing with her but sensing that he was outnumbered and suddenly remembering what had happened to Stonehouse and his other colleague earlier. He couldn't understand why she had such a problem with what he'd been doing. He hadn't done anything wrong. He'd kept quiet and he wasn't putting anyone in danger. He was a skilled professional. He'd spent years training to keep himself out of sight and under cover. He'd even had experience (albeit not that much experience) of having to survive behind enemy lines. He was damn sure Donna hadn't. Bloody woman.

Baxter sighed as he watched the soldier traipse out of the room. He followed but then stopped when something caught his eye on the ground over in the far corner of the classroom. A sudden, quick movement that was over in a second. He turned and walked back deeper into the class, peering into the darkness. He crouched down next to a display of once bright but now sun-bleached reading books. He could tell from the smell and debris on the floor that animals had been foraging in the building. A fox? Dogs? Rats perhaps? Whatever had been there, it was nothing worth worrying about.

Baxter looked up and found himself face to face with the horrifically disfigured shell of what had once been a teacher or classroom assistant. The body (which was so badly decayed that he couldn't tell whether it had been male or female) had laid sprawled across its desk for more than eight weeks. Whatever it was that had been scavenging in the classroom seemed to have taken much of its nourishment from the corpse. The face had been eaten away both by disease and by the sharp teeth and claws of vermin. The yellow-white skull was left partially exposed and bare. In shock and surprise he tripped and fell backwards, knocking over a cupboard full of basic percussion instruments. As triangles, drums, cymbals, maracas and other assorted instruments crashed to the floor the school was filled with sudden ugly sound. With cold sweat prickling his brow and nerves making his legs feel heavy and weak, Baxter froze to the spot and waited for the noise to end. As it finally faded away (it seemed to take forever) he turned and ran out of the room, pausing only to look back again when a body slammed angrily against the large window at the other end of the class and began beating and hammering against the glass. It seemed to be looking straight at him. He could see at least another two behind it.

'You fucking idiot!' Donna hissed at him as he dragged himself back upstairs, his heart pounding in his chest. 'Have you seen what you've done?'

Baxter peered down from the first floor window. There were corpses approaching from all directions.

21

Richard Lawrence flew back towards the dark shadows of Rowley in search of the missing survivors. Bloody idiots, he thought to himself, how difficult could it have been for them to stay together and get to the airfield? This didn't bode well for the future. These were people who, inevitably, he was going to have to rely on in time, and how could he do that when they couldn't even get to the airfield in one piece...? If it hadn't been for the fact that he'd already been airborne he wouldn't even have entertained the idea of going out again tonight. They could have waited until morning. He hated flying in the dark.

Lawrence's journey – already unnecessary in his opinion – was further complicated by the number of people involved. The helicopter was designed to carry a maximum of five – the pilot and four passengers. As if the danger and risks he'd already had to take by flying out in the darkness weren't enough, he now also faced the potential problem of trying to get back to the airfield with six on board. Through necessity he had left his earlier passengers (the people who had helped him to clear the bodies away from the entrance gate) behind at the base and now, alone in the helicopter, he felt isolated, exposed and more vulnerable than usual. Although no-one else knew how to fly the machine, for safety's sake he had always flown with at least one other person with him before. They'd been there to navigate or to help him with the controls or to do whatever else he wanted them to do so that he could concentrate on keeping the machine safe in the air. Tonight he was going to have to do all of it alone. If anything happened to the helicopter he knew he'd have little chance of survival – either the crash would kill him or the bodies would. He didn't even have the comfort of radio communication, the lack of power at the airfield making it impossible. Lawrence was completely on his own, and he cursed the handful of idiots lost in the city beneath him for it.

Like virtually all of the rest of the world, Rowley was a dead place. From the air it appeared to be little more than a slightly darker stain on an already dark landscape. It was a featureless scar. Lawrence had trouble seeing where the city ended and where it began. Christ he wished he'd gone with his instincts and waited until morning. The relentless blackness of the night made him feel like he was flying with his eyes closed and one hand tied behind his back. However difficult it proved to be he planned to fly directly across the city and then retrace the route he'd given the survivors earlier in the day, concentrating his search around the area where he'd been told the missing five had become separated from the others. If they were still on the move he'd probably be able to spot them. Either he'd find them or, given the amount of noise the helicopter made, they'd see him and try to find a way of making their location known to him. He could have done with even a little light to help. Fortunately the earlier fog and mist had lifted but the sky was still filled with heavy cloud. Even the moon would have helped provide some illumination but tonight it was completely obscured from view. He decided he was going to search for no more than an hour before turning round and heading back to the airfield. His fuel supplies were sufficient but not endless. He couldn't justify using any more than necessary on just a handful of survivors when there were many more waiting for him back at the base. Anyway, he thought, if these people had any sense (and he was seriously beginning to wonder whether they did) then they'd probably get their heads down and keep themselves out of sight until they heard him.

Baxter leant against the window and looked down into the car park. There were fewer bodies out there than he'd expected to see. Perhaps the meandering route and far from obvious entrance to the twisting service road which led into the car park had thinned their numbers?

'There are only about twenty of them out there,' he sighed, trying to make the most of a bad situation for which the others seemed (quite rightly) to be holding him completely responsible. 'We can deal with that many, can't we? We've done it before. We can get back to the van and get out of here.'

'We don't have much choice,' Donna snapped. 'I knew we should have kept moving. Bloody hell, we could have been there by now.'

'Or we could still have been driving round in circles, using up our fuel,' Harcourt reminded her.

'Okay,' she said, trying hard to remain focussed and calm, 'let's look at the maps again. We'll plot a route out of here and then make a break for it.'

Baxter opened out the maps on one of the low desks and illuminated the city of Rowley with his torch.

'That's where we are,' he explained, circling the general area on the map with his finger, 'and that's where we need to be.'

'That's the airfield?' asked Donna, unable to quite see what he was pointing to. He moved the torch slightly and nodded.

'That's right, and round here,' he continued, moving his finger back down the page towards the southern side of the city again, 'is where I think we went wrong.'

The map they were studying was of too large a scale to be of any real use in helping them plot a route from their present location back to the road which would take them to the airfield. Baxter took a second book, this one of major town centre street maps, from the rucksack he'd been carrying with him. He flicked through its pages until he found a map of the centre of Rowley and its surrounding districts.

'Where are we now?' he asked. 'What's the name of this place?' His questions were initially met with silence.

'Don't know,' Donna eventually answered. 'I don't remember seeing any place names when we came in. We might have to go out and look for...'

'This is Bleakdale,' Kilgore said.

'How do you know that?' Donna wondered.

'Educated guess,' the soldier replied sarcastically, holding up a child's exercise book which had the words 'Bleakdale Church School' printed across the front cover.

'Bleakdale... got it,' Baxter mumbled. He began to run the torch over the page again as he looked for a school and church in close proximity to each other.

'There,' Donna said, peering over his shoulder. She pointed at the map. 'There's the school and there's the service road leading up to it. That's the turning we took to get in here.'

'That's it. So if we work our way back...' his words trailed away as he concentrated on working out the way back to the traffic island where they had made their original mistake.

'We're going to need to get a move on,' Harcourt warned. She was stood next to the window with Clare, looking down into the car park. Although slow, a constant trickle of bodies were still dragging themselves towards the school building. Many of them seemed to be coming from around the corner, near to the classroom where Baxter had first unwittingly attracted their attention. It was almost as if they had given up looking for the survivors there, and they had now moved on. Now some of them had grouped and had become a small but violent crowd around the front of the van.

'What's happening out there?' Donna asked, turning and whispering over her shoulder.

'More bodies.'

From their first floor viewpoint Harcourt was able to see along several of the surrounding streets of the suburb of Bleakdale. The longer she stood still and stared into the night, the more scrambling, stumbling creatures she was able to see. In the deep-blue darkness of evening the dark figures seemed to move like insects scuttling across the landscape. Staggering along streets and alleyways and crashing clumsily through debris and rubble, all dragging themselves towards the source of the sound that had echoed through the air just minutes earlier. She could now see for herself the full effect that others had previously explained to her. The first figures had originally been drawn towards the school by the noise. Now those few bodies were themselves causing a disturbance which brought more and more of them to the scene. Some stood still with their arms hanging heavily at their sides. Others relentlessly and pointlessly hammered on the sides of the van and on the windows downstairs. The few in the car park didn't bother her unduly. What concerned Harcourt more were the mounting numbers of them she could now see crawling through the shadows of the nearby streets.

Forcing himself to ignore the deteriorating situation outside, Baxter continued to stare at the maps.

'I reckon we should just turn round and go back the way we came, sticking to the main roads,' he suggested. 'We turn left out of the car park and keep following the road round until we reach this roundabout here. Straight across and after a mile or so it looks like it loops back round onto the first road we got onto by mistake. Follow that back and...'

'...and we should be on track again,' Donna said, anticipating his words and speaking for him.

'Why do we have to go backwards?' Harcourt asked, moving away from the window and walking across the room to look at the maps with the others. 'Why not just keep going forward?'

'We could,' Baxter replied with reticence in his voice, 'but that's going to mean going deeper into the city.'

'So? Do you really think that matters now?' she grunted as she studied the maps through her cumbersome facemask. 'According to this we're pretty close to the city centre anyway. I don't think another couple of miles is going to make too much difference, do you?'

Neither Donna or Baxter answered. Both had naturally assumed that the most sensible option available to them would be to turn round and try to get back onto the route they had originally intended to follow. Now that they stopped and thought about it though, the soldier had a point.

'I don't know...' Baxter instinctively mumbled.

'Look,' Harcourt explained, annoyed by their indecision. She leant across the desk and grabbed hold of Donna's torch so that she could show the others what she was thinking. 'We could go left as you suggested, Jack, but then turn left at the next roundabout instead of going straight over. By the time that gets us onto the right road we should only be a few miles short of the airfield.'

A thoughtful few moments of silence followed as the two survivors each considered the soldier's plan. It seemed to make sense and they had to admit she had a point – the risks they were facing were great whichever direction they chose to travel in. So if they were resigned to taking risks anyway, surely it would be more sensible to leave the school and move forwards rather than backwards?

'I'm still not sure,' Baxter said quietly. 'I understand what you're saying but I don't…'

'You lot better make a decision quickly,' Clare said from near the window.

'Why?' Donna snapped.

'Helicopter,' she said, pointing up into the sky at the flashing lights on the tail of the aircraft high above them.

For a second no-one moved.

'Come on,' Harcourt shouted, forcing the rest of the small group into action. With sudden, nervous energy Baxter did up the zip on the front of his jacket and began to collect up the maps and shove them back into his rucksack, all the time keeping one eye on the helicopter circling over the city. He picked up the pack and swung it round onto his shoulders.

'How will they know we're here?' Clare asked.

'They won't,' Donna answered as she grabbed her things and ran over to the classroom door. 'We'll need to get back to the van and get moving. We'll have more of a chance if they see us in the van.'

'Think so?' asked Baxter.

She shrugged her shoulders and glanced around the room at the others.

'Hope so.'

She led the way out of the room and back down the stairs. Weaving through the darkness at speed she pushed open the front door of the school and ran over to the van. The two soldiers, Baxter and Clare followed close behind. Pausing momentarily to look for the helicopter as she opened the van, Donna immediately became aware of a huge swathe of movement all around them. From the shadows in, it seemed, every direction, bodies had turned and were now moving quickly

135

towards them, lurching at them desperately with an ominous speed and purpose. The evening gloom was disorientating and the low light made the perception of distance surprisingly difficult. One of the nearest cadavers reached out for Kilgore and caught hold of him before he even knew it was there.

'Get it off me!' he screamed. 'Get this fucking thing off me!'

The body had grabbed him from behind. He span around, trying desperately to dislodge the emaciated creature or to grab hold of it and drag it round in front of him. The corpse's slimy, rotting skin and constant, writhing movements made it difficult for him to get a grip.

'I've got it,' Harcourt said calmly as she yanked the desperate figure away from him in a single violent movement. She wrapped her hand around its scrawny neck and threw it angrily to the ground. There were many more around them now. Kilgore, shocked by the sudden attack and not thinking clearly, immediately began to check his suit for damage as the others bundled themselves into the van. Harcourt shoved him forward and he scrambled inside, leaving her to stamp angrily on the body at her feet with her heavy standard issue boots. Flesh, muscle and shattered bones were crunched into the ground. Donna started the engine and the sudden noise prompted Harcourt to dive into the back of the van and slam the door shut behind her.

With its engine straining and wheels skidding across the ground, the van roared out of the car park, thudding into body after body as it powered towards the road.

'There!' Clare shouted as Donna threw the van around the second sharp turn. She pointed up at the helicopter which was moving quickly through the sky ahead of them. 'There it is!'

The survivors had only been on the move for a matter of minutes when Lawrence spotted them. The pilot had completed his first circuit of the city centre and was trying to find an excuse for giving up for the night when he caught sight of a momentary flash of light below. The only illumination in the whole of the dead city, the van was easy to pick out and follow.

***

'Left here,' Harcourt shouted from the back of the van, keen to make sure that Donna followed the route she'd shown them in the classroom and didn't screw up again. 'Keep going the way we planned.'

Donna did as instructed, yanking the steering wheel over and guiding the van between the parallel wrecks of a car and a burned out milk float. The van's headlights lit up constant movement ahead of them as bodies emerged from the darkness and stumbled towards the sudden light and noise.

'He'll never see us,' Kilgore moaned from the back.

'Of course he will,' Baxter snapped, sick of the soldier's defeatist attitude, 'there's nothing else to see out here, is there?'

Donna struggled to keep concentrating on the cluttered road ahead of her and resisted the overwhelming temptation to watch the helicopter. It seemed to be flying away from them but she couldn't be completely sure. She just had to keep the van moving and keep hoping that Lawrence would spot them and... the van clipped the kerb, causing its passengers to be jolted and shaken in their seats momentarily. The sudden and unexpected movement forced Donna to return her full attention to navigating along the debris-littered carriageway.

Struggling to follow the van, Lawrence took the helicopter down as low as he dared. This was, perhaps, the hardest and most dangerous part of flying at night above the dead land. Everything was black, featureless and virtually indistinguishable. He had to keep low enough to try and keep track of the vehicle below, but also stay at a sufficient height to avoid any tall buildings, electricity pylons or similar. Fly too low and he knew he probably wouldn't see such obstacles until it was too late.

On the ground below the van had come across an obstruction blocking the road. Nothing too serious, but the tangled wreckage of a three car crash had covered enough of the carriageway to force Donna to slow down to little more than a fraction of her preferred speed. Lawrence, noticing their difficulties, seized on the opportunity to try and make contact. He switched on the helicopter's powerful searchlight and managed to move the concentrated beam of light around enough to gain a general appreciation of the immediate vicinity through which the van was moving. To their right were buildings. On the other side of the road, however, perhaps another half mile further ahead, he could see an expanse of open land - a park or playing fields perhaps? Lawrence eased the helicopter forward to hover above the grassland and saw that directly beneath him were football posts. An important find - he immediately knew that there should be sufficient clear space for him to set down between the two goals. A football pitch would give him more than enough room to land. He moved the searchlight to point down at the pitch in a rudimentary attempt to signal his intent to the survivors on the ground.

'What's he doing now?' Donna asked, keeping her attention fixed on the road ahead and relying on the others to tell her what was happening above them.

'He's moved over to our left,' Baxter replied. 'Now he's hovering.'

'What's he want us to do?'

'How the hell am I supposed to know? I'm not a bloody psychic.'

Baxter stared up at the helicopter hopefully. Having cleared the remains of the car crash, the van sped up again and slammed into a random body, its sudden and brutal disintegration leaving a bloody smear of grease and gore across the area of windscreen through which he was looking. The unexpected noise and movement startled him for a moment. Donna flicked on the wipers.

'He's definitely stopped moving now,' he continued, struggling to see clearly through the smeared glass. 'Try and get closer.'

'I can only follow the bloody road,' Donna snapped. 'What do you want me to do? I can't even see what there is for us to...'

'He's coming down,' Baxter interrupted. His view of the helicopter was clearer now.

'What?'

'He's landing.'

Donna allowed herself to look up from the road for an instant. He was right, the helicopter was descending, but she couldn't see what it was descending towards.

'Stop the van,' Harcourt shouted from the back. 'Stop the van and we'll find him on foot.'

'Are you bloody stupid?' Kilgore protested.

'It's a park,' Baxter said as they passed a momentary gap in the tree-lined fence which ran along the left hand side of the road. 'She's right, Donna, stop the van and let's make a run for it.'

Donna didn't argue. She was cold and tired and frightened and she wanted this wild and pointless chase through nowhere to be over. She forced the van up onto the pavement and climbed out. A body threw itself at her, almost knocking her to the ground. She quickly regained her balance and pushed the rancid cadaver to one side before following Baxter, Clare and the two soldiers who were already sprinting along the fence, looking for a way into the park.

Now that they were out of the van the sound of the helicopter was suddenly deafening. With his lungs already burning and feeling like they were going to explode with fiery effort, Baxter forced himself to keep moving forward, trying to keep up with the others who were all younger and in far better physical condition than he was. He was being left behind. Being at the back of the pack terrified him but he couldn't move any faster. He allowed himself a momentary glance over his shoulder and saw bodies shuffling after them. The light was poor but there seemed to be hundreds of them dragging themselves out of the shadows from every direction. He looked forward again and concentrated on following Donna who was just ahead. He didn't dare look back a second time, but he felt sure that the bodies would be gaining on him. Christ, they were probably catching up. One might even be about to grab hold of him...

Harcourt had also noticed the bodies around them. The disturbance caused by the van had been enough to drive the corpses into a frenzy. Unsurprisingly the helicopter was having even more of an effect. She took comfort in the fact that the aircraft was so loud and its searchlight so bright that in

139

comparison the five of them frantically running along the pavement would hopefully go unnoticed by the dead masses shuffling ever closer.

'Through here,' shouted Clare as she reached an open wrought iron gate. She banked left and ran into the park and was immediately able to see the helicopter in all its magnificent glory. It hovered imperiously some ten feet above the ground.

'Has he seen us?' Donna asked as she tripped through overlong grass which had been left to grow wild for weeks. Conditioned by circumstance to keep quiet and not shout, she began to wave her arms furiously, hoping that the pilot would see her and respond. At first nothing happened. The brilliant white searchlight lit up almost all of the park and illuminated crowds of shuffling cadavers swarming towards the helicopter from the darkness in every direction. The speed of the survivors made them easy for Lawrence to see. He couldn't risk setting down until they were almost directly underneath him. At the last possible moment he dropped the final few feet down to the ground.

'One in the front with me and the rest of you in the back,' Lawrence yelled over the deafening engine and rotor blade roar as Harcourt yanked the helicopter door open. 'Strap yourselves in if you can, just hold on if you can't.'

The pilot's voice was barely audible over the noise. Clare and the two soldiers clambered in, followed almost thirty seconds later by Baxter. Donna waited for him at the side of the helicopter and virtually had to push him up into his seat. Dizzy with exhaustion, he slumped back and sucked in long, cool mouthfuls of damp evening air as she slammed the door shut in his face.

'Come on,' Lawrence hissed under his breath. The bodies were damn close now. He could see the decayed faces of the nearest dead staring back at him.

Donna scrambled into the front and pulled the door closed behind her. By the time her belt was buckled and she looked up they were airborne again. On the ground where they had just been the bodies converged and reached up pointlessly towards the rapidly disappearing machine.

22

The return flight to the airfield took less than fifteen minutes to complete. The silence and stillness when they touched down was overwhelming and filled the five new arrivals with cool relief. Oblivious to the thousands upon thousands of cold, dead eyes which stared at them from beyond the other side of the fence in the near distance, Baxter, Clare, Donna, Harcourt and Kilgore stumbled wearily out of the helicopter and followed Lawrence across the tarmac. In tired silence he led them towards a collection of dark buildings - a large, half empty and skeletal hangar, an observation tower and several smaller buildings which had once been used as offices, waiting rooms and public lounges. Baxter was impressed. The place looked better equipped and more substantial than he'd ever dared imagine it might be. It seemed to have been an unusual cross between a small airport and a flying club and he guessed that it had probably been used for private planes, chartered flights and pilot training. He noticed the prison van and personnel carrier parked a short distance away. The presence of the other vehicles came as an enormous relief. The rest of the group had also made it safely to the airfield.

A dull light was shining out from the top of the observation tower. The survivors followed Lawrence into the building, across a short open area and up two flights of steep, echoing stairs. The events of the last few hours had been physically and mentally exhausting and Baxter in particular struggled to keep moving forward. After what felt like miles of walking and an endless climb they reached the top floor of the building and entered a large room through a pair of heavy double doors. Inside the room was light and warm and was buzzing with noise and conversation, a stark contrast to the cold and enforced silence of the world outside the building. The sight of familiar faces dotted around filled the three weary survivors and two soldiers with a sudden surge of energy again.

'You finally made it then,' Cooper laughed from across the room. 'Where the hell have you been?'

'Piss off!' replied Baxter, managing a tired grin. 'We took a couple of wrong turns, that was all!'

'Just a couple? Bloody hell, we'd almost given up on you. We've been here for hours!'

Donna stood in the doorway and soaked up the atmosphere. The mass of people around her - both those she knew and the twenty or so faces she didn't recognise - seemed relaxed and at ease. She too felt suddenly calmer as if the countless stresses and problems that continually plagued her had begun to be stripped away. Was it because she'd finally reached the airfield that she felt that way, or was she just relieved that Cooper and the others were safe? Whatever the reason, she hadn't been in such a comfortable and welcoming environment for a long, long time. In fact, now that she stopped to think about it, she hadn't felt free like this since the days before the disaster. For a few precious moments the overwhelming relief was such that she couldn't move. The nightmare outside suddenly seemed a thousand miles away. She stood there, overcome and rooted to the spot, feeling full of positive but undeniably painful emotion.

'You okay?' a voice asked from beside her. It was Emma.

'I'm fine,' she answered quickly, suddenly self-conscious. 'I'm sorry, I was just…'

Although Donna had stopped mid-sentence, Emma already understood what she was trying to say. She too had experienced the same bewildering range of emotions when she'd first arrived at the airfield.

'This is really good,' Emma continued. 'These people have really got themselves sorted out here.'

'Looks that way…'

'You won't believe some of the things they've been telling us. You know, when we first saw the helicopter this morning I knew it was going to be important, but I didn't realise just how important. None of us had time to stop and think about it, did

142

we? Christ, these people have been up and down the whole bloody country. They've seen other bases like the one Cooper came from and...'

'I know, I heard Lawrence talking earlier. So how come there's so few of them then?' Donna wondered, sitting down next to Emma.

'Suppose they've just been taking the same approach to all this as we have,' Emma answered, thinking on her feet. 'Mike and I decided right from the start that we couldn't afford to spend all our time looking round for other survivors. We knew we had to forget about everyone else and concentrate on getting through this ourselves. Looks like these people have spent their time doing that too.'

'So how many of them are there?'

'Not sure exactly. I think there are about twenty or so of them here, with another six on Cormansey.'

'Cormansey?'

'The island, remember?'

Donna nodded. She was tired and her brain wasn't functioning properly. Tonight she looked drained and weak, a shadow of her normal self. Emma noticed and passed her a drink. It was a small bottle of lemonade. The sweet liquid was warm and gassy but very welcome.

'Much happened since you've been here?' Donna asked, wiping her mouth dry on the back of her sleeve.

'Not really,' Emma answered, 'we've just been sat here waiting for you lot to turn up. What happened? Did you run into trouble?'

'Stupid cock up,' she admitted, shrugging her shoulders. 'We took the wrong exit on the roundabout where that bloody memorial came down, and then made more mistakes trying to get back on track and catch up with you.'

A sudden peel of loud laughter came from the far side of the room. It was an unexpected and strangely startling noise. Donna looked up and saw that Michael, Cooper and several others were talking to a handful of people she didn't recognise. At first she didn't question who these people might be, or what they might have found amusing. Instead her mind was preoccupied with the fact that she'd just heard laughter. For the first time in many weeks she could hear people freely expressing positive emotions that had previously been suppressed. Whatever the reason for their jollity, it touched an uncomfortable nerve. Normally strong and determined to the point of seeming cold and uncaring, Donna now felt ready to burst into tears. She dismissed her feelings as being just a passing moment of weakness, probably brought on by her tiredness and exhaustion. She turned and looked out of a window behind her before Emma could see the raw emotion in her eyes.

Outside the window the airfield was dark and, although she knew that there were thousands of bodies just out of view, the ground around the observation tower was clear. And the building itself was strong and isolated. She couldn't imagine any of the cadavers she'd seen having the strength, intelligence or coordination to reach the tower, never mind make it up the stairs. Being this high up in the air felt infinitely safer than being buried underground where she'd spent most of the last fortnight.

'See that woman sitting next to Mike?' Emma asked, causing Donna to turn back around, wipe her eyes and look across the room again. Sat between Michael and Phil Croft, the woman Emma referred to was rotund, red-faced and very loud. Donna wondered how the hell she'd managed to survive for so long in a world where silence often seemed to be the strongest form of defence and self-preservation.

'The big lady?' she replied, choosing her words carefully.

'That's right.'

'Who is she?'

'Her name's Jackie Soames.'

'Is she in charge?'

'I don't think anyone's in charge really, but she seems to get involved with most of the decisions round here.'

'She doesn't look...' Donna began.

'She doesn't look like the kind of person who'd be sat giving out advice in a place like this,' Emma interrupted, successfully anticipating what Donna had been about to try and say. 'She's got a lot of respect here, though. I've spoken to a few people who've only got good things to say about her. Apparently she used to run a pub. Story is she slept through everything that happened on the first day. Went to bed with a hangover then woke up at midday and found her husband dead behind the bar.'

'Nice. Who else is there?'

'See the young lad on his own with his back to us?'

'Yes.'

'That's Martin Smith. He's the one who…'

'Supposedly found out how all this happened?' Donna said quietly, sounding less than convinced.

'That's him. And the bloke standing looking out of the window over there,' she continued, nodding across to the diagonally opposite corner of the square room.

'The one with the jacket and the hair?'

'That's the one,' she replied, 'I think his name's Keele. He calls himself Tuggie.'

Donna looked at the man and felt a strange combination of surprise and disappointment and a certain amount of immediate distrust. Whilst just about every other survivor she'd seen wore whatever clothes they'd been able to salvage, this man's appearance seemed to suggest that, for some inexplicable reason, he still considered it important to be well-dressed and presentable. His hair - in contrast to just about everyone else - was surprisingly well-groomed. He looked conspicuously out of place and out on a limb, somehow distant and separate from the others. But was it because he'd chosen not to mix with them, or did the rest of the group not want to associate with him? Whatever the reason, in a room full of people he was very much alone.

'So what does he do round here?' she asked, guessing that the man must have had some relevance to the group for Emma to have pointed him out.

'Did you see the plane in the hangar?'

Donna shook her head.

'No, but I knew they had one.'

'Apparently he's the one who's going to fly it.'

'Why do you say it like that? What do you mean, apparently?'

'Girl over there called Jo told me that he used to fly little tug planes at a gliding club…'

'Hence the nickname…'

'That's right. Anyway, she says he's not flown anything as big as the plane they've got here yet.'

'Does he need to? They've got the helicopter, haven't they?'

'The plan is to keep sending people over to the island in threes and fours to make it safe. When it's all clear they'll load up the plane and take everyone and everything else over.'

Donna nodded and finished her drink.

'Come to think of it, I didn't notice any planes out on the runway when we got here,' she said, stifling a yawn. 'So how did this Tuggie get here? Is his plane in the hangar too?'

'Now that's the part of the story I don't think he wants anyone to know about,' Emma explained. 'Richard Lawrence says that he found him hiding under a table in an office at another airfield when he stopped to refuel the helicopter. He's a bloody nervous wreck. I'm not convinced he's going to be able to fly anywhere.'

'Great,' Donna mumbled.

Jack Baxter crossed her line of vision and began to walk towards her. The tension and fear so evident in his face earlier had now disappeared and had been replaced with a relaxed, almost disbelieving grin.

'You two all right?' he asked. Donna nodded.

'Fine,' she replied. 'What about you?'

'Bloody fantastic!'

'That good, eh?' she mumbled, unable to match his enthusiasm.

'That good.'

'So what are you so happy about?'

Baxter shrugged his shoulders.

'Can't you feel it?'

'Feel what? We've only been here a few minutes, Jack. You can't have had chance to feel anything yet.'

He ignored her flippancy.

'This is going to work out,' he grinned. 'I tell you, it won't be long now before we're out of this mess.'

146

23

The observation tower was the focal point of the airfield and its growing community. The strongest and safest part of the complex by a long margin, it was where people ate, talked, slept, planned, cried, argued and did pretty much everything else together. Not really a tower as such, it was simply the tallest and safest building around and the first survivors to arrive there had naturally gravitated towards it. Its relative height and its distance from the perimeter fence and the dead hordes beyond provided them with a little welcome security. With the arrival of Cooper, Donna, Michael and more than thirty others, however, space was suddenly at a premium. At two-thirty in the morning Michael and Emma found themselves sitting together in a small, dark room off the main entrance corridor at the foot of the stairs. The temperature was icy cold. The couple held each other tightly and covered themselves with blankets and coats to keep warm. Conversation was sporadic. Michael had something on his mind. He'd wanted to talk to Emma about it for a couple of hours since an earlier discussion he'd had with Cooper and Jackie Soames, but for the first time in weeks she seemed relaxed and almost happy and he found it difficult to bring himself to speak knowing that what he wanted to say would inevitably upset her.

After skirting round the subject for what felt like the hundredth time, Michael decided to take a deep breath and tell her.

'Em,' he began slowly, choosing his words with care, 'I was talking to Cooper earlier...'

'I know,' she replied, 'I saw you. The pair of you were as thick as thieves.'

'Remember the conversation we had on the way over here?' he continued, ignoring her.

'Which one?'

'When we talked about the island? I said I wanted to try and get over there pretty quickly so we could make sure we get everything we needed.'

'I remember,' Emma mumbled, already beginning to anticipate what he was about to say next.

'Well…' he began before pausing momentarily, 'I'm going to go over on the next flight.' Michael forced his uncomfortable words out as quickly as he could. Once they were spoken he felt sudden relief at having finally come clean and told her. Emma nodded but didn't say anything. In the darkness it was difficult for him to see her face and gauge her reaction. The silence was awkward and Michael soon felt pressured into explaining further. 'There are a couple of damn good reasons why I should go,' he continued. 'Most important is that I really do want to get over there to try and make sure that this island is everything we need it to be. Second…'

'What happens if it's not?' Emma interrupted. 'What are you going to do? Ask them to bring you back so you can start looking for somewhere else?'

He ignored her again.

'Second,' he continued, 'have you looked at the people left around here, Em?'

'What about them?'

'Just go back upstairs and have a look around. Most of the people here are empty. There's more life in half the bodies outside than in some of them up there. It's not their fault, they just can't handle what's happened and…'

'What point are you trying to make?'

'Jackie Soames says they've already sent some of their strongest people over there but they need more. They're planning to try and clear out the village in the next couple of days and they're going to need as much manpower as they can get.'

'So why do you have to go? Why not send Cooper or some of the others?'

'Cooper's a hard bastard - he'll be more use here keeping this lot moving in the right direction. And if I'm honest, I want to do this. I want to go.'

Emma stopped to think.

'So when are you leaving?' she asked quietly, not really wanting to hear his answer. Her mouth was dry with sudden nervous emotion. Michael shrugged his shoulders.

'They're planning the next flight for sometime tomorrow. It will probably be early afternoon.'

She nodded but didn't say anything. Once again Michael found himself feeling pressured by her ominous lack of words. He desperately wanted to know what she was thinking and feeling. He'd known all along that she was never going to have been happy with the idea, but he didn't know what else he could do. Cooper had implied that he owed it to the rest of the group to go and Michael couldn't help but reluctantly agree. Since arriving at the military base it had been him, Cooper, Donna and a just handful of others who had kept the group together and functioning. The same level of control needed to be applied on the island. They needed representation over there quickly. Keen to keep the conversation with Emma flowing he spoke again.

'It'll be okay,' he began to say, his voice soft and quiet. 'This place seems fairly safe…'

'You say that every time we find somewhere new to shelter and within days we're on the run again,' she snapped.

'This place seems fairly safe,' he repeated, 'but you know as well as I do that it's probably not going to last. Places like this don't stay safe indefinitely. We attract the bodies, and until we manage to find ourselves somewhere that they can't get to this will just keep happening.'

'So you're going to leave now before it happens again?'

Stung, Michael looked at Emma and pushed his body away from hers slightly.

'Come on, that's not fair,' he protested. 'I want to go over to the island to make sure things are moving, that's all. The place could be cleared of bodies in a couple of days and we could all be over there. By this time next week we could be standing out in the open without a hundred thousand bloody corpses watching our every move.'

Emma regretted her comment. He was right, it had been unfair and unnecessary.

'Sorry,' she mumbled apologetically.

'It's okay.'

'It's just that I don't want…' she began to say before stopping.

'Don't want what?' he pressed gently.

'I don't want you to go,' she answered. 'I don't want to be here on my own.'

'But you're not going to be on your own, are you? There are more people here now than we've been with since this all started.'

'No,' she sighed, shaking her head sadly, 'that's not what I mean. You and I have been together since the first few days and I don't want that to change. I've been okay as long as I've been with you. We've had some pretty bloody awful times, but we've got by. I guess I'm just frightened that you'll leave here and something will happen to you or you won't come back or…'

'Shh…' he soothed, sensing her mounting emotion. 'Come on, now you're just being stupid.'

'Am I?'

'Yes. Look, this is nothing. I'll go over there in the helicopter tomorrow and the job'll be done before you know it.'

'You make it sound easy.'

'It is easy.'

'Is it? Is it really? Wake up, Mike. In case you hadn't noticed, nothing's easy anymore. Finding the next meal isn't easy. Keeping warm and dry and out of sight isn't easy. Keeping quiet isn't easy. Driving round the country running from place to place isn't easy so please don't patronise me by telling me that getting in a frigging helicopter and flying God knows how many miles to wipe out this island's already dead population is going to be easy either.'

'Look,' Michael snapped, beginning to become irritated by her negativity and defeatist comments, 'I'm not prepared to sit here and wait for something to happen when I can go and do something about it right now. I've got a chance tomorrow to do something that might guarantee a future for both of us. And if I'm honest, I think I have to do it because I don't trust any of those other fuckers upstairs to do it properly. We can't afford to take any chances with this.'

'I know all that,' Emma replied, her voice equally full of anger and frustration. 'I know why you're going and I know why you have to do it, but none of that makes it any easier to deal with. I just don't want you to go, that's all. You're all I've got left.'

24

'You okay?' Jack Baxter asked. Kelly Harcourt was slumped in a seat in the shadows of the furthest, quietest corner of the room at the top of the observation tower. Kilgore was asleep, curled up in a ball on the ground at her feet like a faithful dog. Harcourt couldn't switch off. She couldn't bring herself to close her eyes, never mind sleep. Her head was spinning with dark, painful thoughts. The hard and bloody fight outside the bunker and the subsequent journey which had brought them to this place had proved to be a long and difficult distraction which had stopped her thinking about the hopelessness of her position. Now, in the silence and calm, there was nothing to stop her thinking constantly about the grim inevitability of her immediate future.

'What?' she mumbled, realising that he had spoken to her.

'I asked if you were okay?'

'No, I'm fucking not,' she grunted with brutal honesty. 'You?'

'I'm all right,' he replied, pulling up a chair and sitting down next to her. He glanced across at the soldier who continued to stare impassively ahead and out of the window and into the darkness. For the first time since leaving the base Baxter thought she looked odd and out of place in her heavy protective suit. In the chaos of the last day and a half he had become used to seeing soldiers, guns and helicopters. Now that things seemed calmer and more organised and controlled, Harcourt and Kilgore suddenly didn't seem to fit in with their surroundings. He didn't know why, perhaps it was because he finally seemed to be starting to feel a little more normal and human again? The soldiers reminded him of the confusion and hopeless battles they had left behind. Baxter could see Harcourt's dark, melancholy eyes behind her facemask. The poor kid could only have been in her early twenties. He felt desperately sorry for her but he began to regret sitting down next to her. He'd instinctively wanted to talk to her to see how she was feeling and make sure she was all right, but he already knew that she never could be. There was absolutely nothing that he or anyone else could do to help her or to soften the blow of what was almost certainly going to happen to her. He'd originally sat down with the intention of trying to start a conversation but now he didn't know what to say. The soldier picked up on his sudden shuffling awkwardness but did nothing to help. He was the least of her concerns.

Baxter was about to get up and walk away again when she spoke. She didn't want to be alone.

'My dad,' she said, her voice flat and empty, 'he would have liked it here. He loved planes. He was turning into a proper old-fashioned grandad. He used to take my sister's boys to the airport and they'd spend the whole day watching the planes taking off and landing.'

'Never appealed to me,' Baxter quietly replied.

'Me neither. Dad loved it though. Should have seen him at my passing out parade. Mum told me she had to keep reminding him to watch me. Spent the whole time looking round the base and staring at the kit instead of looking at me.'

The conversation faltered. Feeling slightly more comfortable Baxter spoke again.

'So tell me, how did you end up in uniform?'

'I had two older brothers in the forces. Like I said, Dad was always interested in the military so I guess I just grew up surrounded by it. Didn't know what I wanted to do when I left school and I just sort of stumbled into it. I figured what was good enough for my brothers was good enough for me too.'

'Glad you did it?'

'I had some good times. I knew some good people.'

'You talk about it as if it's over.'

For the first time since he'd sat down Harcourt turned to face Baxter.

'Come on, Jack,' she sighed, 'you know as well as I do that I haven't got long left.'

'But doesn't this feel like it did every time you went out to fight? What I mean is,' he began to stammer clumsily, 'you knew that you were putting your life on the line every time you picked up your weapon, didn't you?'

She shook her head sadly.

'This is different,' she explained. 'At least on the battlefield you had a chance. Here I'm just sitting and waiting for it to happen, and that's what makes it so bloody hard to deal with. There's nothing I can do about it.'

'I'm sorry, I shouldn't have...'

'Forget it, it doesn't matter.'

Baxter regretted his ill-considered and pointless questions. He wondered whether it would be better for both of them if he just got up and walked away now. Or perhaps he owed it to her to stay and try to talk some more and repair some of the damage he was sure he was doing? The pity he suddenly felt for this young girl was overpowering and humbling. He couldn't even begin to imagine how she must have been feeling. He'd been surrounded by people who were suffering for weeks now, but never anything like this...

'If I could have my time again,' she said quietly, 'then I never would have signed up.' Her voice, although muffled by her breathing apparatus, suddenly sounded tearful and full of emotion. 'I probably would have left school and got myself a normal job like all my friends did.'

'Why do you say that?' he asked instinctively.

'Because,' she answered, 'if I hadn't signed up then I wouldn't be sitting here now waiting to die. If I hadn't signed up then I'd probably have died on the first day like I should have done. I'd have died next to my mum or my dad or my boyfriend, not on my own out here.'

'You're not on your own...'

'I don't know anyone, other than this idiot,' she sighed, gently nudging the soldier on the ground with her foot. 'Honestly, Jack, it would have been so much easier. I really don't want it to end like this. I'd rather have just gone with the rest of them and not known anything about it...'

'Who's talking about dying?'

'How can it not end that way for me? Please don't waste your time trying to make me feel better with bullshit because there's no point…'

'You're assuming you're not immune. You might be able to breathe. There are almost fifty of us here who can…'

'And there are millions of dead people out there who can't,' she interrupted. 'I think it's a pretty safe bet that I'm not immune, don't you?'

'But you've come this far, why stop and give up now?'

'Because now that I have stopped I can see that there's no point carrying on. I'm just prolonging the inevitable. It's going to happen sooner or later.'

'So why not later?'

She shook her head again.

'No, there's nothing to hang on for. You'll all be gone soon anyway.'

'Come with us.'

'Why? It might as well end here as anywhere. If you've got any sense then you won't bother taking me and Kilgore over to your island. We'd be taking up precious cargo space. Might as well use it to take something that's going to be useful to you.'

'There might be somewhere on the island that we can adapt so that…'

'Shut up, Jack, it's not working. What are you going to do? There's only one village on the island for Christ's sake. I don't even know if there's a hospital. There won't be anywhere for me. Are you planning to wrap a plastic bubble round a house so that we can live in a fucking oxygen tent? Thanks for your concern, but it's not going to happen.'

Baxter finally realised that it really was time to stop talking. He meant well but she was right, he wasn't helping. He just seemed to be making things worse for Harcourt and digging a deeper hole for himself.

'So what are you going to do?'

Silence.

'Nothing,' she eventually replied. 'I'll just sit here in this bloody suit until I can't take it anymore. Then I'll end it.'

25

Michael woke up in agony just before seven o'clock the following morning. He and Emma had spent the night sleeping on the floor in the little room where they'd sat together and talked through the early hours. He'd been lying on the hard concrete and Emma had been lying on him. Every bone in his body ached. He slowly opened his eyes and looked around. Seeing their dark surroundings reminded him what had happened and what was already planned for later. Their long and difficult conversation echoed around his head. His heart sank when he remembered that he would be leaving her today.

Emma was still sleeping soundly. Michael carefully eased himself out from underneath her and made sure that she was comfortable and warm before quietly going out of the room and following the corridor down to the building's main entrance. He pushed the door open and stepped out into a bright and cold morning. The sky was clear and blue and the sun strong. A powerful, gusting wind blew across the airfield, waking him fully. A short distance away was the helicopter, the sun glinting on its curved surfaces and reflecting back at him. Remembering what he'd come outside for he found a less-exposed corner of the building, leant against the wall and began to empty his bladder.

'Morning, Mike,' a voice suddenly said from out of nowhere. He looked round and saw that it was Donna. She was sitting on a chair at the edge of the runway, staring out across the airfield. A couple of months ago he would have been mortified at being caught urinating in such a public place. Today he didn't care.

'Morning,' he said nonchalantly as he shook himself dry and did up his fly. 'You all right?'

'Fine,' she replied, shielding her eyes from the sun as he walked towards her.

'What you doing out here?'

'Originally the same as you,' she answered factually. 'Other than that, nothing much. I just wanted to get some air, that's all. Still can't get used to being able to be outside.'

Michael nodded and shoved his hands into his pockets.

'Bloody cold though, isn't it?'

Donna looked up into his face. He was staring into the distance and it was obvious that he had things on his mind.

'You okay?'

He crouched down next to her but didn't immediately answer. From where they sat the bodies on the other side of the fence seemed miles away. From such a distance he couldn't make out individual figures - just a constant, shifting mass of grey-green decay. Phil Croft had mentioned that he thought the corpses might not be able to see the survivors for much longer because of the steady deterioration of their faces and eyes. Their limited eyesight may have reduced, but the fact they remained on the other side of the fence in such vast numbers seemed to be proving the doctor's theory wrong.

'Cooper tells me you're leaving us.'

'You make it sound like I'm disappearing for good,' Michael grumbled in reply. 'I think we're planning to leave later today. All depends on us being able to fly in this wind I suppose.'

'How's Emma feel about it?'

'She's ecstatic,' he answered sarcastically. 'She's really pleased.'

'I bet.'

'She understands.'

'What happens on Cormansey is important.'

'I know.'

'Do you realise how important?'

'I think so.'

'This could make the difference, Mike. This is the best chance we've had. This is the best chance we're going to have.'

'I know,' he said again.

Michael stood up, brushed himself down and walked out onto the runway in front of him. He thought about what Donna had just said, and he found the sudden gravity and importance of the

157

day strangely humbling. Until now he hadn't stopped to think about what he was going to do in any great detail. Sure, he'd considered the practicalities of getting over to the island and he'd paid lip service to starting to build a future for the group. Outside and unprotected, however, with the cold wind biting into his face, he began to fully appreciate the enormity of the task ahead.

Michael was ready to face the bodies again.

After weeks of inaction he was ready to work hard and fight to clear the island of death and decay. He was ready to start planning and working and building and grafting to try and make something positive out of the skeletal remains of the past.

Behind him Richard Lawrence emerged from the door at the base of the observation tower and walked over to where Donna was sitting.

'You all right?' he asked.

'Just taking in the air,' she replied, giving him the same answer she'd given Michael minutes earlier. 'It's been a long time since we've been able to do this.'

Michael turned around when he heard the conversation. He slowly walked back towards the others.

'We'll be looking to leave around midday, okay?' said Lawrence.

'Will we be all right with this wind?'

The pilot laughed.

'This is nothing,' he answered. 'I've been up in far worse than this recently. Trust me, this is a good day for flying. A little breezy, but nothing I can't handle.'

His apparent confidence did nothing to inspire Michael. Much as he genuinely did still want to make the trip over to the island, he'd been quietly hoping for a delay. Although he understood why, things suddenly seemed to be happening at an uncomfortably quickening speed. He wanted to spend some time with Emma before they were separated. They'd spent just about every minute of the last eight weeks together. Now that they were going to be apart, however, every last second suddenly felt more precious.

Without saying anything else Michael turned and jogged back to the observation tower to find her.

26

The morning seemed to be over in minutes. For the first time in recent memory Michael prayed that time would slow down. Take-off was delayed by an hour but that wasn't enough. He'd wanted longer.

The helicopter's powerful rotor blades sliced through the air above their heads as Lawrence flew Michael, Peter Guest and another man called Danny Talbot across the dead land. The spare seat between Michael and Guest was loaded up with their belongings and supplies. What was quickly becoming a regular, almost run-of-the-mill journey for Lawrence was far more of an unsettling experience for his passengers. As well as being used to flying, the pilot had also grown accustomed to the view of the scarred and overgrown landscape from the air. For Michael, Guest and Talbot the turbulent journey was an uncomfortable education - a painful reminder of the incomprehensible scale of the tragedy which had destroyed the world around them.

For the first half of the journey Michael had been preoccupied with thoughts of Emma. He hadn't been able to get her tearful face out of his mind for even a second. As the morning at the airfield had disappeared he'd gradually become more and more uncomfortable with the idea of leaving her behind. Now that it had finally happened and he'd left he felt hollow, empty and alone. He'd looked down from the air and had watched her until the distance between them had become too great and she'd disappeared from view. He tried to comfort himself with the thought that if everything went according to plan they could be back together in less than a week. But there was a lot of work to do before then, and these days things rarely seemed to go according to plan. Michael was already bitterly regretting not being at the airfield to look after her, even though he knew she didn't need him there. It was like she'd said in the early hours of the morning just passed, so far they'd struggled through almost every second of the nightmare together. Being away from her now just didn't feel right.

Forcing himself to try and clear his mind and to focus on what was ahead, not what was (temporarily) behind him, he looked across the helicopter at Peter Guest. Guest was sitting with his head resting against the window and he was staring down. Transfixed, almost unblinking, he watched the ground rush by beneath them at a furious speed. Interested, Michael turned back and looked out of his side. The bright sun of early morning had long gone, leaving the late-autumn sky dull, grey and filled with rain. He peered down and watched as they flew over a small town. Out of view again in seconds, the buildings which made up the town seemed unusually blurred and ill-defined. Everything seemed to be overgrown and covered in a fine layer of green. It was almost as if the buildings and roads were being swallowed up and were melting back into the land.

Below the helicopter the world seemed almost completely still. Danny Talbot - a short and acne-ridden teenager who had arrived at the airfield in the back of the prison truck - found himself instinctively looking out for survivors amongst the ruination. If I was out there on my own, he thought, when I heard the helicopter I'd go outside and I'd made damn sure they saw me. So why couldn't he see anyone down there now? Why could he only see rotting bodies shuffling painfully across the cluttered landscape? Was it because any survivors who heard the helicopter were too scared, too slow or too vulnerable to react? Or was it just because there were no more survivors? On this cold and uncertain day that seemed to be the most probable explanation.

'Cormansey,' Richard Lawrence announced just over twenty minutes later when he spotted the dark shape of the island on the misty horizon. The mainland was behind them now, and the helicopter raced out over the ocean. Michael had somehow managed to close his eyes and had been on the brink of falling asleep when the pilot's words had made him quickly sit up again. His heart began to thump in his chest as he stared out of the window. The longer the journey had taken, the more he had become used to the isolation and protection of the helicopter. The thought that they would soon be back down at ground level in the midst of the mayhem was disconcerting. He couldn't see much through the front of the helicopter from where he was sitting. He peered out over Lawrence's shoulder and was just about able to make out the point in the distance where the dull greens and browns met the grey water as the island emerged from the sea.

Sitting next to Michael, Peter Guest suddenly seemed equally unsure.

'Where is it?' he asked, struggling to see anything through the rain-streaked window. Lawrence couldn't hear him.

'Not sure,' replied Michael, still staring at the horizon. 'I can't see much.'

Lawrence soared over the ocean which appeared deceptively smooth and steady. With a little more confidence and freedom he took the helicopter lower and flew closer to the waves. The frothing surf was now just a few feet below them and, for the first time, the passengers were able to fully appreciate the speed at which they were travelling. The dull, dark blur on the horizon quickly grew in size and definition and in minutes they were over the island.

'This is it then,' mumbled Guest as he peered down at the rough landscape of Cormansey beneath them. It looked just as Michael had expected it to - cold and bleak, with grey rock alternating with lush green grassland and the occasional patches of russet-red and orange-brown vegetation. The sea seemed to be battering the island's coastline relentlessly. Tall waves crashed down on the rocks sending huge plumes of surf and froth smashing up into the air. Below them now was the village, little more than two short roads lined with shops and houses, as yet untouched by those survivors who now inhabited this small pocket of land. Bodies lay motionless in the middle of the street where they had fallen months earlier. Although they were only over the tomb-like place for a matter of seconds, it was time enough for them to see corpses shuffling ominously through the shadows. Strange, Michael thought, that they still seemed to gravitate there.

Lawrence flew straight over the village and continued out further along the length of the island. Michael continued to stare at the land they passed over, the rich colours contrasting vividly with the dark grey-black of the late afternoon sky and the dirty blue-green ocean which surrounded it. The weather had been steadily worsening all day and a storm now looked likely. Down on the ground he could see narrow roads and gravel tracks leading to the doors of isolated small cottages and houses. Virtually every home on the island, although often in view of one or two other buildings, stood a distance apart from even its nearest neighbours. Some were so remote and exposed that they appeared to offer a degree of isolation that even Penn Farm would not have been able to provide.

'Almost there,' the pilot shouted to his passengers as the helicopter climbed again, rising quickly to clear a sudden elevation in the level of the otherwise fairly flat landscape. They passed over a rocky scar which ran across almost the entire width of Cormansey from east to west. Once over the rocks the helicopter and its passengers had a clear view of the rest of the island. In the distance just ahead of them Michael could make out a short landing strip cut into a large area of relatively flat grassland. A little further ahead still and he could see more buildings. From behind a small whitewashed cottage a plume of dirty smoke rose up and climbed into the squally air.

Unperturbed by the swirling winds, Lawrence skilfully touched the helicopter down in the middle of the runway. Neither Michael, Guest or Talbot moved at first other than to unbuckle their safety belts. The pilot, perhaps sensing their understandable unease and uncertainty, turned round to face them.

'They'll be here in a couple of minutes,' he said, lowering the volume of his voice as the powerful engine slowed and died.

'Who will?' asked Guest.

'The others,' he explained. 'Brigid, Harry and the rest of them.'

Michael leant against the cold and rapidly misting window to his right, wiping a section of it clear so that he could still see outside. Now that the helicopter was silent and stationary they could hear and feel the full strength of the fierce wind. It whistled through the rotor blades. They could feel the helicopter being buffeted and battered, feeling as if it was almost being shunted back along the runway. Michael had felt safer up in the air.

'So where are these people coming from?' Guest asked. 'Not that it really matters I suppose. Can't take long to get from one place to the other here.'

'Takes fifteen minutes to drive from one end of the island to the other I think,' Lawrence said. 'We drove a quick circuit when we first got here to try and get the lay of the land. We stopped down at this end because of the airstrip and the hill. Figured the bodies would struggle to get over the hill so they'd mostly stay around the village at the other end…' He stopped speaking momentarily. 'Hang on, here they are.'

Lawrence opened the door to his side and climbed out onto the runway. Immediately being blown about by the wind, he quickly yanked the back door open to let the others out. As he stepped down onto the tarmac Michael saw that a pair of bright headlights was moving along the length of the airstrip towards them. As the vehicle approached he could see that it was a strong, modern-looking jeep. It stopped a short distance away from where the helicopter had landed. A large, stocky woman climbed out of the driver's seat.

'You okay, Richard?' the woman asked. 'Good flight over?'

'Not bad,' he replied. 'How've things been here?'

'Quiet,' she answered, raising her voice slightly so that she could make herself heard over the wind. 'Quieter than I'd expected it to be, actually.'

The woman looked at the three men standing slightly behind Lawrence. The movement of her eyes and the expression on her face prompted the pilot to quickly introduce them.

'Brigid, this is Michael, Peter and Danny.'

The group nodded and mumbled tired and subdued acknowledgments as they struggled to stand their ground against the wind.

'New faces?'

'This lot joined us yesterday,' he explained. 'Remember I told you about the journey we did over here a couple of days back when we saw that crowd of bodies? That was these guys. They'd been holed-up for a while in some military base or other. Had some trouble and ended up having to make a break for it...'

'You can say that again,' Guest interrupted.

'...Karen and I managed to track them down.'

Michael stood next to the helicopter with his arms folded across his chest, looking around anxiously and only half-listening to the conversation. He felt uneasy. It wasn't just the grim conditions and unfamiliar surroundings that concerned him, he felt on edge because of the fact that they were standing out in the open, exposed and defenceless. Were there really so few bodies around here that it didn't matter? And what had the woman meant when she'd said they'd been quieter than expected?

'Come on,' shouted Brigid, 'let's get inside.'

The survivors began to unload their bags and supplies from the back of the helicopter and threw them into the jeep as Lawrence secured the aircraft. Disorientated and slow to react, the three new arrivals squeezed uncomfortably into the back of the vehicle. Their senses suddenly overloaded with questions, emotions, random thoughts and sheer mental exhaustion, they sat in collective silence as Brigid started the jeep, turned it around and drove back down the runway.

'Been keeping yourself busy, Brig?' Lawrence asked.

'I always do,' she replied. 'Anyway, what about you? Everything all right back on the mainland?'

'Okay,' he answered, 'pretty much the same as when you left really. There are a few more of us now, that's all.'

'You going to be able to get Keele to fly that plane over here soon?'

'I bloody well hope so. I'm sick of doing all the donkey work. Christ, the number of times I've flown backwards and forwards between the airfield and this bloody island...'

'Don't make it sound like such an ordeal,' she laughed, leaning forward and wiping condensation from the windscreen with the back of her hand. 'You love it when you're here.'

'I do,' he agreed. 'It's going back to that dead place that I can't handle.'

A narrow dirt track curved away from the end of the airstrip and disappeared between two low, dune-like hills. Brigid drove onto the rough track and followed it round to the right. Sandwiched uncomfortably between Guest and Talbot, Michael looked out through the windscreen and could see that they were getting closer to the billowing cloud of smoke he'd seen from the other end of the runway. He was about to ask where they were going when they rounded another corner and pulled up behind the whitewashed cottage which had been visible from the air when they'd come in to land. A short, athletic-looking man was stood outside, pumping up the tyres of another car. He stopped what he was doing and looked up as the jeep approached.

'Home,' Brigid said as she turned off the engine. 'What you doing, Richard? Coming in or going straight back?'

'I'm knackered. I've told the others I'm stopping here tonight,' he answered. 'There's not a lot of point trying to get back today. I'll wait until morning. I'd rather stay here anyway.'

Once Guest had moved Michael was able to clamber out of the jeep. He stretched his legs. Although short and over quickly, the journey had been cramped and uncomfortable. The man who had been working on the other car walked over to him and held out his hand. Michael shook it.

'Harry Stayt,' the man said brightly. 'How you doing?'

'Good,' he replied, still a little subdued. 'I'm Michael. This looks like quite a place you've found here. I didn't think that I'd get to see anywhere like this again...'

To his embarrassment Michael found that talking coherently had suddenly become ridiculously difficult. This was such a quiet, ordinary and unremarkable place and yet he was struggling to take everything in. It wasn't the location that had affected him and it wasn't the physical appearance of the island (which was very different to the decayed land he'd left behind). It was the atmosphere and the attitude of the people he'd so far met that had taken him by surprise. They seemed to be amazingly relaxed and at ease. They were outside, talking freely, unconcerned by the level of their voices and not looking constantly over their shoulders.

'I tell you,' Stayt said, 'this place is the business. As soon as we got here I knew it. Once we get it cleared up and get everyone else out here we'll be set up for life.'

Michael didn't answer. Instead he just stood still and listened and breathed in the air. Apart from the occasional waft of smoke from the fire nearby everything smelled relatively pure and fresh. The sickly stench of death and decay so prevalent across the rest of the world had much less of an impact here. It was still there, but it was weaker and more diffuse than he was used to. In comparison to the heavy, suffocating, disease-ridden air he had become used to breathing, the air on the island was the purest he could ever remember tasting.

'Is there much left to do?' he asked, finally responding to Stayt's earlier comment.

'Not really,' he replied. 'All that's left now is the big one.'

'The big one?'

'Danvers Lye.'

'What the hell's that?'

'The village. They have told you, haven't they? We're going to clear the village.'

'They told us about it. When?'

'Next couple of days probably. We might even try and make a start tomorrow now there's a few more of us here.'

Michael became aware of the sound of another engine approaching. He took a few steps to his right to look around the side of the cottage and saw that a road stretched out away from the front of the building. A pickup truck was moving quickly towards them. The truck drove past the cottage and carried on towards the source of the smoke a short distance away.

'Who's that?' he asked.

'Bruce Fry and Jim Harper,' Stayt answered. 'They've been cleaning up.'

'Cleaning up?'

Stayt nodded his head in the direction in which the truck had been travelling. Michael followed him as he walked towards another low hill. He heard the sound of the engine stop as they climbed up to the top of the gentle rise. Below them was a natural hollow, the base of which had been filled with a smouldering bonfire. The truck had stopped on the other side of the dip.

'It's the only sensible way of doing this really,' Stayt explained as they watched the two men climb out of the truck.

'Doing what?'

Fry and Harper, dressed in protective boiler suits, got out of the truck and walked round to the back, acknowledging Stayt and Michael when they noticed them watching. With rough, gloved hands they began to drag bodies from a pile on the back of the vehicle and then threw them unceremoniously onto the flames.

'These are mostly the ones we've found lying around. We've got rid of about thirty of them so far,' Stayt explained as he turned round and began to walk back towards the cottage, 'only another few hundred to go. Actually, they burn pretty well.'

'What?'

'Easier to chop up than firewood too,' he laughed as he walked away. 'I can see us sitting in front of the fire in winter with a basket of arms and legs to burn instead of logs!'

'Sick bastard,' Michael muttered. He wasn't relaxed enough yet to appreciate Stayt's humour. He stood and watched the fire for a short while longer, staring deep into the flames. It was difficult to see exactly what was burning, but he could definitely make out charred bones (skulls, hands and feet were particularly distinct) and scraps of partially burned clothing around the edges of the pyre. He turned and followed Stayt back to the others.

'There are six of you here, aren't there?' he asked, jogging to try and catch up with the other man.

'That's right,' Stayt answered.

'So where are the other two, in the cottage?'

'No, they're out. They'll be back in a while. They're scouting around somewhere.'

'Doing what?'

'Just checking the place over. Don't forget we've not been here that long,' he said, waiting by the back door of the small building. The rest of the group had already gone inside. 'We've managed to get quite a bit done, but we wanted to get a little more muscle behind us before we tried anything too risky.'

'Risky?' Michael repeated as he followed him into the dark kitchen of the cottage. The room was cramped and cluttered and the ceiling low. He could see Talbot and Guest sitting in an equally gloomy living room talking to Lawrence and Brigid. 'Bloody hell,' he sighed, 'isn't everything risky now?'

'We've just been taking things steady,' he continued to explain. 'We need to be completely sure of what we're doing before we do anything we might regret.'

Puzzled, Michael walked into the living room. Although as dull and poorly lit as the kitchen, the room was dry and relatively warm and was considerably more inviting and appealing than pretty much anywhere else he'd been in the last two months. It still didn't feel right, standing in full view of the rest of the world like this and talking without a care as if nothing had ever happened. He felt nervous and on edge. What if there were bodies nearby?

'You okay?' Lawrence asked.

Michael nodded.

'Fine,' he replied. 'I'm just a little…'

'Tired?'

He shook his head and struggled to think of the right word to properly express how he was feeling.

'Disorientated.'

'You'll get used to it,' Brigid smiled. 'It doesn't take long.'

Michael sat down on a comfortable armchair next to an unlit fire. Christ, it felt good to be able to sit down like this, he thought. He leant back and stretched his legs out in front of him as he looked around at the others who were continuing to talk. At first he was content to sit and listen without taking an active part in the discussion. He'd been too active for too long now.

After a couple of minutes the conversation changed direction and tone. Another car pulled up outside and the final two survivors entered the cottage, introducing themselves to the new arrivals as Tony Hyde and Gayle Spencer. The two of them (the inhabitants of the island had been travelling in pairs since first arriving) had been out on something of a reconnaissance mission all afternoon. They'd driven to the outskirts of Danvers Lye to check out the situation in readiness for the cleaning-up operation that was inevitably going to begin at some point in the next few days. They'd explained that they had been able to get closer to the village than they'd expected. Michael was confused.

'I don't understand,' he said, looking up at Hyde and Spencer who were sitting on a dusty sofa opposite him. 'How did you manage to get anywhere near the village, and why were you risking your necks out there anyway? Surely the bodies would have reacted to you just being that close to them...'

He stopped speaking. Spencer was shaking her head.

'We were hoping you might be able to shed a little light on this.'

'On what?'

'We thought you might have seen something similar happening where you were.'

'Something like what?' Peter Guest snapped, becoming nervous again.

'We think some of the bodies here are changing.'

'Changing?' he exclaimed, immediately concerned. 'What do you mean, changing?'

'We noticed it yesterday,' she continued. 'Brigid, Bruce and I were the first to get here on Saturday. When we first arrived everything seemed pretty much as we expected, we only had to cough and most of the bodies that were near started swarming around us.'

'So what's changed?' pressed Michael. 'What's different now?'

'When we got up yesterday we were expecting to have been surrounded by bodies because of the noise we'd made and the fire and we'd pretty much decided to play it that way so that we could try and get rid of a few of them. We figured we might as well try and draw them out gradually… you know, bring them to us rather than us running around after them? Anyway, when we got outside there were only a handful of them about. We got rid of them quickly and we assumed that the rest just hadn't managed to make it over to this side of the island yet.'

Hyde took over the story.

'Mid-morning, three of us drove over to the village. We just wanted to see what we were up against and get an idea of what we needed to do to make the place safe. We stopped the car at the end of the main street and waited.'

'What happened?'

'Now this is the weird part,' Spencer continued. 'The bloody things weren't reacting to us. At least, they weren't reacting how we thought they would. Some of them did and they came straight for us, but others stayed out of the way. We managed to get a little closer and we could see them. It was like they were waiting for us.'

'What?'

'You heard me, we could see them waiting in the shadows and inside buildings that had been left open, generally keeping out of our way.'

'So what did you do?'

'Nothing,' Hyde sighed. 'Christ, we didn't want to get too close. The last thing we wanted to do was antagonise them.'

'Antagonise them? So you don't think these things are about to roll over and give up?'

Brigid shook her head.

'So what has happened to them?' Peter Guest asked.

'I've been thinking about this a lot,' she said. The other people gathered in the room turned to listen to her, giving her their undivided attention. 'I don't know what the rest of you have seen, but I've watched these things changing since the day they first got up and started walking round again. In the beginning they were just able to move, then they could hear and see, then they became more aggressive and now it looks like they've started to…'

'Think?' Michael anticipated.

Brigid thought for a moment.

'I suppose you're right. They've gained another level of control. It's a logical progression, if any of this is logical.'

Michael looked around the room.

'I've talked to other people about this before now,' he said. 'We've seen something similar happening, but not to the extent you're talking about. We've got a doctor with us and he said to me that he thinks their brains have survived the infection. It's like they're gradually coming round again, despite the fact that their bodies are falling apart. It's like they've been sedated with drugs that are taking months to wear off.'

'That's good then, isn't it?' Guest said. His mouth was dry and he swallowed hard before speaking again. 'Problem solved, eh? If they're going to be able to think and control themselves, then they're not going to be a threat to us, are they? They'll see it's not a fair contest and just sit there and rot.'

'Possibly,' Michael cautiously responded, 'but I don't think that them being a threat to us is the issue anymore.'

'What are you talking about?'

'I've believed all along that the bodies had been driven by instinct. It's like they're being motivated and controlled at the most basic level. Each time there's been a noticeable change in their behaviour, it's as if they've gained another layer of self-awareness.'

'I don't understand,' Guest complained.

'Have you seen how they sometimes fight with each other?' he asked. Various heads nodded back at him. 'It always seems to be completely random and unprovoked and without reason, doesn't it? But have you ever stopped and wondered why they do it? What have they got to gain from fighting? There's no class or status or other division among them, is there? They don't eat, they don't want shelter, they don't fight for food or possessions.'

'So what are you saying?' Brigid asked. 'Why do you think they do it?'

'I think their fighting is nothing to do with wanting, because they have no obvious desires. I think the only thing they're left fighting for is survival. They're fighting just to continue to exist. It's self-preservation.'

171

'I don't buy any of this,' Guest whined. 'Listen to yourself, will you? Can you hear what you're saying? Can you hear how...?'

'What I'm saying,' Michael added, unfazed by Guest's outburst and with his voice ominously serious, 'is that the bodies aren't a threat to us, it's more that they're beginning to see us as a threat to them. And if they really are driven by instinct, then they'll do whatever they have to do to make sure they continue to survive.'

27
Kelly Harcourt

I can't do this anymore. I've been sitting here for almost a day now and I know that I can't take anymore.

I've listened to everything the others have said and I've tried to understand and see their way of thinking but I can't. My perspective is different to theirs. My priorities are different to theirs. They keep trying to persuade me to stay strong and go with them but I know that there's no point. Doesn't matter what they think they might be able to do for me and Kilgore, it's never going to happen. They're going to have enough trouble trying to look after themselves from here on in. When it comes to the crunch they're not going to put themselves at risk for us and I don't blame them. It would be stupid. It would be pointless. What's going to happen to Kilgore and me is inevitable.

It's the waiting that's hurting me most.

I've had my share of hard times before now. I cried my way through the first half of basic training like a bloody baby. I've been stuck out on the battlefield looking down the barrel of the enemy's gun. I could handle all of that. Hard as it was at the time, I managed it and I got through. When each one of those things happened, no matter how bad it got, I dealt with it.

The difference today is that everything's out of my control. I can't think or fight or negotiate my way out of this one. The end is a foregone conclusion and I've just been putting it off sitting here and waiting. I can't close my eyes anymore without seeing everything that's happened and remembering everything that I've lost. I haven't slept properly for days because my head's been filled with constant nightmares and dark thoughts, even before we came above ground. And it all seems to have come full circle now we're sitting here at the airfield. I look at the people around me and I can see that their faces are full of more hope than ever. They can finally see a way out. The things that are stopping them from moving on now are obvious and clear, and by leaving this place they'll be leaving those problems behind. But it doesn't matter where I go. Location won't change anything. It's not the bodies that will kill me, it's what's in the air. It's going to be the same whatever I do or wherever I go.

Things have changed since we got here. Arriving here felt like reaching the end of the road. I watched the helicopter leave this afternoon and that made me realise that things are moving on without me now and that I should finish this today.

I'm an outsider. Neither living or dead. I can't continue to exist like this.

I'm standing a little way short of the perimeter fence now. The bodies are watching me but they're not reacting as much as I'd expected them to. God, everything sounds and feels different out here. I've spent the last two months either hidden underground or travelling. Now I can hear my footsteps as I walk through the long, wet grass. I can hear birds again and I can see them shooting quickly across the sky. I can see the wind ripping through the tops of trees and I can feel it blowing against my suit.

It's spitting with rain now. Little drops of water are splashing against my visor. If I don't look at the bodies then everything seems green and fresh and clear and all I want to do is breathe the air again. Since we came above ground and left the base I haven't been able to touch my own skin. I want to scratch my arms and bite my nails and rub my eyes and run my fingers through my hair. I want to feel the wind and the rain on my skin one last time.

Kelly Harcourt stood at the edge of the airfield. Oblivious to the bodies standing just metres away from her, and equally ignorant to the watching eyes of the survivors in the observation tower behind, she ripped off her facemask.

And for a moment the sweet relief was overpowering.

Cool, fresh-tasting air flooded her lungs, making her feel stronger and more human than she had felt in weeks. She could smell the grass and the decay and it tasted a thousand times better than she remembered. The seconds ticked by, and it seemed that the impossible had happened. Was she immune? By some incredible chance, did she share the same physical traits which had allowed the people in the building behind her to survive? She didn't dare believe it at first. What were the odds against her managing to survive like this? In a delirious instant her mind was filled with visions of finally making it to the island and actually having some kind of existence where before she'd only been able to think about...

It started.

It was happening.

She knew this was it.

From out of nowhere the pain gripped hold of her like a hand wrapped tight around her neck.

The inside of Kelly's throat began to swell and then split and bleed. With her eyes bulging with pain and suffocation she fell back onto the grass and stared deep into the heavy grey sky overhead, seeing nothing.

Thirty seconds later it was over.

28

The fact that he found himself lying on a relatively warm and comfortable bed for the first time in weeks wasn't helping Michael to sleep. Danny Talbot, in comparison, was snoring from the comfort of his narrow bunk on the other side of the small, square cottage bedroom. It was almost midnight. Michael's head was pounding and he wished that he could find a way to switch off and disconnect for a while. It was impossible. If he wasn't being distracted by the noise coming from the other survivors downstairs then he was thinking about the island and how he had finally managed to get there. When he stopped thinking about the island he found himself thinking about the changing behaviour of the bodies, and when he stopped thinking about that he started to think about Emma. Once he'd started he couldn't stop thinking about her.

Funny how distance alters perspective, he thought. Having spent virtually all his time with Emma over the last two months, he'd grown used to having her around and it felt strange, almost wrong, now that they were apart. He'd always had her there to talk to or to shout at or cry with until now. Whereas they had previously spent most of their time in the same building or the same vehicle together, now it could be argued that they weren't even in the same country. The distance between them seemed immense, almost immeasurable. The sudden physical gulf made him feel strangely guilty and made him question whether leaving the mainland had been the right move. He should never have left her. He knew that she was more than capable of looking after herself (Christ, she'd looked after him enough recently) but that didn't make it any easier. In many ways he felt responsible for her. More than that, he liked being with her and he was missing having her around. He hadn't yet dared say as much to her, but he knew that he loved her and he was reasonably confident that she loved him, as much as anyone could love anyone else in their cold and emotionally-starved world. His sudden solitude this evening (which he still felt despite the fact that he was surrounded by other people) had made him painfully aware of the depth and strength of the feelings he had for Emma but which, because of circumstance, he'd kept hidden and subdued. The constant pressure and danger on the mainland had made it impossible for either of them to fully appreciate how they really felt.

Lying on the bed in the dark was pointless. He wasn't going to be able to sleep. Already fully dressed, he got up and crept back down the narrow staircase to where Brigid, Guest, Harper and Gayle Spencer were sitting in the kitchen.

'You all right?' Brigid asked as he entered the room. His shuffling footsteps on the floorboards above had alerted them to the fact that he was up and awake.

'I'm okay,' he answered quietly.

'Coffee?'

He nodded. The kettle was boiling on a portable gas stove, filling the room with steam and heat.

'Where are the others?' he asked, looking around and trying not to yawn.

'Danny, Tony and Richard are upstairs, Harry and Bruce are outside.'

'Outside? What the hell are they doing out there?'

'Keeping watch,' Gail answered.

'Why? Has something happened?'

She shook her head.

'No, we're not planning on taking any chances, that's all.'

'Bloody hell, just being outside would have meant taking a chance where I've just come from.'

'We know. It's different here, you'll get used to it.'

Michael took a few steps closer to the window and looked out into the darkness. He could just about make out movement a few metres ahead. It was too quick and purposeful to have been a body. It had to have been either Stayt or Fry.

'Here you go,' Brigid said, handing him a mug of coffee.

'Thank you.'

He could see one of the men outside more clearly now. Whoever it was they were walking back towards the cottage. Seconds later the door to Michael's right creaked open and Harry Stayt stepped inside.

'Okay, Harry?' Gayle asked. Stayt nodded.

'Bloody cold out there tonight,' he complained.

'What you come back in for? Anything happening out there?'

'Saw a couple of bodies about half an hour ago, that's all.'

'Give you any trouble?' Michael wondered. 'I mean, did they go for you or were they like the others earlier?'

'They went for us.'

'I don't understand. Why do some of them still react like that when others don't?' asked Harper. A young man, tonight he looked tired and drawn beyond his years.

Michael shrugged his shoulders.

'Who knows,' he replied. 'My guess is that it all depends on what condition their brains and bodies are in.'

'What do you mean?'

'Some of them are more decayed than others. You'd expect their brains to be decaying at the same rate as the rest of their bodies, so it stands to reason that some will be in a worse mental state than others.'

'Bloody hell, they're all in a bad mental state, aren't they?' Stayt grinned. 'Look, sorry to change the subject, but I saw the windows steaming up and guessed you'd put the kettle on. Any chance of a drink?'

Deep in thought, Brigid stood up and spooned coffee into two more mugs. She poured on boiling water, stirred the drinks and then pushed them over towards Stayt who picked them up with one hand. Michael noticed that he was carrying a blade of some description in the other hand. From where he was standing he couldn't see whether it was a sword, a machete or just a long-bladed knife. Stayt noticed that he was looking at it.

'Bloody useful, this is,' he explained as he lifted the blade up into the dull light. It was a long and ornately decorated sword. The other survivors watched him raise it with cautious eyes.

'Nicked it from a museum a few weeks back. I tell you, it's the best thing I've found for getting rid of bodies.'

'Put that damn thing down, will you?' Brigid sighed. 'You're like a bloody kid with a new toy. I used to spend half my time locking up idiots who carried things like that.'

Michael looked puzzled. Stayt explained.

'Ex-Copper,' he grinned. He did as he was asked and then turned round to leave the cottage again.

'Mind if I come out with you?' Michael wondered. His question seemed to surprise the others, Stayt included.

'You can if you want to,' he answered, grinning again. 'If you'd rather spend your first night here out in the dark with Fry and me instead of here in the warm then be my guest!'

'Can't sleep anyway,' Michael grumbled as he zipped up his jacket and followed Stayt out into the darkness. The two men walked away from the cottage together.

'Don't know why they get so wound up about this sword,' Stayt said quietly once he was sure they were out of earshot. 'Don't know about you, but I'd rather carry a weapon like this than a gun.'

'I've never got on with guns,' Michael agreed. 'They're no use anymore. They're too bloody noisy and you have to be a damn good shot to take the bodies out. Miss the head and they'll just keep coming at you.'

'Damn right, and by the time you've got rid of one of them there'll be another couple of hundred following close behind trying to see what all the noise was about.'

'Stick to your sword,' Michael grunted.

'Fry,' Stayt shouted into the darkness. 'Oi, Fry, where are you?'

'Over here,' a disembodied voice replied from the direction of the small hill which overlooked the pyre Michael had seen earlier. The remains of the fire were still smouldering. He could see the faintest of orange glows in the darkness.

'Two of us coming over,' he shouted back. He lowered his voice again to talk to Michael. 'Didn't want him thinking you were one of them and trying to take you out!'

Michael managed half a smile.

179

'Thanks.'

They found Fry crouched over the embers of the fire, warming his hands. Earlier in the evening they'd fuelled the flames with wood and other general rubbish but the remains of the fire's original fuel could still clearly be seen. Michael found it a little unnerving to see so many charred bones. The fact that they were in a natural hollow in the ground gave the area the feeling of being a grotesque mass grave.

'How you doing, Mike?' Fry asked cheerfully as they neared.

'I'm good,' he answered, 'just got sick of sitting in there and staring at the walls.'

'I know what you mean,' the other man said. 'Guess we've all done enough of that recently to last a lifetime.'

'That's why we keep volunteering to come out here,' Stayt added. 'I don't know about you, but I can't stop and relax until I know that we've got rid of all the bodies here and the rest of our people are on their way over from the mainland. I just want to get it done now.'

'How were they all doing when you saw them?' Fry asked. 'Jackie still trying to keep them in line?'

'Seemed to be.'

'Give them a week or so and I reckon they'll all be over here,' Stayt yawned.

'Why should it take that long?'

He shrugged his shoulders and yawned again.

'That's the timescale we've been trying to work towards.'

'So what's stopping us from moving things on more quickly?'

Stayt and Fry both became quiet.

'Apart from getting the village cleared,' Fry eventually admitted, 'nothing really.'

'So we should do it tomorrow, shouldn't we? What reason have we got for delaying it? I feel the same as you two, I don't want to be sitting here talking about what we're going to do when we could be doing it.'

'I'm not sure. I think we should…'

'Be honest, Bruce,' Michael interrupted, 'everyone instinctively makes excuses and tries to put things off because they're scared. I understand because I'm the same, but the sooner we do this and get it done, the sooner we can try and get on with our lives.'

'We know that, but clearing the village is going to be a big job and there's a lot riding on it. We need to make sure we get it right first time.'

'There you go again, more excuses. We don't really have to get it all done on day one, we just have to make sure that things don't go too wrong. Does that make sense?' The blank expressions on the faces of the two men seemed to indicate that Michael had confused them both. 'We just have to make sure we don't take any unnecessary risks,' he explained. 'We should get in there quick, strike, and then get out again. Regroup and then go back and do the same again. Then we do it again and again until the job's finished.'

'Probably won't take that long,' Fry admitted.

'So why are you so keen?' Stayt asked.

'Partly because I just want it over with, partly because of experience,' Michael replied.

'Experience of what?'

'The bodies.'

'But we've all got that. Why should you think any differently to the rest of us?'

Michael shrugged his shoulders and kicked at the ashes on the ground next to his feet, sending a shower of sparks up into the air.

'I don't know about you two,' he answered, 'but I've watched those things change steadily, almost from day to day. I know there's going to come a time when they've rotted down to nothing and they don't get in our way, but what I've seen over the last couple of days has made me think things might get more difficult before they get any easier. Look at what's happened so far - in just a few weeks they've gone from just staggering around to being aggressive and violent and having some control. And now it seems they're starting to watch us and think about what we're doing.'

'What are you getting at?'

'I think that if we don't make a move now, then it'll be the bodies hunting us out, not the other way round.'

29

The dull morning light crept slowly and silently across the airfield. From the top of the observation tower Clare stood and watched as the darkness gradually disappeared. It looked blustery and cold outside but the building protected and isolated her from the brunt of the harsh, almost wintry conditions. From where she was standing she could see right across to the fence and the hordes of constantly moving corpses beyond. As the light improved she could make out the body of Kelly Harcourt lying on its back in the overgrown grass, just metres away from the shuffling feet of the dead.

'You can understand why she did it, can't you?' Emma asked, standing just behind her.

'Such a shame though,' Clare answered quietly, her voice disconsolate and low. 'I liked her. She was nice, much nicer than Kilgore.'

'You can't even begin to imagine what the poor girl was going through,' Emma sighed sadly. 'You just don't know how you'd react if you were in that position, do you?'

'Makes you realise how lucky you are, doesn't it?'

'Suppose so.'

'We are lucky, aren't we?'

Emma shrugged her shoulders. It was a strange question that Clare had asked. On the face of it they had survived where millions had fallen and that had to make them lucky, didn't it? But every day life seemed to be getting harder, and she couldn't help thinking that in many ways it would have been easier just to have fallen and died on the first morning. Feeling suddenly guilty for allowing herself to think so negatively, she forced herself to respond positively to Clare.

'Of course we're lucky,' she said. 'We're lucky to be here. We're lucky to have a chance of getting away from all this.'

Clare wasn't really listening. She nodded and returned her attention to looking out of the window.

'So are we just going to leave her there?' she wondered, staring at Harcourt's body on the ground. 'Shouldn't we move her or...?'

The sudden arrival of Cooper and Jackie Soames into the room interrupted the conversation. Emma quickly turned round. She could tell from the expression on both of their faces that they were far from happy.

'Has anyone seen Keele?' Soames asked, looking around the room hopefully. Her already red face seemed even redder and more flushed than usual.

Clare shook her head.

'I saw him earlier,' Emma volunteered.

'Do you know where he is now?'

'No, have you tried the...?'

She didn't bother to finish her sentence. Soames and Cooper had already turned and were walking away. Donna appeared in the doorway, blocking their way out and stopping them momentarily.

'Any luck?' Cooper asked.

'Not yet,' she replied. 'He's not here then?'

Cooper shook his head.

'He's probably hiding in the outbuildings somewhere,' Jackie Soames suggested. 'We've found him there before, the cowardly bastard.'

Soames and Cooper bustled out of the room again leaving Donna standing alone by the open door. Emma was confused.

'What the hell's going on?'

'Gary Keele's done a runner,' Donna explained. 'We can't find him.'

'Why? What's he running from?'

'Cooper wants him to try and get the plane moving.'

'And?'

'And that's it. Says he can't do it. He suffers with his nerves apparently.'

'Don't we all?'

Donna smiled.

'I hate blokes like him, I really do. They're all bloody talk and no action. Apparently he's spent the last couple of weeks making noises to some of this lot about how he's going to be the big hero and fly them all to safety. When it comes to the crunch he's bottled it.'

'But he can't have left the airfield, can he?'

'Not without getting himself ripped apart or letting a couple of thousand bodies in here he can't.'

'So what happens if they can't get him to fly the plane?' Clare asked. It was a sensible and obvious question.

'Then we'll have to try and get to the island by helicopter I suppose. Lawrence will end up making loads more flights and we'll be limited on the amount of stuff we can take over with us. We'll still get there, it'll just take a lot longer and be more complicated, that's all.'

'But what happens if we can't get…?' she began.

'We'll get there,' Donna assured her, her voice ominously lacking in conviction.

'What the hell are you doing in here?' Phil Croft asked. Smoking one of his last few precious cigarettes and walking slowly through the shadows between the empty airfield buildings, the limping doctor had stumbled across Keele sitting in the corner of a dark and musty waiting room. By chance he'd spotted him moving as he'd walked past a cobweb-covered window.

Keele didn't answer at first. He kept still, hoping the doctor would get the message and disappear. Croft's lack of movement made it obvious that he wasn't planning on going anywhere.

'I'm just trying to get some space,' Keele eventually answered, keeping his eyes fixed on the ground in front of him.

'Christ,' Croft laughed, 'the population of this country has been reduced from millions to probably less than a couple of hundred and you're trying to get some space! Bloody hell, mate, if you want space there's plenty of it out there. You don't need to hide away in here to be on your own.'

'Just piss off, will you?'

'Fine.'

Croft glanced out through the window and noticed Cooper and various other people moving from building to building. He quickly put two and two together and reached the obvious conclusion that they were looking for the man he'd just found. Out of the corner of his eye he noticed that Keele had looked up and was now watching him anxiously.

'So how long you planning to hide in here for?' the doctor asked, still looking out of the window.

'I'm not hiding, I just want to...'

'Come on, they're looking for you, aren't they?'

Keele didn't want to say anything. He forced himself to spit out an answer.

'I'm not hiding,' he mumbled again.

'Yes you are,' Croft insisted. 'So I guess what I heard someone saying last night is true, you're too scared to fly the plane.'

'I'm not scared.'

'Oh, right,' he sneered. 'So let me see if I understand what's going on here. You're sitting in the dark in the corner of this dusty shithole because you want some space, and you're not hiding from the others, you're just choosing not to let them know where you are, is that it?'

'Piss off,' Keele hissed again.

'Keele,' Croft continued, turning away from the window to face the man in the corner, 'let me just tell you something, and I want to make sure you understand what I'm saying, okay? I'm a doctor and I've spent years looking after other people and making sure they get better when they're sick. Things have changed now and if I'm completely honest, I'm not that bothered about anyone else anymore. I'm only really interested in myself and I tell you now, you'll do whatever you have to do to get us out of here or I'll break your fucking legs...'

'You don't...' Keele began to protest.

'You will fly the plane to the island because if you don't I swear I will kill you,' the doctor said in an unnervingly calm and emotionless voice. 'I haven't come this far to have my chances blown by some stupid, cowardly little fucker like you. Understand? Is that clear enough for you?'

Keele didn't respond.

Croft turned and walked out of the building, slamming the door shut behind him. Still smoking his cigarette he began the slow and painful walk back to the observation tower. He passed Donna on the way.

'Have you seen...?' she began to ask.

'He's in there,' he replied, pointing back towards the building he'd just left.

30

Richard Lawrence left Cormansey just after ten o'clock. The nine survivors who remained on the island stood at the end of the runway and watched the helicopter until its bright lights disappeared and were swallowed up by the grey morning gloom. They hoped that it would return later in the day as planned, bringing with it the plane and at least another fifteen people. Michael hoped that Emma would be one of them.

During the long watch the previous evening and early morning he had managed to convince Stayt and Fry to listen seriously to his concerns about the changing condition of the bodies. So much remained unpredictable and uncertain on the island and it seemed sensible to take action sooner rather than later. Never one for diplomacy, Michael had expressed his opinions in blunt, direct and honest terms to the rest of the small group over breakfast and, apart from some initial nervous reluctance, they had been largely receptive. Stayt had pointed out the immediate practicalities of their situation, and that had proved to be the deciding factor. There were already too many of them to shelter comfortably in the single small cottage any longer and they were going to have to expand into other properties. It made sense to try and get a decent foothold in the village now rather than spend the next few days moving unnecessarily from building to building to building. Better to get the bodies cleared away now. It would make the survivor's lives immeasurably easier.

Armed with sticks, axes, clubs and blades of varying descriptions, the small group travelled from the cottage towards the village of Danvers Lye in a convoy of two cars and the pickup truck. It seemed to make sense to use several vehicles. The truck would most probably be needed to help dispose of the piles of bodies which would inevitably be accumulated as the day progressed.

This was the first real opportunity since arriving that Michael, Talbot and Guest had had to see anything of the island. It was a bleak, barren and rocky place covered in patchy grass and bracken. The ocean was almost always in view on one side or the other and plumes of cold grey water seemed to constantly be shooting into the air as tall waves crashed against jagged rocks. Trees were few and far between and the wind howled across the weather-beaten landscape. A basic network of rudimentary roads connected the various buildings, most of which were small cottages and houses; some made of old grey stone, others more modern in appearance. There was a farm over on the southwest of the island and he'd seen a few abandoned fishing boats dotted along the shore, but other than that Michael struggled to think what the inhabitants of Cormansey might have done for a living. This land was harsh and unforgiving and life would surely have been difficult at the best of times. Perhaps it was their isolation and distance from the rest of the world that the people who had lived here had craved. Whatever the reason, he thought to himself, it hadn't done any of them any good.

Despite still wholeheartedly believing in what they were setting out to do, Michael could not help but feel a little uncomfortable, vulnerable and nervous as the village came into view. He stared at the motley collection of unkempt buildings and realised that this was, remarkably, the first time he'd ever gone out actively looking for bodies to destroy in such numbers and it wasn't a pleasant prospect. Until now his time had been spent hiding from them or defending himself against them. Although he knew the corpses would probably offer very little in the way of serious resistance, the trepidation he felt was still substantial. And he wasn't the only one who felt that way. Some of the other faces around him appeared equally unsettled and unsure.

Michael travelled in the jeep at the front of the convoy with Brigid and Harper. He was hot. The entire group had dressed themselves in boots and gloves and either boiler suits or strong waterproofs taken from the empty homes of long-dead fishermen yesterday morning. The advanced decay of the bodies had now reached such a stage that their destruction, removal and disposal was inevitably going to become a bloody, greasy and gruesome affair. The rotting shells would be ripe with disease. No-one relished the thought of close physical contact with them.

'Stop here,' he said when they were just short of the turning onto the road which ran through the heart of Danvers Lye. 'I think we're better off leaving the vehicles here. We don't want to go too far in there and find we've got ourselves cut off.'

Brigid stopped the jeep and turned off the engine. The other car pulled up behind her and the truck stopped alongside it. Quietly and nervously the survivors climbed out of their vehicles and regrouped in the middle of the road.

'So what now? Do we just go marching in there?' Harper asked. Michael shook his head.

'No, I don't think so. Maybe we should take it slow and try and clear the buildings one at a time?'

'Sounds sensible...'

'Look,' Gayle Spencer whispered. She pointed further along the street in front of them, deeper into the shadowy village. Alerted by the sound of the engines, a number of bodies had already dragged themselves out into the open and were moving towards the group with obvious intent. Harry Stayt readied his sword.

'We knew there were going to be a few like this, didn't we?' he said as he anxiously swapped the blade from hand to hand.

'We should try and flush these out,' suggested Fry.

'What?'

'All of the bodies that are still reacting like this - we should try making as much noise as we can to bring them out into the open.'

'Makes sense,' agreed Brigid. 'What have you got in mind?'

Fry ducked into the front of the pickup truck and reached across and leant on the horn. The ugly, unexpected noise echoed across the otherwise quiet island, so loud that for a moment it seemed even to silence the relentless sound of the waves crashing against the grey-stone walls of the small harbour just a couple of hundred metres ahead of them.

'I'll make a start,' Stayt muttered under his breath. He began to walk down the road to meet the gangly bodies staggering the other way, his sword gripped tightly in his hand and raised ready to strike. His stomach was churning with nerves.

'Does anyone else get the impression he enjoys this?' Harper mumbled. 'Sick bastard.'

'At least he's trying,' Spencer snapped. 'We're just stood here looking at him.'

Michael watched anxiously as the lone survivor neared the first two bodies. Like an expert swordsman (which he clearly was not) he lifted the blade above his head and swung it round in a long and surprisingly graceful arc, managing somehow to effortlessly sever the head of the nearest cadaver. The body crumbled to the ground instantly, its decapitated head thumping down onto the tarmac next to it like a rotten peach. Another flash of the blade and the second corpse was also felled, its head removed with equal speed but far less precision.

'I'm behind you, Harry,' Harper shouted as Stayt marched forward with increasing confidence. Harper jogged down the street after his sword-wielding colleague. He had visions of the other survivor thinking he was a body approaching from behind and turning round and striking out at him with his blade. Ahead of them six more dark figures now were near, and six more figures were almost instantly hacked down. Harper, Michael and Spencer began to collect up the bloody remains of Stayt's handiwork which lay scattered around the street. Moving quickly they dragged the corpses over to an area of scrub land on the other side of the road and began to pile them up.

The emaciated remains of Cormansey's most senior police officer lurched at Stayt from behind a wooden fence, knocking him off-balance momentarily. With one gloved hand he pushed the body away, sending it stumbling backwards. It tripped over the twitching torso of another dead islander and fell to the ground. Seizing the opportunity Stayt lifted his sword and chopped down at the corpse, slicing the top of its head clean off, following through and hitting the ground. He winced as the vibration of the impact of the sword on the hard tarmac travelled the length of his tired arms. Breathless he moved onto the next body and then the next and then the next, driven on by a curious combination of adrenaline and revulsion. Fry and Brigid stood together and watched from a distance, listening as Stayt's blade whistled and sliced through the cold October air.

'That's it, Harry,' Harper shouted. Suddenly aware that the clumsy movement around him had stopped, Stayt stood still and looked up and down the street. The previously unremarkable grey scene was now awash with blood and gore and fallen corpses. That seemed to be all of them for now. He couldn't see any other moving bodies.

'Can't see any more of them' Michael shouted to him. Stayt lowered his sword.

'So where are all the others?' he asked, still looking around. 'This can't be it, surely. We were expecting about a hundred of them at least.'

Michael walked over to where the other man stood, staring into the shadowy buildings on either side of the street as he moved slowly along.

'Theoretically they could be all over the island.'

'You reckon?'

Michael shook his head.

'Probably not. I think they're mostly still round here. I think they're hiding from us.'

'Really?'

'I think they're keeping out of the way because they heard us arrive and they've seen you in action with that bloody sword.'

'You've got to be kidding,' Stayt laughed. 'Are you serious? They're not hiding from us.'

Michael continued to stare into one of the nearby buildings.

'Well some of them are,' he replied, pointing into a glass-fronted shop little more than five metres away. 'Look.'

Christ, he thought, Michael was right. Stayt could see bodies gathered inside the building. They seemed almost to be cowering and trying to keep out of sight. The door to the shop was open so they weren't trapped. What the hell was going on?

'So what do we do now?'

Michael shrugged his shoulders.

'Go in and get them out I suppose. Don't see what else there is we can do.'

The two men stood in silence and looked at each other for a moment, both waiting for the other to make the first move. Michael was momentarily distracted by a sudden burst of light and noise which came from the scrubland behind them. Brigid had doused the pile of bodies with fuel and had set light to them. Bright orange flames pierced the grey gloom.

'That should drag a few more of them out into the open,' he grumbled.

'There are only a couple of them in that building over there,' Stayt said quietly, lifting his sword again and pointing across the road at a butcher's shop. He could see at least two dark figures shuffling behind the racks and displays still piled high with the remains of massively decayed and rancid, maggot-ridden meat.

'Let's just see what happens,' Michael whispered and he slowly began to walk towards the shop. Stayt followed close behind. As they neared the bodies they began to move. Unexpectedly they seemed to be retreating further back into the shadows.

'Do you think they're territorial?' he asked. Michael shook his head.

'What, you think that's what's left of the butcher and his wife?' he answered, semiseriously.

'No,' Stayt scowled, 'that's not what I meant. I just wonder if they're aware of their surroundings? Are they really just keeping out of our way or are they standing their ground? Are they just sheltering in there?'

'I don't think they're sheltering. Christ, look at them. They're dead. They're not interested in keeping warm or keeping dry. They just don't want us to...'

He stopped talking. They had reached the doorway of the shop.

'What's the matter?' Stayt asked, immediately concerned. Michael nodded deeper into the shadows.

'Look,' he whispered.

Stayt saw that the two bodies had stopped their clumsy retreat. Now they were standing their ground.

'What the hell's going on?'

'Like I said yesterday, on their own they might not be much of a threat to us anymore, but it looks like we're still a threat to them…'

'Come on, let's just get rid of them…'

'Hold on,' he snapped, grabbing hold of Stayt's arm. 'Take it easy. We've got them cornered. We don't know how they're going to react if we just…'

'I've had enough of this.'

Impatient, nervous and keen to get the job done and the village cleared, Stayt pushed past Michael, lifted his sword and forced his way into the shop. The two bodies shuffled forward slightly and then stopped.

'Careful,' Michael insisted.

Stayt wasn't listening.

'Let's just get this over and done with.'

As he marched towards the back of the shop, the nearest of the two bodies launched itself at him. Taken by surprise and unable to react in time, he impaled the creature on his outstretched sword. Oblivious, the creature grabbed hold of his shoulders and pulled itself forward, dragging itself further onto the antique weapon and forcing the blade out through the small of its back. Stunned by the speed and the savage intent of the sudden movement of the corpse, Stayt did not fully appreciate what was happening until his right hand and forearm had disappeared deep into the grotesque cadaver's decaying chest cavity. He began to gag and choke. The feel of cold, putrefying flesh was vile and the smell was overpowering.

'Get this fucking thing off me,' he wailed as he pushed the body away with his left hand and struggled to free the right. The creature was beginning to flail its arms around his face, trying to grab hold of him again. The other dark figure pushed its way past the first and rushed towards Michael. As Stayt squirmed free from his attacker and kicked the empty shell back across the room and into the window, Michael began to repeatedly punch the face of the body now attacking him. Each hard contact made the corpse's head rock back on weak shoulders before instantly rebounding and drooping forward again. Again and again he hit out, and each time the condition of the head deteriorated further. The features gradually became unrecognisable and indistinct as cold, congealed blood, dripping flesh and brittle bone were ground together. Splits in the weak and rotten skin exposed the cheek and jaw bones and Michael hoped that the continuous beating would eventually smash and mangle what remained of the despicable thing's brain as it rattled round its head. Stayt, having now pushed the first body to the ground and stamped on its head, crushing its skull, grabbed the second figure by the scruff of the neck and pulled it away from Michael.

'I'll sort it,' he said as he lifted the sword and sliced diagonally up across the face of the corpse, from below its left cheek over to just above its right ear.

As quickly as it had begun the sudden frantic activity in the shop ended. Breathing heavily through a combination of their nerves and the unexpected physical exertion, the two men stood side by side and looked down at the gruesome pile of remains at their feet.

'Answers a few questions for us, doesn't it?' Michael gasped, panting.

'Does it?'

'Think so,' he replied. 'For one thing, it proves they're not just going to give up and roll over. Those two went for us with as much force as ever. Difference was they had more about them. They had more control than usual. They were keeping out of our way then we took away their options and backed them into a corner. It was attack us or be attacked.'

'Do you really believe that?'

'Only explanation I can think of.'

'So are we going to have to go through this every time we face them now?'

'Probably.'

'We should tell the others.'

Stayt turned and ran out of the shop, leaving Michael behind continuing to stare into the bloody mess on the floor. He leant down, grabbed as many body parts as he could carry, and then dragged them out onto the street.

31

By mid-afternoon a heavy mist had again descended across Cormansey, limiting visibility. Working their way building by building through the dark shadows of Danvers Lye, the nine survivors had made good progress with their impromptu cull. The group had naturally divided themselves into three threes. Two of the trios had concentrated on emptying buildings whilst the third, with Brigid taking charge, followed behind and cleared the bodies, picking them up from where they had been dumped unceremoniously in the street and driving them back in the truck to the roaring fire still burning at the entrance to the village.

Michael, Stayt and Peter Guest had reached one of the larger and more modern buildings three-quarters of the way along the otherwise relatively quaint and traditional street. An unusual but practical combination of village stores, post office, gift shop, hardware store and supermarket, the shop had almost certainly been one of the focal points of the island's small community before it had been devastated and torn apart. And just before nine o'clock on the first morning of the disaster some eight weeks ago the shop had clearly been a busy place. Michael stood and leant against the cold glass and peered into the gloomy building. He could see numerous corpses on the ground. He could see several others moving nearby.

'What's in there?' Guest asked, trying to look over his shoulder without getting too close.

'There are a few of them in there,' he replied, his face pressed hard against the dirty window. 'I can see them hovering around the back.'

Stayt tried the door. He pushed it open slightly but it was jammed. The slender opening he had managed to force allowed the germ-ridden stench of decay to seep out like a billowing, noxious cloud. He turned his head away in disgust at the sickly-sweet and overpowering smell of death which suddenly filled his nostrils.

'Fucking hell,' he complained, screwing up his face.

'Well what do you expect?' Michael asked, continuing to stare into the dark building. 'Christ, that door's not been opened for over two months. It's full of bodies in there.'

'The light's fading,' grumbled Guest, stating the blatantly obvious. 'We need to get a move on.'

Michael cursed under his breath. He was already finding it difficult trying to see what was happening inside the shop. The place was fairly large and he wanted to try and get a basic appreciation of the general layout before they risked going inside.

'Pete,' he said, turning round to face the other man, 'do me a favour will you and go and bring one of the cars over here.'

Glad to have been given something relatively easy and safe to do, Guest jogged back to where they'd left the cars. The keys had been left in the ignition of an old but well-maintained silver hatchback which Gayle Spencer usually drove. He climbed in and started the engine and then moved slowly through the misty rain until he was level again with the building where Michael and Stayt were waiting. Under instruction from Michael, in a few clumsy movements he managed to turn the car around through almost ninety degrees, leaving the lights shining into the shop on full-beam. Michael pressed his face against the glass again. Because of the dirt and dust much of the light was immediately reflected back but there was some improvement.

'Better?' Stayt asked, also trying to see inside.

'A little,' Michael answered. 'I can see at least six bodies moving, but I think there are more. I can't be sure.'

'Where?'

'Right at the back. Bloody things are doing a good job of keeping themselves out of sight again.'

As he spoke a single corpse slammed against the glass and began to smash its fists against it furiously. Surprised, Michael tripped back and caught his breath, his heart thumping furiously in his chest. The sound the creature made was curious and unexpected. One hand thumped against the glass like mouldy fruit, leaving a greasy residue behind. The flesh on the other hand had deteriorated away to nothing leaving bare bone to clatter against the window.

'Come on,' Stayt muttered as he watched the pitiful figure, 'let's get this done.' Michael nodded in agreement and the sword-wielding survivor immediately began to push and shove the door again. It was blocked by the withered husk of a body and an overturned shopping trolley. With its hinges stiffened after weeks without use, it eventually took the full strength of both men to be able to force a large enough opening for Stayt to squeeze through the gap and get inside. Looking anxiously over his shoulder into the darkness behind he worked quickly to clear the blockage and let the others in.

Each of them holding a makeshift weapon at their side, the three men stood just inside the entrance to the shop, illuminated from behind by the headlights of the car. The body near to the window began to noisily clatter and trip towards them. Grabbing its diseased head in one gloved hand, Michael pushed the loathsome figure away and rammed it up against the nearest wall, managing to wedge it awkwardly between a tall drinks dispenser and a metal magazine stand. He plunged the end of an already bloody crowbar he'd been carrying all afternoon into the body's left temple, pulled it quickly out again, and then watched as the corpse slid clumsily to the ground. Suddenly breathless he returned to the other two, wiping the crowbar clean on the back of his boiler suit trousers.

'Just look at this, will you?' Peter Guest whispered nervously. He nodded deeper into the darkness at the other end of the wide, rectangular shop. The far end of the building seemed to be full of constant, shuffling movement. In the half-light it was impossible to be sure how many bodies they now faced.

'So what do you suggest?' Stayt wondered, wandering forward slightly. They hadn't had to deal with any more than two or three bodies at a time so far today. 'Should we just go for it and see how many of them we can get rid of or...?'

One of the bodies started moving towards him. Spurred on by the sudden movement of the first, the others began to follow.

'What the hell…?' Guest mumbled as the corpses began to stumble towards them *en masse*, moving almost like a pack and with disturbing speed. The building was filled with sudden noise as the clumsy dead collided with fixtures, fittings and each other as they dragged themselves towards the survivors.

'Spread out!' Michael yelled, concerned that he might be caught by Stayt's sword in the melee which was inevitably about to unfold. 'Spread out and hit the damn things until there's none of them left standing!'

He lifted the crowbar again and ran deeper into the building until he reached the first body coming the other way. In a single, swift arcing movement he swung the crowbar up and forced it into the creature's head, shoving it up through its chin and deep into its decaying brain. When the body became limp and stopped moving he lowered his hands and let it slide off the crowbar and onto the floor.

To Michael's right Stayt was cutting his way through the crowd with his now familiar ferocity and intent. Behind and to his left, however, Peter Guest was struggling. He'd so far managed to avoid just about all direct confrontation with the bodies but suddenly there was no escape. He carried with him a cricket bat, and he now cursed his stupid and inappropriate choice of weapon.

'What do I do?' he screamed desperately as the nearest body lashed out at him. He didn't really expect to be given an answer, but in the midst of the close-confined chaos and mayhem he got two.

'Fucking hit them!' Stayt shouted.

'And keep fucking hitting them until they stop moving,' Michael yelled in-between striking out at another two bodies. 'Just do it!'

Half closing his eyes Guest instinctively held the cricket bat as he would have done had he been in the middle of a local club match on a Sunday afternoon. Anticipating the lurching speed of the hideous body which stumbled towards him he took two steps down an imaginary wicket and swung the bat as if he was trying to hit the ball over the bowlers head towards the boundary rope. The wood connected with the underside of the creature's jaw, severing the remains of its spinal cord and practically smashing its head off its shoulders. It flew back into a freezer full of rotten, defrosted food and lay still.

More through luck than judgment, Guest eventually managed to dispose of another body. In the same short period of time Stayt had cut down four more and Michael another two. A total of thirteen of the wretched things had been destroyed.

After dragging more than twenty bodies out of the foul smelling building (including the remains of several which they'd found motionless on the ground) Michael, Stayt and Guest allowed themselves a short break. The long day's work so far had been physically and mentally exhausting. Their eyes now accustomed to the low light indoors, and with the car headlamps still providing limited illumination, they searched through the bloodied remains of the shop, picking through the wreckage as if they were high street window shoppers on a Saturday afternoon.

Michael leant against the nearest wall and flicked through the still glossy pages of a lifestyle magazine filled with pages upon pages of beautiful, immaculately presented men and women. Stupidly and pointlessly, for a second he suddenly became aware of his scruffy, blood-soaked appearance. The pictures in the magazine filled him with deep and unexpectedly bitter feelings of sadness and remorse.

'Look at this,' he mumbled to anyone who would listen, 'just look at this.'

Stayt stood nearby drinking a can of beer and eating a bar of chocolate which was only out of date by a couple of weeks.

'What?' he asked, his mouth full of food.

'All of this shit,' Michael replied, turning the magazine slightly so that Stayt could see the page he'd been looking at. It was a double-page spread of photographs from some celebrity wedding or funeral or other. He recognised some of the faces in the pictures, but he struggled for a second to remember their names or what it was they used to do.

'What about it?'

He shrugged his shoulders.

'Just hard to believe, isn't it? Hard to believe that this kind of thing used to matter. Christ, thousands of people used to buy this crap every week, now there's probably not even a thousand people left alive.'

Stayt picked his way through the rubbish to stand closer to Michael and get a better view of the pictures.

'She was beautiful, wasn't she?' he said quietly, pointing at the face of a television actress he remembered. 'I had a thing about her!'

Michael nodded.

'She's probably like that lot now,' he half-joked, nodding towards the pile of corpses in the middle of the street that Brigid and the others were still moving. 'Hey, remember this?' he asked as he flicked back a few pages to a film review section he'd just passed.

'Bloody hell, yes,' Stayt answered, his eyes darting around the spread of photographs from a long forgotten film. 'Never got round to seeing that.'

'It wasn't that good,' Michael volunteered, 'I saw it about a week before everything happened. Anyway, I bet you could still get to watch it if you wanted to. If we can get the electricity supply working here we could fetch a projector from the mainland and show as many films as we can get our hands on. We'll paint the side of one of the buildings white and we'll project against it. It'll be like a drive in, but without the cars. We'll…'

'No we won't,' Stayt sighed, shaking his tired head. 'Nice idea, mate, but it's never going to happen, is it? If we're lucky we'll get something set up so that we can watch videos or DVDs if we really want to.' He took another magazine from the rack near Michael and began to leaf through its pages. He wiped an unexpected tear away from the corner of his eye. 'Jesus,' he said quietly, 'I'd forgotten about all of this. I hadn't thought about any of it until now.'

Michael continued to look through his magazine as he pondered Stayt's words. He understood completely what the other man was saying. He couldn't vouch for Stayt, but he'd spent the last two months either running at breakneck speed or sitting still and hiding in terrified silence. This was the first time they'd been able to move around freely. This was the first time for weeks that any of them had been allowed the luxury of being able to stop and think and react and remember without having to constantly look over their shoulders in fear of the seemingly endless hordes of bodies which plagued their shattered lives.

Looking back was painful. It hurt more than any of them might have expected it to, but now that they had suddenly been allowed to remember they found it was impossible to stop. They picked through the musty contents of the shop with nostalgia and with heavy, heartbreaking sadness and grief. Two months of repressing and ignoring unhealthy, troubling, gnawing emotions had taken its toll on most if not all of the survivors, and Michael was certainly aware of the damage that had been done. For weeks the speed and magnitude of the events unfolding around him had prevented him from dwelling on the memories of everything he'd lost. Even the brief respite underground in the military bunker had been filled with enough distractions and problems to keep his mind and attention focussed only on the immediate present. Since arriving on the island, however, the pace and urgency of life seemed to have slowed down dramatically and they now had time to grieve.

On the other side of the room Peter Guest was sitting on a counter, crying. Not just sobbing or sniffing quietly to himself, he was wailing with pain, almost screaming with the sudden release of previously pent-up and suppressed emotions. Michael noticed that Tony Hyde was walking past the front of the shop. The noise which Guest was making was of such volume that it made Hyde stop and walk towards the building. Concerned, he leant inside.

'Everything okay?' he asked.

Stayt nodded. Michael walked across to Guest.

'All right, Pete?' he asked pointlessly.

Guest looked up with tears pouring down his tired face. He shook his head and looked down again. In his hands Michael saw that he was holding a small toy. He couldn't see exactly what it was. A car perhaps? Some kind of spinning top or model spaceship? Whatever it was Guest was staring at it as if it was suddenly the most important thing in the world. He wouldn't put it down. He wouldn't let it go.

It wasn't until almost an hour later that Guest had regained his composure sufficiently to be able to talk to the other survivors again. Even now, as he sat next to Michael on the bonnet of the pickup truck and stared into the mass of burning bodies a short distance away, occasional tears still dribbled down his cheeks.

'It's like when you shake a bottle of beer, isn't it?' he said suddenly.

'What is?' Michael asked, confused.

'How we're feeling,' he explained. 'I know you feel the same, I can see it in your face. I can see it in everyone's faces.'

'Still don't know what you're talking about,' the other man grumbled quietly.

'I don't know about you, but there are things that have happened to me that I haven't been able to deal with. There are things I've seen and experienced that I haven't been able to think about because they hurt too much. Things that are too painful. I've wanted to try and sort them out, but I haven't been able to do it yet.'

'So where does the bottle of beer come in?'

'I feel like everything inside me's been shaken up but my top's been screwed down tight. Until you take the top off, nothing can get out. Being here today has been like a release. I wasn't expecting it…'

'So now you're feeling…?'

'Half-empty and flat,' Guest smiled sadly.

Michael nodded thoughtfully as he considered the man's unusual, but accurate, analogy. He was beginning to understand what he was saying.

'What was the business with the toy?' he asked. He could tell from the sudden change in Guest's body language that his nerves were still raw.

'This thing?' he said, taking the toy from his pocket and staring at it again. Michael nodded. 'On the first morning,' he explained, his voice cracking with emotion, 'I was supposed to

203

go and see my lad Joe at school. It was his first class assembly...' He stopped talking when the pain became too much. Although he'd thought about him constantly, he hadn't said his son's name out loud for more than eight weeks and to suddenly hear it again hurt badly...

'What happened?' Michael pressed, sensing that although painful, it would probably help him if he finished what he was saying. 'Did everything kick off before you could get there?'

Guest shook his head.

'I wish that was it,' he sighed, clearing his throat. 'I wasn't anywhere near the school. I was on my way to work when it happened. There was a meeting I couldn't get out of and if I'd missed it I would have...'

'Would have what?'

'Would have got the sack.'

'Was that important?'

'Obviously not, but I thought it was at the time. We'd been working for weeks to close a deal. My bonus and an almost guaranteed promotion hinged on getting the papers signed at that meeting. I would have lost a hell of a lot of cash if things hadn't worked out.'

'But looking back now, was that important? What good would your bonus have been to you now?'

Guest shuffled awkwardly. He knew the answers to Michael's questions already but the admission was still not an easy one to make.

'Are you trying to make me suffer here?' he asked as he sniffed back another tear, his voice little more than a tired whisper. 'I know now that none of it really mattered. The job, the money, the car, the house - none of it. I should have given the whole fucking lot up months earlier but I thought I was doing the right thing. Saddest thing is I'd probably have done it again too. My priorities were all screwed up. I should have been there when it happened. I should have been there with my wife and my boy when they...'

'We've all got regrets,' Michael said wistfully. 'I bet everyone here could tell you at least a hundred things they wish they'd done differently. I don't think we'll ever get over it. I just hope that these feelings get easier to live with, that's all.'

'I loved Joe, you know. That kid was everything to me. Just wish I'd told him.'

'You'd only have embarrassed him,' Michael smiled. 'He wouldn't have understood.'

Guest nodded and wiped his eyes.

'Okay then, I just wish I'd been with him,' he said, correcting himself. 'I just wish I could have held him when it happened.'

The two men stared into the fire again, and for a while the cracking and popping of the flames was all that could be heard.

'So what was with the toy?' Michael asked again, remembering that his question hadn't been properly answered.

'Oh, that,' Guest replied. 'It's silly really. Joe, Jenny and I went shopping on the Sunday afternoon before it happened. We were walking around town for hours and Joe was getting tired and fed up like kids tend to do. I told him that if he behaved himself and if everything worked out at the office over the next few days then I'd get him a present when we next went out, whatever he wanted. I asked him what he'd like, expecting him to go for the biggest and most expensive thing he could think of. Anyway, he dragged his mum and me into a shop and showed us that toy I found today. It wasn't much and it wasn't expensive, but all his mates had one and I was going to get it for him. That was all he wanted. Fucking hell, Mike, I wish I could see him again. Just once more.'

32
Cooper

Progress.

This afternoon it finally feels like we're starting to get somewhere. Things are finally beginning to move. Lawrence has made it back with the helicopter and, even more importantly, we've managed to get somewhere with the plane. We're not airborne yet, but at least Keele's starting to cooperate. I didn't have to say much to him myself, but I heard that there were a few others who threatened him if he refused to fly them out of here.

We've started to move the people and our equipment out of the observation tower. It'll all have to come down eventually so it makes sense to start shifting it now. We're using the small office block nearest to the hangar. There are only a few rooms and it's less comfortable and protected than the tower, but it will do. We should only need to use it for a couple of days, perhaps a week at most.

Keele's finally managed to get the plane out of the hangar now. Actually getting him behind the controls was the biggest step as far as I'm concerned. Now we know that the plane's engine still runs and by moving it to the end of the runway he's got everyone off his back for a while. I can see him sitting in the cockpit from out here. He's looking round like a little kid lost. I know he's not had much experience at flying anything like this before but he has to try. We don't have any choice. As vulnerable and exposed as it leaves us, we're depending on him. I told him that all he has to do is get the plane in the air, get us over there and then land the damn thing. Doesn't matter if it's a complete write-off once we've all made it over to Cormansey. He just has to get us there safely. A couple of crossings, three at the most, is all it will probably take. After that he'll never have to fly again if he doesn't want to. We won't ever be coming back here.

The atmosphere here is still surprisingly positive, if a little muted and more apprehensive than before. The appearance of the plane has generated a lot of anticipation and nervous expectation today. People want to get away from here, but they're not looking forward to dealing with the trauma and uncertainty of leaving. We've been doing some calculations, trying to work out how long it's going to take us to get to the island and how many flights we're going to have to make. Lawrence is happy to keep shuttling between here and Cormansey until everyone and everything's over there. If he can make enough crossings then we can limit Keele to only having to make two flights, although he probably will need to do three. We've got more than enough fuel so time is the only issue. There are fifty of us here now, including the two pilots. The helicopter can carry three - four at a push - passengers at a time. If things go our way we could be out of here in a couple of days but I'm under no illusions. It's been a long time since anything has gone our way.

Baxter said something earlier that's been troubling me. He's been watching the bodies with Croft and they think their behaviour is beginning to change again. The pair of them have been walking up and down the runway because Croft's been trying to exercise his leg. He told me that at one point they just kept walking and didn't realise how far they'd gone until they were close to the perimeter fence. Some of the bodies, he said, continued to react like they always had done, fighting and ripping at each other. Some of them pushed themselves against the fence and tried to get closer to them. It's the others that really concern me. He told me that some of them were just standing there looking at him. He said he felt like he was being watched. A few minutes ago Richard Lawrence told me that they'd seen something similar happening on Cormansey. Apparently there some of the bodies have been keeping their distance from our people, almost hiding from them. There's nowhere for them to go here. They're stuck out here in the middle of nowhere with hundreds more of the bloody things behind them, pushing them closer.

I don't know what this means.

Are the bodies finally about to give up and drop, or is this the beginning of something worse?

We've drawn lots to decide who goes first.

The plane and the helicopter will leave here early tomorrow morning.

The sooner we get away from this place the better.

33

In the frustratingly low light of early evening Jackie Soames was trying unsuccessfully to coordinate the emptying of the observation tower and the movement of anything useful down into the office building below.

'So what's the plan?' Emma asked, returning to the observation tower from outside. She'd watched Keele move the plane from the hangar to the runway earlier and, despite the damp conditions and low temperature, had stayed out there, enjoying the relative freedom and the fresh air. The activity over the last few hours seemed to suggest that things were finally about to start happening and she had assumed that there would be work to be done inside. She could see a few people moving around the room with an apparent purpose, but she could also see many, many more sitting still and staring into space as they always did. Much as she understood their continuing pain and could sympathise with them to an extent, she questioned how long their malaise would last? No matter how bleak or desperate things seemed, they all had to try and face up to what was left of reality sooner or later, didn't they?

'There is no plan,' Jackie replied dejectedly. 'I just thought it would be sensible to get as much stuff out of here as we could before morning.'

'So what exactly do we need to take? Do you know what's already on the island?'

'Not sure.'

'Didn't someone say there used to be about five hundred people living there?'

'Yes.'

'Then there's going to be plenty of clothing and beds and houses and the like, isn't there?'

'Suppose so.'

'So all we really need to take with us from here is any food we've got and any specialist stuff that we know we won't find over there. I don't think there's going to be very much.'

Jackie nodded.

'I know,' she admitted. She looked at Emma and managed half a smile. 'You're right. I suppose I'm just trying to keep myself occupied, that's all. I don't know about you, but I can't stand all this bloody waiting around. It's really starting to get to me. I just want to get on, get things done and get out of here now.'

Emma agreed.

'We've all done more than enough waiting around,' she sighed.

Realising that it was pointless trying to motivate herself or anyone else at the end of the dying day, Jackie sat down heavily. Emma pulled up a chair and sat down next to her. She thought the large, red-faced woman looked unusually troubled. Perhaps it was just tiredness.

'What's on your mind?' she asked.

Jackie shrugged her shoulders and lit a cigarette. She only had a couple left in the box she carried with her. The one she'd just put in her mouth had already been half-smoked.

'This just about sums it up,' she said as she blew out a match.

'What does?'

'These bloody cigarettes.'

'I don't understand.'

'I ran a pub,' Jackie explained, taking a deep, tired breath. 'I used to smoke like a bloody chimney. I used to like having a good time first then worrying about it afterwards. Now I'm down to my last box of cigarettes and I'm hoping there's going to be some on this bloody island when I get there because the last thing I want to do now is give up. I can think of at least another four or five smokers in here and my guess is that none of them want to give up either. Bloody hell, I want to smoke more than ever now.'

'What point are you making?'

Jackie didn't give Emma a direct answer. She knew she wasn't making much sense but she didn't care.

'And drinking,' she continued. 'I never used to get a hangover because I'd never stop drinking. I used to drink every day but there's hardly a drop of alcohol left here now. Christ, I've practically been going through cold turkey for the last couple of weeks and I've bloody well had enough of it.'

'I still don't understand.'

Jackie laughed sadly to herself, shook her head and looked down. She flicked ash from the end of her cigarette and watched as it fluttered down onto the tiled floor.

'Sometimes,' she said, 'I really have to think hard to try and find a reason for why we're bothering to do all of this. You and Michael have got each other and you're bloody lucky because that's more than the rest of us have got. From now on everything we ever want or need we're going to have to fight for. And okay, the bodies might eventually disappear, but we're still going to be out on our own, aren't we? We're still going to have to become self-sufficient for Christ's sake! Bloody hell, I've never been self-sufficient in my life! I've never had anything handed to me on a plate, but I've always been able to go out and get what I want, just about whenever I've wanted it. It's all different now. I'm never going to be able to nip down to the shops to get myself a packet of cigarettes or a bottle of gin again, am I?'

'No.'

Emma looked deep into Jackie's tired face but she couldn't think of anything else to say. She was right, but there was nothing anyone could do about it. Jackie sensed her unease.

'Sorry, Emma,' she mumbled apologetically, 'I didn't mean to go off on one like that.'

'That's okay,' she insisted. 'Really, I understand how you're feeling but…'

'Thing is,' she interrupted, 'I know how lucky I am to still be here and to still be in one piece, but sometimes that's not enough. I can handle this most of the time, but now and then I just want my life back.'

34

Wrapped up in a thick winter coat to protect him from the cold and wearing a baseball cap to keep off the intermittent rain, Michael sat on a low stone wall in the darkness and stared into the distance. He was alone, and at that moment that was just how he wanted to be. The only person he wanted to share his company with tonight was miles away. He'd left the eight other survivors celebrating their day's work and drinking themselves stupid in the dank, dusty and shadow-filled lounge of The Fox, Cormansey's only public house.

The sound of the ocean filled the evening air. It was still refreshingly different to actually be able to hear something instead of the heavy, enforced silence he'd endured during pretty much all of the last eight weeks. The constant crashing of the waves on the beach just ahead of him was a welcome and relaxing sound.

He felt safe being out on his own tonight. Last night he wouldn't have risked being out in the open like this but today the group had worked hard to clear the village and a large number of bodies had been slaughtered and accounted for. From where he was sitting he could still see the bright glow of the huge pyre they'd lit just outside the main part of Danvers Lye. If there were any other bodies nearby tonight (and he guessed that there probably would be) then he knew they would most likely be few and far between and he'd be able to deal with them quickly and easily. In readiness his trusty crowbar remained slung at his side.

Keen to escape from the dead village, Michael had chosen to walk down the twisting coastal road which led back towards the other end of the island. Getting cold, he jumped up from the stone wall where he'd been sitting for the last ten minutes and ambled down towards the sea, his feet grinding noisily into the shingle shore as he neared the ocean. The crashing waves were soon loud enough to drown out the sound of his heavy footsteps.

He'd been busy and preoccupied all day but, now that he'd finally stopped working, he'd again found himself plagued by dark and painful thoughts. Most prevalent in his mind was Emma and the sudden physical gulf which remained between the two of them. Why the hell had he left her on the mainland? Couldn't she have come over to Cormansey with him? She would have been more use than bloody Danny Talbot. Michael had nothing against Talbot but he was young and immature and he'd been of very little help when the group had been clearing the village earlier. Emma, on the other hand, was far more experienced. She had guts and she had strength and when it came to the crunch she wasn't afraid to do whatever she had to do to survive. Looking back now and thinking about some of the survivors sitting in the pub down the road, he decided that some of them seemed to have been chosen to come to the island just because they fitted the stereotypical impression of the kind of person who should have been prepared to fight and clear the land; young, fit and male. A tragic shame, thought Michael, that even now after all that had happened, he and his fellow survivors seemed content to measure themselves and each other according to standards which were once given importance in a society that was long gone.

Michael walked further along the beach. Unlike most of the coastline of Cormansey that he'd seen so far, the shingle here was even and flat and was interrupted by only the occasional large rock. The wreck of a fishing boat had been washed up onto the shore near to where he was walking. He had no way of knowing whether this was a vessel which had originally set sail from Cormansey or whether it had simply drifted and crashed into the rocks here by chance. Wherever it had come from, it had ended its days stranded here on the beach, lying over on one side like a dead whale. As he approached Michael saw that the captain of the boat (if that was who it had been) was still trapped on board. Caught up in rusted winch machinery, the body was particularly badly deteriorated, almost skeletal, no doubt because of its exposure to the harsh and relentless ocean conditions.

Almost all of the visible flesh had been stripped away, washed away by the salty sea water and leaving yellow-white bone exposed beneath.

Months ago the discovery of a body such as the one Michael had found would have mattered and the lives of many people would have been affected by the repercussions of the death and the wreck. Today it didn't mean anything to anyone. Michael pitied the poor sod who had died. It again made him realise just how most of what he had once considered important now counted for nothing. A dead body washing up on a beach would have been headline news in the days before the world had been turned upside down. Now Michael casually walked past it as if it was nothing more than an unimportant piece of driftwood. It was getting harder to remember that all of these bodies had each been someone once. Someone with a life, a name, a history and a personality.

Having previously been forced by circumstance to forget about the past, the change of surroundings and the events of the day now ending had unexpectedly revealed a weakness in Michael's armour. He wasn't alone - most of the others had felt it too. A subconscious refusal to think about the past had until today remained a key defence for many of the survivors. The unprepared men and women on the island, however, had suddenly been given an opportunity to look back and remember what had gone and what they had lost. As a result uneasy comparisons between the past and what remained today were now being made with unhealthy regularity. Looking back was a bloody hard and painful experience. As Michael ambled further down the beach, the driving wind whipping up off the ocean and gusting furiously into his face, he thought about the life he had lived before this nightmare had begun. He thought about the casual approach he had taken to his life and how nothing much had ever seemed to bother him. He thought about how, like everyone else, he'd always taken pretty much everything for granted. He thought about his family and friends. He thought about his home. He pictured his house in his mind as he'd left it, and then tried to drag that image into the present. He pictured the street where he used to live, now overrun with mould, weeds and decay, the pavements littered with the remains of people he used to know.

As the shingle gave way to larger, jagged and more dangerous rocks, Michael found himself turning his attention to the more immediate past. He remembered the early days and finding the farmhouse with Emma and Carl. Christ, they should have done better there. He should have been stronger. They'd let themselves down and had made themselves vulnerable. But then, he thought, if the farmhouse hadn't been surrounded and lost when it had been, surely it would have happened eventually? He thought about the military base and what had happened there, how somewhere which had apparently been so safe, strong and secure could also have been exposed and compromised so quickly and disastrously. Would the island prove to be any safer? He had to believe that it would be. In principle the dangers here were less, but these days the gulf between predictions and reality often proved to be unexpected and immense.

All he wanted was security and shelter. A quiet, simple life with his basic needs satisfied. A roof over his head and Emma by his side was all that it boiled down to.

35

Just after six o'clock the following morning, Gary Keele stood between two of the smaller buildings on the airfield, out of sight of the numerous survivors who were now moving between the observation tower, the office building and the helicopter and plane. This time he wasn't hiding from them, he just didn't want the others to see him. He was literally sick with nerves. He'd already thrown up twice and the sudden cramps in his gut seemed to indicate that he was about to vomit for a third time. He hadn't eaten anything since late yesterday evening and his stomach was empty, but the thought of flying the plane instantly made the bile rise in his throat again.

His legs shaking, Keele crouched down and spat into the overgrown grass and weeds at his feet, trying to clear the sour, stinging taste of vomit from his mouth. This was stupid, he thought to himself. He had literally hundreds of flying hours under his belt, so why was he so worked up about making this flight now? If anything, flying to the island should have been easier than most of his previous flights - apart from the helicopter piloted by Lawrence the skies were otherwise empty. Was it the responsibility of carrying so many passengers and having them relying completely on him that was causing his nerves? That could well have been the reason. In his job as a tug plane pilot at a gliding centre he'd previously almost always flown alone and had no-one's safety to worry about but his own. Or was it because he'd been in the air when the disease had first struck that he now found the thought of flying so hard? On the first morning he'd been tugging the fourth out of five gliders into the air when they'd started falling out of the sky around him.

Get a fucking grip, he thought to himself, forcing himself to stand upright again. Suddenly determined he took a deep breath and marched to the edge of the building but then stopped the moment the plane came back into view. He pushed himself flat against the nearest wall, a cold, nervous sweat prickling his brow once again. He had to do this. He had to make himself do this. He knew he didn't have any choice. Never mind the rest of them, if he didn't get in that bloody plane and fly it then he was stuck at the airfield too.

'Finally, here he is,' Richard Lawrence grinned as Keele walked purposefully past him and towards the plane. 'You feeling all right, Tuggie?'

Keele didn't hear him, concentrating instead on trying to rise above his fear and focussing on the task ahead. Lawrence looked over at Cooper and shrugged his shoulders.

'Don't knock it,' Cooper whispered, 'at least he's here. As long as he gets that bloody plane up in the air I don't care what state he's in.'

The two men stood and watched as Keele climbed into the cockpit of the plane and began to nervously run through his series of pre-take-off checks. In the back of the aircraft twelve equally nervous survivors sat strapped in their seats, surrounded (as they had been for more than half an hour now) by all the bags and boxes of useful supplies the group had been able to safely cram inside. Five more people, Donna and Clare included, emerged from the office building. With her arm wrapped around the shoulder of Dean McFarlane, the youngest survivor at only eight years of age, Clare made her way over to the plane.

'You make sure you don't do anything stupid when you get there,' Jack Baxter shouted to her from where he stood next to Cooper at the edge of the runway.

'I won't, don't worry,' she smiled as she buckled up her safety belt. She glanced across at him nervously. 'I'll send you a postcard. Let you know what the place is like!'

'Don't bother,' Baxter grinned, taking a couple of steps forward so that he could be sure she was safely strapped in. 'We're all planning on being over there with you in a few days time. I'll be with you before the postcard gets here!'

Keele emerged from the cockpit of the plane. He climbed out onto the runway again and looked up and down the length of the aircraft and then up into the sky, obviously psyching himself up for the flight. Richard Lawrence turned and spoke to Donna who was stood nearby, watching anxiously.

'Looks like we're ready,' he said, taking hold of her arm and gently ushering her forward. 'Go get yourself on board.'

Donna nodded and made her way over to the helicopter where three other survivors were waiting. Cooper watched her as she walked away.

'Think this lot are going to be okay?' he asked.

Lawrence nodded.

'Should be,' he replied. 'I reckon as soon as Keele's up there he'll start to get his nerve back.'

'Either that or he'll go to pieces. What if he loses it?'

'Then it'll be a short flight, won't it? And I'll end up spending the next week flying backwards and forwards between this hole and the frigging island.'

Keele was walking towards them.

'Ready?' Cooper asked.

'Suppose so,' he replied, his voice sounding less than certain.

'You know the route, don't you, Keele?' Lawrence checked. Better to be safe than sorry.

'Think so.'

'You shouldn't have any trouble finding the place. If the worst comes to the worst just head for the east coast and then follow it up north until you find the island. You'll see the smoke and the people and they'll see you before you can...'

'I know,' Keele interrupted, 'you already told me.'

Cooper and Lawrence exchanged quick glances. Both were still dubious about the pilot's mental condition and his ability to fly.

'Get going,' Cooper urged. Keele jogged back to the plane.

'We should be back later today,' Lawrence shouted over his shoulder as he walked towards the helicopter. He stopped and turned around to face Cooper and Baxter. 'I'm aiming to be back here by mid-afternoon. Just do me a favour and make sure that everyone's ready to do this again first thing tomorrow. I want to get this done quickly, okay?'

'Okay,' he replied.

Baxter and Cooper, suddenly the only two survivors remaining out in the open, moved away from the runway as first Lawrence and then Keele started the engines of their respective aircraft. A sudden increase in wind and noise accompanied the take-off of the helicopter which rose up and then gently circled the airfield, driving the rotting masses beyond the perimeter fence into a violent frenzy. Keele began to taxi down the runway and then increased his speed. Lawrence hovered high above the ground and watched as the other pilot cautiously coaxed the plane off the ground and lifted it into the air. A few nervous rabbit hops and then it climbed quickly and powerfully towards the grey cloud.

At the edge of the airfield the body of Kelly Harcourt began to move.

The dead soldier had lain motionless where she'd fallen for two days through the wind and rain and darkness. Now, beginning deep inside the paralysed brain of the corpse, and showing itself first at the very tips of its cold and lifeless fingers, the change was starting to happen.

It spread along the body, the movement building gradually until its dead, clouded eyes flickered slowly open and its torso and clumsy arms and legs became animated again. With awkward, involuntary and uncoordinated movements the body hauled itself up onto all fours and then stood and began to stumble forward and then to walk. Gravity and the uneven lie of the land were the only factors which affected the random direction which the dead soldier took. It tripped through the long grass and kept moving until it clattered into the border fence.

In common with the basic reactions of the thousands upon thousands of other bodies which had previously dragged themselves up from the ground and begun to move in this way, the shell that had once been Harcourt turned and tried to walk away. But it couldn't move. It was trapped, held tightly from behind by the grabbing hands of numerous rotting bodies on the other side of the fence. Already agitated by the noise of the plane and the helicopter flying low overhead minutes earlier, the resurrection of the dead soldier had provoked more basic, brutal reactions. The most dexterous of the vicious creatures managed to poke their decaying fingers through the wire mesh and held onto the cadaver's hair, clothing and whatever else they could grab onto. The bodies pulled relentlessly at Harcourt's remains, trying hopelessly to drag them back through the fence, not understanding that the wire barrier was stopping them. Eventually the numb fingers lost their grip and slipped away, allowing the corpse to stumble off again in the opposite direction.

On the other side of the fence, just to the right of where Harcourt's body had been momentarily trapped, another body was reacting in a different way. Eight weeks ago this creature had been a young, intelligent and attractive clothing store manager with a bright future ahead of it. Now it was a mud-splattered, half-naked, emaciated collection of brittle bone and rotting flesh. Unlike the majority of the huge, seething crowd, however, this one was beginning to exhibit signs of real control and determination. Unlike those which simply stood there vacantly or those which ripped and tore at the other corpses immediately around them, this body was beginning to think. Pressed hard against the fence and surrounded by many thousands of creatures on either side and a similar number behind, it knew that it needed to move to survive. On the other side of the mesh it could just about make out the dark blur of Harcourt's body tripping away with relative freedom and it decided that was what it needed to do. It grabbed the wire with cold, bony hands and began to shake it. Other bodies began to do the same.

36

With Danvers Lye now almost completely cleared and the majority of Cormansey's dead population destroyed, the group on the island set about moving from building to building, removing the last remaining corpses and beginning to try and clean and disinfect the various isolated houses and other buildings which were dotted around the bleak landscape.

Michael, Danny Talbot and Bruce Fry had taken the jeep down to the southernmost tip of the island and were beginning to slowly make their way back north along the simple road network. They had cleared and emptied one house already and were now getting ready to start work on the second. In comparison to the gloom of the previous day this morning was bright, dry and relatively warm. Conditions were good and they could see the next building from a fair distance away as they approached. Its red-bricked frontage contrasted obviously and starkly with the rest of the predominantly green, brown and grey land surrounding.

Michael stopped the jeep outside the house. The three men crossed the road and walked the short length of the garden path up to the front door. They paused, partly because they wanted to assess the situation before they barged inside, partly because they were apprehensive about what they might find there. It didn't matter how many corpses they had previously found and disposed of, each new discovery was different to the last and was almost always unsettling. Michael found it especially difficult dealing with those bodies he found in their own homes. Perhaps it was because the corpses they came across in the streets had a peculiar anonymity and detachment from their surroundings. Conversely, when he came across a body which had died in its own environment and surrounded by its own belongings, he instinctively tried to piece together the details of their lives before they had been so brutally cut down. Seeing what these people had once been made it immeasurably more difficult to think of them just as lumps of cold, dead flesh. Whatever the reason for his feelings, they left him uncomfortable and nervous.

'Listen,' he whispered as they stood at the door. Talbot moved a little closer. They could hear something moving inside the house. They'd always known they'd find many places like this. The germ had originally attacked so quickly and so early in the morning that they had always expected to find the occasional building where the occupants had been trapped inside when it had caught and killed them. Fry peered through the windows at the front of the building, first the kitchen and then the living room. He could see the remains of a motionless body lying on the ground next to an armchair. He could also see shadows and faint signs of movement in the doorway. If it was a corpse moving through the house, then it was in the hallway, no doubt attracted there by the sudden noisy arrival of the three survivors at the front of the building.

'Can't see a lot, Mike,' Fry said from a short distance away. 'Might as well just go for it.'

Michael pushed the door and it opened inwards with ease. Instinctively he took a step back as the single moving occupant of the house shuffled and tripped out of the shadows and lurched towards him. His heart sank. This was one of those devastating occasions when he found it impossible to think of the bodies as objects. Sometimes the scale of the tragedy still took him by surprise. Sometimes it still hurt. He stood to one side as the emaciated remains of a small child stumbled towards him. Half his height, the poor kid could only have been five or six when they'd died. The deterioration of the body was such that he wasn't even sure whether it had been a boy or a girl. It continued to move closer with the familiar awkward gait and pointless intent of the dead. It fixed him with its cold, vacant eyes. Funny, he thought, how death had stripped away all individuality from the remains of the population. This thing looked and behaved no differently to the bodies which were twice its size and many more years older.

Danny Talbot stepped forward and, with a sudden grunt of effort, chopped angrily at the body's slender neck with a hand axe. It took five good, hard swipes before the head and spinal cord had been sufficiently damaged to stop the corpse from moving. It fell at Michael's feet and he knelt down next to it.

'Okay?' asked Fry.

Michael nodded. Holding his breath and trying hard to ignore the suffocating smell of the insect-infested body, he picked it up in gloved hands and carried it gently out of the garden and over to the roadside. He placed it down on the grass verge as they'd agreed with the others. Their job today was purely to concentrate on emptying the properties. Others would drive around the island again later, pick up all the bodies in the truck and transport them to a single disposal point. That was all this poor child had left now, he thought sadly as he stared into what was left of its face. No school. No adolescence. No first kiss. No leaving home. No getting a job. No successes. No failures. Nothing.

By the time Michael had stood up again and turned round Fry and Talbot had already disappeared inside. He followed them indoors.

'Anything else in here?' he asked. The smell in the house was typically obnoxious and overpowering.

'Just this one, I think,' answered Fry. He was pointing into the living room at the body on the carpet that he'd seen from outside. Talbot could be heard upstairs checking out the bedrooms. A few seconds later and he came crashing back down, his face flushed red with the sudden effort.

'Clear,' he gasped.

Fry grabbed hold of the bony wrists of the corpse in the living room and dragged it out into the hall. Presumably the mother of the dead child, it had been comparatively well preserved having been maintained in a dry and relatively constant environment. It left behind a dark and sticky stain of decomposition on the dust-covered carpet.

The cold, echoing house was modest and traditional and in many ways it reminded Michael of Penn Farm. The way Fry was disposing of the cadaver was also reminiscent of the way that he and Carl Henshawe had removed the remains of the farmer

Arthur Jones from the farmhouse living room several weeks earlier. The musty smell and lack of fresh air gave the building an antique, museum-like atmosphere.

'You sure you're okay?' Fry mumbled as he came back indoors after dumping the body on the grass verge by the road. 'You seem miles away this morning.'

Michael was still standing in the hallway, looking around at the interior of the house.

'I'm fine,' he replied quickly. Fry had picked up on the fact that Michael seemed distant and preoccupied but, until that moment when it had been pointed out to him, he'd been oblivious to it himself. He did feel different today though, there was no denying it. As well as continuing to worry constantly about Emma and the other survivors back on the mainland, he was also having to contend with a bewildering combination of a number of other unexpected emotions. He felt a strange and unpleasant sense of anti-climax - almost disappointment - and he couldn't initially understand why. He wondered whether it was because he was gradually becoming aware of the limitations of the island. As safe and protected a place as it would no doubt eventually prove to be, he could also see it becoming a restricted and stifling environment. Their isolation and remote location would inevitably make it difficult for them to grow and expand their small community easily. It was already obvious that Cormansey was not going to be the haven that he and the others had naively dreamed it would be. Nothing was going to be easy here, that much was for sure. Michael wondered whether it was what had happened yesterday that was making today so difficult? Was it because he'd suddenly had to face up to aspects of the life he'd lost that was now causing him to feel so much confusion and doubt?

Their brief this morning had been simply to clear the bodies from the homes they visited. Looking around this particular small and unimposing property, however, it was obvious that there was going to be much more work to do to make each building inhabitable again. In the kitchen Michael found that the fridge and cupboards were filled with rotten food. Dust, mould and decay was everywhere. Nothing was salvageable. There were numerous traces of insect and rodent infestations. Some of the taps and the pipe work running through the house were exhibiting signs of severe corrosion. An open window in one of the bedrooms, as well as letting in a supply of relatively fresh air, had also allowed several nesting birds and two month's worth of rainwater into the room. Damp was spreading across the bedroom walls.

The implications of what he saw around him, although he chose not to share them with the others, were immense and humbling in their scale. What he saw today was a world slowly being reclaimed. No doubt the arrival of the survivors on Cormansey would prolong the life and usefulness of this building and others on the island but elsewhere, back on the mainland, the process of decay and deterioration would continue unchecked. The disappearance of man from the face of the planet was inevitably going to cause a massive change and imbalance to the ecosystem. Crops would no longer be grown or harvested. Vermin would be allowed to breed and consume. The decay of millions of bodies would inevitably result in a huge increase in the numbers of insects, germs and disease. The ramifications were endless.

When he'd arrived on the island he'd felt strong, determined and full of hope. Today, however, those feelings had started to fade. In comparison to the almost unimaginable scale of the changes the infection had bought to the entire planet, the minor achievements of this small group of survivors meant nothing.

Unquestionably disheartened, Michael dragged himself back out to the jeep with the other two men.

'Where to next?' he asked.

'Road splits in a while,' Fry replied. 'We'll keep going west. Harper said he was sticking to the east side.'

'Okay.'

Michael sat back in the driver's seat and readied himself for the next building. He stared into the wing mirror and watched the bodies of the child and its mother for a couple of long, thoughtful seconds before turning the key in the ignition and starting the engine. He accelerated away quickly.

'Did that kid bother you?' Talbot asked from the back seat. The way he had asked his question illustrated the level of his comparative immaturity. Nevertheless Michael was surprised that he had even noticed the change in his mood.

'Everything's bothering me today,' he grunted, abruptly and honestly.

'Decent weather,' Fry said cheerfully, doing his best to lighten the increasingly dark and sombre mood. 'Just imagine what this place is going to be like in the summer. Plenty of coastline, good fishing waters...'

'Got to get through the winter first,' Talbot reminded him.

'I know, but that doesn't...'

'What's that?' Michael interrupted. He leant forward and peered up into the sky.

'What?' asked Fry.

'Up there. Look, Lawrence is back.'

He slowed the jeep and pointed up into the clear sky. The helicopter could clearly be seen now, scurrying across the deep blue like a small black spider.

'Bloody brilliant,' Fry sighed with relief. 'Some help at last. Wonder who he's brought with him? Hope it's someone who's going to pull their weight. The last thing we need here is...'

'The plane,' Talbot announced.

All eyes switched from staring at the helicopter to scouring the sky, looking for the plane. Fry spotted it first and pointed it out to Michael. It seemed to be following the exact same course the helicopter had taken. Suddenly feeling more alive and invigorated than he had done at any part of the day so far, he put his foot down and accelerated again.

'Where you going?' Fry asked as they sped past the front of the next house and carried on down the narrow road.

'Just want to see who's here,' Michael muttered, his pulse racing with sudden nervousness and anticipation.

By the time the jeep had reached the airstrip both the plane and the helicopter had already landed. The passengers were quickly being unloaded from the back of the plane. They staggered onto the tarmac strip and wandered towards Brigid and

Spencer who approached on foot from the far end of the runway. The new arrivals looked around in awe at their surroundings like tourists arriving at some long awaited and much anticipated holiday destination. Gary Keele ran in the opposite direction and stopped when he reached a patch of long grass. He bent over double, put his hands on his knees and threw up into the clump of weeds at his feet. Landing the plane had proved to be even more nerve-wracking than taking-off.

Michael stopped the jeep, jumped out and started to look around hopefully. He could see several faces that he recognised immediately. He could see Donna, Clare and Karen Chase amongst others.

There was no sign of Emma.

37

With the first sizable tranche of people now having left, the observation tower had suddenly become something of a hollow and empty place. It wasn't that anyone in particular had gone, Emma thought, it was just that where she had become used to always seeing people, she could now only see empty spaces. Several of those who had now left had done little more than sit in the same spot and wait since they'd first arrived at the airfield. It annoyed her that some of those who had done nothing to help the group had been among the first to get away. The whole day had felt disconcerting and strangely disorientating and her feelings were compounded by the fact that she didn't know if the flight had made it to the island safely. For an hour or two after they'd left she'd half-expected to look up and see Keele bringing the plane limping home, still full of survivors. She didn't have much faith in him, either as a pilot or a human being. But, come to that, she didn't have much faith in anything anymore. If she was perfectly honest with herself, the truth of the matter was that she wanted the plane back so that she could leave. She wanted to get away from this place, and she wanted to get away now, not tomorrow. Whatever had happened they would know if the pilots had been successful in a few hours time. Keele and Lawrence's plan had been to drop off their passengers and get back to the airfield as quickly as they could. They'd planned to travel there and back within the day and had been hoping to return to the mainland by three o'clock. It was already half-past one.

Emma had earlier counted just over thirty people left at the airfield. That included herself and also Kilgore, who had disappeared several hours ago and who she had last seen heading towards one of the outbuildings close to the observation tower. Exhausted, dehydrated and starving, he knew that his time was up but he didn't have the strength or the courage to be able to do what Kelly Harcourt had done. Instead he stayed where he was and festered and waited. The rest of the survivors kept their distance from him. Their most recent approaches had been met with either anger and hostility or with equally unpalatable outpourings of self-pity and grief from the weak little man. With enough confusion, disorientation and doubt of their own to contend with, the survivors did their best to forget about him. Most of them could now be found in the office building, waiting impatiently for the helicopter and plane to return.

Finding it impossible to relax and to stop thinking about Michael and the others, Emma tripped lethargically down the observation tower staircase and stepped out into the cold but bright afternoon. She found Cooper standing outside, scanning the skies and occasionally the perimeter fence with a pair of binoculars.

'See anything yet?' she asked hopefully, startling him momentarily.

'Nothing,' he mumbled. Emma watched him as he shifted his attention from the sky to closer to the ground.

'What you looking for?' she wondered.

'Nothing really,' he replied. 'Just keeping an eye on them.'

Emma shielded her eyes from the sun and looked out towards the fence herself. Without the benefit of the binoculars she could see little more than a constantly shifting and apparently unending mass of cold, dead flesh. The immense crowd didn't look any different today to how it had appeared yesterday or the day before. She soon found herself watching Cooper more than the bodies. His guard was by no means down, but his manner and his whole demeanour seemed to have undergone a subtle change since the first planeload of survivors had left for the island earlier. He now appeared more relaxed and less tense than she'd seen him before. It was as if a heavy weight had been lifted from his shoulders, and with that weight more of the final layers of military discipline and authority seemed also to have been stripped away. As more people left the mainland, so the pressure on him had seemed to lift. Although they still had a long way to go, getting the plane airborne had been a massively important achievement.

'I don't like that,' he said suddenly, focusing his attention on one particular area of fence.

'What?' Emma asked, anxiously.

'Bloody things down there look like they're trying to pull the fence down.'

'What?' she said again in disbelief. Cooper handed her the binoculars and she lifted them to her face. She quickly focussed on the fence and then scanned along to her left until she came to the section that Cooper had been watching. 'Bloody hell,' she gasped.

He was right. In the distance a tightly-packed group of figures had grabbed hold of the wire-mesh with bony, skeletal hands. Together they were pulling it towards them and then pushing it back the other way as if they were trying to work the posts out of the ground. Their coordination and success was haphazard and clumsy and appeared at first to have been gained more through luck than any other means.

'They won't do it, will they?'

Cooper shrugged his shoulders.

'Don't know,' he answered. 'I don't think they've got the strength but...'

'But...?'

'But there are bloody thousands of them out there.'

'So?'

'So, give them enough time...'

Emma looked deep into the mass of bodies again. From where she stood the entire crowd seemed to be writhing and squirming constantly.

'What do we do about them?'

'Don't think there's anything we can do,' Cooper replied, 'except what we're already doing. The number of bodies still following us around is going to cause us problems whatever happens. Anyway, we should be out of here by tomorrow. We'll just have to ride our luck until then.'

'We've been riding our luck since all of this started.'

'True, so one more day's not going to make much difference, is it? I suppose we could go down to that part of the fence, soak the bloody things in fuel and torch the lot of them if we wanted to, but what good's that going to do? It might make us feel a bit better, and it might get rid of a few hundred of them, but will it make us any safer or help us to get out of here any quicker? And if they really are starting to think logically again, then they might see what we're doing as an act of aggression and try and fight back.'

'You're joking, aren't you?' Emma asked in disbelief.

Cooper shrugged his shoulders.

'Stranger things have happened recently,' he reminded her solemnly.

Emma passed the binoculars back to him and turned and walked back to the observation tower, suddenly anxious to get back indoors. Cooper continued to look along the fence. There was another small pocket of what could almost be described as controlled activity by the main entrance gate where more bodies were pushing against the barrier. He turned and walked towards the office building in search of Jackie Soames, Phil Croft, Jack Baxter or someone else who had enough about them to keep the others in order. They needed to keep people indoors and out of sight. They couldn't risk being seen by the bodies and antagonising them unnecessarily. They needed to keep the crowds on the other side of the chain-link fence under control, and the only way they could do that was by keeping their distance.

38

Kilgore lay on a dusty sofa in a dark waiting room, closed his eyes and tried to ignore the pain. He hadn't eaten for what felt like days. He hadn't drunk anything for more than a day and a half. He felt so weak that he couldn't sit upright anymore. He couldn't even lift his arms. Everything felt heavy and leaden. He couldn't bring himself to move his head and so lay facing in one direction, staring out of the windows on the opposite side of the room. The relentless physical discomfort had been hard enough to deal with, but the mental anguish he was now having to endure was in many ways much, much worse.

Kilgore had come to the conclusion that today (or possibly tomorrow) would be his final day alive. His mouth was dry and he struggled to find enough saliva to lick his chapped lips. His head ached and all that he could hear was the sound of his own laboured, rasping breathing echoing around his facemask and the constant hum and buzz of insects which seemed, in his disorientated state, to swarm around the room like circling vultures, waiting for him to die. The end had to be close now.

Lying there and waiting for the inevitable was, bizarrely, beginning to get easier in some ways. The first hours he'd spent in this quiet little room had been long, difficult, painful and confusing. When he'd first shut himself away in here he had still been able to believe that there might have been some slight ray of hope for him. In his tired mind he'd explored every escape route and potential outcome. He'd thought about trying to get back to the underground base he'd originally come from and had made mental plans to take one of the trucks and drive back there alone. But he didn't know whether any of the vehicles had enough fuel and he didn't know how he'd get the gate open and get through the bodies and... and he could come up with a multitude of reasons why every plan he considered would be impossible to follow through. He could still have gone with the others to the island, but what would have happened to him there? He could have done what Kelly Harcourt had done and enjoyed one final breath of fresh air but he knew that he had neither the physical or mental strength to be able to take the final step and remove his mask. No matter how desperate, he couldn't bring himself to do anything like that.

Kilgore was tired. He'd had enough. He wanted it to stop now. He wanted to fall asleep and not wake up again.

He had been hallucinating since early morning, and now there seemed to have been a sudden and dramatic increase in the strength and ferocity of the freakish sights which surrounded him. About half an hour ago he thought he'd been visited by his dead mother and father and one of his teachers from school. In his confused mind the three of them had stood over him and critically discussed his general lack of progress in life. An hour before that and the room he was lying in had appeared to lose all structure and form. The ceiling above him had drooped and dripped down until it had almost touched the floor and the windows on the wall opposite had seemed to close up until they'd disappeared and the room had become dark as night.

The windows were clear again now.

Another hallucination.

He could see Kelly Harcourt in the distance.

Kilgore watched as she came closer. He could tell that it was her because she was wearing the same kind of protective suit that he still wore. He could see her long blonde hair being blown around in the wind. She didn't have her facemask on. Christ, she could breathe! For one irrational moment he forgot everything that had happened in the days leading up to today. And if she could breathe, he thought, then maybe he could too? Groaning with effort he slowly sat up and lifted his hand to his mask. Then he stopped and remembered.

Harcourt continued to come closer. She walked slowly and awkwardly with her head listing over to one side and her arms and legs appearing clumsy, unresponsive and stiff. She must have been hurt. She was dragging her right foot along the ground behind her, not even able to lift it up. And then the sun illuminated her face. A cold and lifeless mask with sunken cheeks and dark, hollowed eyes. Her mouth moved constantly as she approached, seeming to form silent words and moans. Despite his lack of strength and energy, Kilgore forced himself to stand up and walk towards her. His legs as heavy and uncoordinated as his dead colleague's, he hobbled painfully across the room and leant against the window exhausted. Seconds later Harcourt's body clattered against the other side of the glass and for a split second he stood face to face with her before the sudden noise and vibration sent him reeling backwards. Swaying unsteadily for a moment, he watched as the corpse turned and began to walk away.

Each step forward took huge amounts of effort, but Kilgore found himself instinctively trying to follow Harcourt's shell-like cadaver. He wasn't sure why; was it fear, inquisitiveness or nervousness which drove him to do it? Was it that he wanted to properly see what he might still become? He waited in the doorway for a moment to catch his breath before pushing forward again and leaving the building where he'd presumed he'd die. Just ahead of him the body continued to stagger away listlessly, silhouetted against the bright and low late afternoon sun. The sky above Kilgore, so clear and blue for much of the long day now ending, was beginning to darken and was tinged with hints of deep reds and purples and trailing wisps of clouds. Away from the horizon the moon and the first few bright stars could be seen. He followed Harcourt along the runway, past the front of the observation tower and then out towards the perimeter fence.

Kilgore stopped. He couldn't keep up. He'd not gone far but the effort of moving had already become too much to sustain. He put his hands on his knees and sucked in a long, slow mouthful of purified air. Another hallucination was beginning now. More powerful than any of the others he'd had, this one seemed to surround him and swallow him. It began with a noise. Starting quietly and initially seeming to be without direction, it quickly built to a deafening and strangely controlled roar, accompanied by a fierce and angry wind. Exhausted, his lifted his heavy, clouded head and saw the helicopter above him beginning a rapid descent. Wrong footed by the sudden distraction, his weak legs buckled and folded underneath him and he fell onto his backside. Shooting pains ran the entire length of his emaciated body and he winced with sudden agony. Just over ten metres from the perimeter fence he sat in the long grass and watched as the powerful machine hovered in the air above the heads of thousands of seething bodies. Then another sound from out of nowhere and a sudden, sweeping movement as the plane swooped over him before touching down and bouncing along the runway, finally coming to an undignified, lurching halt at the far end of the strip.

Kilgore watched from his collapsed position at the edge of the airfield as people began to emerge from the observation tower. He didn't recognise any of them anymore. They were just dark, shadowy figures now. From where he was they appeared little different to the thousands of corpses surrounding the airfield and as cold and featureless as what remained of Harcourt.

Too tired to stay sitting up, the soldier lay on his back and stared up into the darkening sky above him. The relentless noise of the helicopter changed direction and faded away.

Once he was sure that the plane had safely touched down, Lawrence began to bring the helicopter in to land. He looked down into the relentless, seething mass of diseased cadavers below as he hovered above the perimeter fence. Bloody hell, he thought, the bodies seemed more incensed and animated than he'd ever seen them before. Many ripped and tore at each other. Others were pushing against the fence being crushed, no doubt, by the weight of hundreds more corpses behind them. Many more still were standing their ground as best they could, looking up at him defiantly with cold, unblinking eyes which were filled with anger bordering on hatred. Forcing himself to look away and concentrate again, he flew towards the observation tower and the other buildings.

Cooper was waiting for him by the time he'd landed and had climbed out of the helicopter. With the rotor blades still circulating slowly above him, the pilot ducked down and walked over to the other man. Together they jogged down towards the plane. Keele was sitting in the cockpit trying to recover from the flight. He'd managed to turn the plane round to face back down the runway but he hadn't yet moved. Landing was proving to be the hardest part of flying today.

'Everything go all right?' Cooper asked as they stood and waited for Keele to move. Lawrence nodded. The airfield was suddenly silent now that the plane and helicopter were back and their engines had been switched off.

'Went like clockwork,' he replied.

'And you're both still okay for fuel?'

'Just about.'

'You've got enough to make another flight?'

'Plenty. I should have enough for a good few crossings yet, and I think Keele's got similar.'

'So we'll try and get another load over there first thing tomorrow morning, okay?'

Lawrence sighed.

'Bloody hell, mate,' he protested, 'give me a chance to get my breath back first, won't you. It's been a long day.'

'Get this lot over there and you can spend the rest of your life relaxing,' Cooper grinned.

'You all right, Richard?' a voice asked from behind the two men. They turned round to see that Jackie Soames was walking towards them from the direction of the office building where many of the other survivors still waited for their turn to leave. The relief on her tired face was clear to see.

'Fine,' Lawrence smiled.

Keele had finally composed himself enough to be able to get out of the plane. He walked along the runway towards the others, relieved that the ordeal was over for one day.

'Well done, son,' Lawrence said when he was close enough to hear. 'Told you we'd be all right, didn't I?'

Keele nodded. He was still breathing heavily and his shirt was soaked with sweat. The trauma of landing had exhausted him.

'The lad's done well,' Soames said, wrapping her arm around him and leading him back towards the buildings. 'If I still had the pub I'd buy you a drink!'

'There's a pub on Cormansey,' Keele mumbled, his voice low and tired. 'You can buy me a drink when you get there.'

The four survivors stopped outside the office building. Inside Lawrence could see many faces staring back at him expectantly. For once they seemed positive and happy faces too. A mixture of ages, classes and races all sharing a common desire to get away from this cold and dangerous place. The responsibility he shared with Keele to get these people to safety was humbling. Light from the bright orange sun setting on the horizon reflected off the glass and obscured his view of the people inside momentarily.

'Are they all okay over there?' Soames asked, distracting him.

'What?'

'The people over on the island, are they okay?' she repeated.

'Seem to be,' he replied. 'They've cleared the village and they've managed to get rid of most of the bodies. We left them emptying out houses.'

'So they'll have a place ready for me by the time I get over there?' she joked.

Lawrence shook his head sadly.

'I doubt it,' he said quietly. 'I was talking to Brigid earlier. She reckons it's going to take us weeks to get the place cleaned up.'

'Doesn't matter,' Cooper yawned, stretching his arms up into the cool evening air. 'The one thing we should have plenty of is time. Doesn't matter if it takes us weeks or months to get everything done, does it? As long as we can get hold of enough food and we're relatively comfortable then who cares how long it take us to...'

He stopped talking.

Emma had appeared in the doorway of the observation tower just a short distance away from them. Breathless from the effort of the sudden sprint downstairs, her face looked ashen with fear. Her unexpected appearance and anxious expression immediately silenced the survivor's chatter and in the empty quiet they became aware of another noise coming from a different direction. It was coming from the edge of the airfield.

'They've brought the fence down,' she said.

A moment of shock and disbelief.

'Shit,' Cooper hissed. He turned and sprinted back down the runway, instinctively concentrating his attention on the first section of the rotting crowd that had concerned him earlier in the afternoon. The light was fading quickly and long shadows made it difficult for him to clearly see what was happening from such a distance. He could see bodies spilling onto the field, tripping and trampling over a short section of fallen fence then picking themselves up and lurching towards the buildings. The sudden, deafening noise produced by the helicopter and plane had whipped the dead into a violent frenzy of terrifying proportions and the hysteria of the corpses had driven them forward with increased strength and control. Cooper could see that one of the metal posts had been pushed over until it was almost lying flat on the ground, and now the surging crowd of bodies were trampling the fence further down, their weight threatening to pull down another section of the barrier.

'Fucking things are going to tear the whole fence down,' Jack Baxter desperately shouted as he ran from the observation tower towards where Lawrence, Keele and Soames were standing and watching in numb, terrified disbelief. 'What the fucking hell are we going to do?'

'Block it,' Lawrence suggested. 'Get one of the trucks over there and block it off.'

'Where's Steve Armitage?' Emma yelled desperately. Baxter was one step ahead of her. He ran over to the office building and dragged the truck driver outside. Armitage pounded over to the truck, panting and wheezing with the sudden unexpected effort and exertion. He wasted precious seconds staring out towards the perimeter of the airfield. Already weakened by the collapse of the first, a second section of fence was now close to coming down and still more threatened to topple under the weight of the bodies surging ever forward. They were still several hundred metres away and were moving as slowly and awkwardly as ever, but already an unstoppable deluge of massive numbers of bodies was spilling onto the airfield.

'Too late for that,' Cooper screamed to Armitage as he sprinted past him and back towards the observation tower. 'Keele,' he yelled, 'get that fucking plane back in the air. Get out of here now or you'll never get it off the ground again.'

The furthest advanced of the bodies were close to reaching the end of the runway. Cooper was right. If the pilot didn't act quickly and get the plane airborne in the next few minutes, the runway would be swarming with corpses and take off would be impossible. His earlier nerves suddenly replaced by sheer bloody fear, Keele scrambled back into his still warm seat in the cockpit and restarted the engine. Phil Croft tried to usher people from the office building towards the plane but gave up when they surged forward in a terrified and desperate crowd. The breach in the fence had been visible from the back of the building and word of what had happened had spread quickly. People fought, jostled and pushed each other for position. Cooper tried to head off the crowd, using all his strength to limit the numbers climbing onto the plane. Forced to make a decision that was as selfish as it was selfless, Baxter came round behind him, pushed his way inside and pulled the door shut after him, knowing that there were already enough people on board.

'Out of my fucking way,' Jacob Flynn, a tall, obnoxious and unrefined man, screamed as the plane door closed. He threw himself at Cooper, almost knocking him to the ground. Cooper quickly regained his footing and charged back at Flynn, pushing him back towards the office building.

'Get back, you stupid bastard,' he pleaded as Flynn began to race forward again. The crowd of frightened survivors around him quickly stumbled back out of the way. 'The rest of you get back. It's too late.'

Flynn stopped and looked around. Beyond the terrified faces which surrounded him he could see the dark, scuttling shapes of the dead continuing to advance towards them. He shook his head and turned and ran back to the building behind him, knocking two survivors to the ground as he pushed past them.

Cooper banged his fists against the side of the plane and Keele began to taxi forward.

'Get back inside,' Cooper screamed again at the sea of angry and terrified faces that stared back at him, still hoping to get onto the plane. 'Stay calm and we'll all still get away from here. Get back inside.'

'Come on,' Croft begged tearfully, looking back over his shoulder and realising how close the first bodies were. He limped back towards the office building as quickly as he could move.

A short distance away Lawrence pushed Jackie Soames into the back of the helicopter before grabbing the next three nearest survivors and bundling them into the aircraft too. He jumped back into his seat, started the engine and took off. Emma watched tearfully from the door of the observation tower. She screamed something to Armitage on the other side of the runway but her words were drowned out by the roar of the plane. She watched helplessly as it powered along the concrete strip between them and lifted into the air, it's wheels missing the heads of the furthest advanced cadavers by little more than a metre.

Cooper pushed the final few survivors through the door of the office building and slammed it shut before turning and running back to the observation tower.

'Back upstairs,' he yelled to Emma and Armitage as the truck driver dragged himself across the runway and towards the observation tower, swerving around the first bodies as he did. 'Get up the fucking stairs now!'

There were corpses all around them now. Some slamming into the sides of the office building and trying hopelessly to reach the frightened group of people trapped inside, others lurching towards the observation tower. Still more of them tripped and stumbled towards Cooper as he scrambled to close the door at the base of the tower. Two lumbering cadavers slipped inside, only to find themselves face to face with the breathless Armitage who picked up a metal chair and swung it repeatedly at the pitiful creatures until they had been reduced to little more than a pile of rotten flesh and smashed bone. As

Armitage disposed of the dead, Cooper pulled the double-doors shut and secured them. The two men dragged tables from a small ground floor room and blocked the entrance.

At the top of the staircase Emma collided heavily with another body. Instinctively she scrambled around in the semi-darkness for something to destroy it with. She grabbed the corpse's leg to try and prevent it from getting away. It kicked out at her with surprising strength. The light was poor but in a slender and fading shard of daylight she caught sight of its face. It was another survivor.

'Don't,' the small, mousy woman protested. 'Please don't...'

Emma relaxed and pulled the other woman to her feet. She recognised her as Juliet Appleby, one of the silent majority who had spent their time sat still and hidden in the observation tower for as long as they'd been there. As Cooper and Armitage rushed past them both she shoved Appleby forward. The terrified, shaking woman stumbled across the room to the window directly opposite and looked down over the devastation below. The damaged fence was obscured from view by hundreds of bodies still scrambling through the gap, advancing relentlessly towards the centre of the airfield. Like an unstoppable tidal wave they surged forward. Already there were thousands of them inside the perimeter fence and, beyond them on the other side of the now useless barrier many more followed.

The airfield was lost.

Kilgore lay on the ground and looked up at the sky.

He was aware of movement all around him and sometimes on top of him.

All of the earlier noise seemed to have stopped. The plane had gone again. The helicopter had gone.

It was getting darker.

Too tired to react or fight or even to take off his facemask, he lay there as the last shards of light disappeared and the bodies trampled him into the ground.

39

'So what the fucking hell are we going to do now, Cooper?'
Steve Armitage demanded angrily.

Cooper didn't answer. He walked over to stand next to Emma
and Appleby who both continued to stare out at the desperate
scene outside. Tears of fear and frustration were flooding down
Emma's face.

'For Christ's sake,' she sobbed, 'this isn't fair. This isn't
fucking fair. We were so close to getting out of here.'

'We can still get out,' he said quietly.

'How?' she asked. 'How are we going to get past that lot?'

Emma pointed out of the window and down at the ground,
her tone and body language seeming to demand an answer.
Cooper took a few steps further forward and peered down. From
their high vantage point the apparent hopelessness of the
situation was painfully clear. They could see across the wide
expanse of the airfield. In the distance bodies continued to
stumble and trip through the now sizeable gap in the fence, their
huge numbers showing no signs of reducing. As individual
corpses entered the field, many more followed from either side
of where entrance had been forced. Following each other like a
plague of rats, the entire crowd was slowly being channelled
through the gap. In the clear but rapidly darkening sky above
them the lights of the helicopter and plane could still be seen
disappearing into the night.

'Lawrence will be back,' he said, turning away from the
window and massaging his temples. His head was aching. He
couldn't think straight.

'And what's going to happen then?' Armitage demanded. 'Do
you think those fucking things are going to stand to one side so

that he can land and pick us up? For fuck's sake, just admit it, we've had it.'

For the first time Cooper wondered whether he might be right. The ever increasing crowd of bodies spilled across the land below them like ink steadily seeping across blotting paper. They were congregating around the observation tower and the collection of nearby buildings. He moved round so that he had a better view of the small office block where the others were. By his calculations there were between ten and fifteen survivors trapped there. Jesus, they were surrounded too.

'How are we going to get them out of there?' Emma asked, peering over his shoulder.

'No idea,' he grunted.

'We have to get them out,' she continued. 'We can't just leave them there, can we? We have to…'

'Come on, Emma,' Cooper sighed. 'We're as trapped as they are. There's nothing we can do.'

'What do they want?' Juliet Appleby asked. She had gradually moved away from the window and was now standing in the middle of the room.

'Haven't you ever seen them like this before?'

'No,' she replied, shaking her head. 'I've been here for weeks. I've seen the crowds, but never anything like this. I've never been this close to so many of them. I don't know what…'

'Chances are you're going to get a lot closer to them yet,' Emma interrupted. 'And in answer to your question, I don't know what they want and neither do they. The bloody things don't know anything. They don't know who they were or what they are now. They don't know who or what we are or what they want from us. They don't know a fucking thing and all that I know is they've probably just taken away our last chance of ever getting away from here.'

'No they haven't,' Cooper snapped. 'We can still get out.'

'You keep saying that,' she yelled, sobbing again, 'but I can't see how it's going to happen.'

Dejected and demoralised she sat down heavily and put her head in her hands. Cooper continued to stare out of the window for a moment longer before turning away and looking round the room.

'They're crowding around us because we're a distraction,' he said quietly, 'and we're the only distraction come to that. They go for us because we're different. And I don't know if they do it because they want help from us or because they're scared of us or because they want to rip us to fucking pieces or…'

'It doesn't matter why they do it,' Armitage hissed, his voice strained and hoarse. 'You're right though, the only thing left for them to do is to try and get to us. They won't stop until we're gone.'

'I think,' Cooper continued, 'that all we can do for now is keep out of sight and not make a bloody sound. If they don't know we're up here then we should be okay for a while. We'll wait for Lawrence to come back.'

'Come on,' Emma protested, 'they already know we're up here. Even if just one of them knows and tries to get inside then hundreds more will copy it and will try and do the same.'

'I know.'

'So what if Lawrence does bring the helicopter back?' Armitage asked.

'When he brings the helicopter back,' Cooper corrected him, 'then we'll have to move, won't we? Until then all we can do is shut up, sit tight and wait.'

40

'Just get down, shut your fucking mouth and keep out of
sight,' Phil Croft hissed at Jacob Flynn. Croft was crouching
behind a desk. Flynn was standing in the middle of the room, in
full view of every window. He was a volatile and selfish man
who'd generally kept himself to himself for as long as he'd been
at the airfield. He was different now, desperate and frightened.
He'd been this way since the plane had left and they'd been
forced back into the office. He'd somehow allowed himself to be
left behind and it angered him. As far as he was concerned it was
every man, woman and child for themselves now, and he was
damn sure that he wasn't going to end his time trapped in this
fucking building with these stupid, frightened fucking people.

'What good is keeping out of sight, you frigging idiot?' Flynn
yelled. 'They already know we're in here for God's sake. The
only chance we've got is to open the fucking door and fight our
way out.'

'Fight your way out to where?' Croft asked. 'There's
nowhere left to go.'

One of the survivors cowering in the darkness behind Croft
let out a sudden, painful wail of fear. The doctor turned around
but he couldn't see them. From his position low on the ground,
however, he could see into several of the nearby office rooms.
Thick, angry crowds of rotting bodies stood pressed against
every window, trying to push and force their way inside. Even if
Flynn was right and they tried to make a run for it, he thought,
the sheer weight and number of cadavers outside would stop
them. Sensing that his time was running out, he dragged himself
back onto his feet and walked over to the man still standing in
the middle of the room.

'Open any of the doors,' he said quietly, his face just inches from Flynn's so that no-one else could hear, 'and this place will be full of them in seconds. You won't survive and I won't survive. Open the door and we're all dead.'

Flynn seethed with anger and stared back into the doctor's eyes. A good six inches taller than Croft, his presence was imposing and threatening. He grabbed hold of the other man by the scruff of the neck and pulled him closer.

'I want to get out of here,' he hissed. 'You've got to help me get out of here.'

'You can't,' Croft replied, struggling to keep his balance. 'The only chance we've got is to sit tight and wait.'

'Wait for what?'

He couldn't answer. Flynn let him go and he fell back onto a nearby chair, the sudden movement causing searing pain to run the length of his injured leg from ankle to hip.

'We should all get into one room,' he said, his heart racing, trying to keep calm. 'Let's get everyone together and out of the way. That'll limit what they can see of us.'

Flynn grunted agreement and looked around the dark building. He pushed open a door to his right.

'In there,' he said, gesturing into a small bathroom which contained a single cubicle and a basin. More importantly, the only window in the room was a narrow strip which was above head height. Although out of sight, the shadows and movement of the bodies outside could still occasionally be seen through the frosted glass.

A further nine survivors were cowering in the office building. Slowly and cautiously they emerged from their frantically chosen hiding places, crept towards the bathroom and slipped inside. Flynn stood at the back and shuffled further into the corner as more people joined him. The space was desperately limited. Apart from the toilet in the cubicle there wasn't room for any of them to sit or lie down. Phil Croft, the eleventh and final survivor, pushed his way inside and pulled the door shut behind him.

Someone was crying. He couldn't see who it was. It might even have been more than one person. The bodies outside were reacting to the sounds of movement made by the survivors and the volume of their moans and cries threatened to attract even more of them.

'Whoever that is, you've got to be quiet,' he whispered. He winced in pain and leant back against the door behind him. His leg was hurting again. He didn't know how long he'd be able to stay standing like this. 'Please just be quiet,' he pleaded.

He could still hear muffled crying and sniffing. Whoever it was had tried to stifle their emotions but with only limited success. Other than their cries the room had become frighteningly quiet with no-one daring to speak.

Wedged tightly up against each other and hardly able to move, the eleven desperate people stood and waited.

41

An hour and twenty minutes later the helicopter arrived over Cormansey.

'What the bloody hell's he doing back here?' Donna asked. She'd been walking down the road which ran through the middle of Danvers Lye with Michael and Karen Chase, trying to get used to her sudden freedom and enjoying the unexpected change of pace of life on the island.

'No idea,' Michael answered, immediately feeling nervous and uncertain. He stood still and watched the helicopter for a moment, its dark shape silhouetted against the evening sky.

'Well, either he didn't make it back to the airfield or they've started to bring the rest of them over here early,' Chase suggested.

'But why would they do that?' Donna mumbled to herself, trying to make sense of the situation. Realisation dawned. 'Christ, something's happened, hasn't it? Something's gone wrong.'

'Come on,' Michael said quickly, turning and running back to the jeep.

'They might have just decided to make a move tonight rather than wait for morning,' Chase continued optimistically as she ran after him and climbed into the back seat. She sensed Michael's unease and shared it wholeheartedly. 'Let's face it,' she muttered, 'if you were Keele or Lawrence and you had the energy then you'd probably want to try and get the job over and done with too.'

'So where's Keele then?' Michael asked as he started the engine and turned the vehicle round to drive towards the airstrip.

'There,' Donna replied, pointing up and to her left. She could see the lights on the plane's wings and tail flashing intermittently in the darkening sky. Michael slammed his foot down.

'Take it easy, will you?' Chase complained from the back seat as the car lurched forward. Michael didn't react. Between them they would probably have been able to come up with twenty or thirty plausible reasons why the plane and helicopter had returned to the island so soon. Until he heard otherwise from one of the pilots or their passengers, however, Michael was going to presume the worst.

Driving at speed, the jeep arrived at the airstrip before the plane. The helicopter was just touching down as Michael pulled on the brakes.

'What's happened?' he demanded as the survivors began to jump down from the back of the helicopter. He didn't recognise the first woman who emerged. She looked around the airstrip, shell-shocked, disorientated and frightened. The noise of the engine and rotor blades made it difficult for her to hear what was happening. She knew that someone was shouting at her, but she couldn't see who and she couldn't see where they were. 'What's happened?' Michael yelled again, grabbing hold of the woman's shoulders and turning her round so that she faced him. He stared desperately into her pale and bewildered face.

'Fence came down,' she gasped. Her breathing was wheezy and asthmatic. Michael relaxed his grip, realising that he was frightening her. 'Fence came down and they got in,' she repeated. 'Hundreds of them.'

Michael turned and looked at Donna who was standing directly behind him.

'Fucking hell,' she cursed.

'I think it was the noise we made when we landed back there,' Richard Lawrence explained. 'I'm sure it was. The bloody things went wild and managed to pull down part of the fence. It's been brewing for weeks. All our bloody noise today must have pushed them over the edge.'

'Did you manage to get everyone away?' Donna asked. Michael closed his eyes and dropped his head, almost too afraid to listen to the pilot's answer. He knew that there wouldn't have been room in the plane for everyone.

'We had to leave some people behind,' he admitted quietly. 'There just wasn't enough room. We'd never have been able to get off the ground if we'd brought any more over with us.'

'We'd always said we'd need another flight over after this one,' Jackie Soames said, walking around the helicopter to stand with the others.

'I'll try and get back there tomorrow,' Lawrence continued. 'Christ knows how I'm going to land with thousands of those damn things swarming all over the place though…'

The pilot's voice was drowned out by the deafening noise from the plane as it swooped down behind him. His already fragile nerves shattered by the events of the last couple of hours, Keele was struggling to keep control. His descent was too steep and too fast. The plane hit the ground and bounced back up off the runway before crashing down again, finally stopping at an awkward angle in the grass almost twenty metres over the end of the tarmac strip. After a brief pause the door opened. Keele half-jumped, half-fell down and then stumbled away as his passengers poured out after him.

'It was a fucking nightmare back there,' Jack Baxter shouted over the whipping wind as he tripped along the runway towards Michael and the others. 'Christ, we didn't have a fucking chance. The bloody things were all over us before we knew what had happened…'

Michael wasn't listening. He pushed past Baxter to get closer to the plane, having to fight his way through the stream of frightened people coming the other way. More were still climbing out onto the runway – Jean Taylor, Stephen Carter, several others – but there was no sign of Emma. He stood less than a metre from the door and watched and waited. Still more people – Sheri Newton, Jo Francis – and then the flow of survivors stopped. He moved further forward and leant inside, desperate to see her. She had to be there, didn't she? The plane was empty. Now beginning to panic he turned around again and began to run back towards the area where the frightened survivors had grouped further down the runway. Maybe he'd missed her. He must have done. She must have walked straight past him.

Donna noticed Michael approaching and tugged Richard Lawrence's arm to attract his attention.

'Where the hell is she?' he demanded. 'Where's Emma?'

Lawrence swallowed hard.

'Sorry, mate,' he began, 'she's back at the airfield. We couldn't get everyone over here without…'

'You're going back, aren't you?'

'The plane can't, there's no way we can land it there now…'

'But you're going back, aren't you?' he asked again.

'I will go back, but I don't know what I'll be able to do. I'm sorry, Mike. You don't know what it was like back there. Once they'd got past the fence there was nothing we could do. We couldn't…'

'I'll come with you,' he said, his voice suddenly sounding disturbingly flat and unemotional. 'We'll go now.'

'No, Michael,' Donna sighed. 'You can't, there's no point. We need you here to…'

'I'll come with you,' he said again, ignoring her.

Lawrence shook his head and looked away. Michael fixed him with a desperate, unblinking stare.

'Listen, mate, she's right. There isn't room. There's more than ten people left back there. If I manage to get back to them then I'm going to need all the space I can get to bring as many of them back here as I can, that's if I can get anywhere near them…'

'When are you going?'

Lawrence sighed and looked up into the sky.

'Look, I need some time, okay? Before I do anything we need to stop and think about how I'm going to…'

'Go back now.'

'I can't.'

'Why not? What's stopping you?'

'About fifty thousand dead bodies.'

'You have to go back. You can't leave them there.'

'I don't know what else I can do. It's going to take three or four trips minimum.'

251

'So you make three or four trips.'

'Come on, Mike,' Donna said softly, taking hold of his arm and trying to lead him away from the exhausted pilot. 'It's not his fault…'

He shook himself free of her and stood his ground.

'Michael,' Lawrence sighed, 'I'm not going anywhere until morning, if I go back at all. There's no point taking more of a risk than I have to by flying back at night. Just stop for a minute and think about…'

Michael wasn't listening. He stared at the pilot for a few seconds longer before simply turning away and walking into the darkness, his head filled with dark and desperate thoughts and images of Emma. Donna watched him disappear into the night, knowing that there was nothing she could do to help.

In his heart he knew that Lawrence was right. There was no way he could go back to the mainland tonight.

How could it be, he wondered as the cold wind bit into his face, that just about everyone else could be here when the one person he cared about above all others had been left behind? How could they have done that to her? How could he have allowed it to happen? He cursed himself for ever having left her and the pain he felt increased immeasurably when he pictured her back at the airfield, surrounded by bodies, hundreds of miles away from anyone who could help. The hurt increased still further when he started to consider the limited likely outcomes for Emma and the others. They might remain barricaded away and slowly starve. The bodies might get to them and… and that was a thought too dark to even consider.

He needed to be with her.

They had been apart now for two days and ten hours and his nervousness and pain increased each minute he was without her.

42

What had felt like days had probably been little more than a few hours. The eleven survivors had remained wedged into the small square room together, hardly able to move, almost too afraid to breathe. In complete, terrified silence they had stood and listened to the world outside for what had seemed a painful eternity. Nothing out there had been clear enough to be distinct, but they seemed to have been surrounded by a constant soundtrack of sounds of shuffling bodies, lumbering footsteps and clumsy, barely coordinated movements. Occasionally there were other noises too – most probably single, random corpses attacking others nearby.

Their situation was delicately poised. If they stayed like this then maybe they could last through to the morning, but what then? Croft could sense that the people around him were struggling. The physical and mental pressure seemed to be increasing almost by the second.

'Need to move,' a frightened voice said, the first person to have dared speak out loud for hours.

'Shut up,' Croft hissed under his breath at whoever it was who had broken the precious silence. The cramped confines of the office block bathroom were becoming increasingly claustrophobic and uncomfortable. What he would have given for a seat. The pain in his leg was excruciating. He didn't know how much longer he'd be able to stay standing. Someone else towards the back of the room was also close to reaching the limit of their suffering.

'I've got to move, if I don't I'll…'

'Shut up,' he snapped again, keeping his voice low. The last light of the dying day had now disappeared and the small room was swathed in a cool, inky blackness. He couldn't see who it was that was speaking. Whoever it was they had to keep quiet. They'd all done well so far. They'd managed to remain almost completely silent and somehow they'd stayed safe. The bodies seemed to have lost interest in the office and its occupants for a while. The doctor knew that it wouldn't take much to bring them back again, and even a lone voice could well prove to be enough. The entire airfield would surely have been overrun by now.

'I can't…' the voice moaned. Next to Croft another survivor whimpered pathetically, sensing the danger of their fragile situation. He could see some movement opposite him now. Was it Jacob Flynn again? Whoever it was they were shuffling forward, perhaps trying to grab hold of the person making the noise and silence them.

'Get off me!' a woman's voice yelped. Croft felt his legs weaken with nerves. Jesus, this was all they needed. Potentially they had hours left to spend in here. Everyone just had to stay calm and not panic. If they did that then maybe they still had a chance. All they had to do was…

'Jesus Christ,' he spat. Now it was the doctor's turn to break the silence as another sudden ripple of movement knocked him off his tired and unsteady legs and sent him slamming back against the door behind him. He collided with the door with a loud smack that rang through the empty building like a gunshot. His weakest leg buckled underneath him and he crumbled to the ground, knocking others off-balance as he fell. He lay on the cold, tiled floor, unable to move for a moment. This is pointless, he thought. Absolutely fucking pointless.

A hand grabbed hold of him and yanked him back up onto his feet.

'Come on, mate,' a tired and haggard voice whispered. 'You all right?'

The doctor nodded (forgetting that the other survivor couldn't see) and was about to thank whoever it was that had helped him when he heard it. A single loud bang – the sound of a body slamming a fist against the outside wall of the building close to where they were hiding. He silently willed the rest of the small group of survivors not to respond but he knew that some reaction was inevitable.

'Fucking hell,' someone moaned. 'Oh, fucking hell, they know we're here. Bloody things know we're in here…'

Before they'd finished speaking there was another bang against the outside wall, this time directly behind where Flynn was standing. He instinctively turned round and tried to back away but only succeeded in knocking into more people and pushing them into each other.

Another bang, then another, then another. The sound of rotting fists raining down. Then there were more, the hammering against the wall now coming with such speed that it was obvious there were already several bodies involved.

'Let me out,' a voice next to Croft demanded. He felt his shoulder being grabbed and then pushed out of the way. A hand on his back right between his shoulder blades forced him down again and he hit the ground for the second time in as many minutes, the side of his head glancing against the corner of a cold metal radiator. He tried to push himself back up, aware that the rest of the survivors were suddenly moving past him and out of the bathroom. Don't go out there, he thought. You stupid, bloody idiots. Please don't go out there.

Cooper, Emma, Juliet and Armitage sat in the middle of the room at the top of the observation tower. Armitage gazed down at his feet, not wanting to look up. Cooper looked out at the cold, clear night sky through the wide window opposite him. Emma held her head in her hands and Juliet Appleby stared unblinking into the darkness straight ahead. No-one had spoken for almost an hour. If time had often felt like it had dragged before, then now it seemed somehow to have slowed down again. Each one of the four survivors had made silent mental calculations and each one of them had estimated the length of time it would have taken for the plane and helicopter to reach the island. Similarly they each had an idea how long it would take for the helicopter to return if, of course, it was ever going to come back for them. All of their predictions had come to nothing. They had all hoped that Lawrence would have returned by now. With each minute that passed the likelihood that he would ever come back seemed to reduce still further.

Without warning the sounds of cracking, splintering wood followed by shattering glass fractured the fragile silence.

'What the hell was that?' Emma asked, quickly getting up from her seat and running over to the window. She leant forward and peered down. The darkness was disorientating. She was having difficulty making out any distinct movement in the relentless confusion outside.

'What's happening?' Cooper whispered, standing over her shoulder.

'Don't know,' she replied.

'Oh, Christ,' Steve Armitage moaned from a little further down the room.

'What?'

'The office. Fucking things are inside the office.'

From his position he could see part of the building that was obscured from Cooper and Emma's view. A window had been shattered three-quarters of the way down its longest side. Desperate bodies were already half-climbing, half-falling through the empty window frame. He could see signs that someone was also trying to fight their way out.

'We've got to do something,' said Juliet, moving across the room so that she could see what was happening. 'For God's sake, we have to do something.'

'Like what?' Cooper asked. 'There's nothing we can do.'

'We've got to get the doors open downstairs so that they can get over here.'

Cooper peered into the seething mass of shapes on the ground.

'How they going to do that?'

'What?'

'How they going to get over here? And if they do, how are we going to stop a thousand bloody corpses from pushing their way inside after them?'

'But we can't just leave them,' she protested.

'We haven't got a choice,' Emma mumbled from close behind.

'There are people down there…'

'There are people in here.'

As they watched a lone survivor pushed their way out through the smashed window, the force of their sudden desperate escape sending several bodies flying.

'Who's that?' asked Armitage.

'Not sure,' Cooper replied. 'Jesus Christ...'

Before any of them had time to consider trying to find a way to help the survivor it was too late. Whoever it was had almost immediately been swallowed up by bodies. They crowded around the helpless figure, their numbers meaning that every escape route was quickly blocked, and descended upon it like a pack of starved animals around fresh kill. Elsewhere still more of the bodies surged towards the office, drawn there by the sudden disturbance and noise.

'What the hell's happening now?'

'They know there are more people around here,' Emma answered quietly, 'and they know they're different to them. They're going to force their way inside and...'

'What do you mean, they know there are more people?' Juliet asked.

'Just what I said.'

'But...'

'But nothing. The bodies know we're here. They're looking for us. They've been watching us for days. They've seen the helicopter and the plane and now they're going to hunt us out.'

'Why?'

'Because we're different to them? Because we're a threat to them?' suggested Cooper. 'Who knows and who cares?'

Down below more survivors forced their way out of the besieged building and were swallowed up by the putrefying hordes. Stunned by the speed of events and their absolute, inexorable helplessness, the people in the observation room above could do nothing more than stand and watch.

'So will they come for us next?' Juliet asked, her voice wavering with emotion.

'They probably don't know we're up here yet,' Cooper answered. 'But they will.'

'Give them time,' Armitage muttered.

257

'You're right,' Emma agreed, wiping tears of fear and frustration from her eyes. 'They'll realise we're up here at some point and then…'

'Then what?' Juliet nervously pressed.

'Their physical condition is deteriorating. I don't think they can communicate or reason. So whatever their motives are I think they'll still only be able to react in one way.'

'How?' the now trembling woman asked, her voice a quiet and nervous whisper.

'I think they'll try and tear us to fucking pieces,' she answered in a voice drained of emotion. Her blunt, monotone delivery belied the mounting terror she felt inside.

In the bathroom of the office block, Phil Croft sat on the floor with his back against the door, determined to keep the fucking things which now filled the building away from him at all costs. But he wasn't stupid. He knew it was inevitable. He knew it was only a matter of time.

Reaching into his shirt pocket, he pulled out his last remaining box of cigarettes and opened it up. One and a half smokes left. He lit the first and took a long, beautiful and relaxing drag on it, filling his lungs with nicotine, tar and smoke. He lit the second, and shoved the glowing stub into a wedge of paper towels which immediately began to smoulder and burn. On the other side of the door he could hear thumps, groans and screams. On the other side of the door he could hear the other ten people he'd been trapped with being torn and ripped apart. He tried to fill his head with random, pointless thoughts to distract him from the sounds outside but it was impossible. He'd always been able to block out the horror before, but not tonight. Tonight the terror and hopeless fear was all that was left.

So this is how it ends, he thought sadly as he watched the flames begin to take hold of the paper towels and then begin to scorch and burn the building's wooden wall. He pushed back against the door again (which was now being pushed and shoved from the other side by cadavers) and wedged his feet against the door of the cubicle opposite.

He sat and smoked his last cigarette and waited, wondering whether it would be the flames or the bodies that would get to him first.

From the top of the observation tower high above the ground, Cooper watched the building below him burn. Eleven good people lost. How long before either the fire or the dead got to him and the others? He slumped to the ground and held his head in his hands. He didn't want to look outside any longer.

43

Almost first light.

Exhausted and beaten, Lawrence had delayed his flight for as long as possible, balancing his own physical tiredness with the need to get back quickly to those people they'd been forced to leave behind. Now, seven hours after he'd left them, he flew the helicopter back over the dead land. Beneath him there now seemed to be more movement than ever. Where previously there had only been stillness and an uneasy calm, now the entire dark landscape appeared to be crawling with activity. He could see bodies moving freely across the land, moving pointlessly and constantly from place to place. He wondered whether he was imagining things, whether his nervous mind was exaggerating what he could actually see below him and making it appear worse than it actually was. When he was a child he had shared a bedroom with his younger brother. He remembered how his brother's face had often seemed to twist and contort in the darkness when their bedroom light had been turned off and when shadows and shards of light from the street lamps outside had seeped in and appeared to distort his features. Maybe that was what was happening this morning. The sky was clear and the sun would soon be ready to rise and burn away the darkness. Perhaps it was the dull grey light which made the situation on the ground appear far worse than it actually was.

This was a dangerous and pointless flight. When Lawrence had left the airfield earlier he had felt beaten and disconsolate. What possible hope could the fifteen or so people left there have against the thousands upon thousands of unstoppable bodies he had last seen heading towards the collection of exposed and defenceless buildings. Several times during the journey he had considered turning the helicopter around and heading back, wondering whether there was anything to be gained from even trying. What good would it do? What would he achieve? The base was overrun - if there were any survivors left there, how was he supposed to pick them up? Would his return do anything more than taunt those left behind and prolong their agony? Would he spend his time flying around the complex, watching the others waiting to die?

As bleak and inevitable as the conclusion of his flight appeared to be, Lawrence knew that he didn't have any choice. He had to try.

The slowly lifting darkness of the early morning camouflaged the airfield. In his mind Lawrence still pictured the place as he'd left it hours earlier - a small collection of buildings surrounded by empty space and encircled by the fence and the many thousands of bodies beyond. He knew it would look different now, but it was hard to imagine the extent to which the dark scene would have changed.

Fear, nerves and fatigue had confused Lawrence and made him lose his bearings and pass the airfield. In the uninterrupted gloom everything looked the same and it had not been until he was almost over the centre of the town of Rowley that he realised his mistake. He turned round in a wide, graceful arc and flew back on himself, eventually spotting the airfield (and the fire and smoke to the side of the observation tower) just a mile or so ahead. Like a dark, black scab on the relentlessly bleak and monochrome landscape, as he approached it the airfield already looked overrun and lost. Once again he considered turning tail and heading back to Cormansey. There were hundreds of thousands of bodies swarming constantly around the place. Even if Cooper, Croft and the others were still there and were still alive, what the hell could he do to help them now? How could he hope to reach them?

44

'What are they doing now?' Armitage asked. Too afraid to look himself, the burley truck driver leant against the back wall, as far away as he could get from the window without leaving the room. Cooper and Emma remained close to the glass, watching the bodies shuffling below them with mounting unease.

The rear of the nearby office building had been burning for hours now and more than half of the building had been completely consumed by flame. The fire had attracted the attention of many of the bodies, but many more continued to drag themselves around the rest of the airfield and the other buildings. The physical weight of their immense numbers helped them to randomly gain access to the hangar, waiting room and other places through windows and doors which had been left unlocked and open. Those which strayed too close to the burning building had themselves become engulfed by flames, their remains of their tinder-dry clothing and emaciated flesh quickly igniting. The appearance and movement of the burning bodies was bizarre, unsettling and surreal. Ignorant to the heat and flame which quickly consumed and destroyed them, the corpses continued to stagger around relentlessly, colliding with other random figures and setting them alight too. The fire, although mostly confined to the other side of the remains of the office building, was growing quickly and was eating away at the rest of the structure. Any change in wind direction, thought Cooper, and they might have no choice but to get out of the observation tower and take their chances with the baying masses outside.

'I can see them in at least three buildings now,' Emma said, her voice a barely audible whisper.

'Still reckon we'll be safe here?' Armitage snapped, looking directly at Cooper for an answer.

'I never said we'd be safe,' he replied, 'I just said they don't know we're here yet. They're going to keep sniffing round the buildings because there's nothing else here, is there? Hopefully the fire will keep them occupied and distracted for a while.'

'You think so?' Armitage challenged.

He shrugged his shoulders.

'It might.'

'Assuming it doesn't, how long before they manage to get inside?'

'I don't know if they will. We blocked the door downstairs. They probably haven't got the strength to get past it.'

'We didn't think they'd have the strength to pull the bloody fence down but they managed that, didn't they?'

Cooper didn't answer, knowing that Armitage was right and sensing that the conversation was becoming increasingly pointless and predictable.

'Did you block all the doors and windows downstairs?' Juliet Appleby asked from across the room. She had her face pressed against another smaller window and was trying to look straight down the side of the building.

Cooper shook his head.

'Just the main entrance, why?'

'Because whether they're going to manage it or not, it looks like they're trying to get inside.'

'What's happening?' Emma asked anxiously as she ran over to stand next to Juliet.

'I can see a couple of groups of them.'

'What are they doing?'

'Nothing much, just pressing up against the door I think. It's difficult to see much from up here.'

Emma sighed and held her head in her hands.

'They're going to get in, aren't they?' she whispered.

'Probably,' Cooper admitted.

'But you just said…' Armitage protested.

'I said I'd blocked the door and it wasn't going to be easy for them, but there are thousands of those damn things out there, and a thousand bodies pushing against pretty much any door will open it, won't it?'

'Yes, but…'

'I'm not saying they'll manage it today or tomorrow,' he continued, 'but they're likely to get inside eventually.'

Cooper's use of the word 'tomorrow' made Emma's heart sink. It brought home to her the reality of their situation, and that reality was that they all had very little chance of seeing many more tomorrows, if any. As far as she could see there was no way out of this place.

'Christ, this is fucking stupid,' snapped Armitage, becoming increasingly nervous and angry. 'We can't just sit here and wait for it to happen, can we?'

'That's just about all we can do, isn't it?' sighed Juliet.

'We could make a run for it?' he suggested. 'Fight our way over to one of the trucks and try and get away?'

'Where would we go?' asked Cooper. Armitage couldn't answer. The thought of another directionless drive through the decaying countryside was just marginally more appealing than sitting still and doing nothing. It was a last resort, but they all knew it may well turn out to be their only option.

Emma had made her way back over to the largest window and was now trying to keep hidden in the shadows whilst watching everything that was happening outside. The ground was now completely carpeted in a constantly shifting layer of dead flesh - she couldn't see any grass, pavement or runway. The office building was almost completely ablaze and she knew that there was now no-one left alive inside. Elsewhere the bodies were tightly packed around the other buildings and seemed to be pushing ever closer. Burning bodies still dragged themselves around hopelessly and a thick, smog-like layer of smoke had settled across the scene. The wind was light and directionless and the smoke showed no sign of dispersing.

'What's the roof of this building like?' she asked suddenly.

'What?' Cooper grunted.

'The roof of this building,' she repeated, 'is it flat?'

'Not sure. You can't really tell from the ground. Why, what are you thinking?'

She shrugged her shoulders.

'I'm thinking that if we are going to get out of here, then we need to do a couple of things. First, we need to be somewhere obvious so that Lawrence can see us when he comes back…'

'If he comes back,' Armitage mumbled.

'When he comes back,' Cooper corrected him. 'Whether he can do anything for us or not, I'm sure he'll be back.'

'Whatever.'

'I'm sure he'll be back because any one of us would do the same if we were in his shoes, wouldn't we? You couldn't just sit there on the island knowing that there still might be people left alive and trapped over here, could you?'

No answer.

'Anyway,' Emma continued, 'as well as being visible, we need to make sure that we end up somewhere the bodies definitely can't get to.'

'Like?'

'Like a flat roof,' she replied.

'I think the roof here is sloped,' Juliet said, still standing at the window but now looking up instead of down.

Cooper shuffled round so that he had a better view of the rest of the airfield and, more importantly, the few remaining buildings nearby.

'Not sure about this one, but that one over there's a possibility,' he said quietly, nodding in the general direction of small utility building nestled in the shadows of the hangar where the plane had previously been housed.

'Just a couple of problems as far as I can see,' Armitage grumbled from close behind. 'Getting to it and getting on top of it. Any bright ideas?'

'How desperate are you feeling?' Cooper asked.

'Fucking desperate,' Armitage replied.

'Me too, so we'll just have to find a way of getting up there, won't we? I don't see that we've got any choice.'

'How then?'

'Try the usual tricks,' he answered, 'because they've worked so far. We'll distract the bodies and make a run for it.'

'Shouldn't the fire be distracting them already?' Emma suggested. She was right. Many bodies were continuing to crowd around the base of the observation tower and were ignoring the slowly spreading heat and light of the flames.

'She's right. And anyway, that building is at least twenty feet high,' Armitage sighed. 'What are we going to do? Jump up for Christ's sake? Stand on each other's shoulders?'

'We'll find a way up.'

'Forget about the buildings,' Emma suggested, her mind suddenly racing. 'Using the trucks was a better idea. We could do that, couldn't we? Once they see us on top of one of the buildings we'll have the whole bloody lot of them snapping at our feet. At least with the trucks we'll be able to keep moving...'

'But the trucks are even further away,' whimpered Juliet.

'The prison truck's only on the other side of the runway,' Cooper said. 'Can't see the personnel carrier from here.'

'Still don't know how we're supposed to get to it,' snapped Armitage.

'Better find a way quickly,' Emma yelled suddenly with a new found urgency in her voice.

'Why?' demanded Armitage, worried by her sudden change in tone.

'Because the helicopter's back.'

45

Once he was over the airfield Lawrence allowed the helicopter to drift lower, switching on the searchlight and managing to clumsily guide it around the scene. For a while all he could see were the seething bodies and it took him some time to orientate himself and properly identify the dark shapes and outlines of the observation tower and other buildings through the smoke. Conscious that the noise, light and disturbance that he had inevitably caused was again whipping the rancid crowd below into a bloody frenzy, he moved lower still, stopping only when he was level with the top of the observation tower.

He could see survivors. The nearby office building had been destroyed, but he could definitely see other people at the top of the observation tower. He had to look twice to be sure. Could it have been bodies? Had they found a way inside? From his high position there were no signs obvious of any entrance to the building having been compromised. If the dead had forced their way in he would have expected hundreds of them to have pointlessly crammed themselves inside by now. There didn't seem to be many people there, and those that he could see were moving with direction and control. It had to be survivors. But how could he hope to reach them?

Cooper's face appeared at the window, confirming beyond doubt to Lawrence that his return to the mainland had been worthwhile.

'We have to go outside,' Emma shouted, suddenly having to raise her voice to make herself heard over the welcome noise of the helicopter. 'We have to get out of here.'

'But there is no way out,' Armitage yelled. 'We've just been through this. We're surrounded. They're out the front and they're round the back and...'

'Emma's right,' Cooper interrupted. 'We have to find a way out of here and we have to do it now.'

'Go for the trucks,' Juliet suggested.

'I agree,' Emma said quickly, 'it's the best option. Lawrence will see us moving. If we can get to one of the trucks we can drive through the bodies until we reach somewhere where there are fewer of them. Then he can land and pick us up.'

'Do we just make a run for it?'

'It's not going to be easy,' Emma replied, looking down at the ground immediately around the base of the building. 'I think we should try and distract them and get them away from whichever door or window we decide to use to get out. Then maybe just one of us could try to get across and bring the truck back over here.'

Cooper stood behind Emma, thinking carefully. He glanced up and looked outside and across at Lawrence. The helicopter was hovering so close that, despite the drifting smoke, the pilot's face could clearly be seen. The distance was irrelevant. Cooper thought he might as well have been a hundred miles away for all the good it was doing them. Lawrence looked understandably agitated. Cooper knew he wouldn't wait indefinitely for them to make their move.

'Good God,' mumbled Juliet. 'Just look at that.'

She pointed out of the window down at an area of ground which was almost directly beneath the helicopter.

'What the hell are they doing?' Armitage asked, crowding forward to try and get a better view.

The four survivors peered down. Lawrence had angled the searchlight below the helicopter and slightly to one side. Whilst many bodies continued to react as the survivors had expected them to, others now were beginning to behave differently. A large number of them ripped and tore at those corpses closest to them, but many others did not. Instead those bodies appeared to be visibly agitated and riled by the noise, light and wind coming from the helicopter hovering a short distance above their decaying heads. Many of them seemed almost to be cowering. It was hard to believe, but some of the bodies were trying to move away from the disturbance.

'Fucking hell,' mumbled Cooper.

'This is it,' Emma whispered secretively, 'this is our chance. It's like you said earlier, they're changing. They're finally beginning to wake up, aren't they? Bloody hell, those things down there are starting to get worried.'

'Worried?' Armitage snapped nervously. 'What the hell are you talking about, worried?'

'They're becoming aware of their own limitations,' she explained. 'Some of them are starting to realise that we're capable of causing them a lot more damage than they can do to us. I'm sure that's why some of them fight. They're trying to protect themselves.'

'Bullshit.'

'Might be,' she said quickly. 'Whatever the reason, the point is that this might give us more of a chance of getting past them than we thought we had.'

'How?' asked Juliet.

'Use the helicopter as cover. Make as much of a disturbance as we can and try and get Lawrence's help. Chances are some of them will disappear and keep out of our way.'

'Some of them?'

'The rest will probably still go for us, same as they always do.'

A moment of quiet contemplation followed, disturbed only by the continual noise coming from the helicopter outside. Much as he hated to admit it, Armitage knew that Emma was right. Better to go out there and face five hundred of those bloody things, he thought, than a thousand.

'We should do it,' Juliet Appleby announced timidly.

'Do what exactly?' Armitage instinctively asked.

'Shake them up then go out there and kick their bloody backsides,' Emma answered.

'Because if we don't,' Cooper reminded them, 'then we won't be getting into that helicopter and we'll be stuck here. If we don't go outside and face them now, then we'll be facing them when they finally get in here, that's if we haven't burned to death already. Not much of a choice, is it?'

Dividing his concentration between piloting the helicopter, watching the survivors and watching the bodies below, Lawrence noticed that Cooper and the others had shifted their attention from looking at him to watching what was happening on the ground. He peered down through small observation panels by his feet and watched as the bodies reacted to his presence. He shifted the helicopter slightly and saw that as the disc of light coming from the searchlight moved, so more shadowy shapes stumbled out of the way as if they expected it to burn or maim them. Having seen the behaviour of the creatures on the island change similarly, the actions of the diseased corpses surprised him less than they surprised the others trapped at the top of the observation tower. Perhaps if he dropped lower, he thought, then more bodies would move and he might be able to land and pick up the survivors. He tried briefly, but the number of corpses which stood their ground and still reacted violently was more than enough to convince him that course of action was out of the question. But the presence of the helicopter and the fear (that seemed to be the right word to use) that it seemed to generate amongst the dead was unquestionably important. It would help. It might give the people on the ground a chance, albeit a slight one. Lawrence remembered that the bodies he'd seen acting this way on the island, although quieter and more hesitant than most, had still attacked the survivors eventually when they'd been threatened. The bodies were trying to survive and their most basic instincts drove them to fight when no alternative course of action remained.

From his position above the airfield Lawrence felt uncomfortable and helpless. He had no way of warning the others or telling them what he knew.

Several minutes of frightened inaction passed.

Having stood still and watched and waited for too long, too frightened and unsure to make her move, Emma finally decided that she had to take action. No-one else seemed ready to do it.

270

All the talking in the world wasn't going to get them away from the airfield and, as Cooper had already pointed out, they had nothing to lose and everything to gain from trying to get away. If they did nothing then their last chance would have gone. The prospect of a relatively safe and secure future with Michael was too great a prize to risk throwing away. She had to do something.

'Where you going?' Cooper shouted as she turned and pushed through the doors and began to clatter down the staircase.

'To Cormansey,' she shouted back. 'What about you?'

Suddenly feeling forced into action, Juliet, Armitage and Cooper followed close behind. For all her sudden movement and intent, it was clear that Emma didn't have a plan. They found her at the bottom of the staircase, looking around hopefully for inspiration.

'What now?' Juliet asked.

Through the bitter-tasting, wispy smoke which had seeped inside, Armitage noticed the light leaking in from under the front entrance to the building. A mixture of the natural first light of day and the harsh artificial illumination coming from the helicopter, he cautiously moved towards it. Clambering carefully over the tables and chairs which he and Cooper had earlier used to block the entrance, he peered out through a narrow crack between the double doors. There were still an uncomfortably large number of bodies milling around out there, but their numbers in the light from the helicopter were considerably more diffuse now. He looked up at the aircraft hanging in the air above them. Lawrence seemed to have worked out what was happening. Armitage couldn't be completely sure, but the pilot seemed to be deliberately aiming his light towards the door.

'I reckon we should make a run for it,' he suggested, his sudden positive attitude meeting with surprise from the others. 'We should do it now.'

'We can't risk just throwing the doors open and going out there,' Emma protested. 'What if we get split up? What happens when we get over to the truck? Do we just stand there and wait for you to open it up?'

'Worse than that,' Juliet added, 'if we open the doors and we all go out there, then that leaves this place wide open. We'll have no way back if anything goes wrong.'

'We need to get the truck over here,' Cooper said. 'One of us needs to get over to it then get it back here to pick the rest of us up.'

The sound of the helicopter was deafening and seemed to be amplified at the bottom of the staircase by the long, thin shape of the building itself. Above the mechanical noise the occasional sound of bodies slamming against the walls, doors and windows could be heard. The longer the survivors remained silent, the louder the sound outside seemed to become. Although the helicopter seemed to be keeping some of the creatures at bay, its position next to the observation tower was also drawing more of them closer.

Armitage couldn't stand it any longer. He was generally a quiet man who was content to sit and wait and watch rather than act, but, occasionally, the pressure of a situation proved too much and forced him to take action. It had happened before back in the city when he'd left the safety of the university complex to help collect transport for the group. It was happening again now.

'I'll do it,' he said suddenly.

'What?' asked Cooper, surprised.

'I said I'll do it,' the burley man repeated before he had chance to talk himself out of volunteering. 'Might as well.'

'You sure?'

'No.'

Cooper moved forward and looked through the narrow gap in the doors that Armitage had been looking through just a few seconds earlier. His view was limited, but he could clearly see the prison truck on the other side of the runway where it had been left. It wasn't going to be easy to reach.

'It's got to be a couple of hundred metres away,' he whispered, still looking out through the gap, 'and there are a couple of hundred bodies in your way. Think you can make it?'

'I can do it,' Armitage answered. 'Listen, with enough of those things snapping at my heels, I could run a bloody marathon!'

Cooper nodded and then started moving the tables and chairs which were blocking the doors.

'When you get out there,' he said as he worked, looking back over his shoulder at the other man, 'you just put your head down and run, understand? Keep moving until you reach the truck. Don't stop for anything.'

'I'm not going to.'

Armitage nervously turned round to look at Emma and Juliet as Cooper continued to clear the door. Both women tried to think of something to say but, overcome with nerves and emotion, neither of them were able to speak.

'Ready?' Cooper asked as he dragged the last table away. Armitage turned back towards the door.

'Ready,' he answered.

Cooper nodded. He took a deep, nervous breath.

'Go for it.'

Armitage pushed the doors open and burst out into the cold morning. The light which poured down from the helicopter and saturated the immediate vicinity was momentarily blinding and the unexpected force of the wind bearing down from the aircraft threatened to knock him off his feet. The suffocating smell of burning flesh filled his lungs. For a single disorientated second he stood still and stared at the truck on the other side of the runway. His view was relatively clear and, for an instant, the distance he had to cover seemed reassuringly short. But then he glanced to his left and then to his right and saw that there were bodies all around him. Some remained cowering in the shadows, others began to quickly converge on him from all directions. The sound of the door being pulled shut behind him - barely audible over the constant noise from the helicopter above - prompted him to move.

'Shit,' he cursed as the nearest body reached out for him. It's hands were bony and hard with much of the putrefied flesh having long since been worn and rotted away. Jogging slowly away from the observation tower, and trying desperately to pick up some much needed speed, Armitage grabbed the skeletal figure by the neck and swung it around, sending it flying into a group of four more ragged cadavers and knocking them down like skittles.

He looked ahead again and tried to regain his focus on the truck. Where before he'd seemed to have a clear passage, now a myriad of shuffling figures crisscrossed ahead of him. More vicious hands lashed out, one catching his cheek and tearing three long cuts from just under his left eye and down to his chin. Suddenly pumped full of adrenaline, fear and stinging pain, Armitage again forced himself to ignore the bodies all around him and keep moving forward. His mouth was dry and his heart was thumping like it was about to explode but he knew that he had to keep moving. He lowered his shoulder as two more corpses crossed his path. Charging through the pair of them he smashed one away in either direction.

Almost halfway there.

A heavy and unfit man, Armitage's right knee was hurting badly as a result of the sudden stress he was putting his body under. He knew that he had no option but to keep running through the pain, but every time his foot hit the ground a piercing, shooting pain ran along the length of his leg from his knee to his backside. The pathways and grass under his feet had now given way to the harder tarmac surface of the runway and he knew that he had almost reached the truck. The ground was littered with the random remains of corpses which had been burnt or brought down and torn apart by others and he trod heavily on one which had fallen onto its back. His boot smashed through the rib cage and sent the rotten remains of internal organs flying in every direction. As he frantically tried to pull his foot clear he tripped and fell and in seconds bodies had swarmed all over him.

'Fucking hell,' Cooper yelled from the observation tower as he watched through the crack in the door. More and more bodies piled on top of the helpless truck driver, quickly burying him under a mound of constantly moving, decaying flesh.

'Jesus,' Emma wailed, looking out through a small window nearby and taking care not to be seen from outside.

Cooper moved to open the door.

'Cooper, don't…' Juliet screamed instinctively.

'I can't just leave him out there…'

'Wait,' Emma snapped. She pushed her face against the window. She could see movement from the bottom of the pile of bodies. Armitage was still fighting. High above him Lawrence had moved the helicopter round so that the searchlight was bearing down on him directly. The sudden illumination caused many of the bodies still lurching towards the disturbance to turn and trip away in other directions.

Lying on his back on the cold, hard runway and struggling to breathe because of his tiredness and the choking, abhorrent smell, Armitage began to kick and punch out at the bodies on top of him. They felt hollow and cold and individually offered little resistance. He felt their decayed flesh dripping and dribbling over him and he could feel himself being soaked through by their vile discharge. The more they fought, he found, the quicker they deteriorated. He rolled over onto his front and tried to push himself up off the ground. Still more of them were clinging onto his back. He had no idea how many of the grotesque things were hanging off him and he didn't care. He managed somehow to scramble onto all fours and then pushed hard and stood upright and began to smash the bodies away like flies. With five or six of them already thrown to the ground he found that his torso was suddenly free again and the only bodies still holding on were those which clung onto his legs. He began to move forward again, his powerful strides dislodging more and more of the pitiful creatures until his legs were clear and he could run again. He battered more of the cadavers out of his path before reaching the side of the truck and slamming into it. With one last groan of effort he reached up to the handle on the passenger's door, yanked it open and hauled himself inside. He pulled it shut (severing a single arm that reached after him) and slid across the cab into the driver's seat.

'He's in,' cried Emma from the observation tower window. 'Bloody hell, he's done it.'

Suddenly sensing that a way out may have just been opened up for them, the three remaining survivors crowded together around the main door and waited for the truck to move. Lawrence watched events from the relative safety of the helicopter hanging in the air and continued to drench the scene with harsh, artificial light, giving Armitage some welcome illumination and a limited degree of protection.

Inside the truck Armitage was struggling. His eyes stinging from the smoke, he slumped forward over the steering wheel. Dripping with rancid blood and gore and soaked through with sweat, he fought to catch his breath and keep his tired mind focussed. He reached out to turn the key and start the engine but then stopped. His chest felt tight. He desperately needed oxygen but the deeper he breathed, the more smoke he inhaled and the worse the pain in his chest became. Beginning as an uncomfortable feeling like a localised stitch, it quickly became an uncontrollable searing, burning and ripping pain which started near his heart and which then seemed to spread out across the entire width of his torso. His fingers felt numb and were now tingling with pain. His feet felt heavy and he struggled to move them onto the pedals.

Armitage again tried to breathe slowly and deeply and did his best to ignore the constant distraction of countless bodies which clattered angrily against the sides of the truck. Taking his time, he figured that the slower he moved, the more chance he'd have of getting the truck going. His outstretched fingers eventually made contact with the keys and he somehow managed to turn them and start the engine, pushing himself back into his seat with momentary relief and satisfaction as the truck rumbled into life. Progress was short-lived, however, as another wave of debilitating pain spread quickly across his chest. Groaning with effort he forced himself to concentrate on getting back to the others. He began to move the truck forward and slowly turned the steering wheel to guide the heavy vehicle back towards the observation tower. Still illuminated by the incandescent light from the helicopter, the truck trundled towards the building, mowing down those bodies which foolishly dragged themselves into its path.

'He's coming,' Cooper said, still watching through the gap between the doors. 'Ready?'

Juliet and Emma nodded. Emma's throat was dry and her legs felt weak with nerves. This was make or break and she knew it.

Never mind the immediate danger they faced outside, what happened in the next few minutes would undoubtedly decide the direction and duration of the rest of her life.

'What do we do?' mumbled Juliet anxiously.

'When I open the doors,' Cooper replied, 'you get yourself onto the truck. Doesn't matter if you get in the front or back or if you're left hanging onto the side, just get over to that bloody truck and hold onto it, okay?'

She nodded and was about to ask another question when Cooper threw the doors open. The blood-splattered prison truck ground to a sudden, lurching stop just a few metres ahead of them.

'Move!' he yelled. He grabbed hold of both women by the arm and dragged them forward, virtually throwing them out of the building. Bodies began to surge at them from every imaginable direction. Juliet half-ran and half-fell towards the back of the truck, managing somehow to jump up and yank the back door open. She pulled herself inside and then reached out for Emma who was fighting her way through a dense section of the rabid crowd. She forced herself to keep moving through the tide of rotting flesh which pushed against her and threatened to swallow her up. It seemed that those bodies which had remained on the sidelines had suddenly sensed an increase in the level of their own physical danger and had forced themselves to move and attack before the survivors and their machines attacked them. What felt like thousands of cruel, bony hands reached out to grab hold of Emma. Unexpectedly her speed increased. Running into her at force from behind, Cooper shoved her towards the truck, wedged his hands under her arms and threw her up into the air. With her flailing hands stretched out in front of her she managed to grab hold of the back of the vehicle. Juliet was waiting. She caught hold of the scruff of the neck of Emma's jacket and dragged her inside. The bodies were no match for Cooper's controlled force. He powered through them and jumped up onto the back of the truck after the others. Hanging half-out of the open door he smashed his hand repeatedly on the vehicle's metal side. The noise was more definite and controlled than the relentless battering coming from the bodies. Armitage knew it was his signal to move again. Forcing himself to rise above the constant, agonising pain which still crippled him, he accelerated and turned and drove out towards the gaping hole in the airfield's border fence.

'You okay?' Emma asked from inside the back of the truck.

'Will be when we get to this bloody island,' Cooper replied, still standing in the doorway and holding on tightly with every lurch and sway of the prison truck as it moved across the uneven ground. From every direction bodies turned and stumbled towards the powerful vehicle, some being smashed to the side, countless others being dragged beneath its wheels and crushed into the ground. Ignoring the bloody confusion unfolding all around them, Cooper looked up through the drifting smoke and watched with relief as the helicopter began to slowly follow them away from the buildings.

'What do we do now?' Juliet wondered innocently.

Before Cooper could answer the truck began to slow down.

'Steve,' he screamed at the top of his voice, 'keep moving. For Christ's sake, don't stop here.'

The truck lurched forward again and accelerated for a few metres and then slowed down. The engine stalled as Armitage's foot slipped off the clutch pedal, the sudden movement almost throwing Cooper off the back and into the baying crowds. In the cab the driver's hands and feet felt like lead now and he could no longer make them do what he wanted them to. He knew that he couldn't drive any further. The pain in his chest was unbearable.

'What's he doing?' Emma asked pointlessly as the prison truck ground to a final halt. She ran deeper inside and began to bang on the inner walls. 'Steve!' she yelled. 'Steve! What's wrong…?'

They had stopped just a short distance from the downed section of fence. Even though the crowds were slightly less dense here than they were around the buildings, within seconds of the abrupt ending of the truck's journey masses of rotting corpses were already battering against it's exposed and undefended sides. Cooper kicked out at those which were unfortunate enough to stumble and trip nearest to him.

'We need to get onto the roof,' he said as he surveyed the desperate scene. From all directions hundreds of cadavers turned and began to move ominously towards them. The helicopter hovered overhead, it's noise and light now attracting easily as many bodies as it repelled. Cooper looked down at the sea of swarming creatures in front of him and then glanced up at the helicopter again. 'There's no way he'll be able to pick us up off the ground.'

Turning round he grabbed hold of Juliet and pulled her closer to the door.

'What...?' she stammered.

'Roof,' he snapped. He crouched down and cupped his hands for her to use as a foothold. Groaning with effort and pain he lifted her up. With nothing on the roof for her to hold onto she struggled to get a grip and pull herself up. Cooper dug deep and shoved her a little higher and she managed to dig her elbows down and inch slowly forward. He leant out of the truck and watched until her feet had disappeared over the top. Moments later her head reappeared over the edge.

'Okay?' Cooper asked.

'Okay,' Juliet replied, forcing herself to look anywhere but down into the mass of rotting faces which stared back at her.

Emma was next. With the nearest bodies just inches away from grabbing hold of him, Cooper supported her relatively slight weight until Juliet had caught hold of her hands from above and had pulled her up onto the roof. Cooper then turned and scrambled up himself, using the door at the back of the truck to push himself up.

Breathlessly the three survivors stood together on top of the truck. Emma looked down at the relentless crowd of decayed creatures below her. Their anger and ferocity seemed to increase as Lawrence lowered the helicopter down.

'Get in,' Cooper shouted, having to yell to make himself heard over the deafening noise. Instinctively crouching down and moving on all fours because of the rotor blades which now seemed perilously close and the wind which threatened to blow them off the roof of the truck, Emma and Juliet crawled towards the aircraft. Lawrence now hovered just inches away, although the distance between the roof of the truck and the helicopter's nearest landing strut seemed immense. Taking a deep breath Emma stepped across the gap and pulled herself into the back of the aircraft.

Cooper ran down to the front end of the truck and lay down across the width of the cab. He dragged himself further forward and leant down and banged on the half-open window next to Armitage. He could see the back of his head. The exhausted driver was lying across the steering wheel with his face turned away from Cooper.

'Come on, Steve,' Cooper pleaded. 'We've done it. Let's get you up here.'

Armitage slowly lifted his head, turned to look at Cooper, and then dropped back down again. He closed his eyes.

'Can't,' he gasped, his voice hollow and hoarse and his breathing shallow and intermittent. 'Can't do it.'

'Come on,' Cooper insisted, although he already suspected that it was pointless. Armitage's face was grey and ashen.

He shook his head again.

'Can't.'

Frustrated, for a second Cooper contemplated jumping down and trying to manhandle the other survivor up onto the roof of the truck. He knew that it would be impossible and pointless. He'd have to climb down to do it and even if he managed to shift Armitage's considerable weight, the hundreds of bodies still baying for his blood would prevent him, if not both of them, from getting back up to the helicopter.

'Go,' Armitage gasped, trying to lift his head again. The light from the helicopter suddenly shifted slightly, illuminating the inside of the cab and allowing Cooper to clearly see the pain in Armitage's face. His lips were tinged with blue and it was obvious that he was beyond help.

'Okay, mate,' he said, reaching in through the window and resting his arm on the other man's shoulder. Reluctantly Cooper then stood up and ran the length of the roof to get to the helicopter. Strangely relieved, Armitage closed his eyes again and tried to breathe through the increasing pain until it finally stopped.

'What about Steve?' Emma shouted as Cooper scrambled into the helicopter and pulled the door shut behind him. He shook his head and looked down and watched the roof of the truck becoming smaller and smaller as the aircraft quickly climbed away.

Below them the airfield was a solid mass of crazed, decaying bodies.

46

Almost exactly fifty-nine days since the germ had destroyed almost all of the population of the planet, the final survivors arrived in the air over the island of Cormansey.

Michael had been waiting in the small cottage by the airstrip. Donna and Jack Baxter kept him company although no-one had spoken for what felt like hours. Finally the oppressive silence was broken by the constant dull thud of the approaching helicopter. The distant sound increased Michael's uncertainty and nervousness to an almost unbearable level. Almost too afraid to look he went outside and scanned the skies until he finally spotted the aircraft approaching. He watched every last metre of its painfully long descent to the ground and then sprinted the length of the island's short runway.

Cooper was the first to get out, then Juliet.

Then he saw her.

Michael ran over to Emma and held her. Ignorant to everything else that was suddenly happening around them - the frenzied and excited activity, the tears for missing friends, the cars which approached from various directions, the cheers and cries of relief and sadness - he buried her face in his chest and held her tightly.

'Didn't think you were going to make it over here,' he whispered.

'Neither did I,' she admitted quietly. 'You found us somewhere decent to live yet?' she asked, looking up into his tired and haggard-looking face and smiling through her tears.

'Not yet,' he answered honestly, 'but I'm working on it. I'll show you a few places later. You can choose where we go.'

In a moment of silence Michael stood next to Emma and watched as she looked around her, trying to take in what she could see of the island. He watched her as she tasted the air and listened to the sounds around her and soaked up the atmosphere. He watched her as she relaxed and he held her as she wept with relief.

Cormansey was a bleak, cold and often unforgiving place, but both of them knew it was as good as it was going to get.

Epilogue
Michael Collins
2nd June

I saw Jack Baxter this morning for the first time in almost two weeks. He came by the house earlier. Told me he'd been out walking. I often see him in the distance, marching on his own across the horizon. He told me he walks circuits of the island to keep himself occupied.

Very few people visit us here. There aren't many houses more isolated than ours. That was a deliberate move. We both want to stay close to the others, but at the same time we want lives of our own too. Most people have chosen to live in or around Danvers Lye. There are some people here who want to build a close community and who want to live, sleep and eat in each other's pockets. There are some here who couldn't survive on their own and who need the closeness of others. We don't want that. We don't need that. We've tried it already. We've lived like that for long enough. That kind of life seems pointless now.

Christ, we could do with having Phil Croft here now. We've struggled since Emma fell pregnant. Other people have tried to support her and help her, but it's been difficult and we miss his guidance, company and expertise. It was hard in the winter when she first caught, and it will be hard in the autumn when the baby's born. At least I'll be able to help more then. At the moment I feel useless. The others have been understanding. They told us about the baby that was born when they were back in the city and what happened to it. We know that the same thing could happen to our child. Our medical facilities here are virtually nonexistent and we didn't have any option but to go through with the pregnancy, not that either of us would have chosen to do anything else. I pray that our baby will be all right. I talked to Donna about its chances. She said that although the mother of the baby in the city had survived, it was likely that its father had been killed by the germ. She said that maybe the fact that both Emma and I survived will make a difference. I hope that whatever it is that's kept us both alive had been passed down and will protect our child too.

Jack and I had a long conversation about the future today. I've agreed to go back to the mainland with Cooper and some of the others in a few days time. It'll only be the third time we've been back. Providing the weather stays good the plan is for Lawrence to fly us over to the nearest port. We'll salvage whatever supplies we can and then find a boat of some description and sail back again. There's hardly any fuel left in the helicopter now. We could try to find more, but we need to look for another way of getting to and from the mainland. We're going to have to keep going back there. We'll always need medicines and food and clothing. No doubt we'll become more self-sufficient as time goes by, but at the moment it makes sense to keep scavenging for what we need.

If I'm honest we're struggling here, and I can't see that things are ever going to get any easier. Some people are working on trying to get gas and electricity supplied to the village. They might manage it, but at what cost? It's going to take an enormous amount of effort for questionable gain. How will they maintain the supplies? Who will keep them working? It's all going to take time, but that's the one thing we seem to have in abundance. Nevertheless, I can't help thinking that all of the fighting and the struggling and everything we've been through somehow feels pointless now…

The last time we went back to the mainland (a few months ago now) the bodies were almost all gone. I doubt we'll see any of them moving when we go there this time. They should have rotted away to nothing by now. The last one I saw was slumped at the side of the road just outside a shop we'd been clearing out. Its body was massively decayed and it just lay there and watched me. It tried to move but it couldn't. It managed to lift its head slightly. The remains of its cold, black eyes followed me as I moved between the shop and the helicopter.

For some reason I think about that body a lot. I guess it haunts me. I find myself thinking about what happened to turn it from being a normal, healthy person into that cold, useless mound of decay. I wonder sometimes how aware the bodies were of what was happening to them? They couldn't react, but did they feel anything? I wonder whether their brains were more active and alive than we'd originally thought, and whether it was only the deterioration of their flesh and bone that caused them to react and behave the way they did? Did my friends and family suffer? Did they wander around like that, trying desperately to find comfort or familiarity and a release from their pain? I often wonder whether that last body had been looking at me and remembering what it had once been.

It's getting late. Emma is asleep and has been all afternoon. No doubt she'll wake up soon and then keep me awake all night talking. She still doesn't like to be on her own at night. No-one does.

I'm standing in front of the house looking out over the ocean. It's a bright, warm and sunny day and the water in the distance looks deceptively calm and inviting. Everything is quiet and if I just stand here and listen to the silence then I can almost believe that nothing ever happened. But there's no escaping the fact that our lives have been changed forever and no matter how safe or comfortable we try and make this place, the rest of our days are going to be constantly difficult and hard. We will have to fight for everything we need and if our children survive then they'll spend their lives fighting too.

In getting here we managed to win a small victory, but it was a hollow one. I now know that our achievements are unimportant and insignificant in the overall scheme of things. There might be other people like us. There might be people elsewhere who have been more successful and who are more organised and protected than us. Whoever's left alive and however many of us there are, I think our days are numbered. We are remnants of the past. I sometimes feel like an intruder now, like I shouldn't be here. Baxter says that whatever the reason or cause, what happened to the world was supposed to happen. I agree with him. We've been brushed aside. I can't help thinking that everything we're doing is going to come to nothing. We're just kidding ourselves if we believe any different. The balance of our world has been changed forever. Mankind is being cleansed from the face of the planet. Purification has begun.

All that Emma and I can do is make the most of the time we have left.

That's all that any of us can do.

FOLLOW THE COMPLETE AUTUMN
STORY IN THE BEST-SELLING NOVELS

AUTUMN

AUTUMN: THE CITY

AUTUMN: THE HUMAN CONDITION

ALSO AVAILABLE FROM
DAVID MOODY

STRAIGHT TO YOU
and
TRUST

All books available in paperback and a wide
range of ebook formats from Infected Books

For more information visit:

www.djmoody.co.uk

www.theinfected.co.uk

www.infectedbooks.co.uk

Printed in the United States
51151LVS00001B/1-33